遇到老外英語這樣說

Tony Coolidge　陳華友 ◎著

許可欣 ◎譯

晨星出版

作者序 PREFACE

Moving my family from the USA to Taiwan was one of the best decisions we ever made. Living on this island has truly enriched the lives of my family. No matter how interesting life can be in Taiwan, there are also many differences and challenges that we have to face. The cultural differences often result in uncomfortable situations for foreigners. I appreciated learning the culture through many experiences, and I have met many patient Taiwanese people who were my gracious teachers.

When I was asked to write this book, I felt honored, and saw a duty that I could perform for Taiwanese people and visiting foreigners. First, I believe that this book can serve as an aid to Taiwanese people who wish to understand what foreigners face when they are dealing with everyday situations in Taiwan. I know there are many citizens who want a better understanding, in order to be more effective at relating to people from other countries. The book is also a nice supplement for people wishing to improve their English in practical situations. Finally, I believe that foreigners visiting Taiwan would find this book helpful in gaining insights into the local culture, and learning shortcuts to handling the difficulties they may face. No matter who buys the book, I hope they will enjoy the personal experiences that I have the privilege to share.

Thank you!

Tony Coolidge

目錄

第二篇
Learning about Taiwan
─ History, Culture, Scenery...
人文史地在台灣 / 177

每個單元配置 QR code 掃描供下載音檔,若不便用手機下載者,請輸入以下網址,進入播放頁面後,按右鍵選擇「另存新檔」,即可存取 MP3 檔案。
http://epaper.morningstar.com.tw/mp3/0103353/01.mp3

請依單元編號 key 入下載,例如:01,02,03……

第一篇

Living & Enjoying in Taiwan

食衣住行在台灣

Airport 機場

UNIT 01

My first experience in Taiwan was at the international airport in Taoyuan. To me, the airport seemed cleaner and more modern than Western airports, but it was a bit more crowded. After a long, tiring flight, all I wanted to do was to pass through the immigration checkpoint, claim my luggage and get through the Customs area as soon as possible. I just wanted to find the best local transportation method that would get me to Tainan City. I knew I could conveniently take a taxi to the train station. However, I heard there was a bus that went from the airport directly to Tainan City. That was a cheaper way to get there, and I could take a nap on the bus. There were many signs at the airport in Chinese, which I couldn't read. Luckily, I did find a sign directing me to the taxi stand. But it was not easy for me to find the bus station. It was my good fortune that a nice Taiwanese person realized that I was confused. He asked (in English) if he could help me and direct me to the bus station at the back of the airport. I was so grateful and relieved that I gave him a candy bar that I brought from the USA as a thank-you gift.

If you see anyone who looks like a foreigner at the airport who seems confused or lost, don't be afraid to ask if he or she needs help. Just imagine how you would feel in the airport of a foreign country. You may actually be able provide the information that person needs. If you cannot, at least you can point him or her to someone at the airport who can help.

基本實用會話

Taiwanese (A) Westerner (B)

Helping a lost visitor.
幫助迷路旅人。

B : Please help me. I cannot find my gate.
請幫幫我，我找不到我的登機門。

A : Can I see your boarding pass (ticket)?
我可以看一下你的登機證嗎？

B : Here you go.
在這裡。

A : Oh, you are going on a domestic flight. But you are in the international terminal of the airport.
你要搭的是國內航線。但這裡是國際線的航廈。

B : Oh no! Is the domestic terminal very far?
喔，不！國內線航廈很遠嗎？

A : Go to the end of this hall and catch the Skytrain(PMS). It will take you to the International Terminal in 5 minutes.
走到這個大廳的盡頭搭PMS機場電車，五分鐘就會到國際線航廈了。

Helping a visitor when you don't understand what that person needs.
在不明白旅人需要什麼的情況下，給予他/她幫助。

B : Hello. Could you please help me?
你好，你可以幫幫我嗎？

A : OK. What can I do for you?
好，我能幫你什麼忙？

B : I am having trouble finding the location of the rental car company. Also, I don't know the requirements for driving in this country. If I can't rent a car, I don't know how I will get to my destination.
我找不到租車公司的位置。我也不知道在這個國家開車要具備什麼條件。如果我不能租車，我不知道該怎麼去目的地。

A : I am sorry. I can't understand everything you say. But I know who can help you.
對不起，我聽不太懂你說的話。但我知道誰能幫你。

B : Who?
誰？

A : Someone who can speak English better than me. Please go to the information desk upstairs. If you cannot find it, go to any airline check-in counter.
英文說的比我好的人。請到樓上的詢問處，如果你找不到，也可以到任何一個航空公司的櫃台。

B : OK. Thank you.
好，謝謝你。

NOTES

My advice for people who find a lost 'Westerner' in an airport is to learn how to direct that person to the airport's information desk. If an airport information desk is not nearby, you can direct him or her to an airline company's check-in counter. There is an excellent chance that someone in these places can speak English and provide assistance. Don't forget that being at the airport may be the Westerner's first experience with your language and culture, and it may be a culture shock for him or her. Be patient and speak slowly.

Sentences a Westerner might say
老外可能會說的句子

Hello. Do you speak English?
!嗨，你會說英文嗎？

My flight was short. Although, I'm really looking forward to getting back home.
飛行時間很短，但我真的很期待能回家。

I flew in from Kaohsiung, but, I need to catch another flight to Canada.
我從高雄飛來的，但我必須轉另一班飛機到加拿大。

I came for a business trip. I did spend a few days touring the island.
我是來出差的，也花了幾天遊覽這座島。

I could use some help finding the international terminal.
請告訴我如何找到國際線航廈。

Do I need to claim my luggage?
我得提領我的行李嗎？

Where can I exchange my currency (money) back to Canadian dollars?
哪裡可以將我的錢換回加拿大幣？

Do I have to go through a security checkpoint again?
我得再通過一次安檢嗎？

Oh, I won't. Thanks for your advice.
喔，我沒有。謝謝你的幫忙。

Next time I'll get a visa to allow me to stay longer and explore Taiwan.
下次我會申請時間長一點的簽證，好好探索台灣。

Sentences a Taiwanese person might say.
台灣人可能會說的句子

Yes, I do. How was your flight?
我會。飛行順利嗎？

By the way, where did you fly in from?
對了，你從哪裡飛來的？

Did you visit our country for business or pleasure?
你來這裡是出差還是旅遊？

Do you need help finding anything?
你需要幫忙嗎？

OK. Just go down the hallway and turn left. You will see the signs for it.
好,只要沿著走廊,然後左轉,就會看到指標了。

No. Your suitcases will automatically be transferred to your international flight.
不用,你的行李會自動轉到你的國際線航廈。

There are several currency exchange counters in the Arrivals area of the airport.
在機場的入境大廳有幾家換匯的櫃台。

Yes, you will. Make sure you don't carry any restricted items through there.
是的,以確保你沒有攜帶任何違禁物品來這裡。

You're welcome. I hope you can visit again and see more of our famous sights.
歡迎,希望你再次光臨參觀我們的風景名勝。

Have a safe journey back home.
祝你旅途平安。

Featured Vocabulary

flight attendant (n.) 空服人員

Not long ago in native English-speaking countries, "flight attendants" were known as "stewards" for males and "stewardesses" for females. As more men started to have this job, the airlines chose a name that would be applicable to both male and females. The new term for the job position is also considered less sexist, too.

customs (n.) 海關

When some Westerners enter an Asian country on a flight, they may not understand the Customs rules that apply to that country. They may get into trouble for bringing a plant or fruit in their suitcase. Also, when they return to their own country, the Customs agents there may not allow them to bring certain items into their country. Travelers should be aware of the restrictions at the airport, before they go shopping in Taiwan.

currency exchange (n.) 貨幣交換,換匯

Westerners entering your country may feel uncomfortable not having enough local currency. So they may look for a currency exchange location in the airport. They charge higher exchange fees than banks, but they are more convenient. These businesses are often open only during normal business hours. If they are closed, you can direct the visitor to a large bank that can handle international currency exchange. Not all banks can offer this service.

Transportation 交通

As an American, what I adore about living in Taiwan is the convenience of its public transportation system, and the number of options available to explore the island. The transportation networks are just much better developed and more affordable here than those in America, and even the taxi fares are relatively cheap in Taiwan. The Taiwanese rail system always leaves a positive impression on me. It seems that the trains are always on time. To my surprise, I found mass transit in Taiwan to be so reliable and timely, which contrasts with my experiences back home. In America, being late is commonplace when using public transportation. As for Taiwan's high speed rail system, I can only offer high praise about it. I have never observed any municipal or national transportation system in America that matches Taiwan's in terms of convenience. I enjoy taking visitors to experience a ride on Taiwan's high speed rail. It's remarkable that the HSR allows me to have breakfast in Tainan City, join my friends for a baseball game in Taipei, and make it to Kaohsiung for a late dinner. Technology really makes Taiwan feel smaller and more accessible.

As grateful as I am for Taiwan's transportation system, I have experienced problems when trying to find the right bus or train. Sometimes, there were no English signs on these vehicles, which made them difficult to identify. I often needed to rely on the assistance of strangers to help me during these situations, but it wasn't hard to find a willing helper. Recently, municipal bus systems have improved, and identifying the buses and routes has been simplified. Now, some municipal buses have color codes, and some have English route identifiers. Also, thanks to audio recordings on trains and buses announcing each destination name in English, visitors may avoid missing their stop. It is evident that public transportation here in Taiwan has become more "user-friendly" to native English speakers.

基本實用會話

Taiwanese (A)　　Westerner (B)

A conversation in a taxi.
計程車上的對話。

A : Where can I take you, sir/ma'am?
先生/小姐，請問要去哪裡？

B : Please take me to the Grand Hotel.
請帶我去圓山飯店。

A : OK. That will be no problem. I know the location of your destination.
好，沒問題。我知道那在哪裡。

B : How long will it take for us to arrive?
要多久才會到？

A : The traffic is heavy right now. So, there may be a slight delay. I estimate that it will take about 25 minutes.
現在很塞車，所以可能會晚一點。我估計要25分鐘。

B : Would you please tell me how much the fare will be?
能不能告訴我車費大概多少錢呢？

A : The fare will be approximately NT200.
大概200元。

B : Wow! That is very inexpensive.
哇！很便宜。

> **A conversation at a train station.**
> 火車站的對話。

B : Would you please help me?
可以幫幫我嗎？

A : Sure. How may I assist you?
當然，您需要什麼協助？

B : I am having difficulty finding the train going to Hsinchu City. It is scheduled to depart at 11:20 a.m.
我找不到去新竹的火車，它應該是早上11:20發車。

A : OK. Let me look at your ticket. According to the schedule of departures, you need to wait at Platform 2B.
好，請出示你的車票。根據發車時間，你要在第二月台等車。

B : Where is that platform?
月台在哪裡？

A : Go to that stairway which leads to Platform 2. Section 2B will be on the right side of the platform.
走這個樓梯可以通往第二月台。2B就在月台的右手邊。

B : Thank you very much.
非常感謝你。

NOTES

If you ever have the opportunity, you should recommend to foreigners that they buy an innovation known as the EasyCard. These time-saving cards can be purchased in convenience stores or MRT stations. They simplify the payment of public transportation. If you have the time and want to help foreigners, you can demonstrate how to buy the card and how to charge up the account at a terminal. Explain how the EasyCard can be used for the MRT trains, buses, and even coffee at 7-11! The people you help are sure to be impressed and grateful to you for sharing this time-saving tool.

溝通大加分

Sentences a Westerner might say
老外可能會說的句子

I need to go to the Taipei Main Train Station. How much will the fare be?
我要去台北火車站,車費大概多少?

How long will it be before we arrive at our destination?
要多久才會到目的地?

Where do I get off the bus to transfer to the MRT Brown Line?
我想轉捷運棕線,要在哪裡下車?

At which location can I catch a taxi/a bus/a train?
在哪裡可以搭計程車/公車/火車?

Which city bus do I need to take to get to City Hall?
要搭哪班公車才能到市政府?

I don't require a reserved ticket. How much will it save me, if I purchase a non-reserved ticket?
我沒有訂票,如果現場買票要多少錢?

How much is a business-class ticket from Kaohsiung to Taipei on the HSR?
從高雄到台北的高鐵商務艙要多少錢?

In addition to the taxi fare, should I pay a tip to the driver?
除了計程車費外,我該付小費給司機嗎?

I don't have the small change for the bus fare. Will you accept a NT1,000 bill?
我沒有零錢付公車費。你可以收1000元紙鈔嗎?

The taxi/bus/train ride is taking significantly longer than expected.
搭計程車/公車/火車比想像中的久好多。

Sentences a Taiwanese person might say.
台灣人可能會說的句子

Where (would you like/do you want) me to take you?
你要去哪裡?

The cost of the taxi fare is NT200.
計程車費是200元。

The next (bus/train) is scheduled to leave at 11:00 am.
下一班車(公車/火車)將在早上11點發車。

The taxi stand is directly in front of the main entrance.
計程車候車站就在大門正前方。

The train station is in the center of town across the street from City Hall.
火車站在市中心，在市政廳的對面。

There is a bus station alongside the main highway.
公車站在高速公路旁。

The MRT stands for Metro Rapid Transit, and it is similar to a subway system.
MRT是捷運，跟地鐵系統很像。

Amazingly, the high speed rail train travels at top speeds of over 300 kilometers per hour.
高速火車的速度驚人，時速最快超過300公里。

The MRT trains arrive at this stop at intervals of approximately every 5 minutes.
這一站的捷運大概每隔5分鐘一班。

You can buy the EasyCard at a convenience store and recharge it at this vending machine.
你可以在商店買悠遊卡，然後在這台儲值機儲值。

Featured Vocabulary

fare (n.) 費, 票價

Westerners use the term, "fare," when describing the payment for public transportation methods. This includes taxi fare, bus fare, train fare, etc. Some people in Taiwan use the term, "fee," but that is not typical and may sound strange to a Westerner.

MRT vs. subway vs. tube (n.) 捷運 vs 地鐵 vs 地鐵(英國)

Taiwan is home to two very efficient mass transit rail systems, located in Taipei and Kaohsiung. Westerners often find them to be the MRT systems to be very impressive, because they are usually cleaner and more efficient than similar systems in their countries. However, Americans often describe these systems as "subway" systems and the British describe them as "tube" systems. So, a term like, "MRT train," may be unfamiliar to them. They may instead use the term, "subway train."

High speed rail vs. bullet train (n.) 高鐵 vs 子彈列車

Taiwan's high speed rail system is a technological marvel to most visiting Westerners. It is often referred to as the HSR, which means High Speed Rail. However, the most common term familiar to Westerners is, "the bullet train." This term means, "very fast train," and was originally used to describe the famous high speed rail trains in Japan, known as the "Shinkansen."

Directions 問路

Once, I had difficulty finding a certain cram school in the town of Madou. Finding Madou on a motor scooter was not too difficult. The signs on the main roads leading into the large town were easy to follow. But once I arrived in Madou, the town seemed bigger than anticipated, and the street signs were not all written in Pinyin characters. I stopped frequently to ask for help with my "broken" Chinese language. A few people were too busy to help, or just said, "tiao-buh," which means, "I don't understand," in Taiwanese. But I did get assistance at a 7-11 convenience store. Fortunately, my wife had written down the name of the cram school and the address in Chinese on a piece of paper. The convenience store worker gestured to turn right at the next street and to look for a Family Mart. I found the Family Mart, and a worker there pointed to a gas station and gestured to turn left. I stopped at the gas station, and the attendant pointed to the cram school. Fortunately, stopping at these landmarks made it possible for me to find my way to my destination.

Taiwan is still a place where it is easy to get lost, especially in the urban areas. If you want the ability to give directions to a foreigner in English, I have a few recommendations. First, learn how to say English words that indicate direction and distance. Also, you should know how to say English words like "street," "intersection," "stop sign," and "traffic light." Directing lost visitors to nearby recognizable landmarks is very helpful. It is also helpful to learn how to say the names of these places in English, like "7-11," "Family Mart," "police station," "gas station," or "post office." School campuses also make good landmarks. That should be enough to get the visitor going in the right direction.

基本實用會話　Taiwanese (A)　Westerner (B)

Offering directions to a pedestrian.
向行人報路。

B： I'm sorry to disturb you. Can you help me? I need help finding my destination.
不好意思打擾您。你能幫幫我嗎？我找不到我要去的地方。

A： All right. Where are you going?
好，你要去哪裡？

B： I need to find a post office to mail a postcard.
我要找郵局寄明信片。

A : That's within walking distance. You see that 7-11? Go there and take a right. You will see a Family Mart convenience store. The post office is across the street from the Family Mart.
走路就能到了。看到那家7-11嗎？從那裡右轉能看到一家全家便利商店，郵局就在全家的對面。

B : Hey, that's great. Thank you! How long should it take for me to get there?
太好了，謝謝你！走到那裡要多久？

A : If you walk at a normal pace, you should get there within ten minutes.
如果用一般的走路速度，應該十分鐘內會到。

Offering directions to a driver.
向司機報路。

B : Would you mind giving me directions to Yujing? I am driving my family there to try the famous mango ice cream.
請問往玉井要怎麼走？我想載我的家人去那裡試試有名的芒果冰。

A : First, you want to follow that sign and get on Freeway #8, and go East about 9 kilometers.
你要先跟著指示上八號高速公路，然後往東開9公里。

B : How will I know at which exit to get off?
我怎麼知道從哪個出口下？

A : It will be the last exit, which is the end of the freeway. Take a left to go East on Highway 20. Follow that road 20 kilometers, and you will see a big police station once you reach Yujing. In front of the police station, you want to go straight on Zhongzheng Road.
那是最後一個出口，也是高速公路的盡頭。下公路後靠左往東走20號道路，沿著路走20公里後看到一間大警察局，你就到玉井了。從警察局前，再沿著中正路直走。

B : When I get there, how will I find a good ice cream shop?
到了之後，要怎樣才能找到好的冰淇淋店？

A : Take Zhongzheng Road to get to the center of town. At the intersection of Zhongzheng and Zhonghua roads you will see the most famous place for mango ice cream.
沿著中正路就能進到市中心。中正路和中華路口就能看到最有名的芒果冰店。

NOTES

While touring Taiwan, visitors often have difficulty finding a toilet they can use, especially a western-style toilet. Many stores, and even some smaller restaurants do not have toilets available for public use. This can be very frustrating to a visitor, especially when they are traveling with children. In America, I could always find a restroom in any public building, store or restaurant. It didn't take me long to learn that most reliable places in Taiwan to find western-style public toilets that were clean and functional were the gas stations. CPC has saved me and my family many times.

Sentences a Westerner might say
老外可能會說的句子

I need to go to the Taipei Main Train Station. How can I get there by foot?
我要去台北火車站。要怎麼走呢？

This festival is wonderful, but I can't find a restroom. Would you please direct me to the nearest one?
這節慶很棒，但我找不到洗手間。可以告訴我最近的洗手間在哪裡嗎？

Would you help me to find the nearest MRT station?
可以告訴我最近的捷運站在哪裡嗎？

I need to get a haircut. Can you direct me to a barber shop?
我想剪頭髮，理髮店在哪裡？

We're looking for a good place to eat. Do you know any Western restaurants near here?
我們想找個好餐廳吃飯，你知道這附近哪裡有西餐廳嗎？

I lost my wallet and passport! Please help me to find the nearest police station.
我的皮夾和護照不見了！請告訴我最近的警察局在哪裡。

I heard there was a famous temple in this area, but we can't find it. I think we're lost.
聽說這一區有間有名的寺廟，可是我們找不到。我想我們迷路了。

I need help finding our company's warehouse. Do you know where it is?
我找不到公司的倉庫。你知道在哪裡嗎？

I am late for my presentation at Ren-Ai Junior High School. Would you tell me how to get there?
我去仁愛國中簡報要遲到了。可以告訴我要怎麼去嗎？

I need to drive to Kaohsiung this weekend. I should go via which route?
我這週末要開車去高雄，應該走哪條路呢？

Sentences a Taiwanese person might say.
台灣人可能會說的句子

Go straight down Zhongshan South Road until you see the police station. Turn right at Gongyuan Road and walk for two blocks. You will see the train station in front of you.
沿著中山南路直走，看到警察局後在公園路右轉，走兩個街口就會看到車站在你前面。

You can find a restroom at the CPC gas station just around the corner from the convenience store.
在CPC加油站有洗手間，就在便利商店的轉角。

There is an MRT station on this boulevard three blocks east of here. It will be on your right side.
沿這條馬路往東走三個路口，右手邊就有捷運站。

Go to that 7-11 and turn right. Follow the road to the next 7-11 and turn left. When you get to a Family Mart, the barber shop is next door to it.
從那家7-11右轉，沿著路走到下一家7-11，然後左轉。走到全家便利商店後，理髮店就在隔壁。

Take a walk across this park, and then walk on the driveway around the City Hall building to the other side. You can't miss the Italian pizza restaurant.
走過這座公園，然後沿著車道繞過市政府大樓到另一邊，就能看到義大利披薩餐廳。

After you drive through two intersections, turn right, and you will see the police station immediately on your right.
開過兩個交叉路口後右轉，在右手邊馬上會看到警察局。

Follow Highway 17 north and you will see the road split into two. Stay right, and you will be on Yanhai Road. Follow this road and you will see the signs for Longshan Temple.
沿著17號公路走，會看到分叉路口，靠右走會進入沿海路，繼續直行就會看到龍山寺的指示牌。

If you want to find the warehouse, you need to drive out of the residential area on Highway 10 to the industrial park in the outskirts of town.
如果你想去倉庫，你得先沿著10號公路開出住宅區，然後到市郊的工業公園。

The Ren-Ai Junior High School is five blocks down the road after you turn left at the stop sign.
仁愛國中從這個紅綠燈左轉，再走五個路口就到了。

Both Hwy 1 and Hwy 3 will take you to Kaohsiung from Taipei. But Highway 3 usually has less traffic, so it is usually the fastest way to get to your destination.
國道一號和國道三號都能從高雄開到台北。但國道三號的車通常比較少，所以通常是最快到達目的地的方式。

Featured Vocabulary

intersection (n.) 路口

There are several words that describe where two or more roads meet, or intersect. The most common common word used is "intersection." However, when large roads or highways cross each other at different levels, Westerners call it an "interchange." Also, when two or more smaller roads cross, typically in the countryside, we use a different word. In American English, we use "junction" and in British English, we use "crossroads."

pedestrian (n.) 行人

When touring Taiwan, I have discovered the best way to really know the local culture is to be a pedestrian. That means, there is a much deeper experience available when one explores a place on foot rather than by car. There are different ways to describe this type of activity. We can call it a pedestrian tour, a walking tour, or touring by foot. The term, "walking tour," is more commonly used in the USA, and "touring by foot," is more commonly used in the Great Britain.

Weddings 參加婚禮

I married my wife in the USA, so I didn't experience my first Taiwanese wedding until we moved to Taiwan in 2009. It didn't take very long to be invited to a wedding, because my wife has many relatives. We went to her cousin's wedding in our hometown. My first surprise was finding out that we didn't need to go shoppng for a wedding gift. My wife prepared a red envelope with money inside. We walked to the wedding, which was under a big tent set up on a road. There were balloons and decorations everywhere. I brought my camera and offered to take photos of the wedding. But, I was surprised that the bride and groom already had a big wedding photo album on display, showing them being affectionate in many beautiful locations. I had never seen a wedding album like that before. We sat down at a round table that seated ten people, and proceeded with a ten-course meal. I tried some new dishes, such as fried bumble bees and rooster "balls." The event was festive, with strip dancers, music, and karaoke. Guests went on stage to toast the newly married couple and offer them their blessings. The liquor did flowed freely, and a fair share of people stumbled home. I couldn't help but to have a few beers. At the end of the event, we congratulated the couple and wished them prosperity before they left for their honeymoon. With a full belly and a warm heart, I walked home with my wife, chatting about the new experiences.

We have gone to many weddings after that one, and most have been practically the same. Sometimes the location has been under a tent, and sometimes it has been in a banquet hall. If you invite foreigners to a Taiwanese wedding, you should recommend that they eat small portions of each dish that is placed on their table. They may not realize how many dishes will be served, and they may be too full to enjoy all of them. You can also suggest that they take some of the leftover food home in a doggie bag. A doggie bag is what native English speakers call a bag that carries leftover food. Also remind them that with so many people toasting each other, they need to be careful, because it will be very easy to get drunk.

基本實用會話

Taiwanese (A)  Westerner (B)

Welcoming a guest.
歡迎來賓

A : Thank you for coming to the Hsu Wedding. May I see your invitation?
歡迎您來參加許家的婚禮。我能看看您的邀請函嗎？

B: Sure. Here you go. I am happy to be here. Wow! That is a beautiful wedding album.
當然，在這裡。很高興來參加，哇！這本婚紗照真漂亮。

A: Yes, they got it made last month. Would you please sign this registration book?
對啊，他們上個月拍的。請您在簽名簿上簽名。

B: Who do I give this red envelope to?
這紅包要給誰？

A: I'll take it. Thank you! I hope you enjoy the wedding. The attendant will accompany you to your seat.
請交給我，謝謝您！希望您喜歡這場婚禮，接待人員會帶您到您的位置。

B: Thank you very much!
非常謝謝您！

> **Saying farewell to a guest.**
> 和來賓道別。

B: Thank you for inviting me to your wedding. It was lovely. Congratulations to the both of you. I hope you have a long and prosperous marriage.
謝謝你邀請我來參加你的婚禮。婚禮很感人，恭喜你們，希望你們百年好合。

A: Thank you very much. I hope you enjoyed the food and drink.
非常謝謝你，希望你喜歡今天的餐點和飲料。

B: Yes, I think I enjoyed a few too many beers. By the way, you both make a very attractive couple. I hope you both have a memorable honeymoon. Enjoy your romance together.
喜歡，我覺得我啤酒喝太少了。對了，你們真的很登對，希望你們有個難忘的蜜月旅行，好好浪漫一下。

A: Thank you. We will. Would you like some candy or a cigarette?
謝謝，我們會的。要拿點糖果或香煙嗎？

B: No, thanks!
不用，謝謝！

NOTES

Giving wedding gifts is more complex in the USA than it is in Taiwan. In America, brides register with department stores, and select a list of items she wants. Wedding guests need to go to a store where the bride is registered and select from the list of items. This system was developed to help young couples get what they need to start their lives together, and to allow wedding guests to avoid bringing a duplicate gift. In Taiwan, we simply need to provide a red envelope with money inside. How much money should guests offer? It depends on their relationship to the bride and groom. Close relatives get more money than friends do. Since I am not wealthy, I generally figure out the cost of the banquet meal and multiply it times two or three.

Sentences a Westerner might say
老外可能會說的句子

Hello. I'm here for the Lin wedding. Which banquet room do I need to go to?
你好，我是來參加林家的婚禮。他們在哪個宴會廳？

You want me to sign the registration book here? Who do I give the gift envelope to?
我要在這個簽名簿上簽名？我要把紅包給誰？

Wow! There are so many tables here. How will I know where to sit?
哇！這裡有好幾桌，我怎麼知道自己要坐在哪裡？

The bride is my wife's cousin. It's my first time to be a guest at a Taiwanese wedding.
新娘是我太太的表妹，這是我第一次參加台灣人的婚禮。

In America, we call the round rotating tray in the middle of a table a "lazy Susan."
在美國，我們稱這種中間有旋轉圓盤的桌子為「旋轉餐桌lazy Susan」。

I can't believe it! This is the sixth dish already. What is this called?
真不敢相信，這已經是第六道菜了，它叫什麼？

Wow, this abalone is delicious. Hey! Why is the skin on this chicken black?
哇，這道鮑魚真好吃。嘿，這隻雞的皮怎麼是黑色的？

The bride's mother can really sing. But I think the father had too much to drink. Look at him dance!
新娘的媽媽真會唱歌，但我想她爸爸喝太多了，你看他跳舞的樣子！

Thank you for inviting me. I wish you both a long, happy marriage. What? You want to take a photo with me? Sure!
謝謝你邀請我來，希望你們百年好合。什麼？你們要跟我合照？沒問題！

Sentences a Taiwanese person might say.
台灣人可能會說的句子

Welcome. The Lin Wedding Party is being held in Banquet Room 201. It's right up those stairs.
歡迎，林家的婚禮在201宴會廳，從那邊的樓梯上去就到了。

Welcome to the Lin wedding. Please sign in here. The attendant will seat you.
歡迎參加林家的婚禮，請在這裡簽名，接待人員會引導你。

Please let me see your invitation. OK, follow me. Your assigned seat is right here.
請出示您的邀請卡，好的，請跟我來，你的指定位置在這裡。

Hello. It's nice to meet you. Are you friends or relatives of the bride or groom?
你好，很高興認識你，你是新娘還是新郎的親朋好友？

Please take some food as each dish is placed on the table.
請用。

There will be a lot more food coming, so just try a little of everything.
還有好幾道菜，所以什麼都試一點就好。

That is called shark fin soup. And those are giant, salted prawns.
這叫魚翅湯，那些是鹽烤大明蝦。

This is called "mountain chicken." They always have black skin and dark meat.
這是「山雞」，他們的皮是黑的，肉的顏色也較深。

Would you like a turn singing karaoke on stage?
你想上台獻唱嗎？

Before you leave, say goodbye to the newlyweds. The bride will give you candy and the groom will offer a cigarette.
在你離開前，先向新人道別，新娘會給你糖果，新郎會給你香煙。

Featured Vocabulary

wedding ceremony (n.) 婚禮

Wedding ceremonies in America and Europe are very different than those in Taiwan. Although, it is possible to find something similar to a traditional Christian wedding in a Taiwanese church. Another way native English speakers describe "wedding ceremony" is to use the word, "nuptials." In Western culture, nuptials usually contain several key parts in two different locations, including the procession, the wedding vows, the exchange of rings, and the wedding reception. In Taiwan, a wedding ceremony seems to take place in a large wedding reception, or banquet.

bride and groom (n.) 新娘和新郎

The woman who gets married is called a "bride" and the man is called a "groom." They are the main participants in a Western wedding ceremony. Other participants include the close friends or relatives of the bride (called "bridesmaids) and close friends or relatives of the groom (called "groomsmen"). The best friend of the bride is called the "maid of honor," and the best friend of the groom is called the "best man."

elope/elopement (v./n.) 私奔

In Western society it is more common to find couples who marry without the parents' consent. The act of getting married secretly, without the knowledge of friends or family, is called elopement. The couple elopes to avoid needing their parents' permission. It seems that parental permission for marriage is more important in Asian society than in Western society.

UNIT 05

Funerals 參加喪禮

In December 2004, I was traveling around Taiwan with my wife to shoot a documentary film. During the trip, my wife received grim news that her father was near death in the hospital. Fortunately, we reached the hospital in time to say our final words to him before he passed away. I didn't have the chance to know him very well, but at least I was able to express my gratitude to him, and to let him know I would take care of his daughter. What I witnessed afterwards was an intense emotional ordeal for my wife's family. They stayed together for two sorrowful weeks to make preparations the traditional Taoist funeral ceremony. I stayed with the family for a few days before the funeral to show my sympathy and support. During those few days, I saw Buddhist nuns chant to calm the father's spirit. Their repetitive hymn was heavenly. On the morning of the funeral, there was a gathering of friends and relatives who viewed the corpse in the coffin. They offered their condolences and money in white envelopes to the family. During the ceremony, the family members wore light yellow garments that were draped over their heads. They prayed to the father with incense in their hands. They publicly expressed their agony and grief over their loss. The emotional scene would haunt me forever. At the conclusion, everyone followed the hearse to the cemetery, where the body and coffin were cremated. There is now a small memorial at the cemetery where the ashes are kept, and the family visits regularly to pay their respects.

There are different customs for the funerals of different religions, and Westerners may not be familiar with Buddhist or Taoist funeral customs. If you know foreigners who are invited to a funeral to pay their respects, it may be a good idea to discuss the customs of the ceremony to make sure they don't do anything disrespectful.

基本實用會話

Taiwanese (A) Westerner (B)

Preparing a Westerner for a funeral ceremony. 邀請老外參加喪禮

A: Are you going to Mr. Hsaio's funeral?
你會去蕭先生的喪禮嗎？

B: I'd like to. He was my favorite professor.
B：會，他是我最喜歡的教授。

A : Well, his family members are Buddhists, so there are a few things you should know.
他的家人都是佛教徒，所以有幾件事你要先了解。

B : OK. I've never been to a Buddhist funeral before.
好，我從未參加過佛教喪禮。

A : Make sure you wear a white shirt to show respect for the dead. If you want to make an offering to the family, you can put a little money into a white envelope. You can view the body before it is cremated and offer a blessing.
你得穿白衣，以顯示對死者的尊敬。如果你想對家人致敬，可以放一點錢到白信封裡。在火化前你可以瞻仰遺容，向他致敬。

B : I am not sure if I can bear to view the body, but thank you very much for the advice!
我不知道我敢不敢瞻仰遺容，但謝謝你的建議。

> **A Westerner offering condolences.**
> 老外來致哀。

B : I'm sorry Mrs. Hsiao for your loss. I know this must be so hard for you and your family.
蕭太太，很遺憾你失去親人。我知道您和您家人一定很難過。

A : Thank you for coming to offer your condolences. We appreciate it very much.
謝謝您來致哀，我們很感謝您。

B : Please let me know if there is anything I can do for you during this time of hardship.
這段難過的時間如果有什麼我能幫忙的，請告訴我。

A : I will. Thank you.
我會的，謝謝你。

 NOTES

A traditional Chinese-style grave in a Taiwanese cemetery can be beautifully decorated. These cemeteries may also have large, elegant monuments, in which the bones or ashes are stored. I am amazed by how Taiwanese families can put a lot of thought and care into taking care of the deceased. They even observe a national holiday, known as the Tomb Sweeping Day. On this day, families get together to clean graves and surrounding areas, and to teach their children the importance of respecting ancestors. I think there is something important that Westerners can learn from these traditions.

Sentences a Westerner might say
老外可能會說的句子

Hello. Is this the funeral for the Lee family?
你好，請問這是李家的喪禮嗎？

Do I need to sign this registration book? Who will take this white donation envelope?
我需要在這本簽名簿簽名嗎？這個奠儀該交給誰？

I think I'd rather not look at the body of Mr. Lee. I don't want to be too emotional in front of everyone.
我想我還是不瞻仰李先生的遺容了，我不想在大家面前失態。

Why have people put so many snacks here on the table? Can I take one?
為什麼在桌上放這麼多零食？我能拿一個嗎？

What's going on here? Why is that man chanting and moving that chair around like that?
這是怎麼回事？那個人為什麼一直在吟唱，又把那張椅子像那樣搬來搬去？

Oh my God! They are using a knife to cut the necks of a live duck and rooster? Are they getting sacrificed?
我的天啊！他們用刀子把活生生的鴨子和公雞切開？他們是在獻祭嗎？

That chanting music sounds very relaxing and beautiful. Why is it playing constantly?
誦唱的音樂聲令人好放鬆，好美麗。為什麼要一直吟誦呢？

Where are they bringing the coffin? Where is everyone going?
他們要將棺材搬去哪裡？大家要去哪裡？

Mrs. Lee, I am truly sorry for your loss.
李太太，很遺憾你失去親人。

Is there anything I can do in your time of despair? If there is, please let me know.
在這段難過的時間，我能為你做什麼呢？如果有的話，請告訴我。

Sentences a Taiwanese person might say.
台灣人可能會說的句子

Yes, it is the funeral service for the Lee family.
是的，這是李家的喪禮。

Please sign the book. Also, make sure your name is on the donation envelope.
請在這簿子上簽名，也請在您的奠儀上簽名。

Please have a seat anywhere. If you'd like, you can view Mr. Lee in the coffin and offer your blessings.
請找個地方坐，您也可以瞻仰李先生的遺容，向他致敬。

No! You can't eat that. People often offer snacks to the spirit of the deceased for the afterlife.
不，你不能吃那些點心。那是人們為了讓亡者在來生使用的點心。

The spiritual leader from the local temple is calling on the spirit of the deceased to answer the questions of the family members.
當地廟宇的法師正在召喚亡靈，回答家屬的問題。

No, they're not being killed. Offering the blood of a duck and a chicken is part of a Taoist ritual.
不，不是殺掉他們，取雞鴨的血只是道教儀式的一部分。

The chant is a Buddhist custom to calm the spirit after it leaves the body.
唸經是佛教儀式，是為了使離開肉體的亡靈能得到安息。

Everyone is leaving the funeral home. Some people will go to the cemetery to watch the burial.
大家都要離開喪禮回家了。有些人會去墓地出席葬禮。

Thank you for your condolences. And thank you for paying your respects to Mr. Lee.
謝謝您來致哀，也謝謝您來向李先生致敬。

Thank you for being sympathetic. In time, I will be fine.
謝謝您的心意，過段時間，我會沒事的。

Featured Vocabulary

funeral ceremony (n.) 葬禮儀式

Funeral ceremonies in America and Europe are usually different than those in Taiwan, especially the Taiwanese Taoist or Buddhist ceremonies. Typically funeral ceremonies are events where the public is invited to view the body to say goodbye, and to offer something to the family. In Taiwan, they are typically events where people grieve. In the USA and Europe, many funeral ceremonies are actually as festive as weddings. These ceremonies, called "wakes," are held as a celebration of the life of the deceased.

grave (n.) 墓

A grave is a place where a dead body is placed to rest in the ground for eternity. Graves in the West are typically simpler than those in Taiwan. Westerners have another term for grave, which is "tomb." The word, "tomb," is used to describe a burial place that is ancient. If the remains of the body are placed in a large monument that resembles a building, that is referred to a "mausoleum," "crypt," or "burial chamber."

grieve/grief (v./n.) 哀/悲

In Western society, there is usually a period of time when widows, widowers, and other family members (grief/show their grief) and pay their respects. This is referred to as a "mourning period." They may wear black clothing during this time. Black color is a symbol in Western culture for showing respect for the dead. They may also visit the grave to mourn and offer flowers during the mourning period.

UNIT 06

I have always loved all types of food, and I have always appreciated the opportunity to sample exotic cuisine from other countries. So, when I first visited Taiwan, my eyes nearly popped out when I saw the variety of tasty food there was to try. I was equally amazed by the variety of drinks there were to tempt the tongue. The quality and variety of food and drinks in Taiwan were definitely one of the deciding factors in choosing to move my family to the island. When we moved to Taiwan in 2009, we relocated to Tainan City. How lucky I felt, when I discovered that Tainan was the capital of Taiwanese culture AND CUISINE! There seemed to be more restaurants, tea shops and vendors than I could count in the area. Not to mention, there were unique food and drinks to be found at day markets, night markets, festivals, banquets, weddings, and funerals. Additionally, just about every town we visited had their own specialty food and drinks. I felt like I was in heaven!

What's amazing is that even though I often "overeat" with the incredible variety of food, I am actually healthier in Taiwan than I was in America. I think that says a lot about how much healthier the Taiwanese diet is than the American diet. I believe that most visitors to Taiwan will appreciate the amount of nutritious choices there are. There are many vegetarian restaurants with so many different dishes, it makes my head spin. Even though there are plenty of unhealthy food and drinks available in Taiwan, such as greasy, deep-fried snacks, and sugary drinks, there are also more healthy choices as well. There are many more fruits and vegetables at the local markets than I have ever seen in an American supermarket. I think this is why foreigners who live in Taiwan consider the food and drinks one of the most enjoyable aspects about living here.

基本實用會話

Taiwanese (A)　　Westerner (B)

Sharing a new drinking experience.
分享新的飲食體驗。

A : What did you think about your lunch? You didn't eat much.
你覺得午餐怎麼樣？你吃得不多。

B : I like the soup very much, but please don't ask me to eat that black egg or smelly tofu again.
我很喜歡那碗湯，但別再叫我吃那些黑黑的蛋或臭臭的豆腐了。

A : Oh! Those dishes were preserved duck egg and stinky tofu.
喔！那些菜叫皮蛋豆腐。

B : Whatever it was, I will never try it again. Yuck!
不管是什麼，我都不要再吃了，好噁！

A : OK. Before you go, you should try one of the special Taiwanese drinks.
好。在你離開前，你應該試試台灣的特別飲料。

B : Wow! This tea shop has so many different types of drinks. But I can't read the menu.
哇！這間飲料店賣的飲料種類好多，但我看不懂菜單。

A : They have different types of teas, juice, and even coffees. Which do you prefer?
他們有不同種類的茶、果汁，甚至是咖啡。你喜歡哪一種？

B : Which type of tea will be a good refreshment for a hot day?
哪種茶最適合在大熱天喝？

A : Since you didn't really eat much for lunch, let me recommend the pearl milk tea. The little edible tapioca balls will fill you up.
既然你午餐吃得不多，我建議你喝珍珠奶茶。這個用木薯粉做的小球可以吃，也能填飽你的肚子。

Recommending a Western restaurant.
推薦西餐廳。

B : I don't really feel like having noodles or rice for lunch today. Do you know where I can find a big, juicy hamburger?
我今天中午不想再吃麵或飯了。你知道哪裡可以吃到多汁的大漢堡嗎？

A : I don't eat hamburgers, but my friend told me about a good American-style burger restaurant that he likes. It is near National Taiwan University on Xinsheng South Rd.
我不吃漢堡，但我朋友曾告訴我一家他喜歡的美式漢堡餐廳，在新生南路上，靠近台灣大學。

B : It sounds great! I am willing to try it. Do you know if it is close to an MRT stop?
聽起來不錯！我想試試。它離捷運站近嗎？

A : Yes, it is a 5-minute walk from Gongguan Station. Can I join you for lunch?
近，離公館站只要走五分鐘。我能跟你一起吃午餐嗎？

 NOTES

As much as I enjoy the traditional food in Taiwan, I do often miss good Western food. There aren't as many choices for Western food in Tainan City area as there are in Taipei or Kaohsiung. If you want to help a foreigner in Taiwan feel more at home, find out their favorite type of food, and recommend a Western restaurant in their area. That gesture may even give you a new best friend. You may find foreigners who actually don't like Taiwanese food. If so, they may need help finding a grocery store or convenience store to buy food that they are used to eating.

Sentences a Westerner might say
老外可能會說的句子

I just felt my stomache grumble. It must be lunchtime already.
我的肚子咕嚕嚕叫,現在一定是午餐時間了。

You could say that I am an adventurous eater, because I'll anything once.
我可以說是勇於冒險的食客,因為我什麼都敢試。

I can't read the menu. Can you translate this for me?
我看不懂菜單,能不能幫我翻譯?

I like all types of soups. What can you recommend that I try?
什麼湯我都喜歡。你有什麼建議嗎?

I'll try the beef noodles, but why don't they offer grilled steak here?
我來試試牛肉麵,但他們為什麼沒有烤牛排?

Sure. You can order a special drink for me. The papaya milk sounds delicious to me.
當然,你可以幫我點杯特殊的飲料。木瓜牛奶聽來很美味。

I like pork, but do people really like to eat pig's ears and pig's feet? And are you serious? Pig stomach and intestines?
我喜歡豬肉,但人們很喜歡吃豬耳朵和豬腳嗎?你是說真的?豬胃和豬腸?

I don't know if I will ever get a hang of using chopsticks. Do they have any forks here?
不知道我能不能掌握筷子的用法,他們這裡有叉子嗎?

Watermelon slices and pineapple chunks sound perfect. Do I use these toothpicks to pick up the fruit?
西瓜片和鳳梨塊聽起來棒,我要用筷子夾水果嗎?

Thank you for the new lunch experience. Can I get the receipt? I want to pay for the both of us.
謝謝你帶來這頓新的午餐體驗。帳單能給我嗎?今天我請客。

Sentences a Taiwanese person might say.
台灣人可能會說的句子

Why don't you let me take you to a small restaurant nearby. It will give you a better idea of how the local people eat.
你要不要跟我到附近的小餐館,你會更了解當地人吃什麼。

Are you brave enough to try new exotic dishes?
你敢不敢嘗試新奇的菜餚?

I can translate the menu. But, it might be easier if I just point to the food.
我可以翻譯菜單。不過由我來點菜或許簡單點。

This fish ball soup is famous in this area.
魚丸湯在這區很出名。

Would you like to try a special drink? How about papaya milk or black tea.
你想試試一種特殊的飲料嗎？要吃木瓜牛奶還是紅茶？

When I am in a hurry, I usually order a serving of beef noodles.
我餓的時候通常會點一份牛肉麵。

You can say that Chinese people don't like to waste any part of the pig. They will eat every part.
應該說中國人不喜歡浪費豬的任何一部分，他們每個部分都吃。

I think this restaurant doesn't have foriegners very often, so they probably don't have any utensils besides chopsticks and spoons.
我想這家餐廳不常有外國人來，所以他們可能沒有筷子或湯匙以外的餐具。

After our main course, we usually like to nibble on some fruit and chat for awhile.
主餐之後，我們通常會來點水果，然後再聊聊天。

Nonsense. I will pay the bill. It is customary in Taiwan for the host to pay for the visitor's meal.
胡說，我來付帳。在台灣，主人為客人付帳是習俗。

Featured Vocabulary

restaurant (n.) 餐廳

A restaurant (an eatery) is a place where people pay to eat. However, for native English speakers, there are many words to describe the type of restaurant they are referring to. For example, a "café" indicates a smaller restaurant with outdoor seating. A "buffet" is a restaurant where there are many choices and people serve themselves. A "cafeteria" is a restaurant where there are many choice, but a cafeteria worker serves people. A "diner" is an old-fashioned eatery where a waiter takes the order and serves the food in a short time.

beverage (n.) 飲料

The most common way native English speakers refer to a "drink" is to call it a "beverage." The word, "beverage" is most commonly used in British English to refer to any type of drink, whereas in American English, "beverage" is more commonly used to describe types of drinks. (For example, alcoholic beverage vs. non-alcoholic beverages)

UNIT 07

In America, my wife and I usually cooked our meals, because it was just too expensive to eat out. Fortunately, I loved to cook, especially when I had the chance to create new dishes for my family and friends. I didn't realize that my joy for cooking would be crushed when I moved to Taiwan. We lived with my wife's mother when we first moved to Tainan, so naturally, I wanted to cook a meal for my mother-in-law to show my appreciation. I started to plan my cooking by evaluating her kitchen. I was surprised to find her kitchen lacking a large oven or even a small microwave oven. Almost every home in America had those two essential cooking appliances. There were many other small kitchen appliances I could not find. I went to the local RT Mart supermarket to shop for the ingredients for the special meal. It was a big store, but there were many cooking ingredients I couldn't find. So, I settled for cooking a simple chicken and shitake mushroom dish. My mother was polite and ate the dinner, but I was so disappointed in how bland my dinner tasted. After that, I never had the passion to cook again. On the bright side, with so many varieties of affordable food vendors available within walking distance, I haven't needed to cook for my family. They are quite happy with the meals we eat every day.

If you know foreigners living in Taiwan who prefer to cook their own meals, chances are they prefer to eat food that is similar to what they are accustomed to. They may appreciate your help to find the ingredients that may not be found in Taiwanese stores. Large Western-brand stores like Carrefour and Costco, often have more international ingredients. Occasionally inviting your foreign friends for a shopping trip to one of these stores can be a pleasurable bonding experience. Who knows? They may invite you over for dinner to show their appreciation and teach you something about Western cooking.

基本實用會話　　Taiwanese (A)　　Westerner (B)

Shopping For Ingredients.
購買食材。

A: This supermarket is quite large in Taiwan. You can find many ingredients here.
這家超級市場在台灣算很大。你在這裡可以找到很多食材。

B: Thank you for bringing me here. There seems to be quite a variety of food and drinks here.
謝謝你帶我來這裡。這裡看來有很多種食材和飲料。

A : What will you cook for dinner? What items can I help you find?
你晚餐要煮什麼菜？我能幫你找什麼東西？

B : I am going to make an Italian pasta dish. I am looking for raw hamburger meat, a container of rotini pasta, and a bottle of spaghetti sauce. I also need a few spices, like coriander, thyme and basil.
我要煮義大利麵。我要找漢堡肉、一包螺旋麵、一罐義大利麵醬。我還需要一些香料，像是香菜、百里香和羅勒。

A : (30 minutes later) I'm sorry we couldn't find what you needed here. Maybe, we'll just have to make something else for dinner.
（30分鐘後）很遺憾在這裡找不到你需要的東西。或許我們晚餐得做點別的東西。

B : Or, we can drive into the city and shop at Costco. Do you have a membership?
或是我們也可以開車到Costco買東西，你有會員卡嗎？

Cooking In The Home.
在家開伙。

B : Thanks for letting me cook dinner at your place.
謝謝你讓我在你家煮晚餐。

A : No problem. I will enjoy the chance to try your cooking.
不客氣，我會把握機會試試你的手藝。

B : I bought two nice steaks at Carrefour, an onion, and a few potatoes. Do you like steak, grilled onions and baked potatoes?
我在家樂福買了兩塊不錯的牛排，還有幾顆馬鈴薯。你喜歡牛排、烤洋蔥和烤馬鈴薯嗎？

A : That sounds wonderful! But how will you cook the steaks? I have a wok and some pots.
聽起來很棒！但你的牛排要怎麼料理？我只有炒菜鍋和幾個鍋子。

B : You don't have a frying pan or oven? I guess I can improvise. I'll make stir-fried beef and onions and boiled potatoes.
你沒有平底鍋或烤箱嗎？我想我能改良一下，做個炒洋蔥牛肉和水煮馬鈴薯。

NOTES

If you have Western friends in Taiwan who like to cook, chances are that they may invite you over to their house for dinner. If you receive an invitation, it customary to bring a beverage or dessert as a gesture of gratitude. These are my simple suggestions. If the main course is fish, poultry or pork, I recommend a bottle of white wine. If the main course is beef, I recommend a bottle of red wine. If they are having a barbecue, beer would be suitable. Buy a dessert if the host doesn't drink alcohol, or if you don't know what the main course will be.

Sentences a Westerner might say
老外可能會說的句子

After all you have done to help me adjust to my new life in Taiwan, making dinner for you is the least I can do.
畢竟你幫我適應了我在台灣的新生活，至少我能為你煮頓晚餐。

I will prepare baked salmon as the main course, and asparagus with poached egg as a side dish. It won't be spicy. But I promise you, it will be delicious.
我準備了烤鮭魚當主菜，配菜是蘆筍水波蛋。不會辣，但我保證一定好吃。

Please get the fresh salmon fillets, asparagus, eggs and butter from the refrigerator. I will need bread, garlic, tarragon and the vinegar from the cabinet.
請從冰箱拿出新鮮鮭魚片、蘆筍和蛋。我還需要櫃子裡的麵包、大蒜、龍嵩和醋。

I'm preparing everything from memory. I have made this a few times before. We will crumble the bread crumbs on top of the salmon.
我憑記憶準備這些材料，我以前做過幾次。我們把麵包弄碎灑在鮭魚上。

I know. Butter is very expensive, but the fish wouldn't taste the same without it.
我知道，奶油非常貴，但沒有它，魚的味道就不對了。

Nonsense! It's OK to indulge like this once in while. Live a little!
胡說！偶爾這樣放縱一下沒關係的。就一點。

We don't have an oven in my house, so we won't be able to bake the salmon. I'll have to simmer it in a wok on the stove.
我家沒有烤箱，所以我們不能烤鮭魚。我要把它放在爐子上燉一下。

As for the asparagus with poached egg, we'll steam it in my rice steamer.
至於水波蛋蘆筍，要用蒸飯鍋蒸。

You're welcome! And thank you for the white wine. It goes perfectly with the fish.
不客氣！謝謝你的白酒，和魚非常搭。

Would you like to take the leftovers home with you?
你想把剩菜打包帶回家嗎？

Sentences a Taiwanese person might say.
台灣人可能會說的句子

Thank you for inviting me over for dinner. Do you mind if I watch how you cook the food?
謝謝你邀請我來晚餐。你介意我看著你煮飯嗎？

What dishes will you be preparing? Will it be spicy? I love spicy food.
你要準備什麼菜？會辣嗎？我喜歡吃辣。

What ingredients can I get for you? Are they in the cabinet or the refrigerator?
我要幫你拿什麼食材？都在櫃子裡還是冰箱裡？

Here are all of the ingredients. Will you use a recipe? And what is the bread for? Are we making a sandwich?
所有的食材都在這裡了。你有食譜嗎？這麵包是做什麼的？我們要做三明治嗎？

Wow! You're using a lot of butter with the salmon. Butter is really very expensive in Taiwan.
哇！你煮鮭魚用了好多奶油。奶油在台灣很貴。

Butter has so many calories. I'm watching my weight, so I can only eat a small serving.
奶油的熱量也很高，我正在控制體重，所以我只能吃一點。

Oh! That smells so good. The tarragon gives it an exquisite smell.
喔！聞起來好香，龍嵩的味道很獨特。

So that's what it means to "poach" something. The egg is steamed to be only partly cooked.
那就是「水波」的意思，蛋只蒸半熟。

Steve, this dinner is truly a feast for the senses. I hope you can let me return the favor and cook for you next time.
史帝夫，這頓真是色香味俱全的盛宴，希望你能讓我回報你，下一次讓我為你煮飯。

Thank you, but I really should let you keep the leftovers. I need to watch my weight, remember?
謝謝你，但剩菜還是讓你留著。我需要注意體重，記得嗎？

Featured Vocabulary

measurement (n.) 度量衡

When cooking, ingredients are measured in order to follow a standard recipe. In Western cooking, two sizes of spoons are commonly used to measure ingredients. For example, a recipe for cookies may require a teaspoon of yeast and three tablespoons of sugar. When measuring larger sizes of ingredients, Westerners use a handy tool known as a measuring cup. The same recipe for cookies may ask for three and a half cups of flour.

kitchen appliance (n.) 廚房電器

Kitchen appliances are electric tools that are used in the cooking process. There are many kitchen appliances that Westerners may take for granted in their countries, which may not be commonly found in Taiwan. Sometimes, they need to be creative in their cooking and use what is available. For example, in America, almost everyone has a microwave oven, and it is used to heat or preheat ingredients. But in Taiwan, Westerners can heat food quickly in a wok or in a steamer.

UNIT 08

Vegetarian 素食

Before I moved to Taiwan, I had a bad impression about vegetarian food. I would never consider replacing tasty steak and hamburgers with boring salad and spring rolls. In Taiwan, where a large percentage of people are Buddhists, there are many vegetarian restaurants serving their needs. My sister-in-law invited me to one such restaurant in Taipei, and the experience redefined how I viewed vegetarianism. The restaurant was very large and crowded with people. I stood in line with my tray and I couldn't believe my eyes. There were three types of steamed rice to choose from, and a dozen soups to begin with. That was impressive. Then there was sushi. I absolutely LOVE sushi! There were about a dozen types of sushi rolls with what looked like fish and squid. But those seafood items were actually reproduced from soy bean and gelatins. They had about sixteen ways to prepare about six varieties of mushrooms. There were about twenty other trays with different types of cooked vegetables. In the middle of the serving area was a colorful mountain of fruit. I'm not kidding when I say there were about twenty types of fruit available. After a few fruit drinks, coffee and ice cream, I had a completely satisfying meal. I didn't miss meat at all. If I could eat like this more often, I may even consider being a vegetarian one day.

If you invite foreign visitors to one of Taiwan's popular vegetarian restaurants, chances are that they have ever seen anything like it in their country. It doesn't matter whether they are meat-eaters or vegetarians, they are sure to be surprised. Most vegetarian options around the world are restricted to a few local vegetables and fruits, with salad being the most common vegetarian dish. In America, vegetarians may consider plain steamed tofu and spring rolls to be exotic vegetarian food. Take them to a Taiwanese vegetarian buffet, and they might just want to stay in Taiwan for good.

基本實用會話

Taiwanese (A) :  Westerner (B) :

Eating in a vegetarian restaurant.
在素食餐廳吃飯。

A : What did you think about your lunch today at this Buddhist restaurant?
你覺得今天佛教餐廳的午餐怎麼樣？

B : I just can't believe how many different types of delicious foods that vegetarians can eat in Taiwan.
我不敢相信台灣的素食者有這麼多種美味的選擇。

A : Did you already have some dessert? They have a good selection of ice cream.
你吃點心了嗎？他們的冰淇淋選擇很多。

B : No, thank you. There was just too much food to tempt me. I believe that I might become fat if I were a vegetarian.
不，謝謝你。誘惑我的食物太多了，如果我也吃素，一定會變胖。

A : I don't know about that. Eating here is supposed to be more nutritious than eating too much meat.
這就不一定了。在這裡吃東西應該比吃一堆肉來得有營養。

B : Thank you for buying lunch today. Should I do anything before I leave, like pray to this Buddha statue?
謝謝你今天請我吃午餐。我離開前要做什麼嗎，像是對佛像祈禱？

A : Maybe you can just thank the owner of the restaurant. She is right here.
或許你只要感謝餐廳主人就夠了。她就在這裡。

Asking if someone is vegetarian.
問某人是否為素食者。

B : Oh, I see that this restaurant serves mostly meat dishes. I think I will go somewhere else.
喔，我看到這家餐廳的菜大部分都有肉，我想我還是去別的地方。

A : Wait! We have vegetable fried rice and vegetable soup.
等等！我們有素食炒飯和素湯。

B : Do you use animal fat when you fry the rice? Do you use pork bones when you cook the soup?
你們炒飯時用的是動物油嗎？煮湯時有用豬骨頭嗎？

A : Yes, we do. Are you a vegetarian?
A：有，你吃鍋邊素嗎？

B : No, I'm not. I am a vegan.
不，我吃全素。

 NOTES

When planning the meals for groups of visiting foreigners, it is important to offer vegetarian options, especially with an estimated 5% of people in the world being vegetarians. Be sure that you can ask this question in English, "Do you prefer a vegetarian meal or a meal with meat?" It is also good to give people a vegetarian menu in English. Even if you don't have any vegetarians in your group, it shows kindness and consideration when you ask people for their preference.

Sentences a Westerner might say
老外可能會說的句子

I hope you like this Western-style steak restaurant. It's my favorite place to eat in the city.
希望你喜歡這家西式牛排館。這是我在城裡最喜歡的地方。

I didn't know that. That's OK. You can take what you want from the salad bar for only NT 100.
我不知道，沒關係，你可以吃沙拉吧，只要台幣100元。

While you get your food at the salad bar, I'll order a t-bone steak. I hope you don't mind if I eat it in front of you.
你吃沙拉吧的東西，但我會點一客丁骨牛排，希望你不介意我在你面前吃肉。

My food's not here yet, so I brought some buttered French bread for us to share. What did you find?
我的餐點還沒來，所以我拿了些奶油法式麵包，我們一起吃。你拿了什麼？

Is that enough food for your dinner? You didn't take much.
你晚餐吃那樣夠嗎？你沒拿多少。

I'm sorry! We can go to a vegetarian restaurant, if that's more to your liking.
很抱歉，如果你喜歡的話，我們可以去素食餐廳。

Don't forget, they have a good dessert bar here, and different types of coffee.
別忘了，他們這裡有不錯的點心吧，還有不同種類的咖啡。

My steak is here. Thank you. Oh my goodness! It's huge!
我的牛排到了，謝謝你。喔，我的天啊，好大塊！

Sure, I can finish it. I'm a big guy with a big appetite. But I'll also need to exercise later.
當然吃得完。我是個大胃口的大塊頭。但我晚點還是得做點運動。

You're welcome. If a vegetarian is willing to join me at a steak restaurant, then I am willing to join her at a vegetarian place.
不客氣，如果素食者願意和我一起來牛排館，我也願意和她一起去素食餐廳。

Sentences a Taiwanese person might say.
台灣人可能會說的句子

Well, I don't eat steak. I actually don't eat meat. I am a vegetarian.
我不吃牛排，其實我不吃肉，我吃素。

All right. Thanks! I'll check it out.
好吧，謝謝！我會看看的。

That's no problem. I respect other people's choices.
沒問題，我尊重其他人的選擇。

Well, I did make a salad with olives, carrots, and cucumbers. I added some walnuts for protein. They also had some fried radish cake.
這個嘛，我挑了一碗沙拉，有橄欖、蘿蔔和黃瓜，我還加了一些核桃，補充蛋白質，他們也有煎蘿蔔糕。

Well, this place specializes in meat, so they don't really have a big selection of vegetarian items. But, it's OK.
這地方擅長的是肉食，所以他們的素食選擇其實不多，但沒關係。

No, don't worry about it. You've already ordered your steak. If I'm still hungry, I'll get a serving of squash at the salad bar.
不，別擔心。你已經點牛排了。如果我還是餓，我會從沙拉吧再拿一份南瓜。

Well, I'll definitely have some ice cream and coffee. I'll need to exercise later to burn the calories.
我一定會拿點冰淇淋和咖啡的。我晚點要運動燃燒熱量。

What a huge steak! How big is that? Twenty ounces? Can you eat that by yourself?
好大的牛排！這有多大？20盎司？你自己吃得完嗎？

Thanks for giving me this new experience at a Western-style restaurant. Can I take you to a vegetarian place next time?
謝謝你帶我來體驗這家西餐廳。

Great! We both ate a lot, so how about we go and burn some calories together?
太好了，我們都吃了很多，何不一起去燃燒卡路里？

Featured Vocabulary

vegetarianism vs. veganism (n.) 素食 vs. 素食主義

Most people have heard of "vegetarianism," or the choice of not eating meat. Vegetarians can eat more than just vegetables, so they have many choices, especially in Taiwan. Fewer people have heard of "veganism," or the choice of not eating anything that uses animal products. This means vegans do not eat food made from eggs, dairy products, or animal fats. That includes milk tea, vanilla ice cream, mayonnaise, and pastries baked with animal oil. With so many restrictions, vegans need to show a lot of self-discipline to stick to their diet.

organic (adj.) 有機

The word "organic" is often used to refer to food that is grown or raised naturally, without the use of chemicals or processing. With an increase awareness about the link between nutrition and health, there has been increased demand for organic foods. Even though an "organic food movement" is catching on in Taiwan, the market much bigger in Europe and the USA. Many people would prefer to buy organic rice and vegetables that are not sprayed with pesticides. Likewise, they would prefer to buy organic eggs from farmers who do not feed chemicals to their chickens. The idea is that spending a little extra money on your food now can save you from spending money in the future for medical expenses. An increased demand for organic foods in Taiwan will possibly mean that farmers will have the financial incentive to make their farming practices healthier, too.

Fruit 買水果

It was during my first trip to a local day market that I was introduced to an eye-opening variety of Taiwanese fruits. I recognized some of them in the market, such as bananas, watermelons, pineapples, mangoes, Asian pears, papayas, passion fruit and grapes. In addition, there were so many colorful fruits that I had never seen before. I brought home as many samples as I could afford to share with my family. After washing the Summer sweat off my face, I went to the kitchen, where my wife and mother-in-law had prepared the fruit on the table. My nose was immediately assaulted by a disgusting smell. My wife cut open a very large fruit with spikes on its skin, and its yellow flesh had the aroma of rotten cheese. I did taste a little, but brought the offensive fruit outside. The next fruit I explored was bright magenta, and was known as a "dragon fruit." It tasted fairly sweet, but there was another dragon fruit with white flesh that was even sweeter. One green, crunchy fruit I didn't like very much was a "guava." I noticed an odd-looking, green fruit that my wife called a "Buddha's head." The English name for it was "custard apple." It tasted surprisingly sweet, like custard pudding. The best discovery was a small, reddish fruit with white sweet flesh and a large seed inside. This incredible "lychee" fruit became my favorite of all time. I couldn't get enough.

There are many opportunities for foreign visitors to sample Taiwan's many delicious fruits. There are unique fruits available year round, however the Summer season offers the most local varieties. If you bring visitors to a Taiwanese day market, they may consider Taiwan to be a "fruit paradise." They will find fresh, affordable, exotic fruit, and may even enjoy the opportunity to "haggle" with a fruit vendor to reduce the price.

基本實用會話

Taiwanese (A) Westerner (B)

Shopping for fruit in the day market.
在市場買水果。

A: I thought you would like to try shopping at a typical day market. This one is pretty large.
我覺得你會想要試試在傳統市場買東西。這個市場很大。

B: This place is amazing! I have never seen so many types of fresh fruit for sale in one place.
這地方真棒！我沒在同一個地方看過這麼多新鮮水果特價。

A : Have you ever seen this big, fruit with spiky skin before? It's called a jackfruit. I think it's delicious, but I don't think you'll like the smell.
你以前看過這個皮帶刺的大水果嗎？這叫做榴蓮，我覺得這很美味，但我覺得你不會喜歡這味道。

B : No, I haven't. Oh look! This gigantic fruit is called a breadfruit. While I was in South Africa, I heard it was the favorite food of elephants.
我沒見過，喔，你看！這個超大水果叫麵包果。我在南非的時候，聽說它是大象最愛的食物。

A : I didn't know that. I like breadfruit. My grandmother bakes the seeds. They are also edible.
那我倒不知道，我喜歡麵包果，我祖母會烤麵包果的籽，它的籽也可以吃。

B : Now this massive fruit is one I'm willing to buy. How much is this watermelon? NT600? That's so expensive!
這個大水果就是我想買的。這顆西瓜多少錢？600元？那麼貴！

A : Try to bargain with the vendor. If she likes you, she may give it to you for only NT450.
你試試和老闆殺價，如果她喜歡你，她會算你450元。

Eating fruit after dinner.
飯後水果。

B : I thought dinner was finished. I'm already full. I didn't expect to see this huge plate of fruit brought to the table.
我以為晚餐結束了，我已經飽了，沒想到還有這麼大一盤水果會送上桌。

A : Don't you eat fruit at the end of your meals? It's customary to do so in Taiwan.
你飯後不吃水果嗎？在台灣這是習俗。

B : No. We usually have other desserts after dinner. We occasionally eat fruit as snacks, but not as part of dinner. I'll try some fruit, though.
不，我們晚飯後會吃其他點心，偶爾會吃水果當點心，但不算是晚餐的一部分。但我還是會吃點水果。

A : Wait! Don't use your hand. Use a toothpick to pick up chunks of fruit. Taiwanese don't like people to touch their food with their hands.
等等，別用手。用牙籤叉起水果塊。台灣人不喜歡用手碰食物。

B : I'm sorry. Thanks for the tip!
對不起，謝謝提醒！

NOTES

In Taiwan, fruit a very important part of the peoples' diets. Visitors from other countries may be surprised how many types of delicious fruit are cultivated on this island. Something foreigners enjoy doing in Taiwan is to visit small towns and try the fruits they are famous for. For example, I have enjoyed the pineapples in Minxueng, Chiayi, bananas in Cishan, Kaohsiung, mangoes in Yujing, Tainan City, mandarin oranges in Dongshan, Tainan City, pomelos in Madou, Tainan City, peaches in Hsinchu County, grapes in Nantou County, and custard apples in Taitung County. The fruits make great souvenirs of your trip that you can share with your friends.

Sentences a Westerner might say
老外可能會說的句子

I'm not used to eating a lot of fruit. But, with so many varieties of fruit to choose from in Taiwan, I will probably eat fruit more often.
我不習慣吃太多水果。不過台灣的水果選擇這麼多，我或許會更常吃水果。

I'm nervous about visiting your relatives for the Mid-Autumn Festival. Should I buy some fruit at this market to bring as a gift?
中秋節要去拜訪你的親戚，讓我好緊張。我該到市場買些水果當禮物嗎？

What fruit would be a suitable gift? I have no idea.
什麼水果適合當禮物？我不知道。

What about these? They look like very large grapefruit. I used to enjoy grapefruit for breakfast.
那這些呢？這些看起來好像大型葡萄柚，我以前很喜歡吃葡萄柚當早餐。

I don't want to buy fruit that is so common. I will look for something else.
我不想買那麼普通的水果。我再找找其他東西。

Please tell me a special fruit that you know they will like.
請告訴我他們會喜歡什麼特別的水果。

It's not every day that I'm invited to meet your relatives during an important holiday. Don't worry about the cost.
在重要節日受邀去拜訪你的親戚，這種事不是天天都有，別擔心價格。

You're right. They have grapes from Chile, blueberries from Germany and kiwis from Italy.
你說得對，這裡有智利的葡萄，德國的藍莓和義大利的奇異果。

I found something perfect! These yellow cherries are called Bing cherries. They are very sweet, and they're from Washington State.
我找到完美的水果了！這些黃色莓子是紅肉櫻桃，這水果非常甜，而且是從華盛頓州來的。

Thank you for bringing me to the market. When should I get ready to go with you?
謝謝你帶我來市場。我們什麼時候出發？

Sentences a Taiwanese person might say.
台灣人可能會說的句子

I grew up eating a lot of fruit, because it is just part of our food culture.
我從小到大都吃很多水果，因為這是我們飲食文化的一部分。

That would be a nice gesture. We will certainly eat a lot of fruit on that day.
這是個好選擇，我們那天一定會吃很多水果。

It really doesn't matter. Choose something that shows your style.
都可以。選些能顯示你風格的水果就好。

Those are called pomelos. They are specially-grown in a place called Madou. That is a popular gift this time of year.
那是柚子，是麻豆的特產，是每年這時候很常見的禮物。

Keep looking. There are a lot of fruit vendors at this market.
繼續找。這市場裡還有很多水果攤。

Fruits that are uncommon are imported and expensive. Are you sure you want to spend the money?
進口的水果不常見，而且很貴。你確定你要花這些錢？

OK. This fruit vendor sells a lot of imported fruit.
好，這個水果攤賣很多進口水果。

Yes, they're all costly. How will you choose?
對，他們都很貴，你怎麼選？

That's where you're from, too. That is a perfect gift. It will give you a chance to talk more about where you're from.
那也是你的家鄉，太完美的禮物了。你就有機會聊聊你的家鄉。

I'll pick you up at your place at 2:00 pm.
我下午兩點去你家接你。

Featured Vocabulary

seed vs. pit (n.) 種子 vs. 核

There is often confusion about when to use the terms, "seed" and "pit." Almost every fruit has seeds inside. A pit is a seed. A fruit's flesh is actually the nutrition to help the seed(s) to grow. Typically, when a fruit has more than one seed inside, we refer to them as seeds. Grapes and apples have seeds. When a fruit has one large seed in the center of the flesh, we refer to that seed as the pit. Peaches, cherries, mangoes and lychees have pits.

fruit colloquialisms (phr.) 水果口語

Because different fruit have unique characteristics, they are often used in common English colloquialisms. For example, "You are the apple of my eye," means, "You are someone I cherish above all others." It's the "cherry on top," means something it is extremely special. That's because for Western children, our parents put a cherry on top of our desserts occassionally as a special reward. So, we might say, "My new company offered me great pay, but the three weeks of paid vacation they offered was the cherry on top." If you buy a new car, you can call it a "peach" to say it is excellent, or you can call it a "lemon" to say it is a piece of junk.

UNIT 10

Tea 喝茶

The first time I met Principal Chen at my son's elementary school, he took out a special "tea serving tray" made of polished wood. He had already heated a small pot of water, and proceeded to pour it into tiny porcelain teacups. These teacups didn't seem practical, because they were only large enough to hold three sips of tea. The hot water was used to rinse the cups. He used tongs to put dried tea leaves into a miniature teapot. The principal added hot water, and let it sit for awhile. When he reached for the teapot, I held my cup to allow him to pour the tea inside, but he disposed of the first batch of tea into the sink, leaving only the wet leaves in the teapot. He poured hot water into the teapot again to let the tea leaves "steep," or soak, in the water. This time, the tea was ready to drink. Because the cups were so small, the principal filled my cup many times, making sure it never stayed empty. When the teapot ran out of tea, he repeated the brewing procedure again. The ritual of brewing and pouring the tea was time-consuming, but I believed its purpose was to slow things down. A slower pace allowed people to be respectful and socialize. This tea-drinking experience allowed me to have the time to get to know the principal more personally. In today's technology-driven fast-paced world, opportunities to spend considerable time with people are rare. I appreciated the tea culture that I experienced, which was like going back to a simpler time.

Foreigners may have the privilege of being invited over for tea frequently, because the Taiwanese people are so hospitable to visitors. Like me, they may eventually learn to appreciate the subtle differences between green tea, black tea, oolong tea, and jasmine tea. If you meet a visitor and want to show your hospitality, you can invite them over for tea. The tea culture will be a part of their experience in Taiwan they will remember and appreciate, not because of the tea, but because of the opportunity it offers to socialize.

基本實用會話

Taiwanese (A) Westerner (B)

Buying tea at a tea shop.
在飲料店買茶。

A : Come on, let's go to a tea shop for some refreshments.
走吧，我們去飲料店休息一下。

B : OK. I've seen a lot of tea shops like this one. They are everywhere. How do you choose one?
好，我看到好多這樣的飲料店，到處都是。你要怎麼選？

A： I look for certain tea shop companies that my friends have told me were good.
我聽朋友的建議選擇特定的飲料店。

B： I'll have a pearl milk tea, please. Annie, why don't many young people drink hot tea?
我要一杯珍珠奶茶。安妮，為什麼年輕人不太喜歡喝熱茶？

A： Maybe, because it takes a lot of time to make and drink. It is our ancient custom, but it seems only retired people have time to drink hot tea together.
或許是因為煮熱茶、喝熱茶要花比較長的時間，那是我們古老的風俗，但似乎只有退休的人有時間一起喝熱茶。

B： Yeah, I think that is a problem. The younger generation is always too busy to enjoy spending a lot of time with people. I like things the old-fashioned way.
對啊，我覺得那就是原因。年輕世代總是太忙，沒有時間和人相處。我喜歡這種老式風格。

> **Drinking tea with a friend.**
> 和朋友喝茶。

B： Thanks for dinner, Mrs. Chen. I'm going to join Mr. Chen outside for some tea.
陳太太，謝謝你的晚餐，我要去外面和陳先生一起喝杯茶。

A： How do you like living in Taiwan, Steve? Another cup of tea?
史帝夫，你喜歡在台灣的生活嗎？再來杯茶？

B： Mr. Chen, everyone is so considerate and hospitable. I love it.
陳先生，大家都很體貼、熱情，我很喜歡。

A： My son will attend university in England in the Fall. Do you have any advice for him? More tea?
我兒子今年秋天會去英國上大學。你對他有什麼建議嗎？再來杯茶？

B： Tell him to bring very warm jackets and coats. No more tea for me, please.
叫他要帶非常保暖的夾克和外套。請不要再倒茶給我了。

A： OK. If you don't want me to fill your teacup, just turn it upside down.
好，如果你不希望我再添滿你的茶杯，只要把杯子倒蓋。

B： Thanks for letting me know.
謝謝你告訴我。

NOTES

In Western culture, drinking tea is also a social ritual. This is especially true in Great Britain and former British colonies. Having afternoon tea between the hours of 4 pm-6 pm is a must for many people. They use the time to energize with snacks and tea, usually taken with milk and a lump of sugar. In America, people with leisure time may offer their friends or neighbors a tall glass of iced tea while sitting on their front porch. In either case, the tea-drinking custom is a way to slow down to spend quality time with people.

Sentences a Westerner might say
老外可能會說的句子

Thank you for inviting me to join you for tea, Mr. Lin.
林先生,謝謝你邀請我來喝茶。

I shouldn't drink too much tea, because caffeine keeps me awake all night.
我不應該喝太多茶,因為咖啡因會害我整夜睡不著覺。

Why did you pour the hot water in the teapots and teacups and then pour it out?
你為什麼把熱水倒進茶壺和茶杯,又把熱水倒掉呢?

I'll take a cup of tea. Hey! Why did you throw that tea away?
我喝一杯就好。嘿,你為什麼把茶葉丟掉?

So, can we drink this batch of tea?
那麼,這泡茶可以喝嗎?

Mmmm. The smell is exquisite! And the taste is subtle, but quite extraordinary.
嗯,真香!味道真微妙,但非常出色。

This is my first time drinking jasmine tea. Is it made from flowers?
這是我第一次喝茉莉花茶。這是用花泡的嗎?

Where can I buy some jasmine tea? I'd like to share it with my friends.
哪裡可以買到茉莉花茶?我想和朋友分享。

I can't take this from you. You are too generous!
我不能拿你的東西,你真是太慷慨了!

OK. Since you put it that way. I'll accept your gift, and I will share it. Thank you!
好,既然你這麼說了,我就接受你的禮物,我會和朋友分享的,謝謝你!

Sentences a Taiwanese person might say.
台灣人可能會說的句子

Please have a seat and relax for awhile. Would you like some hot tea?
請坐下休息一會兒,你想喝點熱茶嗎?

The caffeine in the hot tea is not strong. Hot tea always relaxes me, instead of keeping me awake.
熱茶的咖啡因不高。熱茶總是能讓我放鬆,而不會讓我睡不著。

This is a simple way to clean them for our guests.
這是一種簡單的方式,可以為客人清潔茶具。

The first portion of hot water gets the tea leaves ready. But the first amount of tea is not suitable to drink.
第一泡的熱水可以泡開茶葉。但第一泡茶不適合飲用。

Yes. This tea is ready for you to drink. Please let me pour it into your cup for you.
是的，這茶已經可以喝了。請讓我為你倒茶。

Swirl the tea around in your cup a little, and then smell it before you drink it.
讓茶在你的茶杯裡轉一下，在喝之前聞聞它的味道。

This is called jasmine tea. You can smell the scent of the jasmine blossoms in the tea.
這是茉莉花茶，你可以在茶裡聞到茉莉花的味道。

Jasmine tea is made from a blend of green tea, white tea, black tea, and jasmine blossoms.
茉莉花茶是由綠茶、白茶、紅茶和茉莉花混合而成。

Here. Let me give a container of jasmine tea to you. It is from Fujian, China.
這裡，這罐茉莉花茶給你，這是中國福建的茶。

But you must take it. Tea is for sharing with friends. Knowing that you will share my tea with your friends will make me happy.
但你一定要收下，茶是為了和朋友分享用的，知道你願意和朋友分享我的茶，讓我覺得很開心。

Featured Vocabulary

steep (v.) 沉浸

When a Westerner dunks a tea bag into a cup of hot water, they usually say they are "steeping" the tea. Also, during an Asian tea ceremony, Westerners will also use the term "to steep" when referring to the pouring of hot water over tea leaves in a teapot. Another common word used in the West to describe the process is "to brew tea."

For all the tea in China (phr.) 在中國所有的茶葉

A common English colloquial phrase is, "for all the tea in China." For example, one might say, "I wouldn't eat her cooking for all the tea in China." It specifically means, "I wouldn't eat her cooking, no matter what you offer me." Because Westerners perceive that the amount of tea in China is vast and seemingly endless (and valuable), it is a way to express a great quantity of value. However, the quantity is not used in a positive sense. It is used as a way to illustrate a sarcastic expression. If a woman tells a man, "I wouldn't marry you for all the tea in China," she is not declining his offer in a polite manner. The colloquial phrase is used to make the refusal more emphatic.

UNIT · 11

In Taiwanese society, there doesn't seem to be any items more important to the social experience than food. Because of this, there is a lot of thought put into the choice of restaurants and food for social occasions. I have been blessed with many social dinner invitations over the years in Taiwan, and each experience has been unique and memorable. I have enjoyed formal wedding banquets, New Year's company parties, teacher appreciation dinners, birthday celebrations, business club dinners, holiday feasts, outdoor barbecues, and many other types of social meals. One of the most memorable meals was a teacher appreciation lunch, where the parents and teachers enjoyed a catered meal on the school grounds. They served a typical Taiwanese-style banquet on round tables seating ten to a table. As soon as they served the first course, I was surprised to find many parents and teachers drinking beer and wine. I made the mistake of choosing wine instead of juice. The principal and a local legislator were making their way around to all of the tables to give a toast to each guest. The teachers also made their way around to the tables to show their repect. After each toast, I drank a small glass of wine, and it didn't take long before I started to feel the effects. I felt bold enough to visit each table to offer my own toasts to show my appreciation. Needless to say, I didn't have a chance to eat all of the courses of the meal. I was too drunk, and had to go home before dessert was served.

Alcohol seems to be present at every social meal that I attend. I know now to be careful and pace myself. I also know more excuses to use to avoid drinking alcohol. I believe that visitors should understand that social meals in Taiwan are the opportunities to show respect and appreciation in a social setting. It is a time to "show face" as a guest and to "give face" to your hosts. By showing respect properly in public, you have a great opportunity to strengthen your "guanxi," or personal relationships, which is very important in Taiwanese society.

基本實用會話   Taiwanese (A)   Westerner (B)

Being a guest at a social dinner.
參加應酬當客人。

A : Please try this appetizer. It is a local specialty.
請試試這道開胃菜，這是這裡的特產。

B : Thank you. But please take one first, because you're the host.
謝謝你，但您先用，因為你是主人。

A： Ok. Thank you. That is kind of you.
好，謝謝你。你真是太好了。

B： You are the one who is kind. You invited me to share this meal with you. Thank you!
你才是好人，邀請我來吃飯，謝謝你！

A： Would you like to have some Taiwan Beer?
想來點台灣啤酒嗎？

B： Oh, no thank you. I like it, but I should not, because I need to drive my scooter home.
不了，謝謝，我很喜歡，我不能喝，我還得騎機車回家。

Being a host at a social dinner.
舉辦應酬當主人。

B： I would like to make a toast and say thank you to all of my fellow teachers. Cheers!
我想向大家敬酒，謝謝所有的老師伙伴們，乾杯！

A： Cheers, David! It was my pleasure to work with you this year.
乾杯，大衛！今年很榮幸能和你共事。

B： Please make sure you've had enough to eat.
吃不夠一定要說。

A： I'm stuffed. This is a very renowned seafood restaurant. You made a good choice.
我很飽了，這家海鮮餐廳很出名，你選得很好。

B： I did ask the principal for his recommendation.
我請校長推薦的。

A： Let me help you with the bill.
我來結帳吧。

B： Nonsense! I know the custom. I invited you, so don't worry about it. I will pay.
胡說！我知道習慣。是我邀請你來的，所以帳單就別擔心了，我來付帳。

NOTES

In Western society, it is very common for the guest and host of a social dinner to "go dutch," which means everyone pays for their own food and drink. This is not the custom in Taiwan, where it is always the host that pays for dinner when they invite a guest. If you know visitors in Taiwan, let them know about this custom as soon as possible, so they won't need to face any awkward circumstances in restaurants.

Sentences a Westerner might say
老外可能會說的句子

This is my first social dinner in Taiwan. Please help me to avoid making any mistakes, OK?
這是我在台灣的第一場應酬。請提醒我，別讓我出錯，好嗎？

People are making toasts. How do I know when I should drink?
大家在敬酒了。我什麼時候該喝？

What about the food? What should I do about serving myself during each course?
那吃的呢？每道菜我該怎麼挾菜？

I don't know anyone else here at our table.
我不認識同桌的其他人。

It is nice to meet you Mr. and Mrs. Wei, Mr. Lin, and Miss Tang. Cheers!
很高興認識你們，魏先生、魏太太、湯小姐，乾杯！

Almost everything looks delightful. I hope I don't look like a pig in front of everyone.
每道菜看來都好好吃，希望我在大家面前不會看來像頭豬。

OK. I think I'm getting the hang of this. I can gesture to the elders to take their servings before me.
好，我想我懂了。我可以請長輩先挾菜，然後我再挾菜。

But what if I don't want to try one of the dishes? What do I say?
但要是有道菜我不想吃呢？我該說什麼？

The dinner was delicious! I'm glad I didn't eat too much. Thank you for your advice.
晚餐很好吃！還好我沒有吃太多，謝謝你的幫忙。

So, can I offer the host some money for the bill?
那麼，我可以幫主人一起付帳單嗎？

Sentences a Taiwanese person might say.
台灣人可能會說的句子

No problem. Just watch me and the other guests, and follow our lead.
沒問題，只要看著我和其他客人，照著我們做。

When people are making a toast, see if they are looking at you. If they are, it is your turn to drink.
當其他人敬酒時，觀察他們是否看著你。如果是，就輪到你喝酒了。

Since there are a few people at this table who are older than you, you should wait for them, or offer to serve them.
因為同桌有比你年長的人，你應該等他們先挾，或是幫他們挾菜。

OK. Let me introduce you. Everyone, this is Teacher Mark.
好，我來幫你介紹。大家，這是馬克老師。

Cheers! That's perfect! It's nice to offer a toast when meeting someone for the first time.
乾杯！就是這樣！向剛認識的人敬酒就對了。

Don't worry. Just make sure you only take one serving from each course. They usually provide one serving per person at a table.
別擔心，只要確保你每道菜只挾一份就好。他們上菜通常是一桌上一人一份。

Yes, and since I am younger than you, I will wait for you to take a serving.
對，因為我比你小，我要等你先挾菜。

Just wave your hand and say, "No, thank you," in Chinese. "Bu-yao, hsieh-hsieh."
只要揮揮手用中文說「不要，謝謝。」

It's my pleasure. Taiwanese people love to help visitors learn about our culture.
這是我的榮幸。台灣人喜歡幫助訪客學習我們的文化。

In Taiwan, the host always pays. But it might be a nice gesture, if you offered.
在台灣都是主人付帳的。但如果你願意，或許也是不錯的舉動。

Featured Vocabulary

lazy Susan (n.) 旋轉餐檯

Asians often eat their meals on a large, round dining table, which can usually seat 8 to 10 people. In order to help people avoid reaching over the food for the dish that they want, these tables often have a rotating tray in the center. In English, the rotating trays have been referred to as, "lazy Susans" for at least a hundred years, but no one knows where the word originated. But the name infers that servers can be lazy, because they does not have to move the food around to serve the dinner guests. In Western countries, "lazy Susans" are not very common, but they can be found in Cantonese dim sum restaurants.

course (dish) (n.) ～道菜

For most social or formal dining occasions in Taiwan, meals are typically pre-ordered as a package deal that includes multiple dishes (or courses). Westerners typically describe a meal that includes one appetizer, a soup, a salad, an entrée, and a dessert as a five-course meal. This would never be described as a five-dish meal. However, one can say that this meal had five courses or five dishes. But the word "course" is a formal way to describe a part of a meal that includes multiple parts. When describing the meal, one can count how many courses there are and use the number to describe the meal. Look at the following example. "A five-course meal may fill you up, but you may certainly overeat at a formal ten-course meal." Another formal way to describe a meal with multiple parts is to use the term, "full-course meal."

Spiritual Offerings 拜拜

One morning, my mother-in-law asked my family to help her. I saw an abundant spread of delicious food, like pork, chicken, fish, vegetable and side dishes. She also had popular snacks and drinks on the dining table. My children begged to try some of the goodies, but my mother-in-law said that we couldn't eat yet. She asked us to help her bring everything to the third floor of her home. We grabbed armfuls of food and carried them to a special room illuminated with a red light. There was a table in front of the home altar, with smoking incense sticks placed in an incense holder. After we brought all of the food upstairs, she explained that we could not touch anything until the gods and the ancestor's spirits had time to receive the blessing. She called this religious ritual, "bai-bai." We waited for a few hours and retrieved all of the items to enjoy a feast. Over the years, we have helped our mother-in-law many times bring food up and down three flights of stairs for "bai-bai." The work has not been easy, but we have always been rewarded with the most delicious meals at her house.

According to the Taiwanese government, 35% of Taiwan's population are Buddhist and 33% are Taoist. Because of this, a majority of Taiwanese people participate in the ritual of leaving food for their ancestors. This custom may seem strange to a Western visitor, because there is nothing like it in Christian religion. They may see a lot of food left on tables at temples or in front of shrines, or in front of grave sites. You can explain to the visitors that the food is an offering to show respect to the ancestors and other spirits as well as to ask for prosperity. Then they will know that they should never touch the food.

基本實用會話

Taiwanese (A) : Westerner (B)

Visiting a temple.
參訪廟宇。

A : The temple is quite busy during Chinese New Year.
中國新年時，這座廟很忙碌。

B : I see that. Why are people putting piles of food onto the tables outside the temple? Do they give the food to the temple?
看得出來。為什麼大家把成堆的食物放在廟外的桌子上？他們要把食物送給這座廟嗎？

A : No. They are offering it to pay respects to the gods and their ancestors.
不，那是祭品，為了向神明和祖先致敬的。

B： What will happen to the food?
那食物之後會怎麼處理？

A： They will bring it home later to have a feast with their families.
之後會帶回家，和家人一起分享大餐。

B： OK. Are you having a feast tonight? Am I invited?
好，你們今晚也有大餐嗎？我能去嗎？

Being a guest in a home.
到朋友家作客。

B： Is this what we're having for lunch? It looks wonderful! Can I taste it?
這是我們午餐要吃的嗎？看起來好棒，我能嚐嚐看嗎？

A： No! It's not ready to eat. We need to bring it upstairs to our shrine.
不行！還不能吃，我們要先將這些拿到樓上的供桌。

B： Why? Is that where we're eating?
為什麼？我們要在那裡吃？

A： No. That is where the food will be offered to our ancestors' spirits. It's a way to show our respect.
不，那裡是供奉食物祭拜祖先的地方，是我們致敬的方式。

B： OK. I'll help you bring the food upstairs. Will we be able to eat it later? It would be a shame if we couldn't.
好，我幫你把食物拿上樓。晚一點可以吃嗎？要是不能吃就太可惜了。

A： Of course we're going to eat it. We just have to wait a few hours.
當然可以，只要等幾個小時就能吃了。

 NOTES

In Taiwan, it is customary to leave food out for the gods and for the spirits of ancestors. During the annual festival known as Ghost Month, the hungry ghosts are released from "Hell" in mid-July to find food on Earth. People leave plentiful amounts of food out in front of temples and shrines at home for these hungry spirits, so they can return satisfied. In Christian religion, there is nothing like this type of ritual. It might seem very strange to Western visitors to see so much food left out for the spirits. This practice also corresponds to the spiritual activity of burning "ghost money." It is hard for visitors to believe how much real money people spend every year to burn this fake money. I always wondered why people couldn't just leave a pile of real money in front of incense to make a temporary "offering" instead of burning paper and creating pollution.

Sentences a Westerner might say
老外可能會說的句子

What are these stacks of pretty yellow paper?
這堆漂亮的黃紙是什麼？

You burn this paper for your ancestors? How often? Every day?
你把這些紙燒給你的祖先？多久一次？每天？

Where do you burn the ghost money?
你在哪裡燒這些紙錢？

Sure. What else do you do to worship the ancestors?
當然，祭祀祖先還要做什麼事？

Does she need help bringing the food to the altar?
她要人幫忙把食物搬到供桌嗎？

You're right. It is a lot of food. I didn't know she prepared so much for our feast.
你說的對，真的好多食物。我不知道她為今天的大餐準備了這麼多。

Ghosts? Are you kidding me? This food is for ghosts?
鬼？你開玩笑嗎？這食物是給鬼吃的？

Is this food enough for so many ghosts?
這些食物足夠給這麼多鬼吃嗎？

I don't know if I would want to eat this food, if ghosts chewed on it.
如果鬼已經咬過這些食物，我不知道我還想不想吃。

It's a good thing that I don't really believe in ghosts. I will be ready to eat.
還好我其實不相信有鬼，我已經準備好大快朵頤了。

Sentences a Taiwanese person might say.
台灣人可能會說的句子

This is ghost money. We burn it to offer to our ancestors' spirits.
這是紙錢。我們燒紙錢供奉祖先。

We don't do that every day. We burn it during religious ceremonies or holidays.
不是每天都這麼做。只有在宗教儀式或節日時會燒紙錢。

We can burn it in the metal brazier outside. Would you like to help me?
我們會拿到外面的金屬火盆燒。你想幫忙嗎？

Well, my mother already finished cooking our dinner, but we need to bring the food to our home altar first.
我媽已經煮好我們的晚餐，但我們得先把菜拿到我們家的供桌。

That would be very helpful. She would appreciate that. There is a lot of food to carry up the stairs.
那就太好了，她會很感謝你的。要搬上樓的食物太多了。

Actually, my relatives brought some food over, too. They want to have enough to feed the ghosts.
其實我家的親戚也會拿些菜過來。他們想要有足夠的菜供養鬼魂。

Yes, Taoists believe that during Ghost Month, hungry ghosts are released to roam the land to search for food.
是的，道家相信在鬼月，飢餓的鬼魂被放出來，在世間游蕩尋找食物。

Yes. Most people in our village are also offering their food.
夠，村裡大部分的人都會擺放供品。

Haha! The food will be perfectly fine. We will have dinner in a few hours.
哈哈！這食物沒問題的，我們幾個小時後就吃晚餐了。

Great. You have to help us finish the meal. There is too much food for my family to finish.
太好了，你能幫我們吃光晚餐，這些食物對我們家來說太多了。

Featured Vocabulary

Incense vs. joss sticks (n.) 香

Incense is something made from combustible, scented materials, and it has different uses. It can be burned to cover bad smells or to keep insects away. In the West, incense is often used for providing a pleasant scent in the home, or for creating an ideal environment for meditation. Incense sticks are used in Asia for temple ceremonies and spiritual worship. Use of incense has been widespread in Chinese civilization for thousands of years. Another terms for incense sticks used for the purpose of spirtual ritual is "joss sticks."

ghost money vs. joss paper (n.) 紙錢

The burning of "ghost money" is a tradition that often accompanies the offering of food to show respect to the ancestors' spirits. This decorative paper is also known in English as "joss paper." Different types of joss paper is offered to different types of spirits, including different gods. The joss paper can also be folded into shapes to represent items to send to the deceased. For example, they can be folded to resemble items, such as shoes, clothing, or even a house.

Street Vendors 攤販

While sightseeing in the famous Ximending Pedestrian Area in Taipei, something totally unexpected happened to me. I heard some yelling, and then saw a street vendor pushing his food cart towards me at full speed, yelling at pedestrians to get out of the way. He barely missed me with his barbecue grill, which still had flames coming out. I realized that if I had not moved out of the way in time, I could have been hospitalized. I stepped off the sidewalk, as I saw two other street vendors running past me. I was confused, until I saw a policeman on a bicycle following them. What I realized was that some street vendors did not have the proper business permits, and they raced to another location to sell their goods. The policeman could have caught them if he really wanted to, so I believe he just wanted to chase them away from Ximending. He accomplished this goal, but I don't think he realized what a dangerous race he created.

I have not been in a dangerous situation with street vendors ever since that incident. Actually, I am quite fond of Taiwan's street vendors. They often provide a convenient and tasty snack whenever I am hungry. I can find them at street corners or public areas on any day. Of course, there is a gathering of street vendors at local night markets once or twice a week. But on any day of the week, I can find fruit juice, fried food, sausages, and even steak dinners sold from pushcarts. During special occasions like festivals and holiday events, there will be even more tasty treats available from the rows of food stands positioned under tents. There never seems to be a lack of affordable snacks in Taiwan, because of vendors who make a living off of pedestrians.

基本實用會話

Taiwanese (A) Westerner (B)

Visiting street vendors.
逛路邊攤。

A : Let's go to the main boulevard next to the temple. There are always street vendors there.
我們去這家廟旁的大馬路，那裡經常有路邊攤。

B : It's a good time for a late-night snack. What can we find there?
是時候吃點宵夜了。那裡有什麼吃的？

A : There is a guy that barbecues different types of food. Another vendor sells noodle soups.
那裡有個人在賣各種烤物，還有一攤賣湯麵。

B : We must be getting close. I can smell the food. But something doesn't smell so good.
我們一定是快到了，我能聞到食物的味道，不過有個東西不太好聞。

A : That's the stinky tofu cart. That street vendor is quite popular.
那是臭豆腐攤，那種路邊攤很受歡迎。

B : I won't be giving him my business. I'll have the barbecue.
我不會跟他買東西的，我要吃燒烤。

Visiting a local festival.
逛當地慶典。

B : There are so many people here in this town. What are those tents set up along the streets?
城裡這地方有好多人，那些沿著街道搭的帳篷是什麼的？

A : Today is the town's Sweet Potato Festival. Sweet potato is the town's specialty food.
今天是城裡的番薯節。番薯是這城裡的特產。

B : There are a lot of food stalls here under the tents. I didn't realize there were so many ways to prepare sweet potatoes.
帳篷下有好多食物攤，我不知道番薯有這麼多種烹調方法。

A : There are vendors here selling other local products and crafts, too. Do you want to buy a gift for anyone?
這裡還有販售當地特產、藝品的攤販，你想買禮物給什麼人嗎？

B : Sure. There are many things I have never seen before. This festival is pretty cool.
當然，這裡有好多從未見過的東西，這節慶太酷了。

A : Well, if you like this one, there are festivals with food stalls almost every weekend. You just have to find out which towns are having a celebration.
如果你喜歡這個慶典，幾乎每個週末都會舉辦節慶，也都有食物攤，你只要找出舉辦的地點就行了。

NOTES

In Taiwan, street vendors can be found practically everywhere. Some street vendors have developed good reputations in their community, and are quite successful. For most foreigners who are living on a budget, they are seen as a blessing. Not only are they very convenient, they offer a variety of tasty foods, drinks and snacks at a reasonable price. However, not every visitor is willing to buy from street vendors. Some people are concerned about the quality of products sold by street vendors, and believe that they may not follow the same guidelines that licensed restaurant owners must follow.

Sentences a Westerner might say
老外可能會說的句子

Why are so many people going over to those tents?
為什麼這麼多人跑去那些帳篷？

Let's go check it out. I haven't had any lunch yet.
我們去看看，我還沒吃午餐。

I hope they have something good to eat.
希望他們有賣些好吃的。

Hey, look at this. Sesame ointment is good for dry skin. This will make a nice gift.
嘿，你看這個。芝麻軟膏對乾燥肌膚很好，這很適合當禮物。

And look at how many types of sesame oil there are.
你看這裡有好多種類的芝麻油。

Sesame seed crackers and sesame chips. Are these free samples?
芝麻餅乾和芝麻洋芋片。這是免費試吃嗎？

What are these golden fried balls? They smell very good.
那些炸金球是什麼？聞起來好香。

Why is that man yelling? Is he trying to get people to play his ring toss game? In English, we call that type of yelling, "hawking."
那男人為什麼大叫？他想要叫人去玩丟圈圈遊戲嗎？在英國，我們稱那樣大叫為「hawking」（叫賣）。

Now there is something I recognize. I love sausages! Why are some black?
有我認得的東西了。我喜歡香腸！為什麼有些是黑色的？

I'm getting full from these snacks. I won't need to buy lunch now.
吃這些點心就飽了，我不用買午餐了。

Sentences a Taiwanese person might say.
台灣人可能會說的句子

That is the Sesame Seed Harvest Festival. It happens every year in November in this village.
那是芝麻豐收節。這村子每年11月都會舉辦。

All right. You'll see many people selling local crafts, especially those made from sesame seeds.
好，那裡有很多人販賣當地藝品，特別是用芝麻做的。

Of course they will. Wherever there are a lot of people, there will be food stalls.
當然會。哪裡有人潮，哪裡就有食物攤。

Right. The weather is starting to get colder and dryer, so the ointment will come in handy.
沒錯，氣候開始變得涼爽乾燥，所以軟膏很快能派上用場。

During the winter, many people like to make sesame chicken. That is chicken simmered in sesame oil.
在冬天時，許多人喜歡做芝麻雞，做法是將雞浸泡在芝麻油裡。

Yes, they are. That's how they get more customers. They said that you could try some.
對，這樣才能吸引更多顧客，他們說你可以試試看。

It's a mixture of sweet potatoes, batter and sesame seeds. They are fried in sesame seed oil.
這是將番薯、麵糊和芝麻混合後，用芝麻油油炸。

Right. He is trying to get people's attention, so they will pay to play.
對，他想吸引人的注意，這樣他們才會付錢玩遊戲。

Haha! They're not burnt. They are sausages with a lot of sesame seeds in them.
哈哈！那不是烤焦，那些香腸裡加了很多芝麻。

Me, too. Let's go sit in front of the stage and watch the performances.
我也是，我們去舞台前坐著看表演吧。

Featured Vocabulary

street vendor vs. hawker vs. peddler (n.) 擺地攤

Street vendors are people who sell merchandise from a location that is portable, which means, it can be moved. They often sell near streets or public areas that are popular gathering areas. Street vendors, also referred to in English as "hawkers" and "peddlers," typically sell inexpensive merchandise, local crafts or foods. Although in most places, these vendors are required to have a business permit (or license), many do not acquire the required documents because of their expense. Street vendors are often mobile, which means they may sell goods at more than one location. It is quite common to see street vendors in Taiwan and China, as well as in other countries. There are 10 million street vendors in India and 20,000 in New York City. Some say the best hot dogs in America are sold on the streets of New York City, so these street vendors are highly sought after by the tourists.

food stand vs. food stalls vs. food booth (n.) 食品攤

A food stand is a small, temporary structure that serves as a food service facility. These food stands, also known as "food stalls" or "food booths," are typically found in Taiwan at special events, such as festivals, carnivals, graduation ceremonies, and public holiday celebrations. In the USA, food stands are not so common, but they can be found as part of traveling carnivals and circuses. They will sell fast food, including hot dogs, hamburgers, cotton candy, candied apples, ice cream and popcorn.

UNIT 14

My first night market experience was at Huaxi Night Market during my first trip to Taiwan in 1996. It was a memorable experience. The place was like a huge maze that was bustling with activity. There were culinary temptations everywhere. I wanted to try everything, but of course, I needed to be selective. I first wanted to have a pearl milk tea in my hand while I explored the stalls. One area of the market had many drink stalls, so it wasn't hard to find the drink that I wanted. But I did see something interesting there called "frog egg" tea. The back area had many vendors selling clothing, toys, accessories and handicrafts. They were yelling out to the crowd to compete for attention. I slowly pushed my way back to the center of the market towards the delicious smells of food. I saw many popular Taiwanese snacks for the first time, such as oyster omelettes, green onion pancakes, fried chicken fillets, fried mushrooms, and fried squid on a stick. I noticed that there was an abundance of greasy, fried foods. Most of the selections were not healthy, but I tried them anyways. I could not believe it when I saw several peddlers who peddled live snakes. One person placed a large, black snake on a stick, cut it skillfully, and peeled the skin off. He drained the blood and sliced off the meat, as the snake's body writhed. Even though it was hard for me to watch the killing of a snake, my curiosity got the better of me. I tried the snake soup before I left the market.

In my years as a resident of Taiwan, I have visited many night markets in many cities. They are typically similar to each other, but there are famous ones in Taipei, Taichung, Kaohsiung and Tainan. I have heard that the night markets in Tainan City have the best food. From my personal experience, I can't argue with that. Visiting Taiwan's night markets are usually on the to-do lists of visitors. If you have a chance, invite a visitor and be their guide at a night market. It will enhance their experience, because there will be many unfamiliar sights. They will appreciate someone who can explain to them what they are seeing, and it is usually a fun experience for the guide as well.

基本實用會話

Taiwanese (A) Westerner (B)

Ordering food at a night market.
在夜市點餐。

A: Would you like to try this? This is grilled squid.
你要試試這個嗎？這是烤魷魚。

B：It's so big. How will I eat this?
太大了，我要怎麼吃？

A：After he grills it, he will chop it into pieces with large scissors.
烤好之後會用大剪刀剪成一塊塊的。

B：I see. It smells good when they cook it. What is the vendor asking me?
我懂了，烤的時候聞起來真香。老闆問我什麼？

A：He wants to know what type of flavor do you want them to add? Do you want black pepper, spicy pepper, or seaweed powder?
他想知道你想要加什麼調味料？你要黑胡椒、辣椒還是海苔？

B：What do you like? Please choose one, because I want to share it with you.
你喜歡什麼？請你選一個，因為我想和你共享。

Shopping for clothes at a night market.
在夜市買衣服。

B：I can't believe how cheap the clothes and accessories are here. I am looking for gifts to bring back home.
我不敢相信這裡的衣服和配件這麼便宜。我要買禮物帶回家。

A：At the night markets, they are cheap. But they may not be the best quality. Some are knock-offs of popular brands.
夜市裡都很便宜。但他們的品質可能不是最好的，有些是名牌的仿冒品。

B：Some of these items are quite unique. Look at these backpacks designed to look like animal heads. They're so cute.
有些東西真的很特別，你看這些背包的設計，看來像動物的頭，好可愛。

A：You really like to shop, don't you? Let me help you talk to the vendors. I can try to get the best prices for you.
你真的很愛購物，對嗎？我幫你和老闆說說，試試幫你拿到最好的價格。

B：Wow! You can do that? If you can save me some money, you can be my best friend!
哇！可以嗎？如果你能幫我省錢，你就是我最好的朋友！

NOTES

I have had the pleasure of bringing many foreign visitors to experience Taiwanese night markets. They have always told me that their visits to the night market were unforgettable, because there was nothing like it in their country. What they usually appreciate is the opportunity to sample so many types of food and drink in one location. One way to be helpful is to help them to pace themselves. Encourage them to share the food, so they can eat less and sample more. Visitors are usually amazed at how inexpensive the clothing and accessories are. Since they are usually on the lookout for gifts for their friends and family back home, they usually purchase more than they can carry during their first visit to a night market.

Sentences a Westerner might say
老外可能會說的句子

This place is amazing! You call this a "night market?"
這地方太令人驚奇了！你說這是「夜市」嗎？

So, this night market is here on Saturday nights only?
那麼，這夜市只有週六晚上營業？

Wow! There is so much to do. It's like a combination of multiple things back in England.
哇！真是五花八門，就像結合了英國的好多種活動。

Over here, there are little rides and games of chance, just like at a carnival or festival.
在這裡，這裡有小車，還有些賭博遊戲，好像嘉年華還是慶典。

And over there, they are peddling a lot of cheap clothes, purses, wallets and gifts. That's just like our bazaars.
還有這裡，這裡有幾攤便宜的衣服、皮包、皮夾和禮物。就像我們的集市。

And of course, over there, you're got many booths selling food and drinks, just like in our food courts.
當然了，你看這裡，好幾個賣餐飲的攤子，就像我們的美食廣場。

It looks like you have more variety than our food courts. And the prices here are more affordable.
種類看來比我們的美食廣場多，價錢也更便宜。

I'm not hungry. I had dinner recently. But, I would like to play something to win a prize.
我不餓，剛吃了晚餐。不過我想玩遊戲，贏個獎回來。

This game looks very easy. I only need to catch one of these fish with a net made from tissue paper.
這遊戲看來非常簡單，我只要拿這張用衛生紙做成的網子撈魚就行了。

Look! I won! I caught a goldfish. So, what did I win?
你看，我贏了！我抓到金魚了，那我可以贏到什麼禮物？

Sentences a Taiwanese person might say.
台灣人可能會說的句子

Yes. We have night markets all over Taiwan. They are usually at the same location once or twice per week.
對，台灣到處都有夜市。通常會設在固定的地方，一週一到兩次。

No. This is a popular one, so it is also open here on Wednesday nights.
不，這個夜市很受歡迎，所以週三晚上也有營業。

Really? Like what? Please tell me.
真的嗎？像是什麼？說說看。

Yes, it provides something for children in the community to do.
對，這也讓社區裡的小孩有點娛樂。

Yeah. Women like to buy stuff to make themselves look pretty, but don't want to spend too much.
是啊，女人喜歡買些東西妝扮自己，但又不想花太多錢。

Yes. Our night markets serve many specialties and some dishes that are popular all over Taiwan.
對，我們的夜市賣很多特產，有些餐點在全台灣都很受歡迎。

So, are you hungry? Would you like to try something?
那麼，你餓了嗎？你想吃點什麼嗎？

OK. Which game would you like to try?
好，你想玩什麼遊戲？

It's not as easy as it looks. Good luck!
這不像看起來那麼簡單，祝你好運！

You won the goldfish, of course!
你當然是贏得這條金魚！

Featured Vocabulary

outdoor market (n.) 露天市場

Outdoor markets, or open-air markets, are not as common as shopping malls or department stores in Western countries. However, they are quite common and popular in Taiwan. In Western countries there are two types of outdoor markets. There are "farmers' markets," where the local farmers gather to sell their fruits and vegetables. These are similar to Taiwan's "day markets." Customers typically enjoy the opportunity to buy fresh produce to support local farmers, but farmer's markets are not easy to find, and they often occur only once a week or once a month. I have never seen an outdoor market in America that resembles a Taiwanese night market. I have seen outdoor markets called "flea markets" that have many vendors in stalls selling inexpensive or used products. Another fancier named used to describe this type of market in the West is a "bazaar." People go to flea markets, or bazaars specifically to find bargains on clothing, accessories and collectible items.

bargain (n. and v.) 議價, 討價還價

When thrifty people go shopping, and they want to spend less money on items, you can say they are looking for a "bargain." You can also say, they are looking for a special deal, or they want a discounted price. It means they want to spend less than the price that the seller originally offered. Bargain can also be used as a verb. When a person is offering less than what the seller is asking for, you can say that the buyer is bargaining with the seller. In some places, like in the street markets of China, India and the Middle East, bargaining is a common practice. However, it is not a common practice in most Western countries.

UNIT 15

It was my first birthday celebration in Taiwan. I had made a few American friends in Tainan City, and they invited me out experience the local pub scene. We started at an outdoor pub named Tin Pan Alley, which was known for its good food and live music scene. I had a delicious grilled panini sandwich, and a few German beers. There were many foreigners speaking English, and catching up with their friends. There were also Taiwanese locals who, after drinking enough beers, gathered the courage to go out on the dance floor and make new friends. I felt quite at home in this relaxed environment. I didn't need to understand Chinese here. The only drawback was waiting ten minutes for the men's restroom. Women, on the other hand, needed to wait about twenty-five minutes. That was the first stop of my night out. Later, we went to "The Red Wolf," a popular Western sports pub, which featured attractive Taiwanese women pole dancing on top of the bar. There was drinking and dancing happening there, too. The last stop was a small lounge bar popular with foreigners. The first person I met was a Frenchman, who bought me a drink. The foreigners and Taiwanese became fast friends by dancing and drinking. I finally stumbled out of the bar at 7:00 am. This was a crazy adventure, and my 43-year old body was fatigued and in pain for an entire day.

As a family man, I have had relatively few experiences with Taiwan's nightlife, but they each have been memorable for good or bad reasons. There seems to be a difference between the Western and the Taiwanese pub scenes. The Taiwanese seem to have more structure to their drinking rituals. For example, it is common to drink together and offer toasts. People say "gan-bei" and empty the entire contents of their small glasses together. The Taiwanese groups tend to sit together or dance together, whereas foreigners tend to be more independent and do whatever they feel like. In Western pubs, people order their own beverages and drink at their own pace. They dance independently from people in their groups. The Western pubs seem more laid back and casual than Taiwanese pubs, but regardless of which type of pub I have visited, I have enjoyed the social interaction in both environments.

基本實用會話　Taiwanese (A)　Westerner (B)

Drinking in a Taiwanese pub.
在台灣酒吧喝酒。

A: Please let me fill your glass. Would you like Taiwan Beer or Heineken?
請讓我為你倒酒。你想要台灣啤酒還是海尼根？

B: I'll have a Heineken, please. Thank you.
我要海尼根，謝謝你。

A: We should all make a toast and drink together. Here is to the health of our colleagues. Gan-bei!
我們要一起舉杯共飲。敬我們的同事都能健康，乾杯。

B: Gan-bei! In my country, we say, "Cheers!"
乾杯！在我的國家裡，我們會說「Cheers」！

A: Gan-bei and Cheers! Bottoms up!
乾杯，Cheers! 喝乾！

B: No one wants to dance yet? Then, it's my turn to give a toast. Here is to dancing! Gan-bei!
沒人想跳舞嗎？那麼，輪到我來敬酒，敬跳舞！乾杯！

Drinking in a Western pub.
在西式酒吧喝酒。

B: Steve, we've worked hard this week. Let me buy you a beer.
史提夫，我們這禮拜工作很辛苦，我請你喝杯啤酒。

A: Thank you, and I look forward to enjoying a Western pub for the first time. Gan-bei!
謝謝你，我很期待今天的西式酒吧，這可是第一次，乾杯！

B: Don't say gan-bei here, Steve. You can say cheers, and drink as much or as little as you want.
在這裡不說乾杯，你可以說cheers，然後隨意喝一些。

A: OK. So how do I make new friends here?
好，那我在這裡要怎麼交新朋友？

B: Well, if you want to make friends from other countries, don't speak Chinese or Taiwanese.
如果你想交其他國家的朋友，別說中文或台語。

A: That's OK. I do want to practice my English.
沒問題，我也想練練英文。

NOTES

Although, I have enjoyed joining my Taiwanese friends in Taiwanese pubs, most foreigners do not go to these places. If they want to relax and drink alcohol, they prefer to be in an environment where they do not have to translate Chinese. Pursuing relaxation means not having to think too much, and Western pubs provide relaxing surroundings. They provide food, drinks, music and television broadcasts that their guests are accustomed to. Likewise, most Taiwanese people often go to Western pubs out of curiosity, but they prefer to go to a place where they feel the most comfortable.

Sentences a Westerner might say
老外可能會說的句子

This is a fabulous dance club. Do you come here often?
這家夜店很棒，你常來這裡嗎？

So, we can choose one free drink with this ticket?
那麼，我們用這張票能選一杯免費的飲料？

The music is cool, and the dance floor is enormous! The girls are hot! Why are people just sitting or standing around?
音樂很酷，舞池也好大！女孩們都好辣！為什麼大家都只站著或坐著？

If no one is going to dance, let's sit down for a while.
如果沒人跳舞，我們也坐下來吧。

Let me see the menu. How much can the drinks cost? Oh my! The prices are outrageous!
我看看菜單，飲料要多少錢？天啊！這價格太可怕了！

I don't think we'll be drinking too much here. So let's dance to have fun.
我想我們在這裡不會喝太多，所以我們去跳舞玩玩。

Suit yourself. I'm not timid. I'll be out there dancing. Join me when you want to.
隨便，我不是膽小的人，我要去跳舞了，你可以隨時加入。

I just don't care what people think of me. I just respond to the music.
我不在乎別人怎麼想，我只在乎音樂。

Are you having fun yet? I know I am. And look! Someone bought me a drink.
你玩得開心嗎？我知道我很開心，你看，有人請我喝酒。

Actually, this is fun, but I prefer the casual environment of a Western pub. I don't like pretentious places.
其實很好玩，但我喜歡西式酒吧的輕鬆環境，我不喜歡做作的地方。

Sentences a Taiwanese person might say.
台灣人可能會說的句子

No. This club is too expensive, but I thought you would like to see it. I heard about it on the radio.
不，這夜店太貴了，但我覺得你會想看看。我聽收音機才知道這家店。

Yes, just a bottle of beer or basic mixed drink. You can't buy a premium drink with it.
對，一瓶啤酒或基本的調酒。你不能用票換高級的酒。

I don't know. Maybe they'll have the courage to dance later.
我不知道，或許他們晚點就有勇氣跳舞了。

We can't sit at those tables. They are reserved. You have to buy a lot of drinks in order to sit there.
我們不能坐那幾桌，那是保留座。你得買很多酒才能坐在那裡。

Yeah. That's why I have never been here before. But your birthday is a special occasion.
對，所以我以前一直沒來這裡，但你的生日是特殊情況。

No, thanks! I'm not very outgoing. You really have a carefree personality.
不，謝謝，我不是外向的人，你的個性真的很無拘無束。

You really are a good dancer. Look at all of the girls dancing with you.
你舞跳得真好，你看那些女孩都跟你一起跳舞。

Finally, the dance floor is getting crowded. It looks like people here just needed someone to take the first step.
終於，舞池越來越滿了。看來這裡的人只是需要有人帶頭。

It looks like you're fitting in very well here.
看來你非常適合這裡。

I hope you can take me to a Western pub on my birthday.
希望你在我生日時，能帶我去西式酒吧。

Featured Vocabulary

offer a toast (n.) 敬酒

Offering a toast is a ritual that acknowledges someone during a social occasion, and it is usually offered while drinking alcohol. A toast can recognize someone during a wedding or anniversary. Or it can be a way for people to express their gratitude. A toast can include many sentences, or it can be one word. In Asia, people may say, "gan-bei," or "bottoms up," which means they want you to empty your cup at once. In Western countries, people can say, "cheers," or "bottoms up," depending on their mood. When Westerners say, "cheers," they don't care how much or how little you drink. The simplest way to give a toast doesn't require saying a word. You can look at someone, raise your glass or bottle and nod your head. This is a quite common gesture in Western pubs.

a round of drinks (n.) 一輪飲料

When groups of people go out to drink, they can either buy their own drinks, or a host can buy drinks for their guests. Also, people can take turns buying a round of drinks for their group. Buying a round means buying drink for each person in your group. "The first round is on me," is what a person says to buy the first drink for everyone in the group. "Let me get the next round," means a person will buy the next set of drinks for everyone in the group. In Western pubs, foreigners typically buy their own drinks, but if there is a celebration or if friends want to show their gratitude, they can buy a round.

16

KTV KTV

One of my most interesting memories in Taiwan was my first experience at a karaoke box. My hosts in Taoyuan took me to have a nice seafood dinner, and then we toured a local night market. Afterwards, they decided to show me something they enjoyed… karaoke. I didn't want to publicize my poor singing skills, but I was perfectly happy to be an observer. My hosts seemed to really enjoy singing, and their voices were remarkable. I just sat back on the leather sofa and enjoyed the snacks and the Taiwan Beer. My hesitation to sing disappeared after drinking a few beers. I thumbed through the song book and chose a few old English songs. It was a liberating feeling to let go of my fears and sing out loud. It was even more fun when my hosts surprised me by singing an English song with me. I couldn't believe that a 60-yr-old Taiwanese man, who spoke no English, could sing the lyrics with me, "Take me home, country road…" We had a blast together. From that experience, I realized that music was a universal language.

Karaoke, or singing songs accompanied by lyrics on music videos, is an Asian phenomenon. It has been extremely popular in Japan and Taiwan, and its popularity has spread to many other Asian countries. Visiting a karaoke bar, or KTV, is a popular social activity in Taiwan. There are different types of KTV establishments, including some for adult entertainment. If you want to do something fun together, you should invite foreigners to join you and your friends to sing karaoke. This is a fun way for Taiwanese and native English speakers to share their culture with each other. Just make sure you know in advance what type of KTV establishment you are inviting them to.

基本實用會話

Taiwanese (A) Westerner (B)

Selecting a song.
點歌。

A : May I select a song for you?
我能幫你點首歌嗎？

B : Do you have any English songs?
你們有英文歌嗎？

A : Of course we do! Here is this song book, look at the pages that are yellow.
當然有！這是歌本，看黃色的那幾頁。

B： Yes, I do recognize a lot of these songs. But they are all over 20 years old. Do you have anything more recent?

好，我認得很多歌，但他們都超過20年了，你有新歌嗎？

A： I'm sorry, but we don't have many people requesting English songs here. This is all we have.

對不起，但我們這裡沒什麼人點英文歌，我們只有這些歌。

B： That's OK. I remember singing these songs with my father. I'll select a few.

沒關係，我記得和我爸一起唱過這些歌，我會點一些來唱。

> ### Drinking in a KTV.
> 在KTV裡喝酒。

B： Thank you. The snacks look delicious.

謝謝你，點心看來很好吃。

A： Let me know if I can do anything for you. I am your hostess, Mei-ling. May I get a drink for you?

如果需要幫忙就告訴我，我是你的服務員，美玲。需要來點酒嗎？

B： Thank you Mei-ling. I think a glass of whiskey will help me to relax.

謝謝你，美玲。我想要來杯威士忌，有助於放鬆一下。

A： OK. Here is your glass. While you are here, I will sit with you and drink with you.

好，這是你的酒。我會在這裡陪你一起喝酒。

B： Well, OK. The hospitality here is quite nice.

喔，好。這裡的服務挺不錯。

A： Would you like to sing an English song? We do have a nice selection.

你想唱首英文歌嗎？我們有幾首不錯的歌。

B： Not right now. I don't have the nerve yet. I'll let my hosts sing first.

現在不要，我現在還沒有膽量。讓主人先唱。

A： Gan-bei! After a few drinks, you will have the courage, and I will sing with you, too.

乾杯！再喝幾杯酒，你就會有膽量了，我也會陪你一起唱。

NOTES

Because karaoke bars are an Asian phenomenon, chances are that new visitors to Taiwan have not had the experience. In the West, there are very few opportunities to sing karaoke. Some Asian restaurants have karaoke machines, but only if they have a lot of Asian customers who enjoy karaoke. Many Asians overseas have karaoke systems in their homes. So, Western visitors may have had the opportunity to try karaoke only if they had Asian friends. If you invite visitors to a KTV in Taiwan, keep in mind that it may be a very strange experience for them. They may not know what to expect. And they may feel very awkward singing in front of everyone. It could be up to you to offer guidance and encouragement to make the experience more enjoyable for them.

溝通大加分

Sentences a Westerner might say
老外可能會說的句子

Thank you for inviting me, but I don't sing. If I tried, you may never respect me again.
謝謝你邀請我,但我不唱歌。如果我唱了,你就再也不會尊敬我了。

OK. I warned you about my horrible voice. Why do you want me to come?
好,我警告過你我的歌聲很差。你為什麼要我去?

OK. This is it? It looks very plain on the outside. The other KTV across the street looks more attractive.
好,就這樣?外觀看來很乏味,對街另一家KTV看來比較吸引人。

Adult entertainment? What do you mean?
成人娛樂?那是什麼意思?

This room is cozy. Do you want me to sit here on the leather couch?
這房間很舒適。你要我坐在這張皮沙發上?

Like I said before, I won't be singing. Oh, hello! It's nice to meet everyone.
我之前說過了,我不會唱歌。喔,大家好,很高興認識你們。

You're right! They are cute. What is everyone drinking? The first round is on me.
你說得對,他們很可愛。大家在喝什麼?第一輪我請客。

Your friends can sing very well. I can't understand what they are singing, but I know talent when I hear it.
你的朋友唱歌很好聽,我聽不懂他們在唱什麼,但我聽得出來很有天份。

I don't know. Oh, what the hell. Let me see that song book. Are there any American songs in there?
我不知道,喔,管他的。我看看歌本,這裡有英文歌嗎?

Hey! That was fun. With all of these girls as my backup singers, I felt like a singing star. Thank you!
嘿,真好玩,有這些女孩幫我合音,我覺得自己像歌唱巨星,謝謝你!

Sentences a Taiwanese person might say.
台灣人可能會說的句子

That's OK. Our friends will be at the KTV downtown. You won't need to sing unless you want to.
沒關係,我們的朋友會在市中心的KTV。你想唱再唱。

I want you to experience what my Taiwanese friends like to do in their social time.
我要讓你體驗我的台灣朋友在應酬時喜歡做的事。

Yes. We don't go there, because that place is for adult entertainment.
對，我們不會去那裡，因為那是成人娛樂的地方。

They attract men with beautiful hostesses. You don't need them. Tonight, you'll meet my friends and some of them are just as pretty.
他們以漂亮的女服務生吸引男人。你不需要他們的，今晚，我帶你認識我的朋友們，其中有幾個也很漂亮。

Please make yourself comfortable, and help yourself to the snacks. Look at this song book, if you want to sing.
請自便，自己吃些點心，如果想唱歌的話，可以看看歌本。

Everyone, this is my friend Jack. Jack, these are my friends from college.
大家，這是我的朋友傑克，傑克，這些是我的大學朋友。

We will pay for the entire bill when we leave. We can split it.
我們離開時再一起結帳，我們可以分攤。

Actually, the karaoke machine makes everyone sound pretty good. You really should try it out.
事實上，卡拉OK機能讓大家的歌聲變美，你真的該試試看。

Of course. All of my friends can read English, so we'll join you.
當然，我的朋友都會讀英文，我們會一起唱。

You're welcome. My friends enjoyed singing with an American, too.
不客氣，我的朋友也喜歡和美國人一起唱歌。

Featured Vocabulary

karaoke (n.) 卡拉OK

Karaoke is a word that comes from a combination of Japanese words, kara (empty) and okesutora (orchestra). It is no wonder that the origin of the word from Japan, where the form of interactive entertainment was born. Before the invention of karaoke machines in Japan in 1971, lyrics were displayed on television during some live broadcasts of music performances. This was known as a "sing-along" broadcast. When cassette tapes were introduced, versions of popular songs without the vocal track were popular in the Philippines. This was known as "minus one music." The popularity of "minus one music" spread to Japan, and inspired the invention of the karaoke machine. The popularity of the karaoke machine spread quickly throughout Asia, first in restaurants and lounges, and later in people's homes. For some reason, the trend never really caught on in the West.

karaoke box vs. KTV vs. karaoke bar (n.) 卡拉OK包廂vs. KTV vs.卡拉OK酒吧

After the karaoke machines were invented, people created businesses by renting the use of the machines inside of private rooms. In most countries, these rooms are known as karaoke boxes. The businesses may serve food and drinks, and sometimes they offer hostesses to sing and dance with the patrons. In China and Taiwan, kaoaroke boxes are referred to as KTVs. In North America and Europe, there are few of these type of businesses, and they are referred to as karaoke bars.

UNIT 17

Betel Nut 檳榔

The first time I saw betel nut stands, I was in Taipei. To the side of a street were small glass boxes lined up side by side. It was hard not to notice them, as each had decorations of colorful neon lights. Once I looked, what really caught my eye were the young girls inside the glass boxes. Each of these vendors was dressed in bikinis or lingerie. The scene made me wonder if I was in the red light district of Taipei. My friend told me that these glass boxes were betel nut stands. I didn't understand what that meant, so I walked up to them for a closer look. When a car or blue truck pulled alongside, a scarcely dressed woman would come out and give a small package to the driver. I realized that they were not selling any services, but they were attracting (mostly men) to buy their products.

This was my first observation of Taiwan's betel nut beauties. This is a part of culture that is quite unique to Taiwan. It doesn't take long before visitors spot betel nut stands, because they are hard to miss. They are also easier to find away from city centers, where there are fewer restrictions. At first glance, visitors may think they are looking at something that resembles Amsterdam's red light district. But once they understand the tradition, they will realize it is a way for young Taiwanese women to capitalize on a vending business to improve their future.

基本實用會話

Taiwanese (A)　　Westerner (B)

Visiting a betel nut stand.
參觀檳榔攤。

A: Have you seen anything like this in your country?
你在你的國家見過類似的東西嗎？

B: No. Not at all. What is this place?
不，完全沒有。這是什麼？

A: It's a betel nut stand. This one sells betel nuts, cigarettes and beer.
這是檳榔攤，賣檳榔、香煙和啤酒。

B: That's all they sell?
就賣這些？

A: What do you mean?
什麼意思？

B: Well, look at the way this girl is dressed.
這個嘛，你看這女孩的穿著。

A：No. They are not allowed to offer anything else. They dress this way to attract customers. Do you want to try a betel nut?

不，他們不能賣別的東西。他們的穿著是為了吸引客人，你想試試檳榔嗎？

B：No, thank you. But I'll pay her to let me take her photo.

不，謝謝你。但我願意付錢請她讓我拍張照。

Trying a betel nut.
試吃檳榔。

B：I have seen many people chew on these, but I have never tried it. I'll try one just once.

我看過好多人嚼這個東西，但我從來沒試過。我想試一次看看。

A：Betel nuts are supposed to make you feel warm and full of energy.

檳榔可能會讓你覺得發熱，充滿能量。

B：Oh, this tastes horrible! I want to spit it out.

喔，這味道好糟糕！我要吐出來。

A：Don't do that. And don't swallow the juice. Let it sit in your mouth for awhile.

別那麼做，也別把汁吞進去，在嘴裡含一會兒。

B：Ugh! Where do I spit it out? I do feel a little tingling sensation in my head.

噁！我要吐在哪裡？我的頭覺得有點麻麻刺刺的。

A：Spit it out in this plastic cup. Don't spit it on the ground. It makes an orange-colored mess.

吐在這個塑膠杯裡，別吐在地上，會把地上弄得橘色、髒髒的。

B：I'm not going to do that again. But, at least I had a chance to see a betel nut beauty up close.

我不要再吃了，不過至少我有機會近距離見識檳榔的美。

NOTES

I have been offered betel nuts on many occasions in Taiwan, and like any curious visitor, it was an eventuality for me to try one. The taste was bitter and unpleasant, but after a few minutes, the mixture in my mouth did stimulate me. Betel nut users chew them to obtain stimulation. In Western countries, people who want a similar experience use chewing tobacco. Like the betel nut, chewing tobacco offers stimulation. Unfortunately, the repeated use of betel nuts or chewing tobacco will often lead to cancer in the mouth or throat and discoloration of the teeth.

Sentences a Westerner might say
老外可能會說的句子

Why are you pulling over? What are they selling here?
你為什麼停車？他們這裡賣什麼？

Wow! She is gorgeous! Why is she dressed in a bikini on a chilly night?
哇！她好迷人！她為什麼在這麼冷的夜晚只穿著比基尼？

What is she saying? What is she offering?
她說什麼？她賣什麼？

I don't smoke. But I don't know what betel nuts are.
我不抽煙，可是我不知道檳榔是什麼。

That costs NT100? OK. You are very beautiful. Stay warm!
那樣要100元？好，你很漂亮。穿暖一點！

OK. But why do we need this cup? Will we drink something?
好，但我們為什麼需要這個杯子？我們要喝什麼嗎？

Oh, my! This tastes bitter. It doesn't taste as good as chewing tobacco.
天啊，這味道好苦。這和嚼煙草的味道不一樣。

OK. I do feel it now. Can I spit it out now?
好，我感覺到了，我能把它吐出來了嗎？

Oh, that orange saliva looks disgusting. So that's what I see all the time on the street.
喔，那團橘色口水感覺好噁心，那就是我常在路上看到的東西。

Well, that was an interesting experience. I feel like I have more energy now.
這是個有趣的體驗。我覺得我又有能量了。

Sentences a Taiwanese person might say.
台灣人可能會說的句子

I think you will find this interesting. Roll down your window, so the girl can talk to you.
我想你會覺得這很有趣。把窗戶搖下來，女孩才能跟你說話。

She's wearing that to attract us here. It worked, didn't it?
她穿那樣是為了吸引我們過來。成功了，不是嗎？

She wants to know if you want to buy any betel nuts or cigarettes.
她想知道你要不要買些檳榔或香煙。

Let's buy a package of betel nuts and try some.
我們買包檳榔試試。

Get a betel nut out for each of us. And take out that plastic cup.
幫我們一人拿一顆檳榔出來，還要拿出塑膠杯。

No. We'll need a place to spit, after we chew our betel nut.
不，我們嚼完檳榔後，需要一個地方吐汁。

I know. You'll get used to it. Just leave it in your mouth for a few minutes. Then, you'll start to feel it.
我知道，你得習慣它，把它含在嘴裡幾分鐘。然後，你就會有感覺了。

Yes, into the cup. Here. Pass the cup to me after you're done.
對，吐進杯子裡。吐完後，把杯子傳給我。

Some people are rude. They spit on the ground or just throw their cup out of the car window.
有些人很沒規矩，他們會吐在地上，或是把杯子丟出車窗。

Great! Because we're going to stay out late tonight. I will show you the nightlife.
太好了，因為我們晚上得熬夜，我要讓你見識夜生活。

Featured Vocabulary

betel nut (n.) 檳榔

The betel nut, also known as "areca nut," is harvested throughout the tropic zones of Asia and East Africa. They grow on areca palm trees, and are harvested and chewed for their properties as a stimulant. The chewing of betel nuts have been popular for thousands of years in Asia and the Pacific islands. But the popularity of consuming betel nuts has been challenged in modern times as the scientific community has linked the practice to cancer. Also, frequent chewing results in the mouth and teeth to take on an unattractive reddish-orange color. Another criticism is that farmers who cover hillsides with areca palms accelerate the erosion of the land, leading to mudslides and the loss of precious soil.

betel nut beauty (n.) 檳榔西施

Betel nut beauties are young women who sell betel nuts and cigarettes from neon-decorated glass boxes. Their name comes from the addictive betel nuts that they sell, and the fact that they wear revealing clothing to highlight their attractiveness. Betel nut beauties are a uniquely Taiwanese phenomenon, and this tradition originated in the 1960's at the Shuangdong Betel Nut Stand in Guoxing Township (國 姓 鄉) in Nantou County. There is nothing like this tradition in Western countries. However, a similar phenomenon can be seen in the USA and Canada, where young women work in small streetside stands selling anything from coffee to hot dogs. Many wear bikinis to grab attention, but some have even made a name for themselves by wearing nothing at all.

18

Clothes 買衣服

One of the benefits of living in Taiwan has been the affordable cost of clothes and shoes. Perhaps it is due to the fact that most of the world's clothes are manufactured in Asia. In April 2010, I wrote an article for CNN.com titled, "How far does $10 (NT300) go in Taiwan?" (http://ireport.cnn.com/docs/DOC-431199) Almost 2,000 people read it. For this writing assignment, I bought twenty-four pairs of white cotton socks and ten neckties in a local market. I would have spent at least US$50 at a discount store in the USA for the same items. Since writing that article, I have found many other great deals on shirts, pants and shoes in Taiwan as well. My income may be lower in Taiwan than in the USA, but there has been a drastic reduction in the cost of clothing for my family.

When Westerners come to Taiwan, they are usually surprised to see how affordable clothing and shoes are. My friends who visit Taiwan usually buy more clothes than they expect to. Of course, the prices are very attractive, but there are also many "cute" styles that they cannot find in their countries. Asian cultures have influenced their fashion with a lot of "cuteness" for both children and adults. If you bring a visitor to go clothes shopping, expect to wait awhile, because they often take their time browsing through clothes, as the variety is incredible to them.

基本實用會話

Taiwanese (A)　　Westerner (B)

Buying clothes at a night market.
在夜市買衣服。

A : This area of the Feng-Chia night market is famous for clothes.
這一區是逢甲夜市裡有名的服飾區。

B : I'm not really looking for any clothes, but... Oh my! This pink shirt has glitter on it!
其實我沒有要買什麼衣服，可是…喔，天啊，這件粉紅上衣上面有亮片。

A : There is a lot of Japanese influence in the fashion here. You can find "Hello Kitty" on everything.
這裡的服飾受日本影響很深，很多東西上面都有「Hello Kitty」。

B : Even these pink tennis shoes have the cute kitten on it. I have never seen these in America.
就連這些粉紅網球鞋上面都有可愛的小貓。我在美國沒見過這些東西。

A : If you're looking for more shoes, many of these shops have more selections to choose from.
如果你想找鞋，這些鞋店的選擇更多。

B: I already have too many shoes back home, but these prices are hard to believe.
我家裡已經有太多鞋了，但這些鞋的價錢真讓人難以置信。

A: I thought you weren't looking to buy any clothes. Now you have so many shopping bags.
我以為你沒打算買衣服，現在你手上有這麼多購物袋了。

B: I know. There are just too many cute styles, and the prices are too low to resist.
我知道，這些款式太可愛了，而且價錢又低到難以抗拒。

Buying clothes in a department store.
在百貨公司買衣服。

B: The outdoor markets just don't have the glamour I am looking for. I have to wear something gorgeous to the wedding.
這些戶外市場沒有我在尋找的魅力服飾。我去參加婚禮要穿得很迷人。

A: Well, Taiwan has plenty of fashionable department stores. This one is quite famous.
這個嘛，台灣有很多時尚百貨公司。這一家就很有名。

B: This mall looks just like the ones in America, but they are in taller buildings.
這個商場跟美國的商場很像，但美國的建築比較高。

A: I guess that means you don't have to walk as much when you are shopping. Right?
我猜這表示你們逛街的時候不用走太多路，對嗎？

B: Right! This store has formal dresses with the stylish European brand names.
沒錯，這家店有很多歐洲時尚品牌的禮服。

A: Wow! I can't believe the ridiculous prices. Are you sure you want to buy this dress?
哇！我不敢相信這嚇人的價格，你確定你要買這件洋裝？

B: Well, that price is normal in New York City. Besides, I will use my credit card and have my father pay for it.
這價格在紐約市很正常。而且我會刷信用卡，叫我爸付錢。

NOTES

In Taiwan, it is commonplace to see clothing with English words or phrases on them. I have been surprised by some of the most expressions on clothing. Some can be funny and some can be offensive. The sayings on clothes can turn the heads of visitors in Taiwan. For example, I have seen grandmothers and children wearing shirts that have strong sexual language on them. There are plenty of clothes with unsuitable expressions of violence or illegal drug use. When buying clothes with English words on them, I recommend that Taiwanese people get it translated to make sure it is appropriate to wear in public. You never know if what you wear will offend someone or make them laugh at you. They may even take your photo to share with their friends around the world.

Sentences a Westerner might say
老外可能會說的句子

Thank you for bringing me to this market. I heard they have great deals here on garments.
謝謝你帶我來這個市場。聽說這裡的衣服很划算。

I need to start exercising again, so I need to buy clothes and shoes for my workouts.
我得再開始運動了，所以我需要運動服和運動鞋。

This "Nike" t-shirt looks nice. Do you think this will make me look masculine?
那件「Nike」的T恤看來不錯。你覺得那件會讓我更有男子氣慨嗎？

I'll buy a few t-shirts, shorts and sweatpants.
我要買幾件T恤，短褲和運動長褲。

I want to get some "Nike" sneakers to match my shirt.
我要找雙「Nike」運動鞋搭我的上衣。

That's OK. I'll get a pair of cheap sandals while I'm here. My sandals are worn out.
沒關係，我還要買雙便宜的涼鞋。我的涼鞋壞了。

Yeah! Adidas, Reebok, and Nike! But it looks like the one I want is not in stock.
耶！愛迪達，Reebok和Nike！可是我要的好像沒貨了。

That won't be necessary. Wow! The price of these Reebok sneakers is slashed in half! I'll take it!
不需要，哇！這雙Reebok運動鞋砍到半價！我買了！

Well, that's nice of you. I am always interested in saving money. Uh oh!
哇，你真好。我總是很想省錢，喔喔！

I didn't bring enough money with me. Can you help me find an ATM machine?
我身上的錢不夠，你能幫我找提款機嗎？

Sentences a Taiwanese person might say.
台灣人可能會說的句子

Sure. Clothing is affordable here. People come from all over to find bargains.
當然，這裡的衣服很便宜，大家都來這裡找便宜。

OK. I'll help you find what you need.
好，我會幫你找你要的東西。

I don't know if a shirt is enough to make you look masculine. I think you need to work out more.
我不知道這件上衣會不會讓你足夠有男子氣慨。我想你需要再多運動。

What about tennis shoes? Would you prefer a famous brand or something cheap?
那網球鞋呢？你有偏好的品牌還是想找便宜的呢？

We'll have to go to another retail store to find Nike shoes. This store only sells cheap shoes.
我們得去另一家零售店找Nike的鞋子。這家店只賣便宜的鞋。

This retail store has all of the famous brand name shoes that you may want.
這家零售店有你想要的各大知名品牌球鞋。

What do you want to do? Do you want me to help you find another shop?
你打算怎麼辦？要我再幫你找另一家店嗎？

Great! Let me ask the shop owner if he can give you a larger discount.
太好了！我問問店長能不能幫你打更多折扣。

What's the matter?
怎麼了？

Sure! There is an ATM machine in every convenience store.
沒問題！每家便利商店都有提款機。

Featured Vocabulary

knock-off (adj.) 假，贗

Many people buy designer brands of clothing and shoes to be fashionable, or perhaps just to show off. But, they are extremely expensive. Sometimes, people choose to skip the department stores to find knock-offs of the designer brands. The "copies" are often sold at 10%-30% of the price of the authentic products. Some of the copies have slight variations that make them obvious. However, some copies are so similar to the original, they cannot be distinguished with the untrained eye.

off-the-rack vs. custom-fitted vs. tailored (adj.) 成衣 vs. 量身修改vs.定製

In the high-end fashion stores or boutiques around the world, women can sometimes buy clothes that are custom-fitted to their size. A seamstress will take measurements and make adjustments to the design of the clothes. Throughout Asia, expecially Hong Kong, men can go to a tailor, and get a suit measured for his body size and shape. Clothes bought in this fashion are said to be custom-fitted or tailored. This personalized service is more expensive, so most people buy clothes off-the-rack, which means the clothes are manufactured to fit a certain size and are on a rack when they are for sale.

Electronics 買電器

In Tainan City, there is a well-known street named Beimen Road near the main train station. Beimen Road is usually packed with people looking for great deals on electronic merchandise and the latest fashion trends. When I first visited, I was not in the market for new clothes, but I was interested in electronics. The first thing that amazed me was how many shops selling computers, cameras and accessories were so close to each other. There was even a shopping mall that had about fifty small electronics shops in them. The second surprise was how cheap some of the computer parts and accessories were. I found computer memory chips, LCD monitors, computer cables, hard drives, and power cords that were 70% cheaper than what I had found in America. On the other hand, popular electronics brands like Apple and Canon were actually slightly more expensive on Beimen Road than they were in Park Avenue in New York City. What I realized was that many electronics components and goods are actually manufactured in Taiwan, making them more affordable in the local marketplace.

Westerners visiting Taiwan can find and purchase affordable electronics in shopping districts and outdoor markets. Taiwan is the home to many manufacturers that produce memory chips, hardware, and components. This means a good business opportunity for foreigners who can buy electronics directly from suppliers in Taiwan and sell them in their own countries. I know a few foreigners who make a good living by taking advantage of buying electronics from the source… Taiwan.

基本實用會話

Taiwanese (A) :  Westerner (B) :

Buying electronics at an electronics shopping district. 在電器街買電器

A : This is Beimen Road. It means, "North Gate" in English. This street is famous for many types of electronics merchandise and fashion.
這裡是北門路，意思是北邊的門。這條街以各種電器商店和時裝店出名。

B : I'm not interested in clothes, but I am always looking for a bargain on electronics.
我對衣服沒興趣，但我一定想找便宜的電器。

A : What do you want to buy? There are a variety of small shops here.
你想買什麼？這裡有很多種小店。

B： I am always looking for hardware and parts to upgrade my computer system.
我一直想找硬碟，還有升級電腦系統的零件。

A： Then you'll definitely find good bargains here. Do you need a new cell phone?
那你一定能找到便宜好貨。你需要新的手機嗎？

B： No. I am happy with my iPhone. These accessories are very cheap.
不，我很滿意我的iPhone。這些配件非常便宜。

A： Sure. That's because most of it is made here in Taiwan.
當然，因為這大部分是台灣製造。

Buying electronics in a department store.
在百貨公司買電器。

B： This store looks just like an electronics store in my country. It has many famous brands.
這家店看來就像我國的電子用品店，裡面有好多名牌。

A： Hello, sir. May I help you find something today?
先生你好，今天需要我幫您找什麼嗎？

B： I need a new camera. I lost mine during a hike in the mountains.
我要買台新的相機，我去上山健行的時候弄丟我的相機。

A： We have Sony, Canon and Nikon brands. We even have Panasonic and Olympus.
我們有Sony，Canon和Nikon，還有Panasonic和Olympus。

B： Perfect! Those are the brands I know and trust. But, why are they so expensive?
太棒了！那是都是我知道且信任的廠牌，但他們為什麼這麼貴？

A： We import these cameras and need to pay for import duties, so the price is higher.
這些相機都是進口的，必須付進口稅，所以價格較高。

NOTES

Most people in the world are surprised to find out that Taiwan is a leading manufacturer of electronic components, including computer chips, LCD and LED technologies. Taiwan has some leading technology companies, such as Taiwan Semiconductor, Chi Mei Innolux, Everlight, Foxconn, Asus, Acer and HTC. The competitive edge that Taiwan has provided over the years has been its ability to engineer and manufacture with a high level of quality control. This has been good news for Taiwan's economy, but most of these companies now outsource their jobs to China, so more people in Taiwan have had to work overseas.

Sentences a Westerner might say
老外可能會說的句子

I need to buy a new portable computer. What do you recommend?
我要買一台筆記型電腦。有什麼建議嗎？

Taiwanese brands? Which brands are those? I don't think I have ever heard of them.
那是台灣的廠牌嗎？那些是什麼廠牌？我想我沒聽過。

Is their quality reliable? I don't want to buy a computer that will break down soon.
他們的品質可靠嗎？我不想買一台一下子就會壞的電腦。

I still don't know if I can trust a Taiwanese brand. Do you have any American brands?
我不知道能不能相信台灣廠牌。你有沒有美國的廠牌？

Yes! I had a Dell Computer laptop before. I trust that brand 100%.
是的，我以前用過Dell的筆記型電腦，我百分之百相信那個廠牌。

OK! I'll take a look at your laptops from Quanta Computer.
好，我看看Quanta電腦的筆電。

That sounds great. I hope this laptop can handle video editing.
聽來很棒，希望這台筆電能處理影像編輯。

Can you show me your video cameras? Are there any Taiwanese brands?
你能讓我看看攝影機嗎？有台灣廠牌的嗎？

I think I will buy a Sony Handycam. I need to make videos of my English lessons.
我想我要買台Sony攝影機，我需要錄下我的英文課。

You're right. I'm opening up a new language school with my wife. We need this equipment to promote our company.
你說得對，我要和我太太開設新的語言學校。我們需要這些設備宣傳我們的公司。

Sentences a Taiwanese person might say.
台灣人可能會說的句子

We have all of the international brands and Taiwanese brands here.
我們這裡有各種國際廠牌和台灣廠牌。

The two famous brands are Asus and Acer. But HTC and Quanta Computer also make quality laptops.
Asus和Acer是兩個有名的廠牌，但HTC和Quanta Computer也製造高品質的筆電。

Of course, they are excellent. Most LCD screens in all laptops are made in Taiwan.
當然，他們都很優良。很多筆電的LCD螢幕都是台灣製造的。

Yes. We have IBM and Apple. Have you ever heard of Dell Computers?
是的，我們有IBM和Apple。你聽過Dell電腦嗎？

Well, Quanta Computer makes laptops for Dell Computers. And their laptops are cheaper.
這個，Quanta電腦為Dell電腦製造筆電。他們的筆電比較便宜。

If you buy a laptop today, we also offer a free mobile power charger.
如果你今天買台筆電，我們會贈送免費的行動電源。

The Quanta Computer laptops have enough power to handle video editing. Just make sure to get a faster video card.
Quanta電腦的筆電足以處理影像編輯，不過要確認是否配備速度較快的顯示卡。

Unfortunately, there aren't any Taiwanese brands of video cameras. We have the popular Japanese brands.
很可惜，這裡沒有台灣廠牌的攝影機。我們有很受歡迎的日本廠牌。

You are buying a lot of electronics today.
你今天買了很多電子用品。

Good luck with your new business.
祝你生意興隆。

Featured Vocabulary

counterfeit (adj.) 偽造

As a foreigner in Taiwan, it is easy to find great deals on electronics. But sometimes the prices seem too low to believe. Be warned that if a deal looks too good to believe, it probably is not real. I have seen the popular "Beats" brand of headphones, which normally sell for NT 3,000, on sale in outdoor markets in Taiwan and China for only about NT 300. The price was so attractive, that I was excited to make a purchase. Fortunately, I was warned by friends that the products were counterfeit. It means the product was not authentic, and was likely made with cheaper parts. I didn't buy the "fake" version of the "Beats" headphones, because I didn't feel it was worth buying something with lower quality, even if it looked the same as the popular brand. Not only that, I but I was certain that the product would not be covered by a warranty.

electronics store (n.) 電子商店

In Taiwan, there are a few successful chains of retail electronics stores, such as 3C, that sell a variety of electronics at reasonable prices. However, visitors in Taiwan will also find many small shop owners selling electronics. They may sell a variety of products, or they may focus on one type of goods, such as mobile phones, PDA's, cameras, or stereo systems. This may give visitors a different experience than they are used to. In Taiwan, they not only have more stores to choose from, but there are many shops offering great bargains. In the USA, it is extremely difficult to find small mom-and-pop shops selling electronics. The market is dominated by a few chain stores, such as Radio Shack, Best Buy and Circuit City. Their ability to use their purchasing power means they can offer better prices than small business owners.

Cell Phones 買手機

UNIT 20

When I moved to Taiwan, my wife and I bought our own Cell Phones through the A+ store. We didn't expect to make too many calls, so we chose a company whose service would be cheaper. An extra incentive was that every call I made to my wife's cell phone was free. This made our cell phone usage very affordable. Our cell phone was free, as long as we paid for a monthly subscription for service. We chose the least expensive package, which was sixty minutes of service per month for dual users. When we received our monthly bill, my wife yelled at me for exceeding my monthly allocated minutes. But I jumped with joy, after seeing that my cell phone bill for both accounts totalled only NT800, or about US $24.00. After paying an average of US $120.00 per month for cell phone usage for many years in the USA, I was so happy to have such a small monthly cell phone bill.

Westerners living in Taiwan are usually amazed at how inexpensive utility bills are, such as power, water, telephone, and cell phone bills. In Taiwan I pay about 30% of what I paid in the USA. Mobile phone bills in the USA were extremely high, especially for smart phones. Rates for subscriptions can start at US $60.00 per month and go as high as $120.00 per month. If you go over the minutes you are alloted, it is not unusual to have a cell phone bill of over US $200. I am glad I don't have those painfully large bills any more.

基本實用會話

Taiwanese (A) : Westerner (B) :

Buying cell phone at a cell phone store. 在手機店買手機

A : The iPhone 5 is an excellent choice.
這台iPhone 5是很好的選擇。

B : I have always wanted an iPhone. And it is cheaper than I thought.
我一直想到一台iPhone，這台比我想像中便宜。

A : That is because you have to sign up for a 2-year subscription for phone and data service.
這是因為你簽了兩年的電話和電信服務合約。

B : Oh! I didn't know that. How much is the subscription?
喔！我不知道！月租費多少？

A : It depends on how how many minutes of voice and data service you want per month.
這視你每月的通話分鐘數和上網服務。

B： I don't expect to use my phone too much. I don't know many people here.
我應該不會太常用電話。我在這裡認識的人不多。

A： I recommend Package C, which gives you one hour of voice service and unlimited data services. That way, you can keep in touch with your friends back home using the Internet.
我推薦C套餐，你能有一小時通話服務和無限上網。這樣一來，你就能利用網路和家鄉的朋友保持聯繫。

B： Excellent idea! Thank you.
好主意！謝謝你。

> **Paying for a cell phone bill.**
> 付手機費。

B： Excuse me, can you please help me?
抱歉，你能幫我嗎？

A： What can I do for you?
我能幫您什麼忙？

B： I received my first bill for my new cell phone. How do I send them a payment?
我第一次收到新手機的帳單。我要怎樣付款？

A： In Taiwan, the most convenient way is to pay your bill at 7-11 or Family Mart.
在台灣，最便利的方式就是到7-11或全家便利商店付款。

B： What? That is so convenient. Why hasn't anyone thought of doing that in my country?
什麼？好方便。為什麼我的國家沒人想到這麼做？

A： Taiwanese people really do enjoy many conveniences.
台灣人很喜歡便利的生活。

NOTES

Visitors to Taiwan can rent a prepaid cell phone during the duration of their visit, which they can purchase in any mobile phone store. This is a cheaper option that using their own mobile phones from their country, because the roaming charges for operation outside of their country can be excessive. Foreigners who live in Taiwan often purchase a phone and select a monthly subscription fee. This is cheaper than the prepaid option for long-term use.

Sentences a Westerner might say
老外可能會說的句子

I need to get a new mobile phone. What do you recommend?
我需要買台新手機，你有什麼建議嗎？

How do I know which brand is best for me?
我要麼知道哪個牌子最適合我？

Yes, I do want to browse websites, and also check Facebook.
是的，我會瀏覽過網站，也會上臉書。

OK. Then, should I buy an iPhone?
好，那麼，我該買iPhone嗎？

OK, but I don't want my mobile phone to be outdated so quickly. I want to be able to download the latest software.
好，但我不希望我的手機太快退流行，我想要能下載最新的軟體。

I don't know much about those brands. What can you tell me about them?
我不太了解那些品牌。你能向我介紹一下嗎？

Both Samsung and HTC are equally attractive. I guess I should choose Samsung, because it is a little cheaper.
Samsung和HTC都一樣吸引人，我想我應該選擇Samsung，因為便宜一些。

Yes, please. And could you please show me your portable cell phone chargers?
是的，麻煩你。你能再讓我看看行動電源嗎？

I am new here in Taiwan, so I don't have any service yet. Which company do you recommend?
我剛到台灣，所以我還沒用過電信服務。你有推薦的公司嗎？

You've been very helpful. I thought buying a mobile phone would be more difficult.
你幫了大忙。我以為買手機會困難得多。

Sentences a Taiwanese person might say.
台灣人可能會說的句子

Welcome to 3C. We have every major brand of mobile phone here.
歡迎來到3C。每個大廠牌的手機這裡都有。

It depends on what you need? Do you just want to talk on the phone? Or do you also want to surf the Internet and access E-mails?
這要看你的需求？你只是打電話？還是你也要上網、收發電子郵件？

Then you want a cell phone that has the latest technological features.
那麼你需要最新科技功能的手機。

Not necessarily. iPhones are the most expensive phones on the market. You may want to consider some alternatives.
不一定。iPhones是市面上最貴的手機，你可以考慮其他選擇。

You will find all of the features you want in a Samsung or HTC smart phone.
Samsung或HTC智慧型手機都有你需要的所有功能。

Both brands are comparable to the iPhone in capabilities. Samsung may be slightly less expensive than the HTC.
兩種廠牌在性能上都能和iPhone比擬。Samsung或許比HTC稍貴一些。

Just so you know, HTC is made in Taiwan and Samsung is made in South Korea.
你可以參考一下，HTC是台灣製造，Samsung是南韓製造。

Great! Should I show you the latest models of HTC smart phones?
太好了！您要看看最新的HTC智慧型手機嗎？

Of course. Which telephone company do you currently have service with?
當然。你最近使用過哪一家電信服務？

I'll be happy to tell you your alternatives.
我很樂於告訴你其他的選擇。

Featured Vocabulary

cell phone vs. mobile phone vs. smart phone (n.) 手機、智慧型手機

"Cell phones" and "mobile phones" are terms used to describe portable telephones that are connected to a wireless network. "Cell phone" is a shortened term for cellular phone. It was the first term that was used, and later came the term, "mobile phone." After the phones came out data, e-mail and Internet services, the term "smart phone" was introduced to describe the technology.

subscription (n.) 月租費

When purchasing a mobile phone or smart phone, one needs a telecommunications company to provide the phone and data services for the phone. In Taiwan, there are a few major companies competing for these services, and they offer a monthly fee for a limited number of minutes of access. This package of monthly minutes is called a subscription. If you use more minutes than is offered in your monthly subscription, you are charged a higher rate per minute. It is smart to choose a subscription that provides more minutes than you typically use every month in order to save money.

UNIT 21

Banks 上銀行

My first experience with a bank in Taiwan was brief. Nonetheless, I could see a significant difference between it and a typical American bank branch. The space for customers was very small, and there were very few furnishings and decorations. There was also no one to personally greet customers as they walked in. I was there to exchange my currency into U.S. dollars, so I only needed to stand in line and visit the teller. My second visit to a Taiwanese bank was a lengthy experience, as I needed to open my first bank account. I had many documents to fill out, and I had to submit identification, a fingerprint, and a photo. They used these security measures as a safeguard against financial fraud. The teller gave me a pamphlet to sell enrollment in some type of insurance. In the end, I received some paperwork and my checkbook. It looked like a checkbook I would have in America, except that in Taiwan, it could be inserted into a machine to print the latest transactions and balances.

Westerners may find that opening a bank account in Taiwan follows stricter guidelines. However, accessing their money is quite convenient around the island, with many banks and ATM machines available. Taiwanese banks also seem to offer better interest rates for investments and better rates for loans than what I experienced from American banks. The banking fees imposed monthly are also much smaller in Taiwanese banks.

基本實用會話

Taiwanese (A) Westerner (B)

Exchanging currency.
換匯。

A: Please take a number from that little machine over there, and wait for your number to be called.
請從那台小機器抽個號碼牌,然後等待叫號。

B: Thank you. I see that the numbers are displayed above each teller.
謝謝你。我看到每個銀行職員上面都有顯示號碼。

A: May I help you?
需要什麼服務嗎?

B: I need to exchange this currency into Taiwanese money.
我要把錢換成新台幣。

A：OK. I'm sorry, but we cannot accept any bills below $20. And we only accept the newer version of the bills.
好，很抱歉，但我們不接受20元以下的紙鈔，也只接受新版紙鈔。

B：Are you serious? This money is 'real' American money. Are you afraid that they are fake?
真的嗎？這錢是「真的」美金，你們是怕收到偽鈔？

A：I apologize, but that is the bank's policy. You'll find this to be the same with all banks in Taiwan.
很抱歉，但這是銀行政策。台灣的其他銀行也是如此。

Opening a bank account.
銀行開戶。

B： I need to open a bank account.
我要開戶。

A：OK. Are you at least 20 years old? Do you have an A.R.C. (Alien Resident Certificate)?
好的，您滿20歲了嗎？您有外僑居留證嗎？

B：Yes. I'm 21. And I have an A.R.C. through my employer.
有，我21歲了，而且我透過雇主已經拿到居留證。

A：Great! Please fill out this application. And I will need to take your photo and get your fingerprint. You will need to deposit at least NT1,000.
太好了，請填寫這份表格。我需要您的照片，並記錄您的指紋。您至少要先存1000元。

B：OK. Do you have these documents in English?
好，你有英文表格嗎？

A：Oh yes. Sorry. We don't get many foreign customers here.
喔，有，很抱歉，這裡不常有外國顧客來。

NOTES

Foreigners in Taiwan can open a Taiwanese bank account if they want to put their money in a safe place. The most common type of account is called a "Demand Deposit" account. What is required is an A.R.C. and passport, as well as a initial deposit. A local bank may ask for NT1,000, but a larger bank like ChinaTrust may ask for NT10,000. Citibank asks for a minimum balance of NT25,000. HSBC requires a deposit of NT3,000,000. In a recent development, the US government is now requiring all Americans who open a bank account in Taiwan to fill out an American tax document. The U.S. government will make sure that Americans disclose their financial transactions overseas.

Sentences a Westerner might say
老外可能會說的句子

I would like to get a loan.
我想申請貸款。

I want to buy my own house here.
我想在這裡買自己的房子。

I do have an A.R.C. Does that help?
我有外僑居留證，這樣有幫助嗎？

Are you serious? Why do they care about what I want to buy?
真的嗎？他們為什麼在乎我要買什麼？

All right. I guess I'll ask my wife to take me there.
好，我想我再請太太帶我去。

Yes, she is. Why do you ask?
對，她是。為什麼要問？

That's good news. Which way is better?
那是好消息。哪種方式比較好？

I don't think she has ever bought a house. I will need to ask.
我想她沒買過房子。我得問問。

I will ask her and return tomorrow. Is there anything else I need to bring?
我先問她，明天再回來。我還要帶什麼嗎？

Thank you! You've been so helpful. I'll see you tomorrow.
謝謝你！你幫了大忙，明天見。

Sentences a Taiwanese person might say.
台灣人可能會說的句子

What would you like a loan for?
您貸款的目的為何？

That will be extremely difficult for a foreigner.
那對外國人來說是非常困難的。

Of course. But you will need to apply with the Ministry of Foreign Affairs to see if you qualify to buy property in Taiwan.
當然，但您需要向外交部申請，看看您是否符合在台灣購屋的資格。

Basically, foreigners are only allowed to buy property if Taiwanese citizens are allowed to buy property in their country.
基本上，只有臺灣人可以在他們的國家購買房產時，該國國民才能在台灣置產。

Is your wife Taiwanese?
你太太是台灣人嗎？

That changes everything! She can either be a co-signee, or you can apply for the loan through her.
那就不一樣了！她可以是共同申請，或是你可以透過她申請貸款。

If she has never bought property before, she may qualify for a low-interest loan as a first time home buyer.
如果她以前從沒買過房產，她或許符合首次購屋的低利貸款資格。

You will only need to pay 3% interest for that loan, so it is worth it to find out.
你們的貸款只需要付百分之三的利息，所以值得一試。

You should bring your tax records to show your proof of income, and proof of any other property or investments.
你們要帶稅務資料來證明你們的收入，還有其他財產或投資的證明。

You're welcome and have a nice day!
不客氣，祝你有個愉快的一天。

Featured Vocabulary

investment (n.) 投資

Financial institutions offer many types of investments, including different rates of return and different levels of risk. In Taiwan, there are also savings accounts, stocks, bonds and other types of investments. I have seen investments in Taiwan that also provide life insurance or health insurance coverage as an attached benefit. Also, banks and investment companies in Taiwan offer investment in American stocks, but you have to provide American currency to open these accounts. It means in most cases, you need to convert your currency first, and then provide it to open these special investment accounts.

insurance (n.) 保險

There are many types of insurance policies around the world. In Taiwan, however, I have seen some interesting variations on insurance policies. As a rule-of-thumb, I have learned to stay away from insurance policies unless they are backed by the government or the top banks. One of the most interesting types of insurance I have seen in Taiwan is one that grows in value as you make a payment every month, and it provides a payout at the end. It is more like an investment than an insurance policy, but you also get life insurance and/or health insurance coverage. This seems like quite the bargain.

UNIT 22

Driving 開車

In my first six months in Taiwan, I relied on public transportation to get around. Sometimes, I let my wife drive me on her motor scooter. Being a passenger was not easy for me, as I enjoyed the control of being in the driver's seat. I started training myself to drive a motor scooter in Taiwan as soon as possible. After six months of training, I believed I had enough mastery to take the driving test. Fortunately, I did not have to take the written driving test, because my American driver's license was accepted as proof of competence. I only needed to pass the driving test. It was not as easy as I thought it would be. I barely passed, but I did earn my license on the first try, and I achieved my freedom to drive in Taiwan!

Westerners living in Taiwan may also enjoy the freedom of driving, but many I have met choose not to drive for different reasons. First, the process of getting a license may not be easy, because depending on which country they come from, they may need to take a written exam. Second, the busy traffic in Taiwan may discourage people, and in the cities, it is almost impossible to find parking in some areas. Finally, public transportation is so convenient, visitors often feel that driving is unnecessary.

基本實用會話

Taiwanese (A) Westerner (B)

Driving a motor scooter.
騎摩托車。

A: Thanks for driving me to work on your motor scooter.
謝謝你騎摩托車載我來上班。

B: No problem. I am happy to help a friend in need.
不客氣，我很高興幫助有需要的朋友。

A: I have never seen anyone drive so slowly, except for very old people.
我沒看過有人騎那麼慢，除了非常老的老人。

B: Well, I am still not used to how crazy the traffic is here. There are so many people on the streets trying to get to where they are going.
這個，我還不習慣這裡瘋狂的交通。街上有太多人跑來跑去。

A: Everyone has busy lives. Don't you have a lot of traffic in your country?
大家的生活都很忙碌。你們國家的交通繁忙嗎？

B : Sure, but the traffic is less chaotic back home. On these streets, I have to look out dogs, cats, people in motorized wheelchairs, and people driving the wrong way,
當然，不過我家的交通沒那麼混亂。在這裡的街道上，我得注意小狗、小貓、電動輪椅和逆向行駛的人。

A : I know what you mean. You are a safe driver, but after driving in Taiwan, you will be one of the best drivers in the world.
我懂你的意思。你是個安全駕駛人，不過在台灣騎車後，你就會是世界上最好的司機了。

Driving a car.
開車。

A : Could you please pull over at the next rest area?
在下一個休息區你能停一下嗎？

B : OK. I have never seen rest areas like these in my country.
好，我在我的國家沒看過這種休息區。

A : What's different about our rest areas?
我們的休息區有什麼不同？

B : They are so big, and some are like little shopping malls. By the way, I'll go get some gas while you are in the restroom.
很大，有些像小型購物中心。對了，你去廁所時我要去加油。

A : OK, I won't be long. Would you like me to get you a cup of coffee? There's a Starbucks here.
好，我不會太久。你要我幫你買杯咖啡嗎？那裡有家星巴克。

B : That will be great! Another thing I like about Taiwan is how the gasoline prices are the same no matter where you purchase it. In my country, the price of gas at the rest stops are much higher than everywhere else.
太好了，台灣還有一點讓人喜歡的是油價統一。在我的國家，休息站的油價比其他地方高。

NOTES

Foreigners visiting Taiwan for a less than 30 days can drive a car or motor scooter if they bring a valid International Driver's License (IDL) from their country. They are not allowed to own a vehicle in Taiwan, but they can borrow one. They should be covered by the owner's vehicle insurance, as long as they have a valid International Driver's License. If they wish to drive for more than 30 days, they need to go to the local Department of Motor Vehicles and apply for a document called a Driving Visa (國際駕駛執照簽證). If their IDL expires, they should consider applying for a Taiwanese driver's license. They need not worry, because the written test is provided in English.

Sentences a Westerner might say
老外可能會說的句子

Susan, would you give me a ride to the supermarket?
蘇珊，你能載我去超級市場嗎？

No. There's nothing wrong. I loaned it to my friend, and he still has it.
沒有，沒什麼事。我借朋友，現在已經賣給他了。（英文和上下文有點矛盾）

I don't really enjoy driving. It is too stressful.
我其實不愛開車，壓力太大了。

Some people drive their scooters in the wrong direction. Many people don't stop before they merge in front of me.
有些人會逆向騎車，很多人切換到我的車道前不會先停車。

Not to mention how many dogs and cats I almost ran into.
更不用說我差點撞到很多貓和狗。

Not at all. It is a lot less stressful driving in my country. It's a piece of cake.
完全不會，在我們國家開車的壓力少多了，也簡單多了。

No thanks. I'll just take a bus to commute to and from work. Besides, my International Driver's License has exceeded its expiration date.
不，謝了。我可以搭公車通勤上下班。此外，我的國際駕照也過期了。

I don't know if I could pass the written exam. Is it in English?
我不知道我能不能通過筆試。是英文考試嗎？

I will consider it. Would you please give me a ride? It is hard to carry bags of groceries on the bus.
我會考慮。你可以載我一程嗎？提購物袋很難上公車。

Thank you! I appreciate your kindness.
謝謝你！謝謝你的照顧。

Sentences a Taiwanese person might say.
台灣人可能會說的句子

I don't mind taking you, but that's the third time I took you. Is there something wrong with your vehicle.
我可以載你，但這是我第三次載你了。你的車怎麼了嗎？

Why would you loan it out? How will you get around?
你為什麼要賣車？你以後怎麼出門？

Why do you say that?
怎麼說？

I know. You just have to be on alert all of the time.
我知道，你必須隨時保持警覺。

Driving can be quite dangerous. But isn't it like that in your country?
開車是很危險，但你們國家不會這樣嗎？

Maybe you just need more time to get used to the traffic here.
或許你需要時間習慣這裡的交通。

You might consider applying for a Taiwanese driver's license.
你或許可以考慮申請台灣駕照。

Yes, they do have an English version of their computerized test.
有，他們有英文版的電腦試卷。

Of course, I can. I'll pick you up around 5:30 pm.
當然可以，我五點半去接你。

Don't mention it.
不客氣。

Featured Vocabulary

driver's license (n.) 駕駛執照

A driver's license is an issued document that makes it legal for someone to drive a vehicle on the roads. In Taiwan, young people often apply for their license after their graduation from high school. In the USA, students usually get a driver's license while they are still in high school. At the age of 15, they can apply for a learner's permit, and at the age of 16, they qualify to get a driver's license, if they pass the written and driving tests.

driver's visa (n.) 國際駕駛執照簽證

Visitors in Taiwan may legally drive a vehicle for up to 30 days with their International Driver's License. If they wish to extend their driving privileges, until their IDL's expiration date, they need to apply for a driver's visa. They can visit the Department of Motor Vehicles in their area and fill out the International Driving Permit Application Form. They must also bring their driver's license from their country, passport, and submit a photo taken in the past six months.

UNIT 23

Renting 租房子

I sold my home in America to move to Taiwan. The cost of owning and maintaining a home was immense. Even renting a small apartment in the USA is very expensive. When I moved to Tainan, Taiwan, it seemed miraculous to find housing prices that were so low. My family found a spacious 3-story home with 4 bedrooms, living room, kitchen, two and a half bathrooms, and a garage for rent near my mother-in-law's home. The cost was only US $200 (NT 6,000) per month! The price was unheard of in the USA. Needless to say, this allowed me to reduce my family's living expenses and financial stress.

Westerners living in Taiwan may also find the cost of renting an apartment or home much more affordable than in their own country. With the exception of downtown Taipei, rental rates seem very reasonable. Foreigners can usually make a decision about where they want to reside and work, choosing to live affordably in the countryside or conveniently in the city. From my experience, the teaching jobs in the countryside may pay even better than those in the city. In the countryside, a friend of mine found an old-style brick home for rent, with a substantial area of land. The residence was furnished and included a large grove of pomelo trees in his yard. He paid only US $133 (NT 4,000) per month for rent, earned NT1,000 per hour as a teacher, and loved his life in Taiwan.

基本實用會話

Taiwanese (A) Westerner (B)

Renting an apartment in the city.
在市區租公寓。

B: Are you serious? The rent is NT25,000 per month for this small apartment?
真的？這間小公寓每個月租金要25,000？

A: It is hard to find a place to live so close to an MRT Station. It is so convenient.
很難找到離捷運站這麼近的地方，很方便。

B: Yes, it will save me a lot of time getting to my job every day.
對，這樣每天能省下很多上班時間。

A: Think of the time you will save every month. How much is that worth to you?
想想你每個月省下來的時間，這些時間對你來說值多少？

B: Well, fine. I will try to ask my boss for a raise.
好吧，我去試著叫我老闆加薪。

A : Good luck with that. You will need the first month's rent, plus a NT50,000 deposit.
祝你好運，你需要交第一個月的租金，還有五萬元的押金。

B : Yikes! Perhaps I won't be able to live here after all.
什麼！或許我還是無法住在這裡。

> ### Renting a house in the country.
> 在郊區租房子。

A : The rent for this house is NT8,000 per month. The home doesn't have air conditioning. I'm sorry.
這間房子的租子是每個月八千。很抱歉，房子裡沒有空調。

B : That's not a problem. And how much is the deposit?
沒關係。押金要多少？

A : It is NT8,000. Is that OK?
八千，可以嗎？

B : That's no problem. Do the fruit trees come with the home?
沒問題。這棵果樹是這間房子的嗎？

A : Yes, all of the land inside of the fence is included. You can use the courtyard and enjoy the orchard.
對，圍籬裡的土地都包含在內。你可以使用這片院子，也可以享用這片果園。

B : Thank you. I think I will enjoy the quality of life in the countryside.
謝謝你，我想我會喜歡鄉間的生活品質。

A : I believe you will, because this was my grandmother's home, and I enjoyed living here when I was a child.
我相信你會的，因為這是我祖母的家，我小時候很喜歡住在這裡。

 NOTES

Foreigners living Taiwan may sometimes find the process of renting an apartment or home to be an ordeal. Sometimes, there may be problems communicating with a landlord or landlady, and they may be asked to a large deposit payment. Foreigners may be asked to provide letters of reference from their employers, to show their credibility and qualifications. If they are refused, foreigners may feel that they are facing discrimination. However, the owner should have the right to choose who lives in their property.

Sentences a Westerner might say
老外可能會說的句子

Today, I will find out if I am going to move to a new apartment. I applied on Wednesday, and the landlady said she would tell me today.
今天就能知道我會不會搬到新公寓。我週三申請的，女房東說今天會告訴我。

Yes. My apartment is too small for all of my belongings, and is too far from my school.
對，我的公寓太小了，放不下我的東西，離我學校也太遠。

I hope so, too. I am not sure, because the lady asked me so many questions and some of them were very personal.
我也希望可以，我不確定，因為女房東問了我很多問題，有些是非常私人的。

I am not sure if she would ask the same questions to a Taiwanese person.
我不確定她對台灣人會不會問一樣的問題。

She asked me what country I was from, and where I worked. She wanted to know how much money I earned.
她問我從哪個國家來，我在哪裡工作，她想知道我賺多少錢。

She asked for a reference letter from my boss, and his contact information. She even asked me what bank I used.
她要我老闆寫推薦信，還有老闆的聯絡資訊，她還問我用哪家銀行。

Then she asked me if I usually stayed out late at night, and if I had a girlfriend.
然後她問我晚上是不是常出去，我有沒有女朋友。

Should having a girlfriend be a criterion for her decision? That sounds strange to me.
有女朋友會影響她的決定嗎？在我聽來很奇怪。

I hope not. That might be very awkward.
希望不會，那就太尷尬了。

What? Are you serious?
什麼？真的？

Sentences a Taiwanese person might say.
台灣人可能會說的句子

Really? You want to move?
真的？你要搬家？

I hope you are approved. Then, I can come to your housewarming party.
希望你能通過，那麼，我就能去你家的喬遷聚會了。

Maybe she is worried, because she doesn't know you.
或許她會擔心，因為她不了解你。

What kind of questions did she ask?
她問了什麼問題？

I think that is normal to find out if the renter is a stable person who can afford the rent.
我想了解房客能不能穩定給付房租是很正常的。

Maybe she is just a lady who likes to be very cautious.
或許她只是個非常謹慎的小姐。

Hmmm... I think she is trying to make a choice that is considerate of her neighbors.
嗯…我想她想做出對鄰居較好的選擇。

Yes, I cannot explain that one. Maybe she has a daughter she would like you to meet. Haha!
對，那一點我無法解釋。或許她有女兒想介紹給你，哈哈！

You're right. But, do you have a girlfriend? I have a friend that I think you should meet.
你說的對，但你有女朋友嗎？我有朋友想介紹給你。

No. Seriously, don't worry about the landlady. I heard that foreigners get all types of strange questions.
不是。說真的，別擔心那個女房東了，我聽說外國人常被問各種奇怪的問題。

Featured Vocabulary

rent vs. lease (v., n.) 租賃 vs. 租用

In English, "rent" and "lease" mean the same thing, but they are usually used for different situations. "Rent" is more often used to describe the action or cost of paying monthly for the use of a residence or office. "Lease" is most often used to describe the action or cost of paying monthly for the use of an item like a vehicle.

rental deposit (n.) 押金

Landlords may ask for a substantial amount of money in advance, before they approve a renter. This may include the first and last month's rent, and a security deposit for incidental damages. I have heard that foreigners have been asked to pay excessive and unusual deposits, including something called an "appliance" deposit for the household appliances, like the television, refrigerator, and stove. The request of the landlord may seem strange, but they have a right to set their own policies, and renters have a right to look elsewhere.

UNIT 24 Post Office 郵局服務

Thanks to my father, I grew up with a love for collecting postage stamps, as he introduced me to the hobby. I always enjoyed stamps as miniature pieces of art that educated me about faraway places. Before moving to Taiwan, I purchased many Taiwanese postage stamps for my collection, and discovered that many collectors prized these pieces of paper from the Republic of China (ROC). When I moved to Taiwan, I took the opportunity to visit a post office to buy postage stamps directly from the source. I was surprised by how different the Taiwanese post office was from an American post office. Unlike in America, the Taiwanese post office had a waiting area with chairs, and people had to take a number. I wondered, "Was I in a post office or a bank?" I later understood that as a government institution, the post office offered financial services and was considered a reliable place to deposit money. I returned home with recently issued postage stamps, and was amazed about how efficient and versatile the Taiwanese post office was.

Westerners in Taiwan may have an occasional experience with Taiwanese post offices, visiting them to mail a letter or package. However, if they are in Taiwan long enough, foreigners may discover that the post offices also provide other useful services. For example, the post offices provide locations for payment of certain official government taxes or fees. Also, the post offices provide reliable banking and other investment services that offer very competitive interest rates.

基本實用會話

Taiwanese (A)  Westerner (B)

Mailing a package.
寄包裹。

B: I would like to send this package to Sydney, Australia.
我想寄這個包裹到澳洲雪梨。

A: Would you like this sent by regular airmail or express delivery?
你要寄一般航空包裹還是快捷？

B: I would like express delivery, please. It needs to get to my mother before her birthday.
快捷，麻煩你。要在我母親生日前送到。

A: If the contents are valuable, you could purchase insurance. Would you like that?
如果內容物是貴重物品，你可以購買保險。有需要嗎？

B : Yes, please. I think it's the smart thing to do, just in case it gets lost in the mail.
是的，麻煩你。我想這樣比較聰明，以免它弄丟了。

A : All right. The postage will be NT 1,200. The package should arrive in Sydney by Friday.
好的，郵資是1200元。包裹在週五就會抵達雪梨。

B : Perfect! Thank you very much.
太好了！非常謝謝你。

Paying a tax.
繳稅。

B : Hello. I was told that I could pay for my health insurance tax here at the post office. Is that right?
你好，有人告訴我可以來郵局繳健保稅，是這樣嗎？

A : Yes. Please take a number from the machine and have a seat. Your number will be called when it is your turn.
是的，請從機器拿張號碼牌，然後找個地方坐。輪到你的時候會叫號。

B : (Later) Hello. Here is my document. I was told that I would need to pay a tax here in order to receive my payment for my translation work.
（過些時間）你好，這是我的文件，有人說我要來這裡繳稅，才能收到我翻譯的薪資。

A : OK. Please let me see the document. That will be NT200 please.
好的，請讓我看看文件，請交200元。

B : Thank you.
謝謝你。

A : You will need to show this stamp to show proof of payment.
你需要拿這個戳章當繳費證明。

NOTES

In America, post offices only provide mail delivery services. Because of the past reputation of the U.S. Post Office for its bureaucracy and unreliable delivery service, many private-owned delivery companies became very successful. My experience with mail delivery in Taiwan has been very positive. From my experience, the Taiwanese post office delivers mail efficiently and reliably for an affordable rate. Although I have not yet found a Federal Express or UPS mailing center in Taiwan, I have been pleasantly surprised by the package delivery system offered through the 7-11's all over Taiwan. Getting packages shipped within Taiwan is so easy and cheap.

Sentences a Westerner might say
老外可能會說的句子

I need to mail this package to Chicago, in the USA.
我要寄這個包裹到美國芝加哥。

What are my choices for shipping?
有哪些選擇？

That is too slow. What else do you have?
太慢了，還有什麼選擇？

Yikes! That's too expensive.
什麼！太貴了。

All right. Seven days is fast enough. I'll send this package by regular air delivery.
好吧，七天夠快了，我用一般航空郵件寄這個包裹。

I need to fill out a customs form? I am only sending pen pal letters from my students.
我要填這個海關表嗎？我只是寄我學生寫給筆友的信。

OK. No problem. It asks for the value of the contents. I don't know the value.
好，沒問題。上面問內容物的價值，我不知道價值。

Thank you. Can I see your postage stamps? I like to collect them, and I also mail them to friends back home.
謝謝你，我能看看你們的郵票嗎？我喜歡收集郵票，也會寄給家鄉的朋友。

Lovely. I appreciate stamps, and consider them small works of art.
漂亮，我喜歡郵票，我覺得它是小型的藝術品。

Thank you for your help. Have a nice day.
謝謝你的幫助，祝你愉快。

Sentences a Taiwanese person might say.
台灣人可能會說的句子

OK. How do you want this shipped?
好，你要用哪種運輸法？

You can ship this by ocean freight, which is the cheapest rate. It may arrive within 3 or 4 weeks.
你可以用海運，那是最便宜的費率，大概三、四個禮拜會到。

The fastest delivery is express air delivery. They should arrive in Chicago in two days. That will cost NT 2,500.
最快的方法是航空快捷，兩天內就會到芝加哥，費用是2500元。

OK. The regular air delivery should arrive within 7 days. That would cost NT 1,500.
好，一般航空郵件應該七天內會到，費用是1500元。

Please fill out this customs form for the package.
請填寫這份包裹的海關表。

You still need to fill out the customs form to describe the contents.
你還是需要填寫這份海關表，描寫內容物。

That's OK. If you don't want to pay for shipping insurance, you don't need to worry about that.
沒關係，如果你不購買運輸險，就不需要擔心那一欄。

Here are the issues we have now.
這是目前發行的郵票。

In the waiting room, you can find some stamp books that are issued each year.
在等候室可以找到每年發行的集郵冊。

You have a nice day, too.
也祝你愉快。

Featured Vocabulary

postage (n.) 郵資

Postage is a term to describe the fee charged by the Postal carrier or delivery service to deliver a package to its destination. A postage fee can be purchased in advance in the form of postage stamps, or it can be paid at the post office counter. Postage stamps from Taiwan are popular collector's items, and are sought after by people around the world.

Postal insurance (n.) 郵件保險

Postal insurance is a service offered by post offices and delivery services to cover valuable packages in case they are lost or damaged during the delivery process. In a post office, this service is offered as "insured mail," and requires the sender to fill out their contact information and a declaration of the package contents and its monetary value.

expedite (v.) 快捷

To expedite something means to accelerate the speed in which something is done. In terms of mail delivery, post offices offer higher postage rates to expedite the delivery of a letter or package. This type of service is often referred to as express service. Many companies around the world, such as Federal Express (FedEx), United Postal Services (UPS) and DHL, have found success by specializing in expedited delivery services.

UNIT 25

Insurance 保險

After moving to Taiwan, one of my American friends in Tainan told me that one of the biggest reasons he preferred to live in Taiwan was its affordable health care system. He touted the health insurance system of Taiwan as being the best he has ever seen. When he was hospitalized for a few days, the hospital staff told him that it was too expensive for him to have his own room, but he demanded to have privacy. He couldn't believe the room cost US $80 per day, especially when staying at an American hospital might cost US $1,000 per day. He joked that the next time his parents visited, he would put them up at the hospital, because it was so nice and affordable. I have also been very grateful for the affordability of health insurance and medical care in Taiwan. In only a few years, I have saved at least fifteen thousand US dollars in medical expenses by being insured in Taiwan.

Westerners in Taiwan may get health insurance coverage through their employer. They are usually surprised by the quality of healthcare service they get at low prices, thanks to the national health insurance system. The high cost of healthcare in many countries reduces the quality of life for most people. So, I would say that the health insurance system is an important factor for Taiwan's high quality of life.

基本實用會話

Taiwanese (A)  Westerner (B)

Getting a health insurance card.
拿健保卡。

B : What is this application for?
這個表格是做什麼的？

A : As a teacher for our school, you are eligible to receive a national health insurance card.
身為我們學校的老師，你可以收到全民健保卡。

B : Oh. We don't have national health insurance where I come from. How does it work here?
喔，我的國家沒有全民健保卡。這要怎麼使用？

A : You will receive a National Health Insurance ID Card, and you need to bring it with you every time to see a doctor or buy medicine.
你會收到健保ID卡，每次去看醫生或買藥時都要帶著它。

B : So, this will save me money on my healthcare expenses?
那麼，這樣可以節省我的醫療費用？

A : Yes. You will only pay a small premium every month. And when you need medical service, you only pay a much smaller amount by using the card.
是的，你每個月只要付很少的保險費，當你需要醫療服務時，使用這張卡就只要付一些錢。

B : I am sure that will save me a lot of money. Thank you very much!
我確定這能省下我很多錢，非常謝謝你！

Using a health insurance card.
使用健保卡。

B : I was told to come to this counter to pay for my hospital visit.
有人叫我來這個櫃台付診療費。

A : Yes. That's right. May I see your paperwork from the hospital, and your health insurance card?
是的，沒錯。請出示醫院給你的文件，還有你的健保卡。

B : This is the first time I had to visit the hospital. So, all of this is new to me.
這是我第一次來醫院看病，所以對我來說一切都很新鮮。

A : OK. The total amount due is NT800.
好，總額是800元。

B : What? Are you sure? The doctor gave me an x-ray, and a blood test. He also ordered some medicine. Is that included?
什麼？你確定？醫生幫我做了X光還有血液測試，他還開了藥，全都包含在內了？

A : Yes. Take your receipt to the pharmacy and you can pick up your prescribed medicine.
對，請拿著收據到藥局，就能拿到你的處方藥。

B : I would have had to pay at least NT8,000 out of my pocket in my country. God bless Taiwan!
要是在我的國家至少要付八千元。天佑台灣！

NOTES

On March 23, 2010, President Obama signed the Affordable Care Act, giving millions of Americans access to affordable healthcare through a national health insurance system. Before that, I had already been enjoying national health insurance in Taiwan. Not only do foreigners appreciate Taiwan for its high quality of healthcare, but they can save a lot of money by signing up for national health insurance through their workplace. If they are married to a Taiwanese spouse, they can apply for Taiwan's national health insurance. Travelers to Taiwan can get their medical expenses covered if they purchase travel-related health insurance from their country.

Sentences a Westerner might say
老外可能會說的句子

Doctor, thank goodness you can speak English. I was in a motor scooter accident.
醫生，謝天謝地你會說英文。我騎車出車禍了。

I can't put any weight on my right leg. My shin hurts a lot.
我的右腳不能施力，我的脛骨也很痛。

Oh no! That sounds expensive. I don't have health insurance.
喔，不！聽起來很貴，我沒有健康保險。

OK. Thank you doctor. Go ahead.
好，醫生謝謝你，那就做吧。

Geez! I guess I'll need to spend the rest of my vacation in bed.
天啊！我猜我剩下的假期都得躺在床上了。

I hope I will be able to bring the pain killers through customs at the airport.
希望這些止痛藥能通過機場的海關。

I will doctor. Thank you. You have been very kind.
我會的，醫生，謝謝你，你真是好心。

No. I'm sorry I didn't think about it before I came to Taiwan.
不，對不起，我來台灣之前沒想過這種事。

Oh no! I don't know if I can afford this. How much is the total?
喔不，我不知道我付不付得起。總共多少錢？

What? Are you serious? I can't believe it! I'll happily pay with cash. Thank you!
什麼？真的嗎？我不敢相信！我很樂意付現金，謝謝你！

Sentences a Taiwanese person might say.
台灣人可能會說的句子

What is the nature of your injury?
你受了什麼傷？

I see. It does look quite swollen. You likely have a fracture of your bone. But we need to get an x-ray to be certain. We will also need to inject antibiotics.
我看看，它看起來有點腫，你的骨頭可能骨折了，但我們需要照X光確認，也需要注射抗生素。

If we don't get an x-ray, we won't know how to treat your injury.
要是不照X光，就不知道該如何治療。

(later) It was a small fracture, but you need to wear this cast on your leg for about three weeks.
（稍晚）只是小骨折，但你的腳需要上石膏三個禮拜。

I'm sorry for your misfortune. Also, I will prescribe some pain killers for you.
很遺憾你運氣不好，我也會開點止痛藥給你。

Please take it easy and try not to walk during the next few weeks, and keep your cast dry.
接下來幾個禮拜請小心，盡量不要走路，保持石膏乾燥。

(at the payment desk) Do you have national health insurance or traveler's health insurance?
（在出納櫃台）你有全民健保或旅遊保險嗎？

OK. Then you will be responsible for the total healthcare expenses today.
好，那麼你必須全額給付今日的醫療費用。

The total for everything is NT 4,000. How will you pay for that?
總共是4000元，你要怎麼付費？

You're welcome. Go to the pharmacy counter and show your receipt to pick up your medicine.
不客氣，請到藥局櫃台，出示收據就能領藥。

Featured Vocabulary

coverage (n.) 保險

When related to insurance, coverage refers to having the insurance covering various risks. Health insurance coverage, means the policy covers, or pays for, any healthcare that you may require during the specified duration. A person's insurance contract may expire or be terminated because of the lack of payment of the monthly premiums. Then, the person will no longer have coverage.

premium (n.) 保險費

When people have insurance, most make monthly payments to have their policy remain active. This monthly payment is referred to as a "premium." In America my health insurance premiums were very high, with monthly payments of about US $200 per person. In Taiwan my premiums are about US $25 per person, so you can imagine why I am very happy raising a family in Taiwan.

copay (n.) 共付額

When people have health insurance, their health insurance will cover a percentage of the medical expenses. What their insurance does not pay for, they must pay for. This payment is called the "copay." In Taiwan, most basic healthcare services are covered by national health insurance. So, if you go for a routine checkup, your copay will be very low. But if you need specialized surgery, you may still be responsible for a large copay.

Medicine 買藥、推拿

UNIT 26

My family has been blessed with quality, affordable healthcare in Taiwan. But even more significant is the availability of two types of healthcare in Taiwan. There are plenty of Chinese medicine doctors to choose from as well as doctors who practice Western medicine. My wife's brother is a doctor who was trained in both Chinese and Western medicine, so we have been well taken care of by his skills. I prefer to avoid Western drugs, so whenever we had minor issues, such as cold, flu, aches and pains, we sought the help of Chinese medicine. The taste of Chinese medicine herbs took getting used to, but they always worked. Whenever we had a more serious medical emergency, we went to hospitals for Western-style healthcare. No matter what we needed, whether it was Western or Eastern medicine, we received affordable, efficient service, and it was usually covered by national health insurance. God bless Taiwan!

Westerners in Taiwan may not be familiar with Eastern medicine, so they may not ever visit a Chinese medicine doctor while visiting Taiwan. In most Western countries, it is not easy to find a Chinese doctor, unless you go to a place that has a "Chinatown." I have known adventurous foreigners willing to try Chinese medicine, because they prefer to explore alternative healing methods. More people are learning about the "holistic' approach to wellness, so Eastern medicine is gaining popularity around the world.

基本實用會話

Taiwanese (A)  Westerner (B)

Ordering Chinese medicine.
買中藥。

B: I think I have the flu. I don't want to take any drugs or antibiotics, so I thought I would try some Chinese medicine.
我想我感冒了。我不想吃藥或吃抗生素,所以我想試試中藥。

A: Yes, you do have a fever. And there is a lot of mucous in your chest. I will give you a mixture of powder to take home.
是的,你的確發燒了。你的胸腔也有很多痰,我會開一些中藥粉讓你帶回家。。

B: What's in the powder?
藥粉裡有什麼?

A: The powder is a mixture of medicinal herbs. It is all-natural.
藥粉裡混合了各種中藥,是純天然的。

B：Great! That is what I am looking for. I prefer to stay away from man-made drugs.
太好了，這正是我要找的，我想盡量不吃人工製造的藥。

A：Each bag contains one dosage of medicine. Mix one bag with water and drink it. Do that three times a day before each meal.
每一袋都含有一次劑量的藥，每次拿一包藥和水混合，然後喝下去，三餐前服用。

Taking Chinese medicine.
吃中藥。

B：Can you help me to read this package?ou please help me?
你能幫我讀讀包裝上的字嗎？

A：Oh, you're taking Chinese medicine? That's surprising.
喔，你要吃中藥？真令人意外。

B：I thought I would try something new. Western medicine always makes me feel tired.
我想要試點新方法，西藥總是讓我覺得疲倦。

A：The directions say to take one bag of medicine three times per day after each meal.
指示說一次一袋，一天三次，飯前服用。

B：I just drink water with this powder?
我只要喝水配藥粉？

A：Yes. You can mix it in the water or just put it in your mouth and drink water after you swallow it.
是的，你可以混在水裡，或是直接倒入嘴巴，吞下去之後再喝水。

B：Well, the taste is a little foul, but most things that are good for you don't taste good.
這味道有點難吃，但良藥苦口。

NOTES

Around the world, more foreigners are looking for alternatives to man-made drugs to treat symptoms of illness. As a result, there is a growing education about healthy diets and preventative medicine. There is also a growing demand for natural remedies for illnesses. As a result, more foreigners around the world are turning to Chinese medicine. In Western countries, Western medicine still dominates the healthcare industry, but Chinese medicine clinics and pharmacies are gaining momentum.

Sentences a Westerner might say
老外可能會說的句子

Excuse me. Can you treat a migraine headache here?
不好意思，你這裡能治療偏頭痛嗎？

What are my choices of treatments?
我有哪些治療選擇？

That sounds facinating. I never heard that before. What can be done?
聽來很吸引人，我以前從沒聽過，該怎麼做？

Isn't acupuncture the treatment with needles?
針灸是用針做的治療嗎？

I'd rather not have needles in my body, thank you.
我還是不希望有針刺在身體上，謝謝你。

I like how that sounds. I haven't had a massage or neck adjustment in a long time.
我喜歡你的說法，我很久沒有按摩，也很久沒調整脖子了。

Your treatments sound like they are very safe and effective.
你的治療聽來很安全又有效。

Sure I do! You accept that here? That's great news!
當然！你接受嗎？那是個好消息！

I need to thank my friend for suggesting that I visit your clinic.
我需要謝謝我的朋友建議我來你的診所。

This is such a different and interesting way to treat my illnesses. The doctor hasn't started, but I feel better already.
這種治療方式既不同又有趣。治療還沒開始，我就已經感覺好多了。

Sentences a Taiwanese person might say.
台灣人可能會說的句子

Yes, we can. Chinese medicine offers several options to treat severe headaches.
是的，可以，中藥提供幾個不同的選擇，可以治療嚴重的頭痛。

In Chinese medicine, we believe that headaches are caused by a blockage of your "chi" or body's energy flow.
在中藥裡，我們相信頭痛是因為氣不通，或是身體的能量流動不順暢。

So we can unblock your chi by applying acupressure or acupuncture.
因此我們可以用穴位按壓或針灸通你的氣。

Yes, they are very small needles, so you don't really feel them.
是的,用非常小的針,你其實感覺不到。

After your acupressure treatment, we can offer some massage and chiropractic treatment in your back, neck and head.
在穴位按壓治療後,我們可以在你的背部、頸部和頭部按摩或做脊椎按摩。

Before you leave, we will give you some Chinese herbal medicine to help stimulate your blood flow.
在你離開前,我們會開些中藥,幫助刺激你的血流。

Do you have national health insurance or traveler's health insurance?
你有全民健保,或是旅遊保險嗎?

OK. Please come inside and lay down on our massage table.
好,請進來,躺在我們的按摩床上。

Please have some herbal tea. Relax, and the doctor will be with you shortly.
請喝些藥草茶,放鬆,醫生很快就來。

You're welcome. I hope you feel better soon.
不客氣,希望你能快點恢復。

Featured Vocabulary

prescription (n.) 處方

Many medicines are controlled substances, which means they cannot be purchased without permission from a doctor. They are controlled, because they carry a risk of being misused or abused. A doctor provides the patient a prescription, which means an authorized order form. I have noticed that Chinese medicine doesn't require a prescription. Perhaps, it's because this medicine is based on natural ingredients, which do not carry health risks.

Chinese medicine (n.) 中藥

Chinese medicine is an Eastern medicine philosophy that has existed for thousands of years. Unlike Western medicine philosophy, it takes a holistic approach, meaning it addresses the body's own ability to heal itself and helps the body's systems achieve optimal balance. I have seen Chinese medicine has increased in popularity in the past twenty years in Western nations.

Western pharmaceuticals (n.) 西方藥品

Western treatments for illnesses are often made from artifical ingredients or processing, and deal directly with the symptoms of illnesses. These treatments are known as drugs, or pharmaceuticals, which means they are sourced from pharmacists. These drugs may deal directly with symptoms and have successful results, but many people criticize them for not dealing with the source of the illnesses, andthey may often carry side effects.

UNIT 27

Acupuncture 針灸

One day when I had a headache, I was willing to accept someone's recommendation to treat it with acupuncture. I can tell you that the needles were very sharp and fine (thin), and they were not painful. But, as these needles entered deeper into my neck, and touched my nerve endings, it was a strange tingling sensation. When the doctor started putting the needles into my face and forehead, I felt some pain, and I felt like a porcupine with so many needles in my body. I am not sure if the treatment improved my headache, but the pain and discomfort discouraged me from having acupuncture again. Perhaps it was my fear of needles that made it ineffective for me.

Many Westerners may also have a fear of needles, so they may also be unwilling to try this treatment technique. Still, because of the side effects and cost of using drugs to treat symptoms of illnesses, more people are willing to try alternative treatments like acupuncture. Acupuncture has been used and trusted by people for over 2,000 years, so perhaps I will give it another try when a need arises.

基本實用會話

Taiwanese (A)　　Westerner (B)

Acupuncture consultation.
針灸諮詢。

B: My fingers are numb, and I have been diagnosed with carpal tunnel syndrome in my arm. The injury is probably work-related.
我的手指會麻，我曾被診斷出有腕隧道症候群，這傷可能是工作引起的。

A: I heard that can be painful. But there really isn't a cure. All I can do is to give you pain killers.
我聽說那會很痛，但其實無法治癒，我只能給你止痛藥。

B: I don't want to have the side effects from the drugs, doctor.
醫生，我不想要有吃藥的副作用。

A: Perhaps you can consult a Chinese medicine doctor to see if acupuncture can relieve the pain.
或許你可以去諮詢中醫師，看能不能用針灸緩解疼痛。

B: I will put aside my fear of needles, if it will help relieve this pain. I will try it.
我會克服我對針的恐懼，如果真的能緩解疼痛的話，我會試試。

A : And you may want to consider finding a new job that won't require you to use your hand so much.
你或許要考慮找個不這麼需要用手的新工作。

Acupuncture treatment.
針灸治療。

B : Oh! I can feel the needle in my back. But it doesn't really hurt. It just tingles a little.
喔！我能感覺到背上的針，但其實不痛，就是有點刺。

A : Just stay still. It will help me to hit the right meridian points if you don't move.
不要動，如果你不動的話，我更能刺在正確的經絡上。

B : Meridian? What's that?
經絡？那是什麼？

A : They are the focal points through which your life energy flows. Please relax.
那是你生命能量流動時的焦點，請放鬆。

B : I'll relax. It just feels strange to be poked with needles. I've actually been afraid of needles since I was little.
我會放鬆，只是被針扎感覺很奇怪，我其實從小就很怕針。

A : I'm done. Now, just stay here for about ten minutes. I will turn on the heat lamp to transfer the heat to your meridian points.
我完成了，現在，請休息十分鐘，我會打開加熱燈，讓熱量轉移到你的經絡點上。

B : Thanks doctor. Can I make an unusual request? Can you take a photo of my back full of needles with my cell phone? I want to share this experience with my family back home.
謝謝醫生，我能提個特殊要求嗎？你能不能用我的手機，拍張我背後都是針的照片？我想和我家鄉的家人分享這個經驗。

 NOTES

Because acupuncture has been used successfully for such a long time to treat pain and illness symptoms, it has been studied and well-documented by the scientific community. However, there has been no conclusive evidence about why and how well it works. It is believed to remove imbalances in the body's "qi," or life energy flow through channels know as meridians, using needles and heat. Reported results have been mixed, but as long as the needles are sterile, there are no known side effects. The lack of side effects is what attracts foreigners to try it, as most are wary of the side effects of drugs.

Sentences a Westerner might say
老外可能會說的句子

(To receptionist) Hello. Do you provide some services here that could relieve my back pain?
（對接待員）你好，這裡能不能幫我舒緩我的背痛？

Like what? My back really hurts now, and I can barely walk.
像是什麼？我的背現在好痛，我快不能走了。

It hurts so much, I am willing to try anything that brings me the most relief.
好痛，只要能止痛，我什麼都願意試。

OK. I am willing to listen to your doctor's advice.
好，我願意聽聽你們醫生的建議。

(To doctor) Hello doctor. I really need help. My lower back is killing me. The pain is intense.
（對醫生）醫生你好，我真的需要幫助。我的下背部快痛死了，真的好痛。

What can you offer that will provide the most relief in a short time?
你能怎樣在最短時間裡舒緩最多疼痛？

Yes, doctor. I will try everything you suggest.
是的，醫生，你的建議我都會試試看。

OK. Please take it easy. The lower back has a sharp pain.
好，請輕一點，下背痛得很厲害。

That doesn't sound bad. Will that be enough?
聽起來不錯，那樣就夠了嗎？

Which one will be more effective? At this point, I am not afraid of needles. Go for it!
哪一個會更有效？這時候我已經不怕針了，來吧！

Sentences a Taiwanese person might say.
台灣人可能會說的句子

(Receptionist) Yes, we do. Our Chinese medicine doctors are well trained in different techniques.
（接待員）是的，可以，我們的中醫師受過各種技巧的訓練。

Our clinic offers chiropractic adjustments, cupping, acupressure and acupuncture.
我們的診所提供脊椎調整、拔罐、穴位按摩和針灸。

A doctor can offer a combination of these.
醫生可以結合這些方法治療。

(Doctor) What seems to be the problem?
你有什麼問題？

You are very tense. Have some herbal tea, before I begin treatment.
你非常緊張，喝點藥草茶，我再開始治療。

For extreme cases, I can provide a combination of techniques. Did our receptionist already describe them to you?
在極端的案例中，我能結合幾種技巧，我們的接待員是不是已經告訴你了？

I'll begin with a back and neck massage to help you relax, and provide some minor back adjustment.
我會先用背部和頸部按摩幫你放鬆，然後再做點後背調整。

Yes, I'll be gentle. Then I will apply some cupping to your lower back to stimulate blood flow and to draw out the acid in your muscles.
好，我會輕一點。我要在你的下背部拔罐，刺激你的血流，也吸出你肌肉中的酸。

I can then apply acupressure or acupuncture to your meridian points in your back.
然後在你的背部的經絡穴道施以穴位按摩或是針灸。

OK. Acupuncture will likely be more effective, because we will be able to direct heat to the meridian points.
好，針灸會比較有用，因為我們可以直接對穴位加熱。

Featured Vocabulary

acupuncture (n.) 針灸

Acupuncture is an Eastern-based treatment technique for the relief of pain that uses needles applied to the body's meridian points. These meridian points act like the "transformers" or distribution points through which the body's bio energy (qi) flows. The needles allow a Chinese medicine doctor to apply heat energy directly to the meridian points to remove blockages and restore balance to the flow.

acupressure (n.) 穴位按摩

Acupressure is an Eastern-based treatment technique for the relief of pain that uses pressure applied to the body's pressure points. These pressure points correspond to the human body's meridian system, and the meridian points, which act like the "transformers" or distribution points through which the body's bio energy (qi) flows.

meridian (n.) 經絡

Meridians are a channel network in the human body through which the life energy known as "qi" flows. Much of the documentation of the meridians have come from two thousands years of Chinese medicine. For the body to be healthy, and for the organs to work harmoniously, the meridian channels must be kept free from blockage. Removing blockages and restoring "qi" flow is the principle behind acupuncture and acupressure.

Hair Salons 美髮

I have learned to enjoy some of the simpler things in life in Taiwan. One of the simple pleasures living here has been getting a haircut. The service has always been awesome, and the price relatively inexpensive. As a foreigner in Taiwan, I had one of my first memorable surprises when I went to get my first haircut at a local hair salon. My wife ordered the service for me. When it was my turn, the attendant put shampoo in my hair and gave me a 20-minute scalp massage. It was a very relaxing experience and well-worth the extra cost.

My advice for people who work in a hair salon or barbershop, if you offer a scalp massage, don't hasten to offer it to foreigners. Just don't call it a "head massage" as that may make your customer think about a service that is more erotic. Call it a "scalp massage" and use your hands to demonstrate the action, so there is no confusion.

基本實用會話

Taiwanese (A)  Westerner (B)

Greetings at the hair salon
到理髮廳

A： Hello. May I help you?
嗨！要理髮嗎？

B： Yes. I'd like a haircut.
是的，我要剪頭髮。

A： Sure. Please have a seat over here. Would you like to start with a scalp massage? It is very relaxing.
沒問題，請這邊坐。您要先來個頭皮按摩嗎？好好放鬆一下。

B： I have never done that before. How much does it cost?
我沒試過，多少錢啊？

A： The haircut is NT100. The scalp massage is NT50 extra. Would you like a haircut and a massage?
剪髮100元，頭皮按摩外加50元。兩項服務都要嗎？

B： OK. I think I would like to try it.
好啊，我想試一下。

A： Excellent.
好的。

After the shampoo and rinse. Before the haircut.
洗完頭後,剪髮前。

Ⓐ: What would you like me to do to your hair.
你要怎樣的髮型?

Ⓑ: I would like to cut an inch off the top and shave the sides and back.
上面剪掉一寸,兩邊及後面修一下。

After the haircut.
剪完頭髮。

Ⓐ: OK. We're done. How does it look to you?
好了,大功告成。你覺得如何?

Ⓑ: It looks stylish, thank you. How much do I owe you?
帥呆了,感謝。多少錢?

Ⓐ: That will be NT150. Thank you.
就150元,謝謝您。

Ⓑ: Do you accept tips? Here is your tip to show my appreciation.
你們收小費嗎?這小費給你。

Ⓐ: Thank you very much!
感恩!

NOTES

Foreigners often complain that the hairdressers or barbers cut off more hair than expected during a haircut. Sometimes there is confusion in the measurement system. Some foreigners use inches as the measurement system instead of millimeters or centimeters. If you're not sure how much the foreigner wants to cut off, ask your customer to show you with their fingers how much to cut. For your reference, one inch = 2.5 cm.

Sentences a Westerner might say
老外可能會說的句子

I want a haircut, please.
我要剪頭髮。

I want a shampoo, please. (hair wash)
我要洗頭髮。

I'd love a scalp massage (hair massage), please.
我要做頭皮按摩。

Can you dye my hair? What colors do you have available?
我要染髮。你們有哪些顏色可以選？

I'd like to perm my hair, please. (Perm or permanent is a treatment where the hair is curled.)
我要燙直頭髮。

Please trim two centimeters off of the length of my hair.
請幫我的頭髮修短兩公分。

I'd like to get a different hairstyle. Can you show me what you can do?
我想換個髮型，你有什麼建議嗎？

How much does this haircut cost?
這裡剪髮多少錢？

My hairdo looks glorious. Do you accept tips?
我的髮型看來美極了，你們收小費嗎？

I hate what you did to my hair. I look absurd! I want my money back!
我不喜歡你設計的髮型，我看來醜死了，我要退錢！

Sentences a Taiwanese person might say.
台灣人可能會說的句子

Welcome to my shop.
嗨，歡迎光臨。

Please have a seat. We will get to you soon. (or We will get to you in _____minutes.)
請坐，馬上輪到您。（或_____分鐘後就輪到您。）

Please have a seat in the barber chair.
請到理髮椅坐著。

Would you like your hair washed? We use a special protein shampoo.
您要洗頭嗎？我們用的是特殊的蛋白質洗髮精。

Would you like a scalp massage? It will provide instant relaxation.
您要頭皮按摩嗎？可以馬上讓您放鬆。

What would you like us to do to beautify your hair?
您的頭髮要怎麼打理？

How much do you want us to cut off?
您要剪多長？（用您的手指比一下要剪的長度。）

What color do you want your hair dyed? Brown, black, red or blonde?
您要染甚麼顏色？咖啡色、黑色、紅色還是金色？

Thank you and please come back again.
謝謝惠顧，歡迎再度光臨。

I am sorry! Is there anything we can do to fix our mistake?
抱歉，我們要怎麼彌補錯誤？

Featured Vocabulary

trim (n., v.) 修剪

Many Westerners use this word to describe a type haircut that cuts off only a very short length of hair. They may say, "Give me a trim. About 2 centimeters." This means take off 2 cm from all of their hair. Or they may ask you to take a very short length of hair from a specific part of their hair. "Would you please trim a little off the front? About an inch, please."

clippers (n.) 理髮器

For cutting hair, Westerners don't use the word, "scissors." They say, "clippers." Notice that the word is plural form, because there are two parts to every set of "clippers." It's just like we say the plural form, "scissors" and "glasses." Also, there are clippers we use by hand, and there are electric clippers, which are used to cut hair very close to the skin.

sideburns (n.) 鬢角

Many male Westerners prefer to have hair that extends in front of their ears down to the side of their face. It is a popular Western style. Some men like their sideburns long and wild, and some like them short and neat. If you notice the Western customer has sideburns, ask, "How would you like your sideburns?"

UNIT 29

Gym 健身房

Living in Taiwan, I have become a healthier person than when I lived in the USA, the main reason being because the diet seems to be healthier here. It has been easier for me to control my weight with Taiwanese food, except during the holidays, when there is much feasting and drinking. After Chinese New Year of 2010, I gained about 2 kilograms, and made a resolution to start exercising. I looked for a gym, but the closest one I could find was in Tainan City. I signed up for a 7-day free trial pass, and started my workouts in the mornings. The facilities were first-class, and there were many workout options. There were quite a few people, and they were all younger and more physically fit than me. I felt a little self-conscious, but I was determined to lose two kilograms. Even though they normally charged for their services, a personal trainer offered to help me out for a few days for free. He really made a difference and pushed me to achieve my goal.

Gyms are quite popular in Western countries, as there are many people who strive to achieve their optimum fitness. I would say that a greater percentage of young people go to gyms in America than they do in Taiwan, even though the membership fees are much higher. The percentage of young people in Taiwan who pursue weight training or aerobics is much lower than in America, but gyms in Taiwan do provide adequate facilities and support staff.

基本實用會話

Taiwanese (A)  Westerner (B)

Inquiring about a gym.
詢問健身房。

B : I can't believe how much weight I gained during the holidays.
我不敢相信自己在假期裡胖了多少。

A : I know. I also gained about two kilograms.
我知道，我也多了兩公斤。

B : Why don't we find a place to work out together?
我們何不找個地方一起健身？

A : Work out? What do you mean?
健身？什麼意思？

B : I mean, we should find a health club to exercise in.
我是說，我們應該找個健身俱樂部一起運動。

A : I know of a gym inside the mall downtown. We can check on the memberships there.
我知道市中心一家商場裡有健身房，我們可以一起去問問他們的會員。

B : I look forward to seeing what a gym is like in Taiwan.
我很期待看看台灣的健身房是什麼樣子。

> **Signing up at a gym.**
> 加入健身房。

B : Excuse me. How much does it cost for a membership here?
不好意思，加入這裡的會員要多少錢？

A : There is a special deal this week. There is a signup fee of NT5,000. Once you are a member, the membership fee is NT 1,500 per month.
這禮拜有個特別優惠。入會費是5,000元，入會之後，每個月的會費是1,500元。

B : The signup fee is a little expensive in Taiwan. I don't even know everything you offer.
台灣的入會費比較貴一點，我還不知道你們有什麼服務。

A : We do offer a one week free trial. Try us out, so you will know what we have to offer.
我們提供一週的試用。來試試看，就知道我們提供什麼服務了。

B : Thank you. I think I will. What do I need to do?
謝謝你，我想我會的，怎樣才能試用？

A : Do you have a credit card? If so, just fill out our registration form.
你有信用卡嗎？如果有的話，只要填寫我們的註冊表就可以了。

B : I do have a credit card, but it is from South Africa. I hope that's OK.
我有信用卡，不過是南非發卡的，希望可以用。

NOTES

   There aren't as many gyms in Taiwan as there are in Western countries, but there are some reputable brands available. They offer similar services and equipment as gyms in Western countries. Foreigners in Taiwan may find low fees or special incentives to join a gym. However, they should be careful about the contracts. Foreigners should make sure to have a contract that they can read and understand. No one should give into pressure and sign a contract until they have had time to read it carefully. There may be high fees that are hidden, such as useage fees and cancellation fees.

Sentences a Westerner might say
老外可能會說的句子

I'm here to use my free trial for your gym.
我是來試用你們的健身房。

Thank you. I see you have many exercise machines.
謝謝你，我看到你們有很多運動器材。

That's good. But I do prefer free weights.
很好，但我比較喜歡自由重量器材。

Great! Does your gym have weight trainers?
太好了！你們的健身房有重量訓練員嗎？

Hello Steve. I could use some help with free weight training.
哈囉，史堤夫。在自由重量訓練時可能需要你的幫忙。

Actually, I'm from London. I am here to work for a year for my company.
事實上，我是從倫敦來的，我是為了工作來這裡出差一年。

Cool! What do you charge per hour for your weight training?
酷，你的重量訓練每小時收費多少？

Thank you Steve. So how shall we begin?
謝謝你，史堤夫，要怎麼開始呢？

I will. Where should we begin?
我會的，我們要從哪裡開始？

I appreciate your help. Just let me know your work shedule. I am sure I will be back.
謝謝你的幫忙。請再告訴我你的班表，我確定我一定會再來的。

Sentences a Taiwanese person might say.
台灣人可能會說的句子

(Receptionist) OK. Thank you. Just fill out this form, and you can try anything you see.
（接待員）好，謝謝你，請填寫這份表格，全場設備都能試用。

Yes. You can work out every part of your body.
是的，您可以運動到身體的每個部分。

We do have free weights in the back room.
在後面的房間有提供自由重量器材。

Yes, we have two weight trainers. I can introduce you to one. His name is Steve.
是的，我們有兩位重量訓練師，我可以介紹其中一位給你，他叫史堤夫。

(Steve) Hello. Welcome to our gym. I'd be happy to help you. Where are you from?
（史堤夫）你好，歡迎加入我們的健身房，很高興能幫助你，你從哪裡來的？

I love London. I visited there when I was in graduate school overseas.
我愛倫敦，我出國念研究所時去那裡玩過。

Since this is your first visit, I'll help you out for free.
既然這是你第一次來，這次就免費。

You should warm up with some stretches first. You don't want to pull a muscle.
你應該先做幾個伸展暖身，你不會想拉傷肌肉的。

Let's begin with 20 kilograms and work up from there. Put some chalk on your hands to get a firm grip.
先從20公斤開始慢慢增加，手上撲點滑石粉，才能握得緊。

OK. Now take deep breaths and lift every time you exhale. Excellent! Give me ten reps (repetitions).
好，現在深呼吸，每次吐氣時上舉。太好了！重複十次。

Featured Vocabulary

workout (n.) 鍛鍊

A session of exercise is commonly referred to as a "workout." You may have a light workout or heavy workout, depending on the time you put into your exercise session. The act of working out, or exercising, can be referred to as "working out." Many people love to hear the phrase, "You look like you've been working out." It means that they look physically fit.

weight training (n.) 重量訓練

Weight training refers to exercise that involved lifting heavy weights. The purpose of weight training is to build muscle. Because it is not an easy method of exercise, people who are serious with weight training may often hire a personal weight trainer. That is a coach who helps a person to push themselves further in their weight training.

membership fee (n.) 會員費

Gyms earn money by charging customers fees for using their facilities and equipment. This is called a membership fee. Typically the business can charge a fee up front for registration. Then there can be a monthly membership fee for using the gym.

UNIT 30

Hot Springs 溫泉

One of the most relaxing activities I have enjoyed inTaiwan has been soaking in hot springs. My first experience was with my Taiwanese relatives, who invited me to a hot springs spa in Wulai. Every family had their own room with a bath tub. The water was nice and hot, but it felt like taking a bath. It didn't seem so special. The most memorable hot springs experience occurred years later, when my Taiwanese friend brought me to a hot springs resort in Hsinchu County. I was surprised when I realized that all of the men who were bathing were naked. And my friend did not hesitate to take of all of his clothes. So, I followed suit. We both sat in the hot springs pool and enjoyed the mountain scenery around us. It felt strange at first, but I didn't take long to overcome my inhibitions. I had a great conversation with my new friend, and we became best friends since.

It may not be easy for foreigners to bathe while naked in the presence of strangers, but there are many types of hot springs bathing experiences available in Taiwan. There are many luxurious resorts for people who can afford them. There are also many affordable guest houses with spas in them. There are even many natural hot springs that can be found outdoors near rivers. It can be an exciting adventure to find a previously unknown hot spring with a group of friends, and soak together under the stars. There is something for everyone in Taiwan.

基本實用會話

Taiwanese (A)  Westerner (B)

Enjoying natural hot springs.
享受天然溫泉。

B : What a great idea! This water feels warm and relaxing.
這主意太好了！水的溫度很溫暖，讓人很放鬆。

A : I know. We can enjoy each other's company in the mountains and talk about anything we want.
我知道，我們可以在山林裡互相陪伴，聊聊彼此的希望。

B : Please pass me a drink. Thank you. It is very peaceful and private here.
請把飲料傳給我，謝謝你。這裡很寧靜，很隱密。

A : Yes. We're lucky to find this small hot springs. You can find a few along this river, if you look hard enough.
對，我們運氣很好，能找到這個小溫泉。只要仔細找，沿著這條河可以找到幾個。

B： Hey! Did you feel that? Are you trying to tickle me?
嘿，你感覺到了嗎？你是想搔我癢嗎？

A： No! But, look! There are some tadpoles in this warm pool. And they are kissing you.
沒有！不過你看！這個溫泉池裡有蝌蚪，他們在親你。

B： Well, I don't mind staying here if you don't. Little kisses don't really bother me too much.
你不想泡也沒關係，我可以自己留在這裡。這些小小的親吻不會妨礙我享受。

A： Are you trying to tell me something?
你是在暗示什麼嗎？

Visiting a hot springs resort.
參觀溫泉渡假村。

B： This place is beautiful. Will we be going into the hot springs bath together?
這地方很漂亮，我們要一起去泡溫泉嗎？

A： No. There are separate areas for men and women.
不，這裡男湯和女湯是分開的。

B： Would you tell me what I should wear while I am in the public bath?
能不能告訴我去大眾浴池泡湯時要穿什麼？

A： Oh, most people will go in with no clothes on. But you can wear swimming trunks if you prefer.
喔，大部分的人都不會穿衣服去，但如果你想要的話可穿泳褲。

B： Really? Yikes! I didn't bring swimming trunks.
真的嗎？糟糕！我沒帶泳褲。

A： You're a brave guy. I am sure you will get used to being naked in public in no time.
你很勇敢，我相信你很快就會習慣在大家面前裸體的。

 NOTES

Towns that are well-known for their abundance and quality of hot springs are called "spa towns." There are many spa towns around the world, located in areas with geothermal activity. The areas typically sit on fault lines between tectonic plates, where there is often earthquake or volcanic activity. Taiwan is situated where three tectonic plates meet, so there is an abundance of geothermal activity and "spa towns." Some well-known spa towns in Taiwan include Beitou (北投), Jiaoxi (礁溪), Dakeng (大坑), Guanziling (關子嶺), Jhiben (知本), Wulai (烏來) and Yangmingsan (陽明山).

Sentences a Westerner might say
老外可能會說的句子

This is a beautiful town! I didn't realize I could escape into the mountains not far from Taipei.
這是個漂亮的小鎮！我不知道離台北這麼近的地方就有山。

I am excited about trying a hot springs spa. It is my first time.
我好期待去試試溫泉，這是我第一次泡溫泉。

Thank you for your consideration.
謝謝你的貼心。

Will we have our own room, or will we join a public bath?
我們會有自己的房間嗎，還是會去大眾浴池？

OK, I will follow you. Lead the way!
好，我會跟著你，帶路吧！

Oh my! You're not wearing your towel out here in front of everyone? Wow! No one is wearing their towel.
天啊，你沒圍毛巾就站在大家面前？哇！大家都沒圍毛巾。

I don't know. This feels strange.
我不知道，感覺好奇怪。

All right. Don't look. Haha! Oh! This water feels great!
好吧，別看。哈哈！喔！這水溫真好！

Great! And I see that there are water massage areas in the pools. Very nice!
太棒了！我看到池子裡有水療區，太好了！

Definitely! It's time to release some stress. And you're right! The view of the mountains from here is incredible.
沒錯！是時候放鬆壓力了，你說得對，山裡的景色真迷人。

Sentences a Taiwanese person might say.
台灣人可能會說的句子

Wulai is a popular retreat for Taipei residents. People often visit to enjoy the many hot springs.
烏來對台北市民來說是很受歡迎的渡假勝地，人們常來這裡泡溫泉。

Well, there are many we can choose from, but I'll try to pick one that is not too expensive.
我們的選擇很多，但我會選一個不那麼貴的。

This one is well-known for its view. You will see.
這一家以景色出名，你一會兒就能看到。

The best views are from the public bathing area.
最好的景色要從大眾浴池這裡欣賞。

Take the towel, and take off all of your clothes and put them into the locker, including your watch. Your locker key stays on your wrist.
拿著毛巾，脫掉你的衣服，把衣服放到置物櫃裡，包括你的表，再把置物櫃鑰匙戴在手腕上。

Right! That is the only way to really enjoy the feeling of a hot springs spa.
沒錯！這是真正能享受溫泉的唯一方式。

Don't worry. No one here knows you. Go ahead! Lose the towel.
別擔心，這裡沒人認識你，脫吧，把毛巾鬆開。

Look! There are different pools with different temperatures. You can see the thermostats.
你看，不同的池子有不同的溫度。你可以看溫度計。

Yes. It's really time to relax. Would you like to have a beer?
對，是時候放鬆一下了，你想來罐啤酒嗎？

You're welcome. You deserve to try new things while you are here in Taiwan.
不客氣，你在台灣的時候就該嘗試點新鮮事。

Featured Vocabulary

geothermal (adj.) 地熱

Where underground activity produces intense friction and heat, groundwater can be heated to high temperatures. This type of heat is known as "geothermal" heat, or heat from underground. When water that is heated from geothermal energy comes to the surface, they may flow out as hot springs. Geothermal energy can also be captured to produce electrical energy. This is a significant source of energy for New Zealand and the Philippines.

spa (n.) 水療

A spa is defined as a place that provides healthy therapy for the body, with mineral-rich spring water. The concept of spas originated in ancient Greek and Roman times, with the creation of public bath houses. These days, the word "spa" is used to describe a business that provides therapeutic healing, body cleansing and relaxation, not necessarily using hot springs.

mineral therapy (n.) 礦物療法

Hot water can dissolve more solid materials than cold water. Thus, the superheated groundwater naturally dissolves many surrounding minerals before it reaches the surface. Because the human body requires minerals, many believe that soaking in mineral-rich hot springs water is very healthy for the human body. People often visit hot springs as a form of therapy, to improve their health.

UNIT 31

Massage 按摩

In America, massage services are very expensive, averaging about $60 (NT 2,000) per hour, so I rarely had the opportunity to enjoy a relaxing massage. When I moved to Taiwan, I looked forward to finally being able to afford an occasional massage. My first opportunity was during a day off from work. I ventured into the small city of Madou and found a little "Massage Parlor" place not knowing what to expect. It seemed to be a clean, professional place. They offered a 40-minute foot massage for NT500 or a one-hour full-body massage for NT800. I chose the full body massage. It was a massage parlor that did not offer any shady services behind closed doors. I would rate the massage a 7 out of 10, but the price was half of what I would have paid back home.

Foreigners may be attracted to the low rates and good service for the different massage services available in Taiwan. To avoid potential confusion or embarassment, they should try to find out ahead of time if the location offers a legitimate therapeutic massage, or if they offer "happy endings." Happy endings are sexual services offered at the end of massages, and are not offered in most places.

基本實用會話

Taiwanese (A) : Westerner (B)

Searching for a Massage Parlor.
尋找按摩院。

B : Can you tell me where I can go to get a good massage?
你能告訴我哪裡有好的按摩院嗎？

A : What type of massage are you looking for?
你想要找哪種按摩？

B : Ummm. I want a real massage. My feet hurt from hiking in the mountains yesterday.
嗯…我想要真正的按摩。昨天爬山後，我的腳很痛。

A : Of course. There is a place on the corner of Beimen Street and Gongyuan Avenue. They have a good reputation.
沒問題。北門街和公園路的路口有一家，他們的名聲不錯。

B : Thank you. Have you tried it out?
謝謝你，你試過了嗎？

A : No! I can't really afford to pay for massages. By the way, the Chinese word for massage is, "ah-mwo."
沒有，我負擔不起按摩。對了，按摩的中文字是「按摩」。

B : Thank you. If I really like the place, I will take you there next time and treat you.
謝謝你，如果我真的喜歡那裡，下次我請你去。

A : You don't need to do that, but thank you.
不用了，不過謝謝你。

Getting a Massage.
按摩。

B : Ouch! Oh! It hurts!
啊，喔！好痛！

A : Didn't you want a foot massage?
你不是想做足部按摩？

B : Yes. I was told that reflexology was good for my health.
想，我聽過反射療法對我的健康很好。

A : Well, that is what I am doing for you.
我正在為你進行反射療法。

B : But, you're pressing down too hard on my feet. It is painful.
可是你按我的腳按太大力了，好痛。

A : OK. The pain means you are really tense. Are you stressed out? I will take it easy on you.
好的，痛代表你太緊張了，你是不是壓力很大？我會小力一些。

B : Yes. That feels better. Perhaps I have been worried about losing my job.
好，感覺好多了，或許我之前太擔心丟工作。

NOTES

Foreigners will appreciate someone who can guide them to reputable massage services. One of the highlights of their trip to Taiwan may be the affordability of massage therapy. A foot massage can feel extremely satisfying after a day of hiking or a long walking tour of Taipei. Locals should have a better understanding of which massage parlors offer legitimate massage and which offer "happy endings." They may also be able to help visitors avoid "tourist traps," or businesses that charge a much higher price, because they deal primarily with tourists. I know personally, that it is better to go where the locals go to get the best massage experience.

Sentences a Westerner might say
老外可能會說的句子

What should I do now?
我現在該怎麼做？

Oh! These are like pajamas. They look comfortable.
喔，這些好像睡衣。看起來很舒服。

Yes, please. My muscles are pretty tense. Can you focus on my shoulders?
是的，麻煩你了，我的肌肉很緊，你能加強我的肩膀嗎？

Oh! My right knee does have a slight injury. Thank you.
喔！我的右膝受了點傷，謝謝你。

Yeah. That sounds great. Aloe gel may even be more healthy for my skin.
對，聽起來不錯。蘆薈膠或許對我的肌膚更好。

That's OK. Just use what you have.
沒關係，就用你手邊有的。

Oh yes! It feels really good. You're doing a great job on my shoulders.
太好了！感覺真好。你肩膀按得很好。

Mmmm. Feels good. Oh, I'm from the United Kingdom.
嗯，很舒服，喔，我是從英國來的。

Your English is pretty good. And you're really skilled at massage.
你的英文很好，你的按摩技術也很好。

I think you should have plenty of international customers.
我想你有很多外國客人。

Sentences a Taiwanese person might say.
台灣人可能會說的句子

Please change into the clothes on the massage table. I'll return when you are ready.
請換上在按摩椅上的衣服，等你準備好後我再回來。

I'm back. OK, you asked for a full body massage, right?
我回來了，好，你是做全身按摩，是嗎？

Sure. Is there any part of your body that has any pain that I should be careful about?
當然，你身體有哪部分會痛，是我要特別小心的嗎？

OK. You did want me to use massage oil, right?
好，你要我用按摩油，對嗎？

I don't have that, but I do have scented oils.
我沒有那個，但我有香精油。

I hope you like this oil. We heated it for you.
希望你喜歡這種油，我們會幫你加熱。

Your muscles are tense. I will help loosen them up for you. So, where are you from?
你的肌肉很緊，我會幫你放鬆你的肌肉。那麼，你是從哪裡來的？

I thought so. Your accent does sound British.
我也這麼想，你有英國人的口音。

Thank you. I studied English before I received my massage training.
謝謝你，我在接受按摩訓練之前學過英文。

Yes, they do come to this massage parlor frequently. I have opportunities to practice English here.
是的，他們常來這家按摩院，我也有機會在這裡練習英文。

Featured Vocabulary

massage parlor (n.) 按摩院

A "massage parlor" indicates an establishment that does the business of offering massage services. A "parlor" means a store or business that offers a specific type of food or service. Another terms used commonly instead of "massage parlor" is "massage spa."

massuer vs massuese (n.) 男按摩師 vs. 女按摩師

The person who provides a massage is usually called a massuer, if they are male, and masseuse, if they are female. There is another word that is used, but it does not indicate any gender. That word is massagist, however, it is not a commonly used English word.

reflexology (n.) 反射療法

In Chinese, the word for reflexology means "massage." But, in English, reflexology has a more specific meaning. Reflexology is the science that believes that parts of the body, such as the body's main organs, are connected to another part of the body, such as a part of the foot. Reflexology massage is a more specialized type of massage, whereby different areas of the foot are massaged to trigger a response in other areas of the body. You may commonly find reflexology massage parlors, with big maps of the human foot at their entrance.

UNIT 32

Pets 寵物

In America, pets are very popular, and they are treated very well. In the West, dogs are considered "man's best friend." But, when I first visited Taiwan many years ago, I noticed that there were many dogs and cats wandering freely on the streets the streets. Worst of all, I noticed that many dogs were kept in cages outside. I had never seen this type of imprisonment of animals in America. Dogs could be chained in their yard, but Americans always gave their animals a long leash and space to exercise their legs. I felt that most pets in Taiwan suffered from neglect. I didn't see many Taiwanese people keeping their dogs and cats indoors. Recently, I have noticed that many women have lapdogs, treating small dogs like little children. Some women seem to have replaced their desire to have children with taking care of these pets. In contrast to the caged dogs, these "little princes" are treated like special members of the family. So, as far as pets are concerned in Taiwan, I believe they are either pampered or neglected.

As far as foreigners living in Taiwan, I have seen very few who choose to own pets. Unless they are long-term residents, most choose not to commit themselves to having the responsibility of owning pets. They enjoy having the freedom of spending their free time doing whatever they love to do in Taiwan. Owning a pet can be a burden, sometimes requiring the owner to find help taking care of the animals.

基本實用會話

Taiwanese (A) : Westerner (B) :

Finding a homeless dog.
找流浪狗。

B : What a cute little black dog. Where is your mother?
好可愛的小黑狗，你媽媽在哪裡？

A : That's probably the puppy of a wild dog that lives in the streets. You should leave it alone.
這可能是街上野狗的小孩。你該離牠遠一點。

B : Nonsense! It's so cute and reminds me of a puppy I had when I was young.
胡說，牠這麼可愛，讓我想到我小時候養的小狗。

A : It's still young and its mother is probably looking for it.
牠還小，牠媽媽可能在找牠。

B：I don't think so. It looks like it hasn't eaten for a long time. And the traffic around here is very dangerous. We have to do something.
我不這麼認為，牠看來好久沒吃東西了，這裡的車流也太危險。我們得想想辦法。

A：Do you want to keep it? Do you want the responsibility?
你想收養牠嗎？你要負責嗎？

B：Well, no. But, we can't just leave it here. It will get hit by a car. Let's find a new home for it.
不，但我們不能把牠丟在這裡，牠會被車撞到，我們幫牠找個新家。

Asking for help taking care of a pet.
找人幫忙照顧寵物。

B：Nancy, could you help me out?
南西，你能幫我一個忙嗎？

A：What can I do for you?
我能幫什麼忙？

B：I need to go on a trip for a few days. Would you please take care of my cat while I am gone?
我要去旅行幾天，能不能幫我照顧我的貓？

A：I'm sorry. I'm not allowed to have any pets in my apartment. I'm surprised your landlord allows you to have a cat.
對不起，我的公寓不能養寵物。我很驚訝你的房東居然允許你養貓。

B：Well, maybe you can come over to my apartment once a day to feed my cat.
或許你可以一天來我公寓一次，幫我餵貓。

A：I'll be happy to do that. We're practically neighbors.
我很樂意幫忙，我們其實是鄰居。

B：OK. I will give you my house key on Friday morning. Thank you so much!
好，我週五早上給你我家的鑰匙，非常謝謝你！

NOTES

Foreigners typically enjoy having pets in their own countries, but they may avoid pet ownership while living in Taiwan, because animal care may be more of a hassle for them here. For example, they may not fully understand the restrictions of owning pets in their apartment. Or they may not understand the rules and regulations of owning a pet, or what shots are required, or where to get the proper medical care. Also, if they get attached to a pet, and they need to return to their home country, it may be a challenge to transport their pet overseas. Choosing to own a pet can be a much harder choice for a foreigner in Taiwan than for a local resident.

溝通大加分

Sentences a Westerner might say
老外可能會說的句子

Can you please tell me where I can find a veterinarian?
你能告訴我哪裡有獸醫院？

I think its foot was run over by a car or a scooter.
我想牠的腳被車子或摩托車輾到了。

Thank you. This is not a typical Taiwanese dog. I think this is a terrier.
謝謝你，這不是典型的台灣土狗，我想牠是梗犬。

I love dogs. If we can't find its owner, I would like to keep this one.
我愛狗，如果我們找不到牠的主人，我想收養牠。

I will. I don't mind spending money on this deserving little fellow.
我會的，我不介紹為這個小傢伙花錢。

If I am allowed to keep this dog as a pet, I want to ask the vet what type of shots it needs to have.
如果我可以收養這隻狗當寵物，我會請獸醫幫牠注射牠需要的預防針。

Yes, I'm sure. In America, shots are required for pet ownership. I also want to know about neutering the dog.
是的，我確定。美國要求寵物主人帶寵物去打針，我還想知道怎麼幫狗絕育。

I want to make sure this one cannot have more puppies. There are too many dogs in Taiwan having babies.
我要確認這一隻不會再生小狗，台灣有太多懷孕的狗了。

In my culture, we consider dogs our best friends.
在我的文化裡，我們認為狗是我們最好的朋友。

Oh no! I'm not ready to have kids. I haven't even found the right woman for me yet.
喔不，我還沒準備好生小孩，我甚至還沒找到合適的女人。

Sentences a Taiwanese person might say.
台灣人可能會說的句子

Oh no! What's wrong with that dog?
喔不！這隻狗怎麼了？

That happens a lot. There are too many wild dogs living on the streets. I will take you to an animal doctor.
這種事經常發生，街上有很多野狗，我帶你去找獸醫。

Small dogs are more popular as pets in Taiwan these days. This one may have run away from its owner.
近來台灣養小狗當寵物越來越受歡迎了。這隻可能是離家出走的狗。

Really? That is a lot of responsibility. Are you sure you want it? You will have to ask your landlord.
真的嗎？那可是責任重大。你確定你要收養？你必須問過你的房東。

I guess you are not afraid of responsibility after all. OK. We are here.
我想你不害怕負起責任。好了，可以了。

That might be expensive. Are you sure?
可能很貴，你確定？

What does neutering mean?
絕育是什麼意思？

You're right about that. Wow! I didn't realize you care so much about dogs.
你說得對。哇！我不知道你這麼在乎狗的事。

You're so responsible. I think you may even be a good father one day.
你很負責任。我想你有天一定也會是個好父親。

Are you sure? Your "Miss Right" may just be right under your nose.
你確定嗎？你的「真命天女」或許就在你面前。

Featured Vocabulary

lapdog (n.) 寵物犬

A lapdog (or lap dog) is a dog that people give a lot of attention to and treat like their own children. I have seen a growing phenomenon in Taiwan. More people carry their little lapdogs everywhere they go. They bring them on their arms or laps, or they bring them in their purses or bags. It seems that as fewer people want the responsibility of having children, they are opting, instead, to take care of a little, cute dogs. Sometimes, people can describe another person as a "lapdog," which means they are someone who attaches themselves to another person and craves their attention.

veterinarian (n.) 獸醫

A medical doctor that is trained to provide medical services to animals is called a "veterinarian." In English, we often call these doctors, "vets," because Americans like to shorten long words. These doctors practice "veterinary medicine," and work in places called "veterinary clinics" or "vet clinics." Because of the increase in Taiwanese people who have pampered pets, there is a growing demand for verterinary care.

UNIT 33

Weather 氣候

When I moved to Taiwan, many people warned me that it was unbearably hot and humid most of the time. However, I lived in Florida, which is also in the subtropical zone, so it has very similar weather. The year-round temperatures are about the same in Taiwan and Florida, so living in Taiwan was not much of an adjustment. On the contrary, I was pleasantly surprised by how much variety there was in the weather. Florida is flat, but Taiwan has high mountains. This has given me ample opportunity to escape the heat of the lowlands, to enjoy weather that is much cooler and dryer. Going on a mountain retreat has been one of my favorite activities in Taiwan.

Foreigners living in Taiwan may not be used to the stifling heat of the Taiwanese summers, especially if they are from Europe. Hot and humid weather seems to prevail in Taiwan during the months between May and October. Fortunately, Taiwan has two rainy seasons, one at the end of Spring, and the regular typhoon season at the end of the Summer. They provide the rain that the island needs to replenish its reservoirs. Getting around during heavy rainstorms can be a challenge for visitors, especially if they drive scooters to get around.

基本實用會話

Taiwanese (A)  Westerner (B)

Rain Wear.
雨天的穿著。

B: It's starting to pour! We're getting wet.
開始下大雨了,我們會淋濕。

A: Don't worry. I always carry a pair of rain jackets inside of my motor scooter.
別擔心,我的摩托車裡總是帶了兩件雨衣。

B: You seem really prepared for rain showers.
你似乎對下雨做好準備了。

A: Of course. Every summer, you need to be prepared for tropical storms, and even typhoons.
當然,每年夏天都要為熱帶暴風雨,甚至是颱風做好準備。

B: We don't have typhoons where I come from.
我的家鄉沒有颱風。

A: Then you're lucky. Typhoons can cause flooding and mudslides.
那你們很幸運。颱風會造成淹水和土石流。

第一篇

Living & Enjoying in Taiwan

B : Well, on the East coast of America, we call these big storms, "hurricanes." They can cause a lot of damage.
在美國東岸，我們稱這些大風暴為「颶風」，颶風可能導致嚴重的傷害。

Sun Wear.
晴天的穿著。

B : Betty, what in the world are you wearing? It's super hot outside!
貝蒂，你戴的那是什麼東西？外面超熱的！

A : I need to go out to buy something at the store.
我要去商店裡買些東西。

B : Are you going to rob the store? Is that why your wearing a mask? You don't want anyone to recognize you?
你要去搶商店嗎？所以你才戴面具嗎？你不想讓大家認出來嗎？

A : No, silly! It's a sunny day, and a woman has to protect her skin from the sun.
不，傻瓜！今天是晴天，女人要為了保護皮膚防晒。

B : Have you ever tried suntan lotion, or sunblock?
你試過防晒乳嗎？

A : Not really? We only use that when we go out to the beach.
不算有，我們只有去海邊的時候會用。

B : You're going to sweat to death wearing all of those clothes.
你穿著那些衣服會熱死的。

A : I would rather sweat than become darker.
我寧願流汗也不要變黑。

NOTES

Some of the strangest sights to a foreigner is seeing how Taiwanese people dress up for the Summer. Young women wear very short skirts or shorts, and attract the attention of men. However, it seems that women who are over thirty-years-old may wear long pants, long-sleeved shirts, jackets, and even face masks to cover as much of their skin as possible.They may want to avoid being sunburnt, but I always wonder how they can bear the heat.

137

溝通大加分

Sentences a Westerner might say
老外可能會說的句子

I can't believe it! It's only 21 degrees C here today.
我不敢相信，今天這裡才21度。

We must be at a pretty high elevation in order to have this cool weather.
這裡的海拔一定很高，才能有這麼涼爽的天氣。

This is beautiful. There are even pine trees and gorgeous views.
真美，這裡甚至還有松樹，還有迷人的景色。

I don't see why. I can see the trail clearly. It seems safe.
我不懂為什麼，我能清楚看到軌道，看來很安全。

Yeah, you're right. The clouds are so beautiful, and they are coming up right towards us.
對，你說得對。雲看來很漂亮，雲正朝我們飄過來。

The clouds have surrounded us. Wow! It looks like we're in a thick fog. Our view is restricted, and I can't see very far.
雲把我們包圍起來了，哇！看來我們身處濃霧之中，我們的視線受限了，我看不遠。

The wind is really getting stronger. And the temperature seems to have dropped considerably. I wish I had my jacket.
風越來越強了，溫度似乎又降了許多，早知道就帶外套。

We really need a rain jacket now. And my glasses are fogging up. I can't see much at all.
我們現在其實需要雨衣，我的眼鏡也起霧了，我看不太到了。

This is unbelievable! We've just experienced some big weather changes in just a short time.
真是不可思議，我們在這麼短時間就體驗這麼大的氣候變化。

Thanks for bringing me back to our camp safely. Next time I will prepare a jacket.
謝謝你安全帶我回到營區。下次我會準備外套的。

Sentences a Taiwanese person might say.
台灣人可能會說的句子

I know. While everyone is staying indoors, we can enjoy the outdoors and go hiking.
我知道，大家都待在室內，而我們正在享受戶外健行。

That's true. This is Mt. Alishan. We're about 2,500 kilometers high right now.
沒錯，這裡是阿里山，現在的海拔大約2,500公里。

We need to be careful when we are walking on this trail. It can be a little dangerous.
我們走在這步道上要小心，這裡會有點危險。

The weather can change very quickly when you are in the mountains.
在山上的氣候變化非常快。

We'd better head back down the trail now. It will become foggy very quickly.
我們最好快回到步道上，霧很快就會變大。

Let's walk carefully, but keep going. Stick together, and stay on the path.
我們小心走，但腳步不要停。跟緊一點，別偏離步道。

Oh no! It's raining. We're getting wet.
喔，不！下雨了，我們會淋濕的。

Just hold onto my shorts. We'll make it to the trailhead in a few minutes.
披著我的短褲，再幾分鐘就回到登山口了。

I know. I told you that can happen when you are up in the mountains.
我知道，我說過在山上很可能發生這種情況的。

The weather can be very unpredictable, so you can't be too prepared.
天氣變化莫測，所以必須做好萬全準備。

Featured Vocabulary

sunburn vs suntan (n.) 曬傷 vs 曬黑

A sunburn happens when a person is out in the sun for a long period of time, and their skin becomes red and irritated. It becomes damaged, and painful. A suntan is the darkening of the skin caused by prolonged exposure to the sun. The skin produces and accumulates a pigment called "melanin," which darkens the skin and protects it from the sun's rays. Westerners often value a suntan, but in Taiwan, people seem to do everything they can to avoid becoming sunburnt or suntanned. It's likely because there seems to be a cultural preference for lighter skin.

weather forecast (n.) 天氣預報

A weather forecast is information that is prepared to help people predict the upcoming weather. The science of weather forecasting has become more sophisticated, measuring weather patterns, barometric pressure systems, rainfall, and much more. People who present the forecasts are known as weather forecasters. Although weather forecasting has improved over the years, it is still an inaccurate science. Foreigners in Taiwan usually cannot understand the weather forecasts on Taiwan's television stations, so they keep up with the weather forecasts in English from one of two web sites. Taiwan's Central Weather Brueau has an English section: http://www.cwb.gov.tw/eng/. And Taiwan Weather Underground: http://www.wunderground.com/weather-forecast/TW/Taipei.html.

If the weather is severe enough, the American Institute in Taiwan (美國在台協會) will e-mail weather warnings to its citizens.

UNIT 34

Rainy Seasons 梅雨季

As a teacher in Taiwan, I needed to drive my motor scooter to different locations. It wasn't long before I was caught in a rainstorm for the first time. I saw many people jump off their motor scooters to open up their seats and pull out their rain coats. Unfortunately, I did not have a raincoat in my scooter. I kept driving, and eventually arrived at my school. I was totally soaked and shivering, even though it was May. I learned my lesson, and bought a new raincoat the next day. After that lesson, I was never unprepared again for Taiwan's rainy weather.

During Taiwan's late-Spring/early-Summer monsoon season, there may be rainstorms that last for several days in a row. In the north part of Taiwan, it is also very rainy during the Winter. Long, rainy days can be depressing for foreign visitors, and unless they are from a rainy place like Great Britain, they may not know how to deal with the prolonged wet, grey weather. It would be nice to help them to beat the blues by finding interesting indoor activities they can participate in during the rainy times, such as visits to museums, or window shopping in a mall.

基本實用會話

Taiwanese (A) Westerner (B)

Rain Gear.
雨具。

B: I need to buy a rain coat. Where do you keep them?
我得買件雨衣,在哪裡?

A: Follow me. They are at the back of the store. What kind are you looking for?
跟我來,雨衣在店的後面,你要找哪種雨衣?

B: I just need to keep one in the back of my motor scooter in case it rains.
我只是要買件放在摩托車裡的雨衣,以防下雨。

A: These are the cheapest ones, because they are very thin. They won't last very long.
這些是最便宜的,不過很薄,不太耐用。

B: I think I will buy a rain coat that will last a long time.
我想買件比較耐用的雨衣。

A: OK. These are probably what you are looking for.
好,這些或許符合你想找的。

B: Yes, they are perfect. Actually I should get two, in case I have a passenger with me.
對,太好了。其實我想買兩件,以免要載人。

Rain Forecast.
下雨預報。

B : What's the weather supposed to be like this weekend? I'm not really able to understand the Taiwanese newscasts.
這週末的天氣如何？我看不懂台灣的天氣預報。

A : Well, it is supposed to rain this weekend. That is quite common this time of year.
這週末應該會下雨，每年這時候都很常這樣。

B : Oh no. I was really looking forward to my sightseeing trip.
喔，對，我本來很期待去旅行的。

A : I don't know if you will want to go during rainy weather.
我不知道你會不會想在雨天時出遊。

B : It depends. Will the rain be a light drizzle, or will be a heavy downpour?
看情況，只是毛毛雨嗎？還是會傾盆大雨？

A : That is uncertain. Last weekend, we had a moderate, steady rain for two days.
不一定，上個週末就持續下了兩天不大不小的雨。

B : OK. Well, I already bought the train ticket, so I will pack a raincoat and bring an umbrella.
好，反正我已經買了火車票，所以我會帶著雨衣和雨傘。

A : You should still be able to enjoy the special foods from the area. I hope you have a good time.
你應該會喜歡那裡的特產，希望你玩得愉快。

NOTES

Taiwan has over twenty-three million people, and the people on the island consume a large amount of water every year. The agricultural industry also requires a huge amount of fresh water. So, Taiwan's rainy seasons are very important to replenish the fresh water sources on the island. Taiwan's reservoirs are important resources for drinking water, some of which are beautiful tourist attractions. They also provide hydroelectric energy. When we don't get enough rain during the traditionally rainy months, the government enforces the rationing of water. So, the next time it rains, you should appreciate how important it is to the needs of Taiwan's large population.

Sentences a Westerner might say
老外可能會說的句子

It's a beautiful sunny day. Do you want to go to the mountains for a hike?
今天是美好的大晴天，你要去爬山嗎？

I went boating last week. We've had some beautiful weather this month.
我上禮拜去划船，這個禮拜天氣很好。

Why? What's wrong with the gorgeous weather?
為什麼？好天氣不好嗎？

What do you mean? Do you mean the crops need the rain?
什麼意思？你是說穀物需要雨水？

But I thought Taiwan has many of rivers, waterfalls and lakes?
但我以為台灣有很多河流、瀑布和湖泊？

I see. Have the reservoirs become dry before? What has happened?
我懂了，水庫以前乾旱過？怎麼回事？

That sounds serious. The lack of water could affect business, and farmers.
聽起來很嚴重，缺水會影響商業和農業。

I understand. Maybe there is something I can do.
我懂，或許我能幫上什麼忙。

I saw this on television back in the USA. I am performing a rain dance.
我在美國時從電視上看過這個，我在跳祈雨舞。

The American Indians perform a rain dance to ask the spirits for rain.
美國印第安人會向神靈跳祈雨舞，祈求下雨。

Sentences a Taiwanese person might say.
台灣人可能會說的句子

No. I went last weekend. I have a lot of work to catch up on.
不，我上禮拜去過了。我手上有很多工作。

You're right, but I am worried about that.
你說得對，但我有點擔心這一點。

It hasn't rained since Lunar New Year. We need the rain.
從農曆新年後就再沒下雨了，我們需要雨水。

No. I mean everyone on the island needs the rain. Our reservoirs are getting low. That is serious!
不，我是說島上的每個人都需要雨水，我們的水庫缺水了，這是嚴重的問題！

Yes, but they are running dry, too. And the cities only get drinking water from a few reservoirs in Taiwan.
對,但他們也快乾涸了,台灣的城鎮只能從幾個水庫裡取得飲用水。

The government will force everyone to ration how much water they use. Businesses will be limited, too.
政府會要求每個人節約用水,商業用水也會受限。

Yes, so I don't really care about having more sunny weather.
是的,所以我其實不希望再出太陽了。

What are you doing? Why are you dancing like a crazy person?
你要做什麼?你為什麼像瘋子一樣跳舞?

What is a rain dance?
什麼是祈雨舞?

Haha! That's funny. But a drought is not funny, so let me join you.
哈哈!真有趣,不過乾旱可不有趣,我們一起跳吧。

Featured Vocabulary

umbrella vs. parasol (n.) 雨傘 vs. 陽傘

An umbrella is a handheld portable canopy that people use to protect themselves from the rain. There is also a similar item that people use to protect themselves from the sun. This is called a parasol. A parasol is not necessarily waterproof. In Taiwan, people typically use umbrellas for rain or sunshine.

rainstorm (n.) 暴雨

Taiwan has frequent rainstorms during its rainy season at the end of Spring (known as the "monsoon season"). During the end of Summer, there are rainstorm associated with tropical storm and typhoons that pass through Taiwan. In English, severe rainstorms that include lighting and thunder are known as thunderstorms. Another term, "squall," is used for a sudden, heavy wind and rain.

monsoon (n.) 季風

A seasonal reversing of winds usually results in a change of precipitation, or rain. This occurs during the transition between the cold winter season and warmer summer months. During the Winter, temperatures are colder over the mainland, which results in high pressure, which pushes winds out towards Taiwan. In the warmer months, the Pacific Ocean stays cooler, while the mainland heats up faster. This makes the high pressure over the ocean, which blows the moisture-rich winds towards the mainland.

Typhoons 颱風

In my first year (2009) as a resident of Taiwan, I will never forget my first typhoon experience. When it first approached, Typhoon Morakot did not look like a severe storm, yet it was the deadliest and costliest typhoon in recorded history in Taiwan. I remembered the strong winds that peaked at 140 km/hour, but they were nothing like the fierce winds I experienced during hurricanes in Florida. But the heavy rains drenched the island. Even the Jen-wen River flooded over its banks, and most of our small town was under water. Many people had some type of water or wind damage. Sadly, 461 people died in Taiwan, and an entire indigenous village disappeared under a massive mudslide.

Taiwan regularly has a few typhoons every summer, which bring wind and rain to the island. But they typically do not do much damage, thanks to the buffering effects of Taiwan's high mountains. Although the mountain villages and roads are prone to flooding and mudslides, the rest of Taiwan is usually spared the brunt of the damage from passing typhoons. Foreigners visiting Taiwan rarely experience typhoons as anything but a wet and windy inconvenience.

基本實用會話

Taiwanese (A)   Westerner (B)

Typhoon approaching.
颱風接近中。

B: You cancelled your trip to Taoyuan? Why?
你取消了去桃園的旅行？為什麼？

A: Don't you follow the news? The first typhoon of the season is coming this weekend.
你沒看新聞嗎？本季第一個颱風這週末要來了。

B: What is a typhoon? I have never heard that word.
什麼是颱風？我以前沒聽過這個詞。

A: It is a very strong tropical storm. I think you may call it a hurricane where you come from.
那是非常強烈的熱帶風暴。我想你的家鄉可能稱為颶風。

B: Oh, thank you. This sounds serious. What should I do to prepare?
喔，謝謝你。聽來很嚴重，我該準備什麼？

A: You should be fine, as long as you are not in the mountains.
只要你不在山上就應該沒事。

B : I guess I should plan to buy enough food and water, and stay indoors for awhile.
我想我該購買足夠的食物和水，待在室內一陣子。

Typhoon aftermath.
颱風過後。

B : Hello. Betty? Are you and your family doing all right after that typhoon?
哈囉，貝蒂？颱風走了，你和你的家人都好嗎？

A : Well, our house had a lot of flooding, so we are busy shoveling the mud out of our first floor.
這個嘛，我們家淹水了，所以我們忙著把一樓的泥土鏟出去。

B : Oh no! I am sorry to hear that. Is everyone OK?
喔不！很遺憾聽到這個消息，大家都還好嗎？

A : No one got hurt. But my mother lost all of her vegetables in her garden. And the fruit was blown off of our trees.
沒人受傷，但我媽菜園的蔬菜都沒了，水果也都從樹上被吹下來了。

B : I am so glad no one got hurt. I will come over. Can I bring anything?
很高興沒人受傷，我會過去看看，要帶什麼去嗎？

A : Thank you for your offer to help us. Maybe you can bring some drinking water and a shovel.
謝謝你願意幫助我們。或許你可以帶些飲用水和鏟子來。

B : OK. I will be there in thirty minutes.
好，我30分鐘內到。

A : You are so kind. Your visit will make a positive impression on my parents.
你人真好，你的到訪會讓我爸媽留下好印象。

NOTES

As an American from Florida, I have been able to compare the destruction from these natural disasters in Florida and Taiwan. I am always surprised by how little the typhoons damage the infrastructure of Taiwan. The mountains of Taiwan do provide a protective buffer to the damaging force of the winds, but there is always a greater degree of destruction from American hurricanes. I believe that Taiwan has stronger construction standards and have a better-protected electrical grid that what Americans have. Taiwan's practical way of surviving their environment has better prepared them for natural disasters.

Sentences a Westerner might say
老外可能會說的句子

That was quite a storm last night! The rainwater came into our house from the balcony.
昨晚的風暴真大,雨水從陽台流進我家。

The typhoon blew so much stuff onto our balcony, it covered up the drains.
颱風把一堆東西吹到我們的陽台,蓋住了下水道。

Oh my! Did you look outside? Our yard is entirely underwater. Our garden is ruined!
天啊,你有看外面嗎?我們的院子完全淹水了,我們的花園毀了!

I don't think anyone is going to school or work today. There is debris all over the road.
我想今天沒人會去上學或上班。路上到處是碎片。

Do you need to call you friends and family to check on them?
你要打電話給你的朋友或家人問問嗎?

Why did people die in the mountains? I thought there were not many people living in the mountains.
為什麼會有人死在山上?我以為沒幾個人住在山上。

That's horrible news. Is there anything we should be doing now?
真是可怕的新聞,我們現在該做些什麼呢?

OK. I will walk to buy some water. And I'll survey the damage.
好,我走路去買些水,也看看損傷。

I never thought I would see so much destruction in Taiwan.
我從沒想過在台灣會看到這麼嚴重的災害。

Maybe it has something to do with global warming.
或許這和全球暖化有關。

Sentences a Taiwanese person might say.
台灣人可能會說的句子

I know. It's a good thing we woke up to see the flooding in our house.
我知道,還好我們有醒來,看到屋子裡淹水了。

I suppose we can wash all of our wet towels and blankets now. Our floors should be dry.
我們現在應該可以清洗所有濕掉的毛巾和毛毯了。我們的地板應該乾了。

We're lucky to still have electricity. Let me see what's on the news.
還好我們還有電力。我看看有什麼新聞。

Oh no! The schools are closed. But it seems that many people have died.
喔不！學校關閉了，而且看來死亡人數很多。

I'll make some calls, but they should be OK. Most of the people who died were in the mountains.
我會打電話，但他們應該都沒事。大部分的死者都在山上。

That's true, but there were many mudslides in the mountains. An entire village was buried under the giant mudslide.
是的，但山上發生很多土石流，整個村都被巨大的土石流淹沒。

Because of the flooding in our town, the drinking water is not safe for awhile.
因為我們的城市淹水了，飲用水暫時不太安全。

Thank you. And I will call our friends and relatives to see if they are OK.
謝謝你，我會打給我們的親朋好友，看看他們是否安好。

Me, too. This is the worst disaster I have seen in my lifetime.
我也是，這是我這輩子看到最嚴重的災難。

I don't know. But we have a lot to do before life can return to normal.
我不知道，但我們得付出很多心力，才能讓生活恢復正常。

Featured Vocabulary

typhoon vs hurricane vs cyclone (n.) 颱風 vs 颶風 vs 旋風

Taiwan has frequent typhoons at the end of Summer and in early Autumn. Weather patterns in the warm, humid Pacific often generate a lot of energy that hits the Asian coast. Fortunately, Taiwan's high mountains protect most of the populated areas from the destructive power of typhoons, but the mountains often see damaging mudslides. These powerful tropical storms are called "typhoons," if they originate in the Pacific Ocean. They are called "hurricanes," if they originate in the Atlantic Ocean. They are "cyclones," if they originate in the Indian Ocean.

mudslide (n.) 土石流

Also know as mudflows, mudslides are a mass movement of earth triggered by heavy rainfall or melting snow. They are similar to landslides (土崩), which are usually triggered by earthquakes instead of water. The largest mudslide in recorded history happened in 1980, with the eruption of Mt. St. Helens in Washington State, USA. That mudslide displaced 2.8 cubic kilometers of earth.

UNIT 36

Elders 老年生活

During my first trip to Taiwan, I noticed how well the elders were taken care of by their families. I saw many families with three or four generations living under one roof. It was quite touching. I never saw large extended families living together in the USA. Also, the elders were treated with reverence. They were the first to be served at meals, and they were well-cared for. It was very touching to see the older generations treated with the respect they deserve.

I personally feel that foreigners can learn much from the way Taiwan treats their elders. The traditional family values prevail throughout most of Taiwanese society, with parents expecting their children (or eldest son) to take care of them during their old age. This is not the case in most countries. Sadly, I have learned that more families in Taiwan are leaving traditions behind, choosing to send their parents to live in nursing homes.

基本實用會話

Taiwanese (A)  Westerner (B)

Greeting an elder.
向長者打招呼。

B: That was nice of the old man to invite us to have tea with him. What should I say to him?
這位老人真好，邀請我們和他一起喝茶。我該對他說什麼？

A: Yes, it was nice of him. That is Taiwanese hospitality for you.
是的，他人很好。這是台灣人的熱情。

B: Cindy, how should I address him?
辛蒂，我該怎麼稱呼他？

A: You should call him "a-bei." It is a respectful term for an elder. And it might be nice to bow to him.
你該稱他「阿伯」。這是對老者的尊稱，如果能對他敬禮也很好。

B: A-bei, hsieh-hsieh. Did I say it right, Cindy?
阿伯，謝謝。辛蒂，我這麼說對嗎？

A: Yes, you can raise your cup to drink when he raises his cup to you. I think he likes you.
是的，當他朝你舉起杯子，你也可以舉起杯子，再喝茶。我想他喜歡你。

B: Thank you, Cindy. He reminds me a lot of my grandpa. Please tell him I appreciate his hospitality.
謝謝你，辛蒂。他讓我想到我的祖父。請告訴他我很感激他的款待

Discussing a nursing home.
討論養老院。

B: Honey, have you ever thought of finding a place to take care of your mother?
親愛的，你想過找個地方照顧你母親嗎？

A: No. That's impossible. We can't send her away to a nursing home.
不，不可能。我們不能把她送到養老院。

B: Then what should we do? She needs medical care and supervision. We are too busy to offer that.
那我們該怎麼做？她需要醫療照護和監督。我們太忙了無法兼顧。

A: You're right, but I can't bear sending her away. Could we hire a caregiver to come to our home to take care of her?
你說得對，但我無法忍受把她送走。或許我們可以請個看護來我們家照顧她？

B: I am willing to consider all of our options. Please get the information about our choices.
我願意考慮所有選擇，找找所有選擇的資訊吧。

A: Thank you for your thoughtfulness.
謝謝你的體貼。

B: You don't need to thank me. She is part of our family.
你不用感謝我，她也是我們家人。

A: I hope we can take care of her after all of the years she took care of me.
希望我們能照顧她，畢竟她照顧我這麼多年。

NOTES

Most Americans can expect to retire by the age of 65, and then enjoy their retirement years while they still have good health. However, once they lose the ability to take care of themselves, most Americans end up in a nursing home. Nursing homes in America are very expensive, and can be a drain on a family's finances. Even though they may have well-trained, friendly staff and comfortable facilities, to an older person, nursing homes cannot provide the love and attention that a family can.

Sentences a Westerner might say
老外可能會說的句子

It is so nice of you to volunteer as a social worker.
你人真好，志願來這裡當社工。

Why do you care so much for the elderly?
你為什麼這麼在乎老人家？

You must have become very close to her.
你一定和她變得很親近。

I see. So, now you feel like you can help other elders instead.
我懂了，那麼，你現在覺得你也能幫助其他長者。

Do families in Taiwan send their older parents to retirement homes?
台灣的家庭會把家中的老人送到養老院嗎？

So many elders are left in their homes with a lack of care and attention?
那麼很多老人都被留在家裡，缺乏照護嗎？

Can I come with you next time? I would like to see what I can do to cheer them up.
我下次能跟你去嗎？我想看看我能做些什麼，讓他們開心一點。

Maybe you and I can teach them how to play a card game called "Bridge."
或許我們能教他們如何玩一種叫橋牌的紙牌遊戲。

My grandparents and their friends used to play "Bridge" all of the time. It is very popular with retired people.
我祖母和他們的朋友常玩橋牌。這是退休人士中很受歡迎的遊戲。

I am sure I will learn something from being with them, too.
相信我也能從他們身上學到一些事。

Sentences a Taiwanese person might say.
台灣人可能會說的句子

I really like to take care of older people who cannot take care of themselves.
我很喜歡照顧無法自理的老人家。

When I was little, my mother needed to work, so my grandmother took care of me.
我小時候，我媽得工作，所以是我祖母照顧我。

Yes, we were very close. She taught me a lot. But, she passed away before I could care for her in return.
對，我們非常親近，她教會我很多事。可是，她在我能回報她之前就去世了。

Yes. I know that a lot of families are so busy needing to make a living. So there are many retired people who are neglected.
對，我知道很多家庭都忙著賺錢盈生，所以有很多退休的人都被忽略了。

Some people do, but I think it is too expensive for most families.
有些人是，但我想對大多數家庭來說太貴了。

Yes, especially in the villages far from the cities.
對，特別是離城市較遠的村莊。

OK. A lot of them may never have seen a foreigner before.
好，很多人以前從沒見過外國人。

Why do you think they would like to play a card game?
你為什麼覺得他們會喜歡紙牌遊戲？

That's fine. Maybe it will catch on here in Taiwan.
沒關係，或許在台灣也會流行起來。

I am happy to have you join me. It seems you are a very respectful young man. Older people really deserve our respect.
很高興有你的加入，看來你是個非常有禮貌的年輕人，我們要尊敬老人家。

Featured Vocabulary

nursing home vs. retirement home (n.) 護理之家 vs. 退休之家

When a person retires, they may want to change their lifestyle. Most retired people don't want to spend much time taking card of a big house. Some people want different levels of assistance when their age and health requires it. Most elderly people in the USA are taken care of by a nursing home. In Taiwan, people have traditionally taken care of their parents, but there are more retirement homes and nursing homes these days. The word "retirement home" is a generic term that describes a center or community where the elderly live together with limited care. A "nursing home" is used to describe a center where the elderly patients are given more substantial healthcare services.

social security vs. pension (n.) 社會保障 vs. 退休金

Many people look forward to a secure retirement income. If the retirement income comes from a job, that is referred to as a "pension." If the income is a form of social support provided by the government, that is usually referred to as social security income. In the USA, the government takes a percentage of a person's monthly income as social security tax. Then, they provide this money as income when the person retires.

elderly vs senior citizens (n.) 老人 vs. 老年人

People who are of retirement age, typically over 65 years old, may be referred to in English as the elderly. The word, "elderly" is used to describe an age group, not an individual person. Another term has become more popular in recent times. The term, "senior citizens" is a more respectful way to describe this group of people. If you are referring to a person, you can call someone "an elder," "a senior," or a "senior citizen."

37

Superstitions 迷信

Living in Taiwan, I have experienced many customs or actions that seemed to lack a reasonable explanation, only to later discover that they are common superstitions. Not being skilled with chopsticks, I once stuck a pair into a bowl of rice to keep them from getting the table dirty. I was scolded and told not to leave them standing upright in a bowl of rice. I found out that this resembled incense standing in a bowl of rice, which reminded people of funerals. Basically, I was told that it was rude to remind people of funerals and death during dinnertime.

Foreigners in Taiwan may find many strange customs that have no logical purpose behind them. These can include what to do and what not to do in a temple, or in a guest's home. They can be about what to do or what to wear during weddings, funerals and holidays. There are many occassions and circumstances that may have superstitious customs. To me, they seem to be linked to Chinese culture or religions. Visitors to Taiwan usually have no way to know if they are breaking a superstitions taboo, except by accident. Perhaps, it would be wise for someone to write a handbook for visitors titled, "The Superstitions of Taiwan" to help them avoid making a faux pas.

基本實用會話

Taiwanese (A) Westerner (B)

Avoiding the number 4.
避開號碼4。

B : I finally found a new apartment. I will be living in the Gongyuan Square Towers, apartment 404.
我終於找到新公寓了。我要搬到公園廣場大廈，四〇四號公寓。

A : Are you on the 4th floor? Are you sure you want to live there? Is it too late to cancel your contract?
你住四樓？你確定你要住那裡？來不及取消合約嗎？

B : Yes, I am. Why wouldn't I want to live there? The manager gave me a discount.
對，為什麼不要住那裡？經理還幫我打折。

A : Of course the manager gave you a discount. It's probably hard for him to rent that apartment out.
經理當然幫你打折。他或許很難把那間公寓租出去。

B : Why? It is a beautiful apartment in a nice location.
為什麼？那間公寓很漂亮，位置也很好。

A : I am sure it is, but the number 4 is very unlucky. And people even try to avoid living on the 4th floor. In Chinese, the number 4 sounds the same as the word for "death."
我相信是，但四號代表不幸，大家都避免住在四樓。在中文裡，四號聽起來和「死」一樣。

B : Thank you for the advice, but I will keep the apartment. In my culture, the number 13 is unlucky, so I am quite happy with number 4.
謝謝你的建議，但我會留住這間公寓。在我的文化裡，十三號才是不幸的代表，所以我能接受四號。

> **Lucky mole hair.**
> 幸運的痣毛。

B : Cathy, I am happy to attend your big family reunion, but I have a personal question.
凱西，很高興能參加你的家族大聚會，但我有個私人的問題。

A : Thank you for coming. My family is happy to meet you. What is your question?
謝謝你來。我的家人也很高興能認識你，你有什麼問題？

B : Quite a few of your older relatives have moles on their face. I have seen moles before.
你有幾個長輩臉上都有痣，我以前也看過痣。

A : Oh, you mean the dark spots? Yes, they are common with older people.
喔，你是說那些黑點嗎？對，在老人家身上很常見。

B : But why do the men and women let long hairs grow out of their mole? It looks so strange.
但為什麼男人和女人會讓他們的痣上長出毛來？看起來好奇怪。

A : In Chinese culture, the hair from the mole is a symbol of longevity and good luck.
在中華文化中，痣上的毛是長壽和好運的象徵。

B : I believe you, but I can't help it. It feels weird. I want to find some small scissors.
我相信你，但我總覺得奇怪，我好想找把小剪刀來。

 NOTES

Ghost Month, which occurs at the end of every summer, contains many superstitions related to ghosts. Visitors may wonder why a hotel porter would knock on the hotel room door before letting you in. That is done to scare away the ghosts that may be inside. It is also superstitions to avoid swimming in lakes or the ocean during Ghost Month, because a ghost can drown you. And never whistle at night, or you may attract an unwelcome guest into your room.

Sentences a Westerner might say
老外可能會說的句子

I am ready to go to your sister's wedding. I am looking forward to my first Taiwanese wedding experience.
我已經準備好參加你妹妹的婚禮了，我很期待我的第一場台灣婚禮體驗。

Yes, I have their gift money right here. Is NT 5,000 enough?
是的，他們的禮金就在這裡。五千元夠嗎？

OK. So I'll put it in your red envelope. It looks like the lucky money for Lunar New Year.
好，我把錢放在你的紅包裡。看來像是農曆新年的紅包。

Why did you give NT 8,000? Is there any meaning to that amount?
你為什麼給八千元，那個數字有什麼意義嗎？

OK. The number you chose means we are wishing them good fortune. That sounds good to me.
好，你選擇的數字代表我們祝他們能發財，聽起來不錯。

I'm listening. I don't want to embarrass myself in front of your family.
我洗耳恭聽，我不想在你家人面前丟臉。

What's wrong with that?
那有什麼問題嗎？

Fine. I will keep the chopsticks on the table.
好，我會把筷子放在桌上。

I see. No one wants to think about death or ghosts. I got it.
我懂了，大家都不願想到亡者或鬼。我懂了。

All right. Living in Taiwan can be very complicated.
好，在台灣生活真困難。

Sentences a Taiwanese person might say.
台灣人可能會說的句子

Did you put some money in an envelope?
你把錢放在信封裡嗎？

No, no, no. That won't do. First, you can't have a white envelope. That is the color used for funerals.
不，不，不是那樣。首先，你不能用白包，那是喪禮用的顏色。

Also, it is not lucky to give an odd number. Let's give NT 8,000.
還有，奇數也不是代表幸運的數字，我們包八千吧。

In Chinese culture, the number eight is a very lucky number. It is pronounced "ba," which sounds like "fa." That means fortune.
在中華文化裡，八這個數是非常幸運的數字。它的發音聽起來就像「發」，代表財富。

Since it's your first wedding, let me teach you some customs that you should not forget.
既然這是你第一場婚禮，我再告訴你一些習俗，不要忘記喔。

When you're eating the dinner, don't put the chopsticks standing up in your bowl of rice.
當你吃晚餐時，不要把筷子插在飯上。

It reminds people of the incense used at a funeral.
會讓人想到喪禮用的香。

Second, do not mention anyone who has died. And never mention the word, "ghost."
第二，別提到任何已經去世的人。也絕對不到提到「鬼」這個字。

Also, don't point to anyone. That is not polite.
還有，別指著任何人，那樣不禮貌。

Hey! I am just trying to help you avoid any embarrassment.
嘿，我只是想幫你避免發生任何丟臉的事。

Featured Vocabulary

superstition (n.) 迷信

Chinese culture has many superstitions based on its culture and religions. The word "superstition," comes from "supernatural causality," which means something that happens because of a supernatural source. Another way of describing the meaning of "superstition" is that it is a folk belief, or a belief localized to a certain culture. It seems that the superstitions of Taiwan revolve around what will bring good luck and what will bring bad luck. And they also help people avoid dealing with ghosts. There are superstitions in Western culture as well, including many involving bad luck. The number "13" brings bad luck, and the number "7" is very lucky. Walking in the path of a black cat is unlucky, and finding a four-leaf clover will bring you good luck. Breaking a mirror will bring you 7 years of bad luck.

auspicious (adj.) 吉利的

To be "auspicious" means to be conducive to success or a favorable condition. Another way to simplify the meaning is having the quality to make a person have good luck or good fortune. In Taiwan, there are many symbols or traditions that are auspicious, such as lucky numbers. The number 8 is auspicious. Also, there are some Chinese zodiac signs, such as the Year of the Dragon, that are considered very auspicious. In Western culture, we have some auspicious symbols, such as a four-leaf clover, a rabbit's foot, a rainbow, and the number 7.

Legal 法律

During my first visit to Taiwan, I had the impression of an island ruled by tough and foreboding laws. I saw a sign at the international airport which read, "Bringing drugs into Taiwan is illegal, and those found guilty are punishable by death." That seemed very severe to me, because in America, the worst that could happen to an offender is a jail sentence. Fortunately, during my stay in Taiwan, I have had no legal problems. But, I did have a run in with police on one occasion. The first time, I was driving my car, and I saw a police car behind me with its lights flashing. I stopped, because in the USA, seeing flashing lights means you must pull over. Confused, I got out of my car. The policeman in the car honked his horn and waved at me to keep driving. He seemed as confused as I was, wondering why someone would stop in front of him for no reason.

Foreigners in Taiwan usually have no problems during their visits or stays, but some do break the law when they are under the influence of alcohol, or sometimes they may break the law, because they are not aware of Taiwanese laws. But generally, the police in Taiwan show patience and understanding with foreigners, usually letting them get by with small infractions. I often wonder if the police let foreigners go because they are nice, or if they just don't want to try to speak English.

基本實用會話

Taiwanese (A)　Westerner (B)

Traffic accident.
交通意外。

B: Are you OK? Are you hurt?
你還好嗎？有受傷嗎？

A: I'm fine. How about you? My car only has a small scratch. How about your motor scooter?
我很好，你呢？我的車只有點小擦傷，你的摩托車呢？

B: The damage is minor. Should we give each other our phone numbers or what?
只是小傷，我們要交換電話號碼嗎？

A: Oh. The legal requirement is to call the police, even if it is a minor accident.
喔，法律要求得叫警察，就算只是小車禍。

B: Are you sure? No one got hurt, and the damage is not significant.
你確定？沒人受傷，損傷也不嚴重。

A： You're right, but if you don't have a police report, you will not be legally protected in Taiwan.
你說得對，但在台灣如果沒有報案紀錄，就得不到法律的保護。

B： That is very nice of you to provide this advice to me.
你真好，告訴我這項建議。

Finding an attorney.
找律師。

B： Jean, I need help finding an attorney. My landlord locked me out of my apartment and is trying to sue me.
珍，我需要幫忙找個律師。我的房東把我鎖在我的公寓外，還想告我。

A： What? Why is this happening?
什麼？怎麼回事？

B： I was late paying this month's rent, because I went on a trip out of the country, and was delayed in returning.
我這個月的房租遲交了，因為我出國旅行了，回來的時間也延遲了。

A： Oh, he doesn't sound very understanding. I think you'd better hire an attorney and bring your rental contract.
喔，他聽起來不太諒解你，我想你最好雇用一名律師，而且帶著你的租賃合約。

B： How expensive is it to hire a lawyer?
雇一名律師要多少錢？

A： It's much more affordable than in the USA. But if you can't afford one, you can call the Legal Aid Foundation at 02-6632-8282.
比美國便宜多了，但如果你負擔不起，你可以打給法律扶助基金會，02-6632-8282。

B： Thank you Jean. You are a lifesaver!
謝謝你，珍，你救了我的命！

NOTES

If a foreigner gets into legal trouble in Taiwan, the first place they often go to is the government representative office for their home country. However, the people in these offices are usually very limited in the amount of assistance they can provide. Fortunately, there is an organization, called the "Legal Aid Foundation," that can help foreigners who are legally residing in Taiwan. Their mission is to provide legal assistance to people who cannot afford it.

Sentences a Westerner might say
老外可能會說的句子

Jamie, can you please help me? I don't know what this letter is about.
傑米，你能幫幫我嗎。我不知道這封信在說什麼。

Late traffic fines? I never remembered getting any traffic fines.
罰單遲交？我從不記得有收到交通罰單。

But I don't think I have ever received a notification in the mail.
可是我想我沒收過任何信件通知。

What can I do to straighten out this mess?
我要怎麼處理這件事？

(At the Adjudication Office) Thank you for accompanying me here.
（在裁決所）謝謝你陪我來這裡。

I don't think I forgot breaking the law. What's going on?
我不記得我有違法。怎麼了？

Yes, but that's not me driving. Hey! That's my roommate. He often borrows my motor scooter. He must have been hiding the traffic fine notifications.
對，但不是我開車。嘿，那是我的室友，他經常借我的摩托車，他一定是把罰單藏起來了。

That's impossible. I don't have this amount of money. What are my options?
不可能。我沒有這筆錢，我還有什麼選擇？

This doesn't sound very fair at all. Can an attorney help me?
聽起來一點也不合理。有律師可以幫助我嗎？

Thank you. Please let this lady know that I will come back tomorrow.
謝謝你，請讓這位小姐知道我明天會再來。

Sentences a Taiwanese person might say.
台灣人可能會說的句子

Oh, no. It is a letter to pay your late traffic fines at the Taipei City Adjudication Office.
喔，不，這是台北市裁決所判你遲繳交通罰單的信。

Well, there are many traffic cameras. If they catch you speeding or running through a red light, you are automatically fined and notified.
這個嘛，有很多測速照相，如果抓到你超速或闖紅燈，就會自動寄罰單通知你。

I see. It looks like there are many tickets here. And since they were not paid on time, the late fees have added up.
我懂了，這裡列了很多張罰單。因為罰單沒及時繳交，滯納金就累積了。

Let me go to this office with you to translate for you.
我陪你去裁決所，幫你翻譯。

Sure. No problem. Show them your letter and your identification.
不客氣。把你的信和通知單拿出來。

They said they have proof. Look at these photos. This is your motor scooter, right?
他們說他們有證據，你看這些照片，這是你的摩托車，對嗎？

I see. I explained this to the lady, and she said you still need to take care of the fines.
我懂了，我向這位小姐解釋了，她說你還是得繳交罰金。

She said you can take care of this and work it out with your roommate, or face more fines.
她說你可以先繳，然後再和你的室友算帳，或是面對更多罰金。

Perhaps they can help. Tomorrow, I will help you find one.
或許他們可以幫忙。明天我再幫你找一個。

You're welcome. I think there is even a legal aid service that can help you.
不客氣，我想還可以找法律援助服務幫助你。

Featured Vocabulary

attorney (n.) 律師

If a person has legal trouble, he or she can hire an attorney. An attorney is a licensed professional in the practice of law who can represent you and protect you. Another common way to refer to an attorney is "lawyer." An attorney or lawyer can also be referred to as a counsellor, who one who counsels you on legal affairs. In Taiwan, attorneys are much more affordable than those in the USA. In the USA, if a person is convicted of a crime and they cannot afford to pay for an attorney, they may be assigned a public defender for free. These attorneys are often inexperienced, or they may be people who want to offer some of their time "pro bono," which means free of charge.

judge (n.) 法官

When a person goes to court, their court case is overseen by a person known as a judge. Another term used to describe a high-level judge is "magistrate." In the USA, it is polite to address a judge as "Your Honor." In some cases, a judge can make the final decision (or verdict) for a case, or they may refer the decision to a jury, which is an impartial group of citizens.

court (n.) 法院

A court is an authorized government institution or building where legal cases are heard and decided on. In Taiwan, there are two high courts, the Taiwan High Court (臺灣高等法院), which oversees most of Taiwan, and the Fuchien High Court (福建高等法院), which oversees Kinmen. The Taiwan High Court has Branches in Taipei, Taichung, Tainan, Kaohsiung, and Hualien. Under these High Court Branches are District Courts. All of these courts can handle civil law and criminal law. Likewise, in the USA, there is a structure of district courts, appellate courts (regional), and the Supreme Court, which is the ultimate legal authority.

UNIT 39

Greetings 問候

I have always been impressed by the respect people show each other in Taiwan. Even in something as simple as their greetings and goodbyes, the Taiwanese people I have met have always been respectful. Almost always, a greeting has been accompanied by a nod of the head or a bow. Also, I have noticed that people oftentimes include a respectful title with their greetings or parting expression. The titles include "little sister" or "little brother" for younger people, or "elder brother" or "elder sister" for the older people. To show respect for people of older generations, I have heard people call them "uncle or "auntie" or "grandpa" or "grandma." This has endeared me to people much more easily when meeting them.

If you would like to greet a foreigner, you may consider offering a handshake during your welcome. It is extremely common in Western cultures. If you are brave, you may even consider surprising them and giving them a hug. This will be something they may not expect in Taiwan, but they will likely appreciate the gesture. You can say, "Hello," "Hi," or "Greetings." If they are from the southern USA, you may hear them say, "Howdy!" Alternatively, you may say, "It's nice to meet you" or "I am glad to meet you." A good response would be, "The pleasure is mine."

基本實用會話

Taiwanese (A) Westerner (B)

Greeting someone.
和人打招呼。

B: Hello, it's nice to meet you. I am David.
你好，很高興認識你，我是大衛。

A: It's nice to meet you, too. I am Cindy.
很高興認識你，我是辛蒂。

B: Why don't you shake my hand?
你為什麼不握我的手？

A: Oh, no thank you. It is not our custom, especially between a man and a woman.
喔，不，謝謝你，那不是我們的習慣，特別是男女之間。

B: OK. I guess a hug is out of the question, right?
好，我想擁抱就更不可能了，對嗎？

A : Of course. We've just met.
　　當然，我們才剛認識。

B : Perhaps we will become good friends in the future.
　　或許我們未來能成為好朋友。

> ### Saying goodbye.
> 和人道別。

B : Mr. and Mrs. Lin, I appreciate the hospitality that you offered.
　　林先生、林太太，謝謝你們的熱情款待。

A : Please take this box of tea back home as our token of friendship.
　　為表達我們的友誼，請收下這盒茶。

B : Thank you, Mrs. Lin. You shouldn't have.
　　謝謝你，林太太，你不用這麼客氣。

A : Where did you learn to bow like that? You are so respectful.
　　你從哪裡學到這樣鞠躬？你太敬重了。

B : My good friend told me I should learn the local customs. I have seen many people bow here during my visit.
　　我的好友說我應該學習當地習俗。我在這裡時，看到很多人這樣鞠躬。

A : Take care. Have a safe journey back home. Come back again.
　　保重，祝你一路順風，歡迎再來。

B : Thank you, so much. God bless you and your family. Farewell.
　　非常謝謝你，願主祝福你和你的家人，再見。

 NOTES

　　When having a business meeting in Taiwan, foriegners should learn the proper etiquette for meeting a person for the first time. In the USA, businesspersons exchange business cards, but the process in Taiwan and China seems to be more formal and ritualized. Whereas at an American business meeting a card can be handed to a person at any time, the Taiwanese prefer to exchange the cards at the first opportunity. In America, a business card may be slipped into a folder, or stapled to a piece of paper, or thrown onto a table. In Taiwan, it is customary to present the business card with two hands and offer a slight bow of the head. A show of respect seems to be important to this exchange process in Taiwan.

Sentences a Westerner might say
老外可能會說的句子

I am here to drop off a package. What's your name? I am glad to meet you.
我來送貨。你叫什麼名字？很高興認識你。

Hey! I know you. Steve, hello there.
嘿！我認識你，史帝夫，你好。

Just another delivery. Sally, greetings!
只是來送貨。莎莉，你好！

I have. Excuse me. What's your name? Bill? It's a pleasure.
吃了。抱歉，請問您的名字是？比爾？很榮幸認識你。

Oh Steve! Aloha, buddy!
喔，史帝夫！阿囉哈，兄弟！

Everything is going well. I have to make another delivery. I have to go now. Bye Steve!
一切都很好，我還得去送貨，我得走了，史帝夫，再見！

Right! Aloha can mean hello or goodbye. Ciao, Bill!
對！阿囉哈表示你好或再見。掰掰，比爾！

Sally, I hope to catch you later.
莎莉，我們晚點再聊。

Steve, see you later, alligator!
史帝夫，晚點見，再見！

Jamie, I hope you have a good day. Farewell.
傑米，希望你今天順利，再見。

Sentences a Taiwanese person might say.
台灣人可能會說的句子

I am Jamie. Thank you, Sam. I am also happy to meet you.
我是傑米，謝謝你，山姆，很高興認識你。

Hello Sam. What brings you here today?
哈囉，山姆，什麼風把你吹來？

Oh, hello Sam! Have you had lunch yet?
喔，哈囉，山姆！你吃午餐了嗎？

Yes, it is. And you are Sam? The pleasure is mine.
對，你是山姆嗎？我也很榮幸認識你。

Hey Sam! How's it going?
山姆！你好嗎？

Aloha, Sam!
阿囉哈，山姆！

OK Sam. See you later!
好，山姆，晚點見！

Sure, Sam. See you next time.
好，山姆，下次見。

After awhile, crocodile!
晚點見，再見！

You're quite the social delivery man. Be safe!
你真是友善的快遞人員，注意安全！

Featured Vocabulary

greeting (n.) 迎接

A greeting is an expression people make when they meet someone. A person can greet another orally, such as saying "Hello" or "How are you?" Or, he or she can also include a physical gesture, such as a handshake, hug, or even a kiss. There are informal and formal greetings as well. Greetings that are considered socially acceptable vary around the world. In Taiwan, people are typically conservative, with people asking, "How are you?" or "Are you full (have you eaten)?" Taiwanese may offer a slight bow or nod their heads, but they typically do not make physical contact. In Eastern countries, a bow may be appropriate in formal situations to show respect. In Western countries, handshakes are common, and if the people are familiar with each other, a hug or a kiss on the cheek is not out of the question. Two people who don't want to show too much affection may give high-fives with their hands, or bump their fists together, or they may offer a salute. In some indigenous cultures, touching noses is a common greeting. Different cultures have their preferable way to signal their recognition, affection, friendship or reverence when greeting people.

parting (n.) 離別

When parting, or leaving a person, one can offer parting words as a signal of acknowledgment. A person can part by saying their goodbyes (parting phrases). Just as in a greeting, there are verbal and physical expressions for parting, and they may be quite similar to the greetings. I have seen that during goodbyes, Taiwanese seem to be more relaxed about physical contact. I have seen that handshakes and hugs are more common at parting. In Western countries, it is very common to part with a handshake or hug. There are MANY English phrases used for parting for different occasions. These include: goodbye, bye, bye-bye, bless you, farewell, cheers, so long, take care, take it easy, talk to you later, and catch you later. Also, some foreign words are commonly used for parting words by English speakers. These include: Adieu (French), Au revoir (French), Ciao (Italian), and Aloha (Hawaiian).

UNIT 40

Feelings 感受

My wife told me that when she grew up in Taiwan, her parents told her it wasn't polite to sing or dance in public. She was told that expressing one's emotions in public wasn't suitable for a young lady. When I moved to Taiwan, I did notice people's hesitation to speak or laugh out loud. I noticed women who covered their mouths with their hands when they laughed, and their laughter was barely audible. My wife has spent enough years in America to adjust to the American ways of emotional expression, and she is still polite in public, but she is just not afraid to express her happiness. I did notice that the indigenous people were an exception to this rule. On my trips, my wife and I have enjoyed singing and dancing loudly to the moon when we were out with our indigenous friends. The indigenous people seemed to be as expressive as American people, if not more so.

Western visitors may be surprised to find how muted the emotional expression is in Taiwan. I have seen Westerners lose their temper in public, and crowds of people will stop to watch. It seems very rare that an emotional outburst will happen in public. Perhaps Taiwanese people have resorted to politeness and consideration to respect others and to avoid conflict. In a tiny, crowded island, it is not hard to see why people will want to stay harmonious. The stress of daily life is already very high for the Taiwanese. They don't need more to worry about. However, they should be aware that foreigners may be more expressive with their emotions, and be understanding of this cultural difference.

基本實用會話

Taiwanese (A)  Westerner (B)

A happy reaction
快樂的反應

B : Happy birthday, Rose! I hope you like it.
生日快樂，蘿絲，希望你喜歡。

A : Oh my goodness. That is a funny birthday card.
我的天啊，這張生日卡真有趣。

B : Yeah, I was rolling on the floor when I read it at the store. I knew you would get a kick out of it.
對，我在店裡看卡片差點笑倒在地。我就知道你也會喜歡。

A : It is brilliant. And what's this inside? Tickets to a concert?
太好笑了，裡面是什麼？音樂會的門票？

B : Sure. I'd like you to go with me. By the way, why did you cover your mouth when you read the card?
當然，我希望你跟我一起去。對了，你讀卡片的時候為什麼蓋住你的嘴巴？

A : I didn't want to laugh out loud and bother everyone in the office.
我不想要笑太大聲，打擾了辦公室其他人。

B : Yeah. I have noticed that people in Taiwan are usually very quiet.
對，我注意到台灣人通常都很安靜。

Expressing anger
表達憤怒

B : Hey you! How dare you? You almost hit us with your car.
喂，你！你好大膽？你差點開車撞到我們。

A : Steve! Take it easy. You're causing a scene.
史蒂夫！放輕鬆點，不要惹事。

B : What? Are you kidding? We were almost killed. Aren't you angry?
什麼？你開什麼玩笑？我們差點被撞死，你不生氣嗎？

A : Yes, I was scared. But I will keep my feelings to myself.
對，我嚇到了，但我不會表達情緒。

B : Why? I can't calm down unless I let it out.
為什麼？除非發洩一下，否則我無法冷靜。

A : But what good will that do? The guy is gone. And you are just attracting a lot of attention.
但那有什麼好處？那傢伙不見了，你只是在引人注意。

B : Is there anything wrong with that? I don't care about attracting attention. I am just angry. I'll calm down later.
那有什麼不對嗎，我不在乎引人注意，我很生氣，我晚一點就會冷靜了。

NOTES

Saving face is an Asian phenomenon that is an important fixture in Taiwanese social behavior. People are taught to show a good face to the public, and keep anything bad out of public view. For Westerners, they are used to people expressing their feelings directly. I personally like knowing when someone is sad or upset. It gives me to find out what the problem is so I can fix it. But more often than not, Taiwanese people will say everything is fine, and not share their feelings. They deal with their feelings in other ways, when other people are not around. I wouldn't say that is better or not than the Western way, but it does make it hard sometimes for foreigners to understand Taiwanese people.

Sentences a Westerner might say
老外可能會說的句子

Guess what? I have a new job. I'm on cloud nine!
你猜怎樣？我找到新工作了。我要飛上天了！

No! I'm not working on a cloud. I said that I'm a happy camper today.
不是！我不是在天上工作，我是說我今天是個快樂的露營者。

No, no! I'm just telling you that I am very happy today.
不，不！我只是說我今天非常高興。

I was hired as a lead actor for a TV travel show. It's my dream job.
我成為電視旅遊節目的男主角了，那是我夢寐以求的工作。

Why are you down in the dumps?
你為什麼跌入谷底？

Being down in the dumps means that you are feeling sad. Why are you blue?
跌入谷底的意思是你感覺很難過。你為什麼憂鬱？

I am sorry to hear about you losing your job. No wonder you are down in the mouth.
很遺憾聽到你失去工作了。難怪你嘴角下垂。

I am just saying, "no wonder you are sad."
我只是說，「難怪你很難過」。

I'm just using common English phrases to express happiness and sadness.
我只是用一般的英文片語表達快樂和傷悲。

Jamie, I hope you have a good day. Farewell.
傑米，希望你今天順利，再見。

Sentences a Taiwanese person might say.
台灣人可能會說的句子

What? Your job is on a cloud? How is that possible?
什麼？你的工作是在天上？怎麼可能？

Your job involves camping? Really?
你的工作還要露營？真的嗎？

OK. So what is your new job?
好。那你的新工作是什麼？

Well, that's the way to think positive. I can help you improve your Chinese if you'd like.
那麼想很正面，如果你需要的話，我能幫你改善你的英文。

I'm not in a dump. Why do you say that?
我沒有在谷底，你為什麼這麼說？

But I am not blue. I am sad. Why? Because, I lost my job today.
但我不憂鬱，我很難過。為什麼？我今天丟了工作。

Why are you talking about my mouth? You are confusing me.
你為什麼關心我的嘴巴？你的話讓我很困擾。

Why don't you just say so? Why are you saying all of those crazy things today?
你為什麼這麼說？你今天怎麼都說些亂七八糟的話？

Well, I guess I should learn more English phrases. I may need to improve my English to get a better job.
好吧，我猜我應該多學學英文片語。我得加強英文才能找到更好的工作。

I'd like that very much. Thank you.
我也很希望，謝謝你。

Featured Vocabulary

happiness (n.) 幸福

Happiness is the state of being happy. Another English word for happiness is "euphoria." There are many ways to express happiness in the English language. One can say, " I am delighted," or " I am pleased." To add more emphasis, one can say, "I'm over the moon," or "I'm pleased as punch." If one is happy with a situation they are experiencing, they can say, "I'm having a whale of a time," or "I'm having the time of my life." If a person says, "I'm on cloud nine," it means they are so happy that they feel like they are near heaven.

sadness (n.) 悲傷

Sadness is the state of being sad. Other English words for sadness are "sorrow" and "melancholy." There are many ways to express sadness in the English language. One can say," I am filled with grief," or " I am blue." To add more emphasis, one can say, "I'm in anguish," or "Woe is me." If one is sad because of a relationship, they can say, "I'm heartbroken," or "I have a heavy heart." If a person says, "Everything is looking bleak," it means they are so sad that they feel like they have no hope.

anger (n.) 憤怒

Anger is the state of being angry. Other English words for anger are "upset" and "ire." There are many ways to express anger in the English language. One can say," I am vexed,"or" I am miffed." To add more emphasis, one can say, "I am outraged," or "I am furious." If one shows their anger out loud, you can say, "they are throwing a tantrum" or "they are having a hissy fit."

UNIT 41

In Taiwan, I have received many offers and invitations from people, especially during social occasions involving meals. Hosts have insisted that I try their dishes, and encouraged me to eat more, even when I have been too full to eat. Many times, when I tried to refuse another dish or drink, their insistence became stronger. I usually gave in. Whenever I was invited to a social meal, I resigned myself to being stuffed until I was almost sick. Declining invitations have seemed harder to do in Taiwan than in the USA. But I can't complain. The hospitality in Taiwan has been marvelous. Instead of trying to decline invitations, I have learned to avoid the invitations, through distraction or by leaving the situation. I have gone to the bathroom a lot to avoid excessive eating and drinking.

Because they are often considered special guests, foreigners visiting Taiwan get invited often to join locals for meals and events. The invitations can be more than the visitor can handle, so they need to learn how to politely decline offers. My advice for Taiwanese people, when offering a foreigner a dish or drink to try, give them the feeling of choice. Don't say, "try this" or "you need to try this." Instead, ask the person, "would you like to try this?" and if they say "no," you shouldn't ask them again. The visitor may feel pressured and won't have a good impression from the experience. If you want a foreigner to try something, just show them how enjoyable it is, and their curiosity may take over.

基本實用會話

Taiwanese (A)  Westerner (B)

Making a request
提出請求

B: You are a good karaoke singer. You sounded very professional up there on stage.
你很會唱歌，你的聲音在舞台上聽來非常專業。

A: A: I chose an English song for the next one. You should come up and join me.
我下次會選首英文歌，你應該上台和我一起唱。

B: B: No, thanks. I don't sing very well.
不，謝謝，我不太會唱歌。

A: A: Please come up on stage with me. I chose the song just for you.
請跟我一起上台？我是為你選了這首歌。

B: B: No. Really. I don't want to embarrass myself.
不，真的，我不想丟臉。

A : A: Pretty please? It would mean a lot to me if you could join me for this song.
拜託啦？如果你能和我一起唱，對我意義重大。

B : B: Well. If you put it that way, how can I refuse?
好吧，你都這麼說了，我怎麼拒絕呢？

Declining an offer
拒絕請求

B : Thank you Mrs. Wu. Your dishes are delicious.
吳太太，謝謝你，餐點很好吃。

A : A: Teacher Steve, please try this one. It is a local specialty. It is part of a rooster, and the dish is stir fried.
史帝夫老師，請試試這道菜，這是特產，這也公雞的一部分，用大火快炒的。

B : B: Umm, what part? I think I will refuse your offer this time, Mrs. Wu.
嗯，哪一部分？我想這次要拒絕您的好意了，吳太太。

A : A: Are you sure? How will you know you won't like something unless you try it?
你確定？你沒試怎麼知道自己不喜歡？

B : B: You are right, but I don't want to try this one. I will pass on it.
你說得對，但我不想試這個，還是算了。

A : A: But a young man like you should eat more. Don't be afraid. Please help yourself.
但像你這樣的年輕人應該多吃一點。別害怕，自己挾。

B : B: Thank you for your hospitality and graciousness. I appreciate your offer. I will respectfully decline this time. I really am too full.
謝謝你的熱情和慷慨，也謝謝你的款待，這次真的要拒絕了，我已經太飽了。

NOTES

Declining an offer is an art form in Western culture. Not wanting to burn bridges for future opportunities, Westerners try to decline offers and invitations with respect and tactfulness. The key to preface the phrase with appreciation for the offer. For example, one can say, "Your offer is extremely attractive, but I have to decline at this time. Perhaps next time." It is often valuable to leave the door open for future opportunities. Sometimes, declining an offer can be a form of negotiation. "I would say yes to such a great offer in most circumstances, but at this moment, I need to politely decline." This statement allows the person making the offer to ask what the circumstances are, so he or she may have the opportunity to adjust the offer.

Sentences a Westerner might say
老外可能會說的句子

Cindy, would you like to go to the classical concert with me?
辛蒂，你想跟我去聽古典音樂會嗎？

Are you sure? I have two tickets. You won't have to pay anything for it.
真的？我有兩張票，你不用付錢。

Is there any reason you don't want to go?
有什麼不想去的理由嗎？

Sally, I just asked Cindy to go to the concert with me. But she refused.
莎莉，我剛邀辛蒂和我一起去聽音樂會，但她拒絕了。

It's a classical concert. Do you know why she would decline? She didn't give me a reason.
古典樂，你知道她為什麼拒絕嗎？她連理由都沒說。

Would you please tell me? I am puzzled.
可以告訴我嗎？我被搞糊塗了。

Thank you for telling me. I thought there was something wrong with me.
謝謝你告訴我，我還以為是我做錯了什麼。

Thanks. What will I do with this extra concert ticket?
謝謝，這張多出來的票要怎麼辦？

Oh, right. Sally, are you free Saturday night? If you are, would you like to go with me to the concert?
對，莎莉，你週六晚上有空嗎？如果有的話，你想跟我去聽音樂會嗎？

You're welcome. I'll come by and pick you up at 7:00pm.
不客氣，我七點來接你。

Sentences a Taiwanese person might say.
台灣人可能會說的句子

I appreciate the offer, Bob. But, I have to say no.
謝謝你的邀約，鮑伯。可是我得拒絕。

It's not about the money. It's a nice offer, but I will decline.
不是錢的問題，謝謝你的邀約，但我得拒絕。

Sorry, I have to go.
對不起，我得走了。

Really? What concert did you invite her to?
真的？你邀她去聽哪種音樂會？

Cool! I love classical music. I think I know why she didn't want to go with you.
酷！我喜歡古典樂。我想我知道她為什麼不想跟你去。

I don't think her boyfriend would like her going with you, and she doesn't want people to know she has a boyfriend.
我想她的男朋友不會希望她跟你出去，她也不想讓人知道她有男朋友。

I don't think there is anything wrong with you at all. I think you have good taste in music.
我想問題完全不在你身上，我覺得你對音樂很有品味。

Why don't you invite someone else?
你為什麼不邀請其他人？

Thank you. I would love to go. I appreciate you thinking of me.
謝謝你，我很想去，謝謝你邀請我。

I look forward to it.
我很期待。

Featured Vocabulary

request (v.) 請求

To request means to ask someone for something. There are several other English words that can be used. Using the word "request" or "desire" is more polite, whereas using "demand" is more forceful. There are many ways to ask for something, and most important word to use when making a request is "please." Some examples are, "May I please have some?" and "Would you please come with me?" Some people like to use terms of endearment when making a request. Such as, "Excuse me dear, but would you help an old woman cross the street?" Other common ways of making an invitation include, "Would you like to…," "Would you care to…," and "I would be very happy if…"

decline (v.) 下降

To decline means to turn down a request. There are several other English words that can be used. Using the words "no, thank you" is a polite response, whereas using "I refuse" or "I reject your offer" is more forceful. There are many ways to decline an offer, but it is important to use the words "thank you" to show appreciation to the person who made the offer. Other respectful ways to refuse an invitation include, "I'd like to, but…," "Thank you for asking, but…," and "Unfortunately, I can't…"

accept (v.) 接受

To accept means to agree to an invitation. There are other English words that can be used. Using the word "agree," "affirm" or "consent." There are many ways to respond with acceptance, and most important words to use when accepting is "thank you." Some examples are, "I accept your offer, thank you" and "Thank you, I am honored." Other common ways of accepting an invitation include, "I'd very much like to," "That's very kind of you," and "With great pleasure."

UNIT 42

One of the frustrations I have faced in Taiwan is how to deal with Taiwanese people's preference to avoid confrontation and conflict. There have been misunderstandings that have led to the unexplained disappearance of friends and acquaintences. What has been frustrating is that the misunderstandings could have been resolved through discussion, but they did not have the chance. What's worse is that misunderstandings are sometimes spread as gossip. I have grown up being taught that it is better to deal with problems with people face-to-face, take responsibility, listen to other people's perspectives, and try to work out a compromise. On many occassions, I have wanted to apologize or repair a relationship, and I never had a chance. I could say that this is one of the most disappointing aspects of living in Taiwan. Fortunately, I have become more familiar with the language, customs, and culture, and the conflicts have become less frequent.

With the combination of a culture gap and a language barrier, conflicts are common occurrences between foreigners living in Taiwan and local residents. Misunderstandings between foreign residents and locals just happen all of the time, but knowing how each culture deals with conflict and confrontation can make the difference between a successful relationship and a serious fight. Foreigners can learn how to deal with the locals' avoidance of negativity and confrontation. Taiwanese people can learn the value of being direct with foreigners. By understanding each other's culture better, there can be improved cross-cultural cooperation and harmony.

基本實用會話

Taiwanese (A) :  Westerner (B) :

A hopeless argument
絕望的爭論

B : I never agreed to work on Saturday mornings. This is unfair to expect me to do so.
我絕不同意週六早上工作。要求我這麼做是不公平的。

A : You need to do it. I am your boss.
你必須這麼做，我是你老闆。

B : But, when you hired me, I told you that my Saturdays were not available for work.
但當你雇用我時，我說過我週六不工作。

A : You foreigners are all the same. You only want to have fun and do what you want.
你們外國人都一樣，你只想玩樂，只想隨心所欲。

B : Us foreigners? Are you being prejudiced? I don't need to work for a prejudiced boss.
我們外國人？你是歧視嗎？我不需要為一個有歧視的老闆工作。

A : Really? Do you think it's so easy to get a good job like this one? Go find out for yourself.
真的嗎？你以為找到這樣的工作很容易嗎？自己去找找看。

B : I will. I am sure I will find a boss that will respect their promises.
我會的，我一定會找到一個講話懂得尊重的老闆。

A compromising negotiation
讓步的協調

B : I never agreed to work on Saturday mornings. This is unfair to expect me to do so.
我絕不同意週六早上工作。要求我這麼做是不公平的。

A : You are right, Susan, but this is a special case.
你說的對，蘇珊，但這是特殊案例。

B : My Saturdays are very precious me, Mr. Wu.
我的週六對我來說非常珍貴，吳先生。

A : We consider you an important part of the team at our school, and sometimes members of our team really need help. This time Teacher Mark has an emergency and needs a substitute.
我們認為你是學校團隊的重要份子，有時候我們的團隊需要幫助。這一次馬克老師有急事，他需要找人代課。

B : Well, thank you for making me feel important here.
謝謝你讓我覺得自己很重要。

A : We like to think that each of us can count on each other when the need arises. Can you help us?
當有需要的時候，我們彼此都要互相幫助，你能幫助我們嗎？

B : OK. I'll make an exception this time. Thank you for being forthcoming about the problem.
好，這次就當是例外，謝謝你用友好的態度解決這個問題。

NOTES

Prioritizing a harmonious society has been a cornerstone of Chinese culture for countless generations. This has contributed to one of the biggest differences between Chinese and Western cultures. From their perspective, Westerners may consider the way that Chinese people deal with disagreement and conflict is counterproductive and cowardly. In actuality, the Chinese culture teaches the avoidance of conflict and negativity in negotiation as the path to social harmony and unity. This includes the avoidance of confrontation and dominance. For Westerners to be effective at relations and negotiations with Chinese people, they should understand and practice this cultural difference, or they may just be avoided in the future.

Sentences a Westerner might say
老外可能會說的句子

Good morning, Frank. That was a lot of fun we had last night, right?
早安，法蘭克，我們昨晚玩得很開心，對嗎？

Where did you go? Why did you leave early?
你去了哪裡？你為什麼提早離開？

Really? I hope everything is OK at home.
真的？希望你家裡一切平安。

Is there anything wrong? Did something happen last night that I should know about?
還好嗎？我該知道昨晚發生什麼事嗎？

Steve, what's wrong with Frank? He hasn't talked to me all day.
史帝夫，法蘭克怎麼了？他整天不跟我說話。

Oh, no! Why does this happen so often in Taiwan? How can I know what went wrong if no one is willing to discuss it?
喔不，為什麼在台灣常發生這種事？如果大家不願意討論，我怎麼知道出了什麼問題？

No. Please tell me, so I can do something about it. I don't want to lose Frank as a friend.
不，請告訴我，我才能想想辦法。我不想失去法蘭克這個朋友。

Frank is Cindy's boyfriend? I had no idea she had a boyfriend when I asked her.
法蘭克是辛蒂的男朋友？我邀她的時候不知道她有男朋友。

Now I understand. Now I can do something to resolve it. Thank you, Steve.
現在我明白了，我能想辦法解決這個問題。謝謝你，史帝夫。

Frank, I am sorry about asking Cindy to the concert. I didn't know you two were going out. Let me make it up to you. I'll give you the two concert tickets to take her on a date.
法蘭克，邀辛蒂去音樂會的事我很抱歉，我不知道你們倆個在約會。讓我補償你，我會給你兩張音樂會門票，你帶她去約會吧。

Sentences a Taiwanese person might say.
台灣人可能會說的句子

(Frank) Yeah, sure.
（法蘭克）對，當然。

I had an emergency I had to take care of at home.
我家裡有急事得處理。

Sorry, I have to get back to work.
抱歉，我得工作了。

No, nothing. Really.
不，沒事，真的。

(Steve) He just wants to avoid a confrontation with you.
（史帝夫）他只是想避免和你起衝突。

You don't know why he is upset?
你不知道他為什麼生氣？

All right. He found out that you asked his girlfriend Cindy to go to a concert with you.
好吧，他發現你邀他的女朋友辛蒂去音樂會。

I know you asked Sally, but, Steve feels threatened by you.
我知道你約了莎莉，但史帝夫覺得你威脅到他了。

Maybe you're right. It's just not part of our culture to confront people.
或許你說的對，但我們的文化不喜歡和人起衝突。

(Frank) Well, I guess everyone can make a mistake. I appreciate your offer.
（法蘭克）嗯，我想每個人都可能犯錯，謝謝你請客。

Featured Vocabulary

conflict (n.) 衝突

When people disagree about something, they can have a conflict. Disagreements are natural with different points of view, but the wrong choice of language can intensify conflict. There are some language skills that can help reduce conflict with Westerners.

1) Avoid using negativity or insults to label the other person. For example, saying "You foreigners are all liars" will likely destroy any chance of compromise.
2) Don't ignore or minimize the feelings of the other person. For example, don't say something like, "Honestly, I don't care what you think. You're not from around here."
3) Don't blame the person with "you" statements. For example, you shouldn't say, "We wouldn't have this problem, if YOU did what I asked."
4) Don't be condescending. An example of a condescending phrase is, "You mean to tell me that you have only now understood what the problem is?"
5) Don't question the other person's honesty, integirty or intelligence. For example, you shouldn't say, "Do you expect me to believe that you didn't have time to come to our meeting?"
6) Finally, don't base the meanings of what the other person is saying based on stereotypes of prejudice. An example of this would be, "All you foreigners ever think about is having things the way you want."

apology (n.) 道歉

Apologizing, of giving someone an apology, can be an effective to diffuse a conflict or confrontational situation. The most common way to apologize in English is to simply say, "I'm sorry." It doesn't admit fault, nor does it add any more friction to the situation. You can also say, "I apologize for the difficulty you have having with this situation" to reduce the friction without taking responsibility for the conflict. Apologizing can help lower the level of conflict, but the most effective way I have found to settle a conflict completely is to accept responsibility for conflicts, because being compassionate and generous has offered more rewards than being righteous.

Learning about Taiwan — History, Culture, Scenery...

人文史地在台灣

UNIT 43

History 歷史

Growing up in the USA, I had little opportunity to know about Taiwan's history. I only knew that settlers from China lived in Taiwan for hundreds of years before Japan took over the territory, and then it was ceded to the Republic of China after World War II. Once I decided to move to Taiwan, I did more research and increased my knowledge of the history. Traveling around Taiwan to its historic sites also expanded my understanding. I have been very surprised about the diversity of Taiwanese history, with its indigenous peoples, the mainland Chinese immigrants, the European colonists, the Japanese empire, and the Republic of China. The more details I have learned, the more fascinated I have become about this island. Unfortunately, almost all of the Taiwanese college students I have met have only a superficial knowledge of Taiwan's history outside of its relationship with China. To me, it is sad, because they cannot fully appreciate Taiwan's place in the world, without a broader context.

Most people outside of Taiwan know little about Taiwan's history, but when they tour the island, they are usually surprised by the historic complexity that they find. When they visit the ancient indigenous sites, or the Dutch forts, or the Japanese-style hot springs, they usually marvel at the many international influences that were a part of Taiwan's history. This historic and cultural diversity is actually something that add value to the experience that foreigners have in Taiwan.

基本實用會話

Taiwanese (A) : Westerner (B) :

Tourist discovering Taiwanese history
觀光客探索台灣歷史

B : Fort Zeelandia used to be the capital of the Dutch colony in Formosa almost 400 years ago.
荷蘭在四百年前殖民台灣時,安平古堡曾是首都。

A : That's right. Taiwan was colonized by the Dutch during the 1600's.
沒錯,台灣在17世紀時曾受荷蘭殖民。

B : That's amazing. I thought Taiwan was just populated by Chinese people.
太神奇了,我以為台灣一直都只有中國人居住。

A : Actually, during that time, Taiwan already had many other indigenous cultures.
其實,那時候台灣已經有許多原住民文化。

B : Really? I didn't know that. I never heard about indigenous cultures in Taiwan.
真的嗎？我不知道。我從沒聽過台灣的原住民文化。

A : Also, settlers from mainland China arrived in Taiwan about 500 years ago.
還有，大約五百年前，中國大陸就開始有人來台灣定居。

B : I am looking forward to learning more about Taiwan's history during my trip.
我很期待在旅行中學習台灣的歷史。

Taiwanese student's view of history
台灣學生的歷史觀

B : Didn't you learn about Taiwan's history when it was a territory of Japan?
你們的台灣史有沒有學到，台灣曾是日本領土的一部分？

A : Yes, in 1895 the Japanese conquered Taiwan.
對，在1895年時日本占領台灣。

B : Well, actually, the Chinese Qing Dynasty gave up Taiwan to Japan with the Treaty of Shimonoseki.
事實上，是中國的清朝在馬關條約中將台灣割讓給日本。

A : I heard that the Japanese were ruthless occupiers during their time in Taiwan.
我聽說日本占領台灣時非常殘忍。

B : That may be true. But many older Taiwanese people preferred the way they were governed by the Japanese rather than by the Republic of China.
可能是吧，但許多台灣老人比較喜歡日據時期，而非中華民國。

A : How do you know so much about our history?
你怎麼這麼了解我們的歷史？

B : I just took the time to read the history books that are available in English.
我剛花了點時間閱讀英文歷史書。

NOTES

I personally believe that Americans have had a chance to heal from the wounds of past atrocities committed by authorities when the U.S. government formally apologized for those past mistakes. Sharing the voices of the victims and holding people responsible for acts like the massacre of millions of American Indians and the enslavement of Africans has helped society to heal and avoid repeating the mistakes. In Taiwan, I don't believe there has been enough done to teach the younger generation about the horrors and atrocities of the "White Terror" period (1949-1987) of Taiwanese history under martial law. Most young adults I talk to know very little about this period of history, so I believe there should be more done to educate younger generations. Without these efforts, the freedoms that Taiwanese have won with their blood and tears may vanish in the future.

Sentences a Westerner might say
老外可能會說的句子

I just came back from a one-week tour of the island.
我剛結束一週的環島行程。

It was fascinating. I learned so much about this island's history.
太棒了，我學到好多這個島的歷史。

I toured the National Museum of Prehistory in Taitung and learned that people settled here more than 10,000 years ago.
我去了台東的史前博物館，知道這裡超過一萬年前就有人居住。

And many groups came to Taiwan since then, with their own language and culture.
許多族群從那之後遷移來台灣，帶著他們的語言和文化。

And I saw the ancient obelisks in Peimen Culture Park. Did you know the Bunun had a form of written language 2,000 years ago?
我還到北門文化公園看了古老的方尖碑。你知道布農族在兩千年前曾經有文字嗎？

Then, we went up to Ruifang District near Keelung.
我們還去了基隆附近的瑞芳。

I learned a lot about the colonial Japanese history of that place. The Gold Mine Museum and the hot springs were nice attractions.
我聽了許多那個地方的日本殖民史。黃金博物館和溫泉都是很好的景點。

I visited old Fort San Domingo in Tamsui. I didn't realize the Spanish colonized Taiwan.
我參觀了淡水古老的紅毛城。我不知道西班牙也殖民過台灣。

That's something I already knew, because I have visited Fort Zeelandia in Tainan City before.
那我已經知道了，因為我已經去過台南的安平古堡。

I look forward to sharing the history of Taiwan with other people. I don't think people in my country know much about it.
我很期待跟其他人分享台灣的歷史。我想我家鄉的人不知道這些事。

Sentences a Taiwanese person might say.
台灣人可能會說的句子

Welcome back. How was your trip?
歡迎回來，旅行好玩嗎？

Really? Please share what you learned with me.
真的，請和我分享你聽到了什麼。

Yes, I learned about that in school. They crossed over a land bridge from the mainland.
對，我在學校學過。他們從大陸跨過陸橋而來。

Right. We have fifteen indigenous groups now, but we had many more than that before.
對，我們現在有十五個原住民族，但以前更多。

That is something I didn't know. That's quite an accomplishment.
這一點我不知道，真是了不起的成就。

That's a beautiful area of Taiwan.
那裡很漂亮。

I've been there. The Japanese ruled Taiwan for 60 years until 1945.
我去過那裡，到1945年前，日本統治台灣六十年。

That was almost 400 years ago. And the Dutch also colonized South Taiwan.
幾乎是四百年前的事了，荷蘭也殖民過南台灣。

There was a lot of Dutch influence in Taiwan for a long time.
荷蘭對台灣的影響持續了很長的時間。

I think Taiwanese people also have a lot to learn about their own history.
我想台灣人對自己的歷史也有待學習。

Featured Vocabulary

colony (n.) 殖民地

A colony is an area of land settled and administered by an occupying country without being given autonomy. During the time an area is ruled by an occupying country, it is known as a colonial period. Taiwan had several colonial periods, being ruled by the Chinese Dynasties, Spanish, and Dutch. Some Taiwanese consider the authoritarian rule of the KMT under the Republic of China to be a colonial period. With the development of Taiwan's democracy, some people feel that Taiwan is finally a self-ruled island, although international recognition is complicated by politics.

martial law (n.) 戒嚴

After the Kuomingtang (KMT) took over the island in 1945, the leader, President Chiang instituted Martial Law. Martial law is the suspension of the rule of law by a military government. The time of martial law in Taiwan lasted from 1949 to 1987, giving the leaders of the Republic of China great powers and control over the people of the island. Because of the constant fear of infiltration by Communist spies, the human rights of many were abused by the enforcers of this law. There are many published account in English by the survivors of the "White Terror" period of Taiwan's history, which shines the light on untold abuses and misery suffered by ordinary Taiwanese people during that time. With the lifting of martial law, Taiwan could plot a course towards normalcy, and eventually democracy.

Geography 地理

Before I came to Taiwan in 1993, I expected to see a Pacific island with beaches, palm trees, farms and cities. During my first visit, I was stunned by the variety of geography and climate. I visited the metropolitan city of Taipei, and settled in the mountainous village of Wulai. I was dazzled by the butterflies, waterfalls and mist that surrounded me. It was like a fairy tale. Then we went to Sun Moon Lake in Nantou, and I was surrounded by alpine forests. Then we drove through the Cross-Island Highway, and my breath was taken away, literally. The scary road though the center of the island revealed grand mountains and treacherous cliffs. When we stopped at a rest area, the elevation was so high, that I lost my breath after walking just a few steps. Once we arrived in Hualien, I took a walk on a beach under palm trees, and went whale watching in the sea. I returned to America after that trip and told everyone I knew that Taiwan had the geography and beauty of an entire continent in a small, beautiful package.

If they leave Taipei City to explore the island, most visitors in Taiwan are stunned by the beauty and geographic diversity that is offered. Because of this diversity, there are many amazing types of landscapes to explore, as well as many outdoor activities. The land not only offers much to do, but provides the abundance that supports the splendid flora and fauna that make Taiwan a natural paradise. Many people leave Taiwan feeling like the Taiwanese are very fortunate to have so much in such a small place.

基本實用會話

Taiwanese (A)  Westerner (B)

Tourist discovering Taiwanese geography
觀光客探索台灣的地理

B : We are so high up. I can barely get enough oxygen. Do I see snow on that mountain peak?
這裡好高,我快吸不到氧氣了,在山頂上能看到雪嗎?

A : Yes, you do. Did you know Taiwan has the second tallest mountain range in Asia?
可以,你知道亞洲第二高山在台灣嗎?

B : I didn't know that. The Himalayas are the tallest. That makes for great mountain climbing.
我不知道,喜馬拉雅是最高的山,所以登山客很多。

A： And hiking, bungee jumping, paragliding and white water rafting. There is so much to do.
還有健行，高空彈跳，滑翔傘和泛舟，有很多活動。

B： I look forward to trying them all out. What's next for us during this trip?
我很期待全都試試。這趟旅行接下來要做什麼？

A： I was hoping we could travel south of the Tropic of Cancer and spend a few days at the beach.
我想要去北回歸線以南旅遊，在沙灘上停留幾天。

B： Great idea! I like relaxing as much as I enjoy being active.
好主意！我喜歡放鬆，也喜歡到處活動。

Taiwanese student learning about geography
台灣學生學習地理

B： Jeff, you are truly fortunate to live in a place with so much geographic diversity.
傑夫，你運氣真好，能住在地理這麼多樣化的地方。

A： What do you mean?
什麼意思？

B： When I lived in Florida, which is larger than Taiwan, all we had was flat land, pine forests, swamps and beaches.
佛羅里達比台灣大多了，但我住在那裡時，我們只有平原、松林、沼澤和沙灘。

A： I like beaches. But, I heard that Florida is a fun place to live.
我喜歡沙灘，不過聽說住在佛羅里達很有趣。

B： That may be true. But Taiwan has much more to do because of your mountains and valleys.
或許是真的，但台灣可以做的事比較多，因為你們還有山脈和峽谷。

A： I haven't had a chance to explore much of Taiwan yet. I have been too busy studying.
我還沒機會探索台灣，我都忙著念書。

B： If you travel more, you will be able to understand how lucky you are to live in Taiwan.
如果你多花點時間旅遊，就知道你住在台灣有多幸運了。

NOTES

I have lived around the world, and have enjoyed the unique beauty offered by each country I visited. After exploring Taiwan, I believe that the island is a diamond amoung pebbles. It offers so much diversity, and the reason why is its diverse geography and climate. Sitting on fault lines, the island was formed by extreme geological forces, forcing high mountains into the sky. Its position in the Pacific Ocean on the tropic of Cancer also affects the climates that Taiwan posseses. With tropical, subtropical, temperate and alpine climates, there is also an amazing diversity in plant life, animal life and food available to the Taiwanese. This has attracted people throughout the centuries, giving Taiwan its variety of cultures. There is also an incredible variety in activities available. This diversity that is unique to Taiwan makes the island one of the most unique places on Earth.

Sentences a Westerner might say
老外可能會說的句子

I just came back from a trip to Penghu.
我剛從澎湖旅遊回來。

I did! But what was amazing was that I felt like I was in another country. The terrain there was quite different.
有，但最棒的是我覺得自己好像出了國，那裡的景色非常不同。

Well, it was dry, like a desert with many cacti. I enjoyed the cactus ice cream there.
那裡很乾，就像有很多仙人掌的沙漠，我喜歡那裡的仙人掌冰淇淋。

Sure, they do. But nice beaches are not unique there. Actually they have very unique rock formations.
對，是有沙灘，但並不十分獨特。其實他們獨特的是岩層結構。

Jimmy, you are so lucky to live in Taiwan.
吉米，你好幸運能住在台灣。

Here, you have so many types of terrain within a short distance.
你們在這麼短的距離裡就有很多種不同的地形。

You're right. But you have to travel great distances to reach different types of terrain.
你說得對，但你得走很遠，才能看到不同的地形。

Exactly! In Taiwan, no matter where you are, you are only a few hours away from beaches, tall mountains, lush forests, waterfalls, or even deserts.
沒錯，無論你在台灣的哪個地方，只要幾小時就能抵達沙灘、高山、茂密的森林、瀑布，甚至是沙漠。

Sure. And I am thoroughly enjoying your homeland while I am here.
當然，我非常喜歡你的家鄉。

Of course! A foreigner is an unlikely tour guide for a Taiwanese man, but I'll be happy to.
不客氣！外國人最不可能當台灣人的導覽了，但我很樂意這麼做。

Sentences a Taiwanese person might say.
台灣人可能會說的句子

How was your experience? Did you enjoy the seafood?
玩得如何？你有吃海鮮嗎？

I haven't been to Penghu yet, so please tell me what is different about it.
我還沒去過澎湖，請告訴我那裡有什麼不同。

Wow! That is surprising. I only heard that those islands had nice beaches.
哇！太令人驚訝了，我只聽說那裡有很漂亮的沙灘。

Your photos are very interesting. They make me want to visit there.
你的照片看來非常有趣，讓我也想去看看了。

Well, I always wanted to live in the UK or the USA.
這個嘛，我總是想住在英國或美國。

I know that can be very expensive.
我知道那可能很貴。

But the USA has all types of terrain as well.
可是美國也有各種地形。

Indeed! I have much to explore in my own homeland before I explore the world.
的確！在我探索這個世界前，我的家鄉還有很多地方等著我探索。

Can I join you on your next weekend trip.
下個週末我能跟你一起出去玩嗎？

Thank you, Steve. I appreciate your guidance.
謝謝你，史帝夫，謝謝你的導覽。

Featured Vocabulary

terrain (n.) 地形

In English, if you are referring to the type of geography area in an area, you are describing the "terrain." Someone may ask you, "What type of terrain do you live in?" or "What types of terrain does your country have?" You can tell them that Taiwan offers an incredible variety of terrains, such as beaches, lakes, rivers, flatlands, highlands, high mountains, pine forests, and subtropical forests.

lowlands (n.) 低地

When describing an area that is typically flat, you can use the English word, "lowlands." Ninety percent of Taiwanese people live in the lowlands of Western Taiwan, which covers only twenty percent of the island. In the lowlands of Taiwan are most of Taiwan's major cities, industry, and agriculture. It is hard to imagine that almost 27 million people can live in such a small area.

highlands (n.) 高地

When describing an area that is hilly or mountainous, you can use the English word, "highlands." Eighty percent of Taiwan is considered highlands. This terrain can also be separated into two types of terrain; hills and mountains. Taiwan's highlands is comprised of five rugged mountain ranges, which are parallel to each other. They also have six mountain peaks that are over 3,500 meters tall. Mt Yu Shan rises 3,952 meters above sea level, which makes Taiwan the 4th highest island in the world.

Religions 宗教

Wandering around Taiwan, I couldn't help but to notice how many temples there were. In America, I was used to seeing churches everywhere, but not temples. So, the temples seemed so fascinating to me, with intricate carvings and statues that seemed to tell moral stories. I have seen some incredibly large, lavish temples and many very tiny temples or altars by the roadside. There is quite the variety. Most people's homes seem to have an altar of some type in a room dedicated to prayer. I learned that most of the temples I saw were for the Taoist religion, which is practiced by 1/3 of Taiwanese citizens. They usually borrowed their intricate design from Southeast China. Some temples I visited were for the Buddhist religion, which is practiced by a little over 1/3 of the Taiwanese. There were some temples dedicated to famous historical or religious figures, such as Confucius and General Guan Yu.

Most visitors to Taiwan practice a religion other than Taiwan's predominant religions, so they often are interested in exploring the unfamiliar sights and sounds from Taiwan's temples. Christian visitors staying in Taiwan may be relieved to find out that there are plenty of Christian churches available for many different denonimations. Taiwan's indigenous communities have been predominantly Catholic or Protestant since the Europeans brought their religions to Taiwan hundred of years ago, replacing their worship of nature. Christian churches are abundant in most cities and towns, but foreigners may have a hard time finding a service offered in English, unless they go to a big church in a big city.

基本實用會話

Taiwanese (A)  Westerner (B)

Discovering the Tainan Confucian Temple
探訪台南孔子廟

B: Why are all of these students lined up outside of this temple?
這些學生為什麼在這座廟外面排隊？

A: We are at the Tainan Confucian Temple (台南孔子廟). There are a few others in Taiwan.
這裡是台南孔子廟。台灣還有幾個地方也有孔子廟。

B: It does look different than the other temples. There are no statues of gods in here.
看起來和其他廟不同，這裡沒有神像。

A: It is also called the "Scholarly Temple" and promotes the teachings of Confucius.
這裡是所謂的「學術聖殿」，推崇的是孔子的教學。

B : I heard of him. He is one of the wisest people in Chinese history.
我聽過他，他是中國歷史上最聰明的人之一。

A : Today is Confucius Day, or Teacher's Day. The students are here to participate in an ancient ceremony to worship the greatest teacher, Confucius.
今天是孔子誕生日，或稱為教師節。這裡的學生都是來參加古老的儀式，向最偉大的教師孔子致敬。

B : I see. So, in Taiwan some people are actually worshipped like a deity. Amazing!
我懂了，那麼在台灣，有些人真的會像神致敬，真神奇

Discovering a Buddhist Temple
探訪佛教寺廟

B : This temple is beautiful! It doesn't have the ornate dragons and gods of the other ones.
這座廟好漂亮，裡面沒有雕龍，也沒有其他神祇。

A : That's because this is one of the Buddhist temples. Their designs are simpler.
因為這是一座佛教寺廟，這裡的設計比較簡單。

B : I heard of Buddha. He came from India, right?
我聽過佛陀，他來自印度，對嗎？

A : Yes, but there are different incarnations of Buddha that people worship in Taiwan as deities.
對，但台灣人視為神祇崇拜的佛陀有不同的形象。

B : Which deity is worshipped here? This does not look like a Buddha statue that I recognize.
這裡崇拜的是什麼神？看起來不像我認識的佛陀雕像。

A : This deity, or bodhisattva, is named Kuanyin, or the Goddess of Mercy.
這座神祇，或說是菩薩，名叫觀音，是大慈大悲之神。

B : There is much I can learn about Buddhism, because there is more variety to it than I thought.
佛教要學的事還好多，因為比我想像的複雜多了。

NOTES

In many countries, foreigners are actually introduced to Taiwanese religion and culture through the Buddhist Compassion Relief Tzu Chi Foundation (慈濟基金會). Taiwanese who live all over the world learn Buddhist teachings at Tzu Chi centers around the world, and share Buddhists principles to communities in many countries. But the main focus of their teaching is spreading love and compassion through "action." As a result of the mission of this organization, thousands of people every year are beneficiaries of their relief efforts, and the organization is held in high esteem worldwide. As a result, Taiwan also gets positive public relations from the efforts of the compassionate and generous members. Tzu Chi also builds hospitals and schools to help even more people learn how to give their professional skills to more people in the world.

Sentences a Westerner might say
老外可能會說的句子

This temple looks very ancient. The carvings and paintings seem to tell different stories.
這座廟看來非常古老。裡面的雕刻和繪畫似乎在訴說不同的故事。

This is confusing. Why are there altars for so many different statues? Are these deities?
我搞不懂了，為什麼祭壇上有這麼多不同的神像？這些是什麼神？

I have only learned how to worship one god. And this statue looks like a Buddha.
我只知道如何敬拜一個神。這個雕刻看來好像佛陀。

Wow! So Buddhists aren't the only ones who worship Buddha. I didn't know that.
哇！那麼佛教不只敬拜佛陀，我不知道這一點。

I think this religion must be very complicated. Look at these sculptures. They each seem to tell a story.
我覺得這宗教一定非常複雜，你看這些雕像，他們每一尊看來都有一個故事。

In my religion, there is a heaven and hell. We are also taught how to go to heaven.
在我的宗教裡有天堂和地獄，我們也學習如何才能上天堂。

But these sculptures look very scary. They show beings with cow heads and horse heads.
但這些雕像看來非常嚇人，他們有牛頭和馬頭。

And look at all of these people being stabbed, cooked or crushed. They have to endure so much pain!
你看這些人都被刺、被煮或被壓碎了，他們得承受好大的痛苦。

Churches preach about the consequences of evil, too. But this seems too gruesome.
教堂也宣講邪惡的下場，但這看來太可怕了。

Could you please help me find one that is convenient? I really want to find one to go to.
能不能幫我找家方便一點的？我真的想找家教堂。

Sentences a Taiwanese person might say.
台灣人可能會說的句子

It's true. This is a Taoist Temple. There are many throughout Taiwan.
是的，這是道觀，台灣有很多道觀。

Yes, these are different gods worshipped by the Taoists.
對，道教崇拜的神祇很多。

It is a statue of Buddha. This is only one of the deities that are part of Taoist folklore.
這是佛陀像，他只是道教傳說裡的其中一個神祇。

Correct. And this very old wooden doll is Matsu, the goddess of the sea.
沒錯，這尊看來很舊的木偶是媽祖，海神。

Growing up, we are taught many Taoist stories to help us to avoid being bad and going to hell.
我們長大的時候都學習很多道教的故事，教我們不做壞事，才不會下地獄。

Taoists also have a heaven, but there are different "levels" of heaven.
道教也有天堂，但有不同「層次」的天堂。

Look here. We also have demons, just like in your religion.
你看這裡，我們也有惡魔，就像你們的宗教一樣。

I think the temples are meant to scare the Taoist followers to become good people.
我想廟宇是為了嚇阻道教徒，要他們成為一個好人。

I would be interested in seeing how different it is going to a church.
我也想看看教堂有什麼不同。

No problem. There are many, but it may be difficult to find one that speaks English.
沒問題，教堂有很多，但要找家英文教堂可能有點困難。

Featured Vocabulary

god vs. deity (n.) 神

In English, if you are referring to a "god" or "deity," they both have the same meaning, but "god" is often used to describe "the only being" of supreme power. Whereas "a deity" is used to refer to a being" of divine power, when there is a belief that there is more than one deity. Worshipping only one god is called "monotheism," and a religion that worships only one god is known as a "monotheistic" religion. One example of a monotheistic religion is Christianity. Worshipping multiple deities is know as "polytheism," and a religion that worships multiple deities is known as "polytheistic" religion. One example of a polytheistic religion is Taoism.

house of worship (n.) 祭祀處所

House of worship is a general term used to describe a place where people gather to worship deities or a god. It is a general term. Specific terms are used for different religions. Christians use the term, "church." Jews use the term, "synagogue." Islamist use the term, "mosque." Buddhists, Taoists, and Hindi use the term, "temple."

Taiwan's religions (n.) 台灣的宗教

The original religions in Taiwan were the paganistic religions that worshipped nature. These were practiced by Taiwan's ancient indigenous peoples. Hundreds of years ago, immigrants from the South Chinese mainland introduced Buddhism and Taoism. Around the same time, Dutch settlers introduced Protestant Christianity to the indigenous people. Spanish settlers introduced Catholicism to the locals on the island. With the arrival of the Japanese in 1895, other Buddhist religions and Shintoism were introduced. After World War II, some members of the Kuomingtang introduced Islam from Westrn China. Taiwan is a religious melting pot, showing how tolerant people of different religions can be living together on a small island. According to government figures in 2005, the predominant religions of Taiwan are: Buddhism (35%), Taoism (33%), Yiguandao (3.5%), Protestantism (2.6%) and Catholicism (1.3%).

Languages 語言

During my first tour of Taiwan, I was offered greetings wherever I went. However, the greetings were sometimes different, depending on where I was in Taiwan. Most people I met offered me the phrase, "ni hao ma?" This is, of course, Mandarin Chinese, for "How are you?" This is the official language on the island, but in Southern Taiwan, most people said, "li huh buh?" This is the same phrase in Taiwanese language. In some communities, people greeted me with, "ng hoh!" I later found out that these were Hakka communities, where people spoke Hakkanese. In a mountain village, I was greeted with, "Loka su ga?" This is the same phrase in the indigeous Atayal language. Also, some Taiwanese elders actually greeted me in Japanese, saying, "Genkidesu ka?" I couldn't believe how many languages I heard during my first trip to Taiwan. It was confusing and frustrating sometimes, when I couldn't rely on my Chinese-English dictionary.

Visitors to Taiwan prepare to communicate with the locals by studying Mandarin Chinese or bringing a dictionary or phrase book. That is fine, as Mandarin is spoken by a majority of Taiwanese, because it has been taught by the school system since 1945. However, you will often find locals speaking their native languages. Taiwanese is spoken by about 70% of the population. Most Taiwanese people are descendants of immigrants from what is today the Fujian Province of mainland China. Only about 3% of the population can speak Hakka language and Hakka people in Taiwan immigrated from another area of South China. There are about 2% of the population who are indigenous people, and there are 15 official indigenous tribes with their own languages.

基本實用會話

Taiwanese (A) Westerner (B)

Listening to village elders
聽村裡的老人說話

B: Do you hear that, Jenny? Those two women are talking to each other in a strange language.
你聽到了嗎，珍妮？那兩個女人在聊天。

A: Well, we are in a remote village. Let me hear what they are speaking.
這裡是偏遠的村莊，我來聽聽他們在說什麼。

B: How interesting. I never thought I would hear anything other than Chinese spoken in Taiwan.
真有趣，我沒想過在台灣能聽到中文以外的語言。

A : Well, we are in an indigenous area, so they might be members of a tribe.
這裡是原住民區，所以他們可能是部落的成員。

B : I heard there are fifteen tribes left in Taiwan, each with its own language.
我聽說台灣有十五個部落，每一個都有自己的語言。

A : I think I heard the ladies speaking Japanese, too. That is what they were taught as children.
我還聽到他們也說了日文，他們小時候學了日文。

B : I see. So, Taiwan is truly a place that is diverse and rich in language and culture.
我懂了，所以，台灣真的是個多元化的地方，語言和文化都很豐富。

Talking to a local farmer
和地方農夫聊天

B : Hello! Can you help me? I am lost. "Ni hao ma? Ni kuei bangmang wo, ma?"
你好！你能幫我嗎？我迷路了。「你好嗎？你可以幫忙我嗎？」

A : "Tia buh. (我聽不懂)"
我聽不懂。

B : Please look at this map. Do you know where to find this school? "Je-ge xieshiao tsai na li?"
請看看這張地圖，你知道這學校在哪裡嗎？「這個學校在哪裡？」

A : "Gua em tsai. (我不知道)"
我不知道。

B : Excuse me. This lady doesn't seem to understand my English or Chinese. Can you help me?
抱歉，這位小姐似乎聽不懂我的英文或中文。你能幫幫我嗎？

A : Sure. She is an elder who can only speak Taiwanese. She probably doesn't know much Chinese.
當然，這位老人家只會說台語，她或許不太會說中文。

B : Thanks for letting me know. I thought my Chinese was not good enough for her.
謝謝你告訴我，我以為我的中文對她來說不夠好。

NOTES

The Japanese language is not considered one of the native languages of the Taiwanese people, but from 1895-1945, it was the official language, and the only language taught in public schools. It is not surprising to find many people who still know how to speak Japanese. People who are over 80 years old were taught Japanese during their childhood years, but they may not remember much, if they had not used it frequently. But there are many elders, especially in the remote indigenous villages who continue to speak to each other in a mixture of Japanese language and their own native indigenous language. These days, I have seen many of the younger generation choose to study Japanese, because of their interest in Japanese pop culture. It may be possible that the Japanese language may be heard more often in Taiwan in the future.

Sentences a Westerner might say
老外可能會說的句子

It's nice to meet you, too, Stephanie. I am here to study the Chinese language.
我也很高興認識你，史蒂芬妮。我是來這裡學中文的。

No. I am studying to be a linguist. I am actually fascinated by language.
不，我是語言學家，其實我很著迷於這個語言。

Well, sort of. A linguist is a person who studies linguistics, or the science of language.
算是吧。語言學家是研究語言的人，或是研究語言科學的人。

Yes. I think I will be studying languages my entire life. There are so many of them.
對，我想我這輩子會一直研究語言，語言的種類很多。

It's possible. For now, I will enjoy learning about the languages of Taiwan.
有可能。目前我很喜歡學習台灣的語言。

I would like to study Taiwanese and Hakkanese.
我想學台語和客家語。

They don't have their own written language, but their oral language is very different from Chinese.
他們沒有自己的文字，但他們的口說語言和中文非常不同。

I have read about them. They are part of the Austronesian language family.
我讀過這個，他們屬於南島語族。

No. "Austronesian" means from the south islands.
不，南島語族的意思是來自南邊的島嶼。

Well, what are you studying here at the University, Stephanie.
史蒂芬妮，你在大學都學些什麼？

Sentences a Taiwanese person might say.
台灣人可能會說的句子

Oh, are you here to learn Mandarin for business?
喔，你是來學商業中文的嗎？

What is a linguist? Is that a job?
什麼是語言學家？那是一種工作嗎？

Oh! So, your future job is to be a scholar?
喔，那你未來的工作是當學者嗎？

Perhaps you will be a professor one day.
或許你有天會成為一名教授。

Well, there are quite a few. You may be surprised.
種類還不少，你或許會感到驚訝的。

Why do you want to learn them? Most foreigners don't learn those languages.
你為什麼想學？很多外國人不會學那些語言。

You might be surprised that Taiwan has 15 languages from its tribes.
你或許會驚訝，台灣有十五種部落語言。

What does that name mean? Did they come from Australia?
那名字是什麼意思？他們來自澳洲嗎？

Oh yes. "Nándǎo"(南島) It means the same thing in Chinese, too.
對，南島語族，在中文也是一樣的意思。

I am studying Japanese, because I like the Japanese pop culture.
我在學日文，因為我喜歡日文的流行文化。

Featured Vocabulary

linguistics (n.) 語言學

Linguistics is the scientific study of language and its structure. Some branches of linguistics focus on historical comparisons, and help people to trace the roots of language. Many international linguists are attracted to Taiwan, because of its wealth of spoken languages. Many choose to study and preserve the disappearing Austronesian languages of the indigenous tribes. While others studying the Austronesian language family in the Pacific Islands find their way to Taiwan to study the language family's origins. Through the study of language, linguistics can actually help paint a clearer picture about the history of human migration and ancestry.

Austronesian language family (n.) 南島語族

There are many language families in the world. Most of the European languages, such as Spanish, Italian and Portuguese belong to the Latin language family. Mandarin, Hakka, Cantonese and even Taiwanese belong to the Sino-Tibetan language family. According to linguistic scholars around the world, Taiwan is also considered the homeland to the Austronesian language family. There were over 20 Austronesian languages in Taiwan, before colonization by the Japanese and Chinese. Some of the languages have disappeared, because many lowland tribes were assimilated and wiped out by the colonizing powers. Autronesian languages spread out from Taiwan beginning 2,000 years ago, and now are spoken in territories stretching from Madagascar to Indonesia, to the Philippines to Hawaii, New Zealand and most of the South Pacific Islands.

UNIT 47

Scenery 風景

On my first trip to Taiwan, I truly felt like I was in paradise. My first morning in Wulai District in New Taipei City, I woke up early because of jetlag. I stepped out to the patio and what I saw made me feel like I was in a dream. I was surrounded by steep, green mountains, with lushs forests. The trees were teeming with wildlife, including monkeys, flying squirrels and many beautiful birds. There were low-hanging clouds and mist brushing over the landscape in front of me. The butterflies of many colors were playfully dancing in the air. To my left and right, there were waterfalls, providing a soothing rush of sound and spray. Below me was a majestic river, cleaner than any river I had ever seen. I walked through the village with my camera in-hand, and explored the natural scenery. When I returned to the USA, I had many photos to show my friends proof that paradise really exists on Earth.

Outside of Asia, most foreigners don't consider Taiwan a popular tourist destination. There is very little information available about tourism in Taiwan. So many of the foreigners who visit, come for education, a job or for business. Once they are in Taiwan, those who take the time to travel around the island are taken by surprise. They experience a level of natural beauty that is unexpected, and their initial experiences usually leave them wanting more. I have found that when they return home, these visitors are the best sources of word-of-mouth advertising for Taiwan's tourism industry. Their photos and descriptions of their experiences in Taiwan often result in more visitors coming to experience the island for themselves.

● 基本實用會話　Taiwanese (A)　Westerner (B)

Discovering the mangrove forests
參觀紅樹林

B : What should I be looking for with these binoculars? Are we birdwatching?
我拿著這個雙筒望遠鏡要找什麼？我們要賞鳥嗎？

A : Look at the wading birds in the water, next to the mangrove forest.
找找水裡的涉禽，就在紅樹林旁邊。

B : Yes, I see them. They are feeding on crabs and shellfish. What's so special about them?
有，我看到他們了。他們正在吃螃蟹和甲殼動物。他們為什麼這麼特別？

A : Just be patient. You may see something that you have never seen before.

耐心點，你或許會看到以前沒看過的東西。

B : Hey! You're right. Look at those big white birds. They have black faces and long black bills that look like a spoon.

真的，你說得對，你看那些大白黑，他們的臉是黑的，像湯匙的長喙也是黑的。

A : Those are called black-faced spoonbills (黑面琵鷺). They migrate every year from Korea and Japan.

那些稱為黑面琵鷺，他們每年從韓國和日本遷徙到此。

B : That is something special that I have never seen in the world. This area should be protected.

好特別，我在世界上都沒看過，這地區應該好好保護。

A bird lover's paradise
愛鳥者的天堂

B : According to the Taiwan International Birding Association (TIBA) handbook, that is a blue magpie. It's the national bird of Taiwan.

根據台灣愛鳥協會的手冊，這是藍鵲，這是台灣的國鳥。

A : That's a beautiful creature. Taiwan has so many beautiful birds and butterflies.

真是美麗的生物。台灣有好多美麗的鳥類和蝴蝶。

B : You're right. This island is a birdwatcher's paradise.

你說得對，這座島是愛鳥者的天堂。

A : There are many native birds, but also many seabirds and migrating birds stop in Taiwan, too.

這裡有很多原生鳥類，也有很多候鳥和海鳥會在台灣停留。

B : Next time I go birdwatching with you, I will bring a nice camera. I might just catch a glimpse of a rare bird.

下次我和你去賞鳥，會記得帶台好相機。我剛似乎看到一隻稀有的鳥類。

A : Of course. I have taken photos of fifty different types of birds already.

當然，我已經拍了五十種不同的鳥類了。

NOTES

As ecotourism increases in popularity in Taiwan, there is a growing awareness about the importance of protecting the environment in Taiwan. Ecotourism provides economic incentives for the preservation of natural habitats, which does help get the attention of policymakers. Groups in Taiwan like Taiwan Ecotourism Association (T.E.A.) have helped to spread awareness about these opportunities and benefits to the general public. Their efforts have showcased the natural beauty of Taiwan, and they have also partnered with the indigenous peoples of Taiwan, who have traditionally practiced the ways of living harmoniously with nature. These people are leading the way for a greener Taiwan, and I believe they deserve more attention and support.

Sentences a Westerner might say
老外可能會說的句子

Thank you for inviting me to go out, Wendy. I have never gone river trekking before.
謝謝你邀請我出來，溫蒂。我以前從沒溯溪過。

I usually stay indoors during the Summer, but this is a great way to cool off.
我夏天都常待在室內，不過這種涼快的感覺不錯。

This is like hiking, but more refreshing. What a gorgeous view we have.
這就像健行，不過更涼爽，這裡的風景真迷人。

Let's catch up to our group, so we can hear what guide has to say.
我們快跟上隊伍，才能聽到導遊說什麼。

I have my camera inside of a big waterproof bag. The bag even floats on the water.
我把相機放在大防水袋子裡，這袋裡還能浮在水上。

Of course! It sounds like ecotourism is alive and well in Taiwan.
當然！聽來生態旅遊在台灣很興盛。

Hey look. On the rocks in front of us. Those are monkeys.
你看，在我們前面的岩石上，那裡有猴子。

That's something I would never see back home in Ohio.
我以前在俄亥俄州沒看過這種猴子。

Amazing. What's that sound ahead of us? It is getting louder.
太棒了，前面那聲音是什麼？越來越大聲了。

It's a huge waterfall! There's a rainbow over our heads, and it's like heaven here.
好大的瀑布，我們頭上還有彩虹，這裡好像天堂。

Sentences a Taiwanese person might say.
台灣人可能會說的句子

My friends just recently learned about this type of activity. We really enjoy it.
我朋友最近在學這種活動。我們真的很喜歡。

Yes, it is. These rivers in the mountains stay cold, even during the Summer.
對啊，山裡的這些河一直很清涼，連夏天也一樣。

Also, if we are quiet and pay attention, we will see many native animals and plants.
如果我們安靜下來仔細觀察，可以看到很多原生動植物。

He says you need to keep your valuable items protected in waterproof bags.
他說你要把貴重物品收在防水袋裡。

More importantly, you need a trash bag. We cannot leave any trash behind, or we will disturb the environment.
更重要的是，你需要一個垃圾袋。我們不能把垃圾留在這裡，也不能影響環境。

OK. Follow the group and stay close. Don't forget to speak quietly.
好，跟緊隊伍了，別忘了說話小聲點。

Right. They are macaques, which are native to Taiwan.
對，那是獼猴，是台灣的原生種。

I don't think you will see one of those either. It is a flying squirrel.
你以後應該也看不到。那是飛鼠。

You will see. That is our final destination for our trek.
等一下就會看到，那是溯溪的最終目的地。

This is where we can swim and play for awhile. This will definitely cool us off.
我們可以在這裡游泳，玩一陣子，這一定可以讓我們涼快一下。

Featured Vocabulary

scenery (n.) 風景

In English, the appearance of the land within your view is known as the "scenery" or the "landscape." The scenery can be beautiful, or it can be an "eye sore," which means "ugly." While most visitors to Taiwan come for business or culture, more foreigners are discovering the immense beauty offered by the travel destination. It is this growing reputation spread by word-of-mouth that is starting to attract more visitors to Taiwan. The combination of high mountain vistas, tropical flora, and fine beaches is found in very few places in the world. Furthermore, because the natural attractions are becoming a growing reason for tourists arriving in Taiwan, a growing segment of island's tourism industry is "ecotourism."

ecotourism (n.) 生態旅遊

Ecotourism is a relatively new term, which means a type of tourism that does not damage the natural environment. The term is derived from "eco," which is short for ecology, and "tourism." Ecotourism involves the acts of visiting, viewing and experiencing the natural wonders of a location, and it usually includes an educational element designed to teach people about how to maintain ecological harmony with nature. Because Taiwan has many types of natural attractions with a growing worldwide reputation, ecotourism is on the rise. Many ecotourists come to the undeveloped areas of Taiwan to see birds (birdwatching or birding), monkeys and other wild animals in their natural environment. Hiking in the mountains has always been popular, but an emerging ecotourism activity is called river trekking, where groups of people walk upstream along rivers through a natural environment. These tourists are taught the importance of preserving these habitats, or these animals will disappear. Ecotourists who enjoy exploring marine environments may choose to snorkel in the coral reefs or go whale watching in Hualien. Other growing types of active tourism allow for the viewing the beautiful scenery of Taiwan in different ways, such bicycling, hot air ballooning and paragliding. Ecotourism has brought new economic opportunities to undeveloped areas in Taiwan that have traditionally been lacking in job opportunities.

UNIT 48

During my 2003 trip to Taiwan, I was brought to a theme park. But after visiting Disney World about 10 times in my life, I had a different idea of what a theme park was. Back then, I was expecting thrill rides, but in reality, the rides could only provide thrills for children under 12. I can only describe them as being "low-budget" experiences, because I was spoiled by the American theme parks. But the park did have the "theme" of indigenous culture that was very attractive to me. They had cultural attractions featuring the 12 official indigenous tribes. This included replicas of the different types of traditional villages the tribal people once lived in. They had performers who wore the traditional colorful costumes. And they also served indigenous food, such as a barbecued mountain pig. Even though the culture that I saw was superficial, it did provide a glimpse that attracted me to want to learn more. I was happy that the theme park was not something like an American theme park, because the discovery of Taiwan's indigenous culture helped me to decide to live in Taiwan.

Most Westerners usually have a different experience with theme parks than the Taiwanese. Millions of Western tourists visit the famous Disney theme parks in the USA every year. Also, there may be well-developed, high-budget theme parks in their own countries. If a Westerner goes to a Taiwanese theme park, and compares the experience, they may be somewhat disappointed. For one reason, the Taiwanese theme parks are typically much smaller than Western theme parks. Also, Western theme parks are usually developed with a higher budget. The Western rides may be more thrilling and more dangerous, to suit the tastes of the Westerners. But personally, I will say that the level of quality of the Taiwanese theme parks have increased in the past decade.

基本實用會話

Taiwanese (A) Westerner (B)

Visiting the National Palace Museum
參觀國立故宮博物院

B : There are so many tourists at this museum. It is crowded in here.
這家博物館的遊客好多，這裡好擠。

A : Most are probably from mainland China. They come here to see their cultural treasures.
很多遊客都是從中國大陸來的。他們來這裡看他們的文物。

B: These Chinese antiques are just incredible. They are so finely-detailed.
這些中國古董真是不可思議，好精緻。

A: This collection of royal antiques is the largest in the world.
這是世界最大的皇室文物。

B: How did they end up here in Taipei?
他們為什麼會在台北？

A: The Chinese Nationals escaped the Communist revolution, and they brought them to Taiwan.
台北的故宮逃過共產黨革命，將文物帶到台灣。

B: I heard the Communists destroyed Chinese cultural artifacts, so I think the Chinese are lucky that these precious cultural relics were saved.
我聽說共產黨毀了很多中國文物，所以我想中國人很幸運，還保留了這些珍貴的文物。

Visiting Taipei 101
參觀台北101

B: According to the travel guide, this building is the second tallest in the world.
根據旅遊手冊，這棟大樓是世界第二高樓。

A: It was the tallest in the world not long ago. And it had the fastest elevator in the world.
不久前，這裡還是世界第一高樓，它還有世界上最快的電梯。

B: Taipei 101 still is incredibly impressive. It is an engineering marvel.
台北101還是令人印象深刻，它是工程上的奇蹟。

A: It is a famous landmark in Taipei. What is a famous landmark where you come from?
它是台北的著名地標。你的家鄉有什麼著名地標？

B: Many people who visit my town of Seattle like to visit the Space Needle.
很多人來西雅圖會去參觀太空針塔。

A: I hope I can see your landmarks when I visit your city one day.
希望有天去你的家鄉時，也能參觀你們的地標。

NOTES

When I lived in America, I saw no marketing for tourism in Taiwan targeting Americans. Actually, compared to most countries, Taiwan has seemed to do very little to promote tourism in Taiwan to Westerners. In the 6 years I have lived in Taiwan, I have met very few Western tourists. Those who I have met have come to Taiwan because they worked here in the past, and already know what it has to offer. Some people who came to Taiwan as travelers told me it was because they were invited by a friend, or because of word-of-mouth. As a Westerner, the many wonderful reasons for traveling to Taiwan have been a secret to most Westerners. On the other hand, a lot of marketing efforts have been focused on people in mainland China. As a result, Chinese tourists have become commonplace in Taiwan.

Sentences a Westerner might say
老外可能會說的句子

Come on! Let's go on the roller coaster again.
快點！我們再去搭雲霄飛機。

Just one more time. This is the only ride that is thrilling enough for my taste.
再一次就好，對我來說，只有這個設施夠刺激。

That was fun! Now I will follow you. Please lead the way.
真好玩，我現在願意跟著你走，請帶路。

In English, we call that area the "midway." It is where they have the food booths and games of chance.
在英文來說，我們稱這裡為「遊樂園」，那裡有食物攤，還有一些機率遊戲。

I will try. But I'm not a gifted athlete. I will do my best.
我會試試，但我沒有運動天份，我會盡力的。

Come on, Gina! That little train ride is for small children.
拜託，吉娜！這個小火車是給小孩玩的。

Well, that's a very big ferris wheel. We should have a good view of the scenery up there.
這個摩天輪好大，在上面應該能看到很好的風景。

The view is amazing! I can even see the Gukeng coffeeshop we visited earlier.
這風景好動人！我還能看到之前去的古坑咖啡店。

Huh? Oh, yeah. OK. Here you go.
啊？好啊，給你。

I plan to go to Hualien to see the Taroko Gorge.
我想去花蓮看太魯閣峽谷。

Sentences a Taiwanese person might say.
台灣人可能會說的句子

But we've already been on that ride five times in a row. Can't we check out the other rides?
但我們已經連搭五次了，我們不能去搭其他設施嗎？

OK. But I warn you. My stomach is not feeling well.
好，但我警告你，我的胃已經不舒服了。

Let's go to the area where they have the games. Maybe, you can win a prize for me.
我們去有遊戲的地方玩。或許，你可以幫我贏個獎品。

OK. Can you win something cute for me at the midway?
好，你能在遊樂園贏個可愛的東西給我嗎？

(Later) Well that's OK that you didn't win anything. Let's go on this ride. It looks safe.
（稍後）沒贏到也沒關係，我們去搭這個，這看來很安全。

But, you said I could choose. How about this one? Does that look interesting to you?
可是你說我可以選擇。那這個呢，你覺得這個有趣嗎？

What do you think of the view? The Janfusan Fancyworld theme park is built on a scenic mountain.
你覺得景色如何？劍湖山世界主題樂園是依美麗的山景而建。

It's a little chilly up here. Would you mind loaning me your jacket?
這裡有點冷，你能借我外套嗎？

Thanks! You're a gentleman, Steve. What attraction would you like to visit tomorrow?
謝謝！你真是紳士，史帝夫。你明天想參觀什麼景點？

Do you have a tour guide over there already? If not, I would be happy to join you.
你已經找到導遊了嗎？如果沒有的話，我很樂意和你一起去。

Featured Vocabulary

tourist attractions (n.) 旅遊景點

Tourist attractions are well-known places or objects that attract people to visit. There are several general types of attractions, including natural attractions, historical/cultural attractions, shopping attractions and famous landmarks. In Taiwan some of the most famous and popular natural attractions for foreign visitors are Taroko Gorge National Park and Mt. Alishan. Some of the most famous cultural/historical attractions are the National Palace Museum (國立故宮博物院), Taiwan National Museum of Prehistory, Lukang Longshan Temple and Jioufen (九份). Some popular shopping attractions include Ximending (西門町) and some of the most famous night markets. While the most famous landmark in Taiwan, known by foreigners, is Taipei 101.

theme park (n.) 主題公園

A theme park is a popular type of attraction, especially for families with children. The name refers to the fact that these parks have a theme. But usually, theme parks have rides, entertainment and restaurants, all designed for families' amusement. Thus, they are also referred to as "amusement parks." They have become places for families to have fun, and to spend their money. Although, they are not in the same league as DisneyWorld and Universal Studios, there are some notable theme parks in Taiwan. They include E-Da in Kaohsiung, Janfushan Fancyworld in Yuenlin County, Formosan Aboriginal Culture Village in Nantou County, and Leofoo Village Theme Park in Hsinchu County. There are also amusement parks that focus on water rides and activities. These are referred to as, "water parks." In almost every amusement park in the world, the most famous rides are roller coasters and ferris wheels. Westerners usually refer to more generic, smaller parks with rides as "amusement parks," whereas, the larger, parks with a theme" or "brand name" like DisneyWorld, SeaWorld and Universal Studios, is usually referred to as a "theme park."

In October of 2012, I took the opportunity to bring my family to visit Penghu Islands. It was a very short, inexpensive flight from Tainan City to Magong on Uni Air. The small city of Magong seemed like a typical Taiwanese port city to me. They had hotels, shops, 7-11's, schools, post offices and police stations. They did have very good seafood restaurants and some historic areas. There was an excellent aquarium that my kids enjoyed, and a beautiful beach in front of our hotel. When we rented two scooters and toured the island outside of the city, we actually felt like we were in a different country. There were dry areas, with cacti, providing the fruit for cactus ice cream. There were very unusual rock formations, and picturesque fishing villages. The journey was short and pleasant, but it provided many surprises and a feeling that we were in a different world.

A few visitors to Taiwan are lucky enough to discover Taiwan's beautiful offshore islands. These islands attract visitors with their unspoiled beauty, history, and unique offerings. For example, just off the coast of Xiamen, China is the island of Kinmen, which is famous for it sorghum liquor known as Kinmen Kaoliang Liquor. This drink is very popular and prized by people throughout Asia. The Matsu Islands were at one time the site of intense fighting between the ROC soldiers and the PRC army. Long after the cease fire of 1958, Matsu Islands have converted their reinforced military defenses into tourist sites. Matsu residents approved the building of gambling casinos in 2012, so the island may attract more tourists in the future. Green Island off the East Coast was a former penal colony. Penghu Islands offer many water activities during the Summer and delicious seafood. Orchid Island is home to a tribe of people whose culture is similar to the Polynesian people. The islands outside of the main island of Taiwan offer pristine landscapes, unique historical and cultural sites, and peaceful rest and relaxation.

基本實用會話

Taiwanese (A)　　Westerner (B)

Visiting Kinmen
金門旅遊

B : This is a pretty island, but I don't think there is much to do here.
這是座漂亮的島嶼，但我不認為這裡有什麼事好做。

A : You may be right, but Kinmen has its bright spots.
你或許說得對，但金門有它的亮點。

B : There is a world-famous liquor produced here called Kaoliang. You should try it.
這裡出產世界知名的酒，稱為高粱，你應該試試看。

A : "Gan-bei." Wow! It's so strong! I think I'd better not drink anymore of this.
「乾杯」。哇！好烈！我想我最好別再喝了。

B : There are also delicious noodles made here. You can try a free sample.
這裡還生產好吃的麵，你可以免費試吃。

A : Yeah, it's nice. But I have tried many types of noodles already in Taiwan.
很好吃，但我在台灣已經試過很多種麵了。

B : Kinmen is also very convenient to Xiamen, a beautiful city in mainland China. Let's check it out.
金門到廈門也很方便，那裡是大陸一個美麗的城市，我們去看看。

Visiting Matsu Islands
馬祖旅遊

B : What an interesting place. It's small, but it has many historic sites.
真有趣的地方，這裡很小，但有很多歷史古蹟。

A : We're right off the coast of mainland China, so there are a lot of Chinese cultural sites.
這裡是中國大陸的沿岸，所以有很多中國的文化遺址。

B : I really want to see the old military defense tunnels. I heard there were serious battles before.
我真想去看看以前的軍事防空洞，聽說以前發生過激烈的戰爭。

A : We can take a tour. I know the Americans helped to protect these islands before I was born.
我們可以參加旅行團。我知道在我出生前，美國人曾協助保護這裡的島嶼。

B : Did you know my grandfather was a pilot, who helped with the defense of Matsu?
你知道我祖父也協助保護馬祖的飛行員嗎？

A : Really? It's cool that you are able to be here and see these islands that he helped to protect.
真的嗎？你能來這裡看看他曾經幫忙保護的島嶼，真是太酷了。

NOTES

In 1945, after the leaders of the Republic of China retreated from Mainland China, they settled on the outskirts of China, including territories now administered by Mongolia, Russia, Tibet, India, Bhutan, Pakistan, Afghanistan. Chiang Kai-shek took a majority of his forces and settled in what is now Taiwan and Hainan Island. He eventually pulled out of Hainan Island, and focused on Taiwan as the seat of the government in exile. The smaller islands of Kinmen, Matsu and Penghu became the front line of the ROC to prevent the advance of the Communists towards Taiwan. Now, these islands are no longer war zones, but they have become popular tourist sites, and a reminder of a different era.

Sentences a Westerner might say
老外可能會說的句子

I am excited about visiting the Penghu Islands. Thanks for inviting me.
要去澎湖玩了，好興奮。謝謝你邀請我。

I always enjoy exploring new places, but why did we have to take the ferry?
我總是很喜歡參觀新地方，但我們為什麼要搭渡輪？

It's not just that, but I am feeling a little seasick.
不只是那樣，我也有點暈船了。

I should be fine in a little while. What's the name of this port?
我應該一下子就沒事了。這港口叫什麼名字？

Oh, so there is more than one island to explore?
喔，那麼這裡不只一座島？

Where do we start our adventure?
我們的旅程從哪裡開始？

That sounds like a good plan.
聽來是個好計畫。

I'll enjoying trying any kind of seafood, except for whale or dolphin meat.
我喜歡嘗試各種海鮮，除了鯨魚或海豚肉。

Ugh! Let's stay away from those places. So what will we do after lunch?
啊！我們還是不要去那些地方了。我們午餐後要做什麼？

Really? I have never tried cactus ice cream before. That sounds interesting.
真的？我以前沒吃過仙人掌冰淇淋。聽起來很有趣。

Sentences a Taiwanese person might say.
台灣人可能會說的句子

No problem. I thought you should see other types of attractions while you are in Taiwan.
不客氣，我以為你在台灣時應該到其他景點參觀過了。

All of the airplane tickets were sold out. I know that would have been more convenient.
所有機票都賣完了，我知道那樣比較方便。

I'm sorry to hear that. I hope your sickness passes soon, because I want you to have an appetite to try the local cuisine.
很抱歉，希望你的暈船能快點好，因為我希望你會有胃口嘗嘗地方美食。

This is Magong, the capital city of the Penghu archipelago.
這裡是馬公，澎湖群島的縣轄市。

Yes. And, these islands were once known as the Pescadores when they were ruled by the Dutch.
對，這些島在荷蘭統治時期曾經稱為澎湖列島。

We can casually stroll around the historic sites, until you have an appetite again.
我們可以在歷史古蹟輕鬆散步，等你恢復胃口。

Then, we can enjoy the fresh seafood for lunch. The seafood is highly regarded here.
然後，我們午餐可以去吃海鮮，這裡的海鮮備受好評。

It is illegal to sell whale and dolphin meat in Taiwan, but I have heard that people still sell it at some places.
台灣販賣鯨魚和海豚肉是違法的，但我聽說某些地方有賣。

It's going to be a hot day, so we can cool off with some cactus fruit ice cream.
今天天氣會很熱，所以我們可以吃仙人掌冰淇淋涼快一下。

After that, we'll hit the beach and cool off in the ocean. Penghu is well-known for its recreational water activities.
在那之後，我們可以再去海邊玩水涼快一下。澎湖的水上活動很有名。

Featured Vocabulary

archipelago (n.) 群島

Archipelago is an English word derived from Greek words for "chief of the sea," which was a name used to refer to the Aegean Islands off the coast of Greece. Now, the word is used to refer to any chain, or group, of islands that are clustered closely to each other. The largest archipelagos are actually the countries of Indonesia, Japan, the Philippines, New Zealand and the British Isles. The government of Taiwan claims several archipelagos, including the Penghu Islands, Kinmen Islands, and Matsu Islands.

islets (n.) 胰島

An islet is a name used to describe an island that is very small, especially for islands that are uninhabited. Other words describing different types of small islands include "atoll," "sandbar," or even "rocks." Taiwan has many islets off of its coasts, some of which are frequently visited by tourists. Some well-known small islands include, Sansiantai, Turtle Island, and Liouciou. There are many islets in the disputed Paracel and Diaoyu Island Groups.

disputed islands (n.) 爭議島嶼

Between Taiwan and Japan are the Senkaku/Diaoyu Islands. They are so small, they are barely inhabitable. However, after they were determined to contain possible oil reserves in the 1970's, the People's Republic of China took interest in the islands, and the dispute has been a concern in the international community ever since. Lost in this dispute is the fact that the Republic of China (Taiwan) has claimed sovereignty over these islands since 1945. The Paracel Islands are an archipelago of tiny islands in the South China Sea between the Philippines and Vietnam. They are claimed by the Republic of China, but the PRC military took them over from the PRC in 1950 during the Chinese Civil War. Even though it retains its claim, the ROC government has no presence on the islands.

Animals 動物

UNIT 50

This past summer, I took my family to the Taipei Zoo. I have seen many zoos in the USA, and I was impressed with the size of this zoological park. I would rate it a world-class zoo. They had all of the popular, well-known animals, like elephants, giraffes, zebras and now, they have panda bears. But my biggest surprise came from visiting areas of the zoo that displayed the animals native to Taiwan. I discovered many animals that are endemic to Taiwan, which means they live nowhere else in the world. I also couldn't believe how many species of animals made their home on this island. Taiwan is truly an island of diversity and abundance. There were muntjacs and serows, mountain pigs, and the very odd-looking pangolin. There were curious Formosan rock monkeys, acrobatic flying squirrels, and the majestic Formosan Black Bear. There were many species of birds, insects and sea creatures on display at the zoo. I stared into the exhibit for the Formosan Clouded Leopard, and found it very difficult to see the beautiful animal. I wasn't sure if it was hiding, or if it just wasn't there.

It was reported in the news last year that the Formosan Clouded Leopard was likely to be extinct in the wild. This would be sad news indeed for Taiwan to lose one of its most beautiful creatures. The health and diversity of the island's creatures are important indicators of the health of the island for human beings. So if we cannot protect the natural habitats of Taiwan for our precious creatures, we cannot provide a healthy home for our children and future generations. This is why it is crucial that Taiwan cooperates with the international community to educate its citizens about the importance of protecting natural habitats and wildlife. This includes limiting pollution and habitat encroachment. By working together with people around the world, Taiwan's endemic species will have a chance to survive.

基本實用會話　Taiwanese (A) 　Westerner (B)

A visit to Taipei Zoo
參觀台北動物園

B: This is a big zoo. What does this sign say?
這動物園好大，這個指示牌說什麼？

A: This area has animals that are native to Taiwan.
這一區是台灣原生動物區。

B : There are quite a variety of animals here. You have several species of deer.
這裡有好多種動物，鹿也有好幾種種類。

A : Yes, Taiwan used to have an abundance of deer a long time ago.
對，台灣很久以前有很多鹿。

B : We have a lot of deer in Virginia, too. Taiwan also has a black bear, just like Virginia does.
維吉尼亞州也有很多鹿。臺灣也有黑鹿，跟維吉尼亞州一樣。

A : I think we have quite the variety of animals for such a small island.
我想我們這個小島上的確有很多種動物。

B : Yes, you have many animals that we don't have, including monkeys, flying squirrels and clouded leopards.
是的，你們有很多我們沒有的動物，包括猴子、飛鼠和雲豹。

A visit to the mountains
去爬山

B : This path looks dangerous. It's not very wide, and we're on the side of a mountain.
這條道路看起來好危險，不是很寬，我們就站在山邊。

A : In order to show you the wildlife of Taiwan, we need to take you deep into their habitat.
為了讓你看看台灣的野生動物，我們要帶你深入他們的棲地。

B : I'll take the risk, because I really want to take good photos for my nature magazine.
我願意冒險，因為我真的想為我的自然雜誌照些好照片。

A : Look! Over there on the side of the mountain. What a cute little deer.
你看，在山的那一邊，好可愛的小鹿。

B : That's a Formosan Serow. Or perhaps a Reeve's muntjac. Where can we find a leopard?
那是台灣長鬃山羊，也可能是山羌。哪裡可以看到豹？

A : The clouded leopard may already be extinct. No one has seen them in years.
雲豹可能已經絕種了，這幾年沒人看過他們。

 NOTES

The Republic of China Wildlife Protection Act was enacted in March 31, 1990 by the government. It provides for the classification and determination of wildlife categories, to help with the protection of native fauna. It establishes a conservation donation fund that can help with the preservation of habitats, also referred to as ecosystems. The act also established a format for international cooperation for wildlife protection. The laws provide important education to the public about the importance of habitat protection. Finally, it provides penalties against companies and individuals that damage the habitats of protected animals.

How was your weekend? My trip to Hualien and Taitung was fantastic.
你的週末過得如何？我的花東之旅棒呆了。

I learned a lot about the native marine life in Taiwan.
我知道了很多台灣的原生海洋生物。

First, I went whale watching on a boat from Hualien Harbor.
首先，我從花蓮港搭賞鯨船出海。

Yes! We saw a humpback whale, and a few other cetaceans.
有，我們看到座頭鯨，還有其他鯨目動物。

A cetacean is the name of the family of animals that whales belong to. It includes dolphins and killer whales, too.
鯨目動物指的是鯨魚所屬的亞目，裡面也包括海豚和殺人鯨。

Then you should come with me next time. I swam with dolphins at FarGlory Ocean Park.
那麼你下次應該和我一起去。我曾在遠雄海洋公園和海豚一起游泳。

I'd love to. In Taitung I visited the Shanyuan Ocean Ecology Community.
我很樂意。我在台東去了杉原海洋生態社區。

An instructor took me and a group of people out to the coral reef to go snorkeling.
有個指導員帶我和一群人去珊瑚礁浮潛。

When you go snorkeling, you just breathe air through a tube, and you need to stay near the surface.
浮潛的時候，只透過管子呼吸，而且需要待在海面附近。

Yes, it is easy. Scuba diving, on the other hand, requires more training. You go deep underwater and breathe from an air tank.
對，很容易。另一方面，潛水就需要更多訓練。你會潛到較深的地方，用氣瓶呼吸。

Sentences a Taiwanese person might say.
台灣人可能會說的句子

I just stayed home and rested. I had a lot of housecleaning to do. What did you do?
我只有待在家裡休息，我得打掃家裡。你做了什麼事？

Unfortunately, I don't know much about the marine life, except for what I can see in the seafood restaurants.
很不幸的，我不了解海洋生物，除了在海鮮餐廳裡可以看到的那些。

That sounds so interesting! Did you see any whales?
聽來很有趣，有看到鯨魚嗎？

What is a cetacean? I have never heard that English word before.
什麼是鯨目動物？我以前沒聽過這個詞。

I love dolphins! They are so cute and smart. I will make sure I learn the word, "cetacean."
我愛海豚！海豚又可愛又聰明，我會記得這個字「鯨目動物」。

What? That's my childhood dream! Please take me with you next time.
什麼？那是我童年的夢想！拜託下次帶我和你一起去。

What did you do there? Taitung is a beautiful part of Taiwan.
你去那裡做什麼？台東是台灣很漂亮的地方。

What's the difference between scuba diving and snorkeling?
潛水和浮潛有什麼不同？

I'd like to try that. Is it easy to learn?
我想試試，好學嗎？

I hope I can have some vacation time soon to learn how to get closer to the creatures of the sea.
希望我很快就能有假期，學習如何接近海洋生物。

Featured Vocabulary

fauna (n.) 動物

The word, "fauna," means the different types of animal life (wildlife) that lives in an area. If the types of animal life is native to the terrain, you can say that this is "native fauna." There are times that species introduced from other areas can adapt or even take over the local habitat. You can call animals that come from other places living in the local habitats, non-native fauna or "exotic species." If it is one type of animal, you call it a "species," if it is group of animals you are referring to, you can say "fauna."

endangered vs. extinct (adj.) 瀕危 vs. 滅絕

There are many species of animals in Taiwan that are protected, because they are endangered. The reason for their endangerment, is that their habitats have been encroached upon by human settlement. Other reasons include the building of highways and railroads, which disturbs the natural migration and feeding routes. Also, air and water pollution can have serious effects on the natural habitats and food sources of Taiwan's native animals.

habitat (n.) 棲息地

In civilization, the word "habitat" is a general term that can be used to describe a person's home or peoples' homes. In nature, a habitat is the area of land that houses and supports wildlife. When describing a natural habitat, the land not only provides shelter, but also a sustainable food and water supply. Taiwan is a small island with 27 million people and well-developed agriculture and manufacturing industries. This human development has reduced the reduced the natural habitats to the point that many native animal are extinct or endangered.

51

Flora 花卉

During my early explorations of Taiwan, there was constant excitement discovering the variety of landscapes, animals, ethnicities, culture, food, and just about anything else that can be discovered. Not lost in the excitement, was the discovery of the amazing fauna of this semi-tropical island. Plant life seemed to find refuge in every type of terrain. I found trees and grasses covering the tallest peaks, while Taiwanese alder made even the inaccesible cliffsides green with life. I wandered through large bamboo forests, where the breeze made the bamboo trunks creak deeply and made millions of leaves fill the air with a soothing song. I climbed large moss-covered rocks to enjoy the spray of waterfalls. I walked through a forest of tall pine on Mt. Alishan and was reminded of similar forests of Mt. Rainier in Washington State. I walked through mangroves, which reminded me of the Everglades near Miami, Florida. Every place I visited in Taiwan, the plant life provided much character to the surroundings.

I have truly enjoyed discovering the wild flora of Taiwan, although visitors can find many unique experiences involving the domesticated flora of Taiwan. During the Spring and Fall, there are flowers almost everywhere, filling the scenery with splashes of color. Flowers are an important attraction in Taiwan, especially Taiwan's orchids, which are popular all over the world. There are frequent floral expos attracting visitors to the island. There are also many tours for visitors, to tour tea and coffee plantations. Also, foreigners may enjoy visiting orchards and farms for the experience of picking their own fruit and vegetables. I have enjoy picking my own peaches, mangos, bananas, longains, watermelons, cantelopes, custard apples, and Asian pears. They just seem to taste fresher when you pick them yourself.

基本實用會話

Taiwanese (A)　　　Westerner (B)

A visit to a botanical garden
參觀植物園

B： This is one of the most beautiful gardens I have ever seen in a big city.
這是我在這個大城市裡看到的最美麗的花園。

A： People have been visiting Taipei Botanical Gardens (台北植物園) since 1921 to get away from the stress of city life.
從1921年台北植物園成立後，人們常來參觀以抒解城市生活的壓力。

B : I love those flowers on the water. They look like water lilies.
我喜歡那些水裡的花，看來好像荷花。

A : They are lotuses. They are quite beautiful and they are also edible.
那些是蓮花，不僅漂亮，也可以食用。

B : There is quite the variety of plants here. My mother had a "green thumb."
這裡的植物種類好多，我母親是「綠手指」。

A : There are over 100 species of plants. What does that mean, that your mother had a green thumb?
這裡有超過100種植物。你母親有綠手指，那是什麼意思？

B : That is slang. It means that she enjoyed growing and cultivating plants in her garden.
那是句俗語，意思是她喜歡在花園裡種種花植草。

A visit to a farm
參觀農場

B : You told me we were going to eat vegetarian food tonight, but I didn't know we were going to harvest our own food.
你說我們晚上要吃素食，但我不知道我們得自己收割我們的食物。

A : I wanted to make it a surprise. Just follow what everyone is doing now.
我想將這當作驚喜，只要跟著大家一起做就行了。

B : Can I have a little shovel, too? What are we digging for here?
我也可以拿個小鏟子嗎？我們在這裡要挖什麼？

A : Carrots, sweet potato and taro root. We will be making a stew.
蘿蔔，地瓜和芋頭。我們可以燉湯喝。

B : We're really going to eat fresh food tonight. That is a cool experience.
我們晚上的菜真新鮮，這體驗真酷。

A : Right after this, we will go to the orchard and choose our own peaches and pears for dessert.
在這之後，我們要去果園，為我們自己的點心選擇桃子和梨子。

 NOTES

The Botanical Society of America is the most famous organization dedicated to promoting the appreciation and protection of plant species. This organization of dedicated scientists, gardeners and everyday people work together with local communities to provide education and they often provide gardens where the public is invited to learn more about plants. Taiwan has a chapter of this organization. It is called The Botanical Society of Republic of China, and its web site is http://www.tspb.org.tw. The group was formed in 1975, and has annual meetings.

Sentences a Westerner might say
老外可能會說的句子

Well, I never thought I would go to a flower show, but sure, I'll go with you.
我從沒想過我會來看花卉展，但當然，我們可以一起去。

I assume that it would. The word "international" is in the event's name.
應該是吧。「國際」這個字只是活動名稱。

Look at the crowds. This event sure is big.
你看那些人，這活動真的很大。

I can read this itinerary. It's in English. Wow! A professor from Texas A&M University is speaking. That is where I went to college.
這議程我看得懂，是英文的，哇！德州農工大學的教授要來演講，我從那裡畢業的。

(Later) Well, that was interesting. Who knew that so much scientific effort went into perfecting a flower?
（稍後）真有趣，誰知道在一朵花背後，在科學上付出那麼多心力？

It is amazing how beautiful these flowers are. There are more colors than I ever imagined possible.
這裡的花太美了，真是驚人，花卉的顏色更是超過我的想像。

I think the Taiwanese floral designers must be getting more creative every year.
我覺得台灣花卉設計師的創意一定每年都越來越好。

That is a dream worth pursuing. For now, just learn everything you can about flowers.
那是個值得追求的夢想。你現在要盡可能學習花卉的一切。

Here you go. This is for you.
給你，這是送你的。

You opened my eyes today. I have a new appreciation for flowers, thanks to you.
你今天讓我大開眼界，我對花有了新的認識，謝謝你。

Sentences a Taiwanese person might say.
台灣人可能會說的句子

Steve, I think you will enjoy it. The International Orchid Show attracts people from all over the world.
史帝夫，我想你會喜歡的。國際蘭花展吸引了世界各地的人。

Give it a chance. I think you will be impressed.
試試看嘛，我想你一定會覺得印象深刻。

The orchid industry is big in the world. And there are symposiums here given by notable guest speakers in the industry.
這裡的蘭花業是全世界最大的，還邀請業界裡最知名的客座講師來這裡參與座談會。

Would you like to attend the lecture? We might learn something interesting.
你想參加演講嗎？我們或許能學到有趣的東西。

There is a competition to see which country has the most beautiful floral displays.
那裡有國家花卉競賽。

I think the Taiwanese floral exhibits have a chance to win this year.
我想台灣的花卉展有機會在今年勝出。

I would love to be a florist. My dream is to have my own flower shop.
我也想當個花商，我的夢想是開家自己的花店。

I agree. That is why I wanted to attend this expo. Thanks for coming with me.
我同意，所以我要來參加這個展覽，謝謝你跟我一起來。

What? Why are you giving me these orchids? They are beautiful. Thank you.
什麼？你為什麼要給我這些蘭花？好美，謝謝你。

You're welcome. I appreciate you as a friend, too. You are always willing to try new things.
不客氣，我也很感謝有你這個朋友，你總是願意嘗試新鮮事。

Featured Vocabulary

flora (n.) 植物

The word, "flora," means the different types of plant life (wildlife) that lives in an area. If the types of plant life is native to the terrain, you can say that this is "native flora." But if the plant grows natively AND it is found nowhere else in the world, it is called "endemic flora." There are times that plant species introduced from other areas can adapt or even take over the local plant ecosystems. This is why the transport of plants is controlled at airports.

endemic (adj.) 地方特有種

If a plant is "endemic" to Taiwan, it means that the plant grows natively nowhere else in the world. According to botanists (scientists who study plants), 26% of all plant species in Taiwan are endemic to the island. Many of the endemic plant species are actually endangered, and may disappear forever, because of damage to the ecosystems. Currently, Taiwan needs more education and help to protects its fragile ecosystems and the diversity of plant and animal life.

pollinate (v.) 授粉

Plants reproduce by producing and distributing seeds. For flowering plants, pollen (tiny reproductive material from the male organ) is produced to fertilize the female organs in the flowers. Once fertilized, a flower can become a fertilized fruit or seed that can reproduce. This process is important for the survival of human beings and other animal species. Flowering plants are the dominant types of plants in the world, and they provide much of the food we need, in the form of grains, nuts, fruit and some vegetables. Plants have adapted to work symbiotically with insects like bees and butterflies to aid in the pollination process. Without the help of these beneficial insects, we would lose many of the food plants that we currently consume. Thus, as responsible citizens, we should look for alternatives to pesticides that are used on our crops, as they have been shown by scientists to kills the insects that the flowering plants need.

52

UNIT

Treasures 珍寶

I have always considered Taiwan an island full of cultural treasures to discover. While visiting someone in Douliou City (斗六市), I toured the sites of Yunlin County (雲林縣) and Changhua County (彰化縣). I can't remember where my host brought me, but we visited some very large shops in an area popular with tourists. In these shops were special treasures… petrified wood. There were small pieces sold as jewelry. There were larger pieces and logs that were polished as stools. I couldn't believe that there were also large tables made from petrified (fossilized) wood. In America, I had been aware that petrified wood was selling as rare treasures. A typical petrified log that weighed 45 kg (100 lbs.) might sell for $300-$400 in the American marketplace. In the stores I visited in Taiwan, they were less than half that price. What I saw in front of me made me realize that Taiwan had treasures that were valued around the world. I immediately wondered what type of money-making opportunities were available for me here. What were the costs of shipping and taxes? After that, I found other treasures, such as jade, pearls and coral, which made me ponder the business opportunities.

Many visitors to Taiwan enjoy the experience of shopping and finding great values around the island. They can find great bargains on electronics, clothing, and other merchandise, but they may also find treasures that are considered far more valuable in other parts of the world. For example, Tainan City is famous for its oyster industry, and as a result, there are local markets selling one of the industry's by-products… pearls. One of my friends from South Africa bought genuine pearl earrings at an outdoor market in Tainan for NT 2,700 (US $90). She had them appraised at a jewelry shop in South Africa for NT 9,300 (US $300).

基本實用會話

Taiwanese (A) : Westerner (B)

Shopping for jade jewelry
購買玉石首飾

B : Thanks for helping me to find a gift shop. I need to find some souvenirs for my family.
謝謝你幫我找到這家禮品店。我得為我的家人找些紀念品。

A : No problem. There are many attractive trinkets here in this temple gift shop.
不客氣,這家廟宇的禮品品有很多吸引人的小玩意。

B : I would like to find something precious and unique to Taiwan.
我想找些比較珍貴的,是台灣特有的。

A ： You should buy some jade jewelry for your family. Jade is a semi-precious stone that is supposed to have healing and protective qualities.
你應該為你的家人買些玉石首飾，玉是半寶石，具有療癒和保護的特性。

B ： There are so many choices. How do I know what to get for each family member?
這裡選擇好多，我怎麼知道要怎麼選擇送家人哪一個禮物？

A ： That's easy. What year was each person born? This chart tells you their zodiac sign.
很簡單。他們各是哪一年出生的？這個表可以告訴你他們的生肖。

B ： Oh yeah! I can buy a necklace for each zodiac sign. Perfect!
太好了，我可以每個生肖各買一條項鍊。太完美了！

Looking for treasures in a stream
在河流裡找寶石

B ： Why did you bring me to this small river? Why are there so many people here?
你為什麼帶我來這條小河流？這裡為什麼有這麼多人？

A ： This is one of Taiwan's special experiences. We are at Baibao Creek (白鮑溪).
這是台灣的特殊體驗。這裡是白鮑溪。

B ： Everyone is looking in the water. What should I be looking for?
大家都在水裡翻找，我們要找什麼？

A ： Look for beautiful stones. Some of them are semi-precious gems. You may even find jade.
找漂亮的石頭，有些是半寶石，你甚至可以找到玉。

B ： Isn't that valuable? Cool! Let's go find a place upstream where there are fewer people.
那不是很珍貴嗎？酷！我們去上游人少一點的地方找。

A ： OK. Let's just look along the ground along the way. You never know what we may find.
好，我們沿路找上去，你永遠不會知道我們能找到什麼？

NOTES

While other industries may be suffering, the Taiwanese jewelry industry has experienced healthy growth. In particular, many international buyers have treasured the precious red coral from the sea off the coast of Taiwan. Master craftsmen have created beautiful jewelry and art from the coral. Many mainland Chinese tourists come to Taiwan seeking these precious objects, and every tour of Chinese tourists seems to be begin and end at a coral jewelry shop. Prized for their beauty, the red coral, which are found in deep waters, are disappearing because of overharvesting. One should remember that these precious items are the skeletons of living creatures, and that their habitats are usually destroyed by collecting them.

Sentences a Westerner might say
老外可能會說的句子

I am glad you offered to be my business partner. I really need someone reliable here in Taiwan.
很高興你願意當我的生意夥伴，我在台灣真的需要一個可靠的人。

Where shall we start? Let's find some sources for less expensive jewelry first.
我們要從哪裡開始？我們先找不那麼貴的寶石。

What is special about this studio?
這工作室有什麼特別的？

OK. I am sure the beads are beautiful. I only hope they are durable and affordable.
好，我相信珠子會很漂亮，我只希望他們很堅固，價格也合宜。

(Later) Well, that was a good start. I think we can work with them. What's next?
（稍後）那是個好開始。我想我們可以跟他們合作，接下來呢？

Great! Cultured pearls are always popular with our customers.
太好了，我們的客戶很喜歡養殖的珍珠。

(Later) That was a great source for pearls. And the oyster omelettes were delicious, too.
（稍後）這個珍珠貨源很好。蚵仔煎也很好吃。

I heard that Hualien was a beautiful place. What do the suppliers there offer?
我聽說花蓮是個漂亮的地方。那個供應商賣什麼？

(Later) Amazing. The jade here has a clear, emerald color. These will be very valuable.
（稍後）太了不起了。這裡的玉很清澈、翠綠。這些將會很有價值。

I don't know if coral will be popular with my buyers. They are very environmentally-conscious. But, thank you so much for your tours.
不知道我的買家會不會喜歡珊瑚，這具有環保的爭議性。不過謝謝你的安排。

Sentences a Taiwanese person might say.
台灣人可能會說的句子

You're welcome. I am all but happy to help you find sources of jewelry and gemstones in Taiwan. There is much Taiwan has to offer.
不客氣，我非常樂意幫助你在台灣尋找玉石、寶石，台灣這類寶石很多。

OK. The first place I will take you is to a studio in Sandimen Township (三地門鄉) in Pingtung County.
好，我先帶你去屏東縣三地門鄉的工作室。

You will see. There are glass beads made by the local indigenous women.
你一會就知道了。那裡有很多原住民婦女製作的玻璃珠。

They are. Each bead is so colorful and unique. They are already sold worldwide.
是的，每個珠子都色彩豐富又獨一無二，他們已經銷往世界各地。

I arranged for you to visit a few oyster farms in Tainan City and Chiayi County.
我安排你去參觀台南縣和嘉義縣幾個牡蠣養殖場。

I think you will be very happy with the quality and price of Taiwanese oysters.
我想你一定會滿意台灣牡蠣的品質和價格。

Next, we will tour suppliers in Shoufeng Township (壽豐鄉) in Hualien County.
接下來，我們要去找花蓮縣壽豐鄉的旅遊供應商。

That is one of the most famous places in the world for jade gemstones.
那裡的玉石在世界上是很出名的。

Before we leave, I think you will be interested meeting the supplier of red coral.
在我們離開前，我想你會想見見紅珊瑚的供應商。

You're welcome. I do hope that you are successful in building your business.
不客氣，希望你的生意順利成功。

Featured Vocabulary

jade (n.) 玉

Jade is a semi-precious stone that has been prized for thousands of years, and it is a favorite gemstone of people who believe in feng shui (風 水). Because of its light color and purity, jade is believed to provide nourishing energy to the human body. Jade is found in the USA, Russia, China, and Southeast Asia, but Taiwan is the source of a special type of jade, known as Taiwan Jade. This jade comes from Shoufeng Township (壽豐鄉) in Hualien County (花蓮縣). These gemstones have a emerald green color that is prized by collectors. Also, there are some of these stones that have a waxy surface. Finally, you may be lucky to spot a variety that is known around the world, the Taiwan cat's eye jade.

pearl (n.) 珍珠

Pearls are produced by oysters and other shellfish as a way to protect itself from foreign objects in their body. The substance of the pearl is calcium carbonate, which the shellfish use to cover the inside of their shells for comfort and protection. "Natural pearls," which are found in nature are very rare, so humans have produced pearls by inserting foreign objects into oysters that they raise on farms. These are called "cultured pearls." Taiwan has a large oyster farming industry, so it is natural that there are farms set up to produce cultured pearls. You can find pearl jewelry in Taiwanese marketplaces for a great bargain, selling for much lower than international prices.

jewelry (n.) 珠寶

Jewelry, also known as jewellery, are decorative items worn for personal adornment. These beautiful crafted items can be made from all types of materials, from precious gemstones and metals to common objects like seashells and wood. Taiwan's jewelry industry is showing healthy growth for its exports. One reason is that Taiwan offers many natural resources that are used in jewelry-making, including jade, pearls, coral, and petrified wood. Another reason is that there are many creative craftspeople in Taiwan who design unique and exquisite pieces. In Pingtung, the glass beads made from Paiwan tribal women are highly prized in Europe, because of their bright colors and unique patterns. As a result of Taiwan's proficiency in the industry, the annual Taiwan Jewellery and Gem Fair attracts many buyers from around the world.

UNIT 53

Cultures 文化

After visiting Taiwan for the first time, I realized how misunderstood Taiwanese culture was in the world. I also realized that cultural identity was also evolving in the minds of the Taiwanese people. My first experience with culture in Taiwan was in Wulai, where I was exposed to Taiwan's Austronesian culture unexpectedly. The colorful Hakka culture was evident during my trip to Meinong District (美濃區) in Kaohsiung. In Tainan, I visited a village that still preserved the Siraya (西拉雅) culture, a lowland (平埔族) tribal culture that has all but vanished. Visiting some districts, especially those with hot springs resorts, I saw Japanese architecture and culture on display. In most big cities, the influence of international culture is easy to find. Starbucks, McDonalds, and American movies can be found in most Taiwanese cities. I was also surprised to see German restaurants and stores in Taipei. I realized that Taiwan was not only a melting pot of Asian and Western cultures, it was also a blend of ancient and modern.

If foreign visitors take the time to explore Taiwan, they may begin to understand the diversity that is the melting pot of Taiwan. Although the blend in Taiwan is dominated by Han Chinese culture, it also consists of Confucianist, Taoist, Buddhist and Hakka cultures, and to some extent, the indigenous cultures. There are also the external influences of Japanese culture and American culture in Taiwanese society. Taiwan's multiculturalism is more obvious today, even though politics have historically hindered the recognition and acceptance of multiple cultures in Taiwan's identity. You can also see the identification of modern Taiwanese culture through other factors, such as the "convenience store culture," the "tea shop culture," or the "cram school culture."

基本實用會話

Taiwanese (A) Westerner (B)

Watching a religious procession
看宗教儀式

B: This is quite a colorful parade. What are they celebrating?
這個遊行的色彩真鮮豔，他們在慶祝什麼？

A: People from the local temples are marching to pay a visit to the largest temple in Tainan.
各地廟宇的人來這裡進香，參觀台灣最大的寺廟。

B: There is so much Chinese culture on display here. What's the occasion?
這裡展示了好多中國文化，這是什麼活動？

A: The large temple is celebrating their deity's birthday. So each smaller temple is bringing their deity to pay a visit to show respect.
這座大廟正在慶祝殿內神祇的生日，所以小廟都會帶他們的神來拜訪，以示尊敬。

B: I see. Look at all of these performers, dancers, musicians and warriors. It is very lively.
我懂了，你看這些表演者、舞者、音樂家和戰士，真的很熱鬧。

A: Yes, these are customs that go back hundreds of years to Southern mainland China.
對，這是數百年前中國南方的習俗。

B: I can't believe that guy over there. He is hitting himself with a spiked stick. Is he bleeding?
我不敢相信那裡的人正在做的事，他正用狼牙棒打自己，他在流血嗎？

Attending a music concert
參加音樂會

B: Wow! Taiwanese culture has come a long way. I love this music! What's the name of this band?
哇！台灣文化有很大進步，我喜歡這個音樂！這個樂團叫什麼名字？

A: Their name is Chthonic (閃靈樂團). They are a metal band that is famous internationally.
他們的名字是閃靈樂團，他們是國際知名的重金屬樂團。

B: I love their fast-paced, highly-charged music, even though I can't understand the words.
我喜歡他們節奏又激烈的音樂，即使我聽不懂他們在唱什麼。

A: Their leader likes to write emotional songs about Taiwanese culture and history.
他們的團長喜歡寫些台灣文化和歷史的情緒性歌曲。

B: Cool! He's even playing an old Chinese instrument. What is that called?
酷！他甚至還演奏古老的中國樂器，那叫什麼？

A: It's an "erhu." That is one of his trademarks, combining the traditional sounds of the erhu with modern music.
那是「二竹」。那是他的標誌，將傳統二竹和現代音樂結合在一起。

NOTES

The culture of a people is closely tied to the language and other things, like the food, religion and industries. Another important factor in culture is music. In Taiwan, traditional music, or folk music, is borrowed from mainland China. One can still find classes teaching how to play traditional Chinese instruments, such as the erhu (二胡) or the pipa (琵琶). For at least twenty years, Taiwanese people have enjoyed listening to recordings of popular songs in Taiwanese (Minnan) language. These days, modern pop stars from Taiwan have shared their music and Taiwanese culture with millions of international fans.

Sentences a Westerner might say
老外可能會說的句子

I'm really going to miss Taiwan. I will miss all of you, too.
我一定會想念台灣,也會想念你們的。

There is just so much to the Taiwanese culture that I will miss, but there are some aspects I won't miss.
台灣文化令人想念的事物太多了,不過有個部分我不會想念。

I will miss the thoughtful, respectful, hospitable ways people treat visitors, such as the tea ceremonies.
我會想念人們對待遊客的體貼、有禮、熱情,例如茶道。

I will miss eating in Taiwan, with the convenient and affordable take-out meals.
我會想念台灣的食物,還有方便又便宜的外帶餐點。

Oh yeah. I will definitely miss the way people in Taiwan respect teachers.
對了,我一定會想念台灣人尊重老師的方式。

I have never felt this much respect from students in the USA. I guess it's not really taught in our culture.
在美國,我從來沒感覺過學生會對老師這麼尊敬,我猜我們的文化裡沒教這個。

Let's see. There is a convenience store on every corner, and several tea shops on every block. It seems like overkill.
我想想,每個街角都有便利商店,每幾個路口就有飲料店。感覺太多了。

I also don't really like the cram school culture, even though it provides more jobs.
我也不喜歡補習班文化,即使它能提供更多工作。

And the competition is so extreme here. People push each other to their limits, so their quality of life is reduced.
這裡的競爭也太激烈了,人們總是將對方推向極限,所以生活品質也減少了。

But, Taiwan offered so many positives, that I really have nothing to complain about.
可是,台灣的優點很多,所以我其實沒什麼好抱怨的。

Sentences a Taiwanese person might say.
台灣人可能會說的句子

Steve, we're really going to miss you when you return to the USA. What will you miss the most?
史帝夫,等你回美國,我們一定會想你的。你最想念的會是什麼?

What aspects of our culture will you miss most?
你會最想念哪部分？

Sure. We do learn to show our appreciation to visitors, because, what comes around goes around.
當然，我們學習對遊客表示感謝，因為付出總有回報。

If I live outside of Taiwan, I think I will miss the food culture the most.
如果我住在台灣以外的地方，我想我會最想念飲食文化。

Yes. That part of our culture was influenced by Confucius.
對，我們的文化受孔子影響。

And what parts of our culture won't you miss?
你不會想念我們文化裡的哪個部分？

I would tend to agree with you. Sometimes, you can have too much of a good thing.
我同意你的說法。有時候會適得其反。

Memorization is overemphasized, instead of developing creativity and problem-solving.
過份強調記憶，而不是發展創造力和問題解決的能力。

I tend to agree with you. It means we work longer hours for less pay to survive in a shrinking job pool.
我同意你的說法，這表示我們在縮水的工作機會中，得付出更多工作時間，收入卻更少。

We benefitted from knowing you, too, Steve. Best wishes for your future.
史帝夫，我們能認識你也受益良多，祝你未來萬事如意。

Featured Vocabulary

Han Chinese (n.) 漢族

Han Chinese, or the Han people, are an ethnic group that comprise of the majority of the population in mainland China and Taiwan. The word, "Han" originated from the Han Dynasty (206 BC – 220 AD), and the Han Dynasty was named after the region of Hanzhou, which was named after the Han River. Han Chinese culture began dominating the island of Taiwan over 500 years ago with the arrival of settlers from mainland China. Although some people consider these ancient Taiwanese settlers as "Minnan" from the southern part of the mainland, with a different language and culture, today, they are politically categorized as "Han Chinese."

Taiwanization (n.) 台灣本土化運動

Taiwanization (臺灣本土化運動) is a term to describe the Taiwan localization movement that began after 1975. This gradual movement embraced the importance of a separate Taiwanese culture, economy and society. This movement began some important changes in the education system, including the teaching of Taiwanese history. It also included the teaching and preservation of the other languages locally established on Taiwan. Today, most of the people in the younger generations of Taiwanese people identify themselves with a pluralistic society that is centered on the unique history and cultures of the island.

Indigenous 原住民

When I first traveled to Taiwan in 1996, one of my first journeys was to Wulai Township in New Taipei City. A tour guide told me that there were indigenous people in Taiwan, but I knew nothing about them. He said they were called Taiwan's aboriginal people, and that they constituted a small minority (2%) of the island's population. I took the bus from Xindian to Wulai Township to find out about this culture for myself. After passing lush, green mountains and many waterfalls, I reached my guest house in the late morning hours. I unpacked and was greeted by my personal tour guide, Lawa. She told me that she was from the Atayal tribe, and she was excited to share authentic cultural experiences. On my first day, I discovered that the Atayal people had their own distinct language and unique customs. Over the next 5 days, I enjoyed the colorful traditions, celebrations, songs, dance, and music that my guide proudly shared in her community. Unexpectedly, the tribal culture seemed more like the culture of the Pacific Islands than that of mainland China. My hosts at the guest house generously offered tasty indigenous cuisine, like grilled mountain pig, flying fish, and millet wine. What made everything more special was how my new aborigine friends treated me like part of their family.

I have brought other foreigners to visit indigenous areas, and they have been fascinated by their experiences. If you have visitors, you should recommend that they visit one of Taiwan's 16 officially-recognized tribes. They include the Amis, Atayal, Bunun, Hla'alua, Kanakanavu, Kavalan, Paiwan, Puyuma, Rukai, Saisiyat, Sakizaya, Sediq, Thao, Truku, Tsou and Yami. The visitors can find many similarities between the cultures of Taiwan and the Pacific, indicating that Taiwan truly has cultural links around the world.

基本實用會話

Taiwanese (A)  Westerner (B)

A conversation at a tourism information center.
遊客服務中心的對話

A : How can I help you?
有什麼我能幫忙的？

B : I heard a lot about Taiwan's indigenous culture, so I'd like to go to an aboriginal area to do some sightseeing.
我聽說過台灣的原住民文化，所以我想去原住民區域觀光。

A: No problem. The most accessible indigenous area near Taipei is around Wulai Township, one of the villages inhabited by the Atayal people. It's located in the mountains of the Wulai District about 40 kilometers south of here.
沒問題，離這最近的原住民區域在烏來，那裡住著泰雅族，離這裡約40公里。

B: Atayal people? Is that the name of one of the aboriginal tribes?
泰雅族，這是原住民部落的名字嗎？

A: Yes, they are the second largest tribal group in Taiwan. They were once known for being fierce warriors. They had facial tattoos and they used to cut off the heads of their enemies.
是的，他們是台灣第二大原住民族，曾經是非常勇猛的戰士，臉上有紋面，而且以前會割下敵人的首級。

B: That sounds fascinating, and a little scary. Should I be concerned about visiting Wulai? 聽起來真迷人，也有點可怕。我去烏來參觀要注意什麼嗎？

A: While you're in Wulai, visit the Atayal Museum to learn more about the history and culture, and enjoy the local cuisine. Try the barbecued mountain pork and buy some souvenirs. Don't forget to take photos of the enormous waterfall, while riding in the cable car.
你去烏來時，可以參觀泰雅族博物館，了解更多歷史和文化，也能享用地方美食，試試烤山豬肉，也可買些紀念品。別忘了在搭纜車時和大瀑布合照。

B: Wow! That sounds like a memorable experience. Thank you!
哇，聽來會是趟難忘的經驗，謝謝你！

A conversation in an indigenous village.
在原住民部落的對話

B: No more millet wine, please, although it's delicious. I shouldn't drink too much wine, because there is so much I want to explore here.
請不要再倒小米酒了，雖然它很好喝。我不該喝太多酒，因為我還想多看看這裡。

A: Thank you for dining at our restaurant. I hope you liked our traditional food. If you want to see more of our culture, I recommend you visit our cultural center. You'll see our local boys and girls rehearsing for the annual Amis Harvest Festival. Their costumes are quite spectacular.
謝謝你來我們餐廳用餐，希望你喜歡我們的傳統食物。如果你想更了解我們的文化，建議你可以去文化中心參觀。你會看到我們這裡的男孩女孩為了每年的阿美豐年祭正在排練，他們的服裝很特別。

B: Right, I have my camera ready. What activities will they perform?
好，我已經準備好相機了，他們要表演什麼活動？

A: They will practice their songs and dances. But be prepared. They may just invite you to join them. 他們會練習歌舞，不過小心點，他們會邀請你加入。

B: What? But I'm not very good at singing or dancing.
什麼？但我不太會唱歌，跳舞。

A : Don't worry! The Amis people, or Pangcah, are very hospitable to visitors. They are very patient, and they will probably welcome you like you were part of their family. Have a good time!
別擔心，阿美族人對遊客都很熱情，他們非常有耐性，或許會熱情歡迎你，好像你是他們家族的一份子。祝你玩得瑜快。

NOTES

Most foreign visitors in Taiwan spend their time in the Taipei area, so they seldom have the opportunity to see the 16 tribal cultures of Taiwan. If they wish to experience more than what is available in the Taipei area, you may recommend that they visit one of the two aboriginal cultural theme parks in Taiwan. The largest one, Formosa Aboriginal Culture Village (http://www.nine.com.tw), is located in Nantou County. The other one, Taiwan Indigenous Peoples Culture Park (http://www.tacp.gov.tw), is located in Sandimen, Pingtung County. These parks give visitors a sample of all of Taiwan's tribal cultures in one location.

溝通大加分

Sentences a Westerner might say
老外可能會說的句子

I've never heard about the tribal people of Taiwan. Can you tell me more about them?
我沒聽說過台灣的部落，能再多說一些嗎？

How do I say "hello" in your language? "Lokah su!"
你的語言怎麼說「哈囉」？「Lokah su！」

Can you direct me to the nearest indigenous village?
你能帶我到最近的原住民村莊嗎？

Did you say that the east coast of Taiwan has the largest indigenous populations? How can I travel there?
你說台灣東海岸有最大的原住民族群？我要怎麼去那裡？

What? You want me to try that? I don't think I'd dare to eat flying squirrel meat.
什麼？你要我試？我覺得我應該不敢吃飛鼠肉。

Mmm. This is pretty good. May I have some more millet wine, please? Cheers!
嗯，這很好喝，我可以再來點小米酒嗎？乾杯！

These colorful Paiwan glass beads are beautiful and very creative.
這些色彩繽紛的排灣族玻璃族很美，而且很有創意。

Which tribes in Taiwan have traditional tattoos?
台灣哪些部落有傳統的紋身？

Is this souvenir actually made by an aboriginal artist?
這個紀念品真的是由原住民藝術家做的？

Sentences a Taiwanese person might say.
台灣人可能會說的句子

The traditional houses of some of the tribes were elevated above the ground to prevent rats and snakes from coming inside.
有些部落的傳統住屋高於地面，以預防老鼠或蛇跑到室內。

The next performance of traditional tribal dance begins at 5:00 p.m.
下一場傳統部落舞蹈的表演在下午五點開始。

You may take photos with the beautiful cultural performers after the show is over.
節目結束後你可以和美麗的文化表演者合照。

Most of the tribes cultivate a wild grain called millet to eat as food or to make into wine.
很多部落種植一種稱為小米的野生穀物，可以當食物也可以釀酒。

Our traditional costume has unique patterns and colors to signify what tribal group we belong to.
我們的傳統服飾有獨特的花紋和色彩，以標示出我們所屬的部落族群。

Our people, the Bunun, have an ancient writing system that is over 1,000 years old.
我們布農族的古老文字已經超過一千年。

The two-headed snake is a sacred symbol to both the Rukai and Paiwan people.
雙頭蛇是魯凱族和排灣族的神聖象徵。

The Amis are talented musicians, and one of their unique instruments is the nose flute.
阿美族是很有天份的音樂家，他們的特殊樂器之一是鼻笛。

Before the 1930's, members of the Atayal, Truku, Sediq, and Saisiyat tribes received facial tattoos as symbols of honor.
在1930年代之前，泰雅族、太魯閣族、賽德克族和賽夏族會紋面，那是榮譽的象徵。

If you'd like to support the local tribal artists, please buy their handicrafts at the gift shop. 如果你想支持部落藝術家，請在禮品店購買他們的手工藝品。

Featured Vocabulary

indigenous peoples vs. aborigines (n.) 土著人 vs 原住民

In most countries, people refer to their original inhabitants as indigenous peoples. Only in Australia, do residents refer to their original inhabitants as aborigines. When Westerners hear people use the term "aborigines" to talk about the Taiwanese tribes, they are often confused. This is why I believe we should follow international convention and refer to Taiwan's tribal people as "indigenous," instead of "aboriginal."

tattoo (n.) 紋身

Getting a tattoo is very common in Western culture. When visiting Taiwan, Westerners are often surprised to see the traditional tattoos of the aboriginal tribes, and this is an aspect of the culture many find fascinating. Facial tattoo culture was once a part of the Atayal, Truku, Sediq, and Saisiat tribes. People from the Paiwan tribe still wear traditional tattoos on their arms and legs.

Moon Festival 中秋節

UNIT 55

I happily accepted an invitation to join a Mid-Autumn Festival celebrated by the family of a student that I taught. I enjoyed the opportunity to get to know their family better, and to experience more traditional Taiwanese customs. I arrived with a bottle of wine, and was greeted with a box of moon cakes. I tried these delicacies for the first time, and felt they were a little rich and heavy, but not too sweet. These appetizers went down very well, especially with cups of hot tea. Instead of a traditional Chinese feast, we sat in front of several barbecue grills. That was a big surprise for me, but I did enjoy this method of cooking. We sat and talked while the coals were getting hot. My student shared with me the traditions and meanings behind the "Moon Festival" customs. Her parents, grandparents, aunts, uncles and cousins were sharing in the conversation, and I shared about the traditional Thanksgiving holiday in America. It was a pleasant exchange of culture. I could see how much the family enjoyed being together, and how close they were, even though their busy lives limited their opportunities to be together. The holiday activities with a Taiwanese family gave me a new appreciation for family time and how Taiwanese people like to express their love through sharing of their food and blessings.

If they are fortunate, visitors to Taiwan will have the opportunity to explore the experiences of the Mid-Autumn Festival with a host family. They will have the opportunity to see what happens when Taiwanese put their busy lives aside to be with their families and share their love and gratitude through familial activities, culture, and food. Being with a family on this occasion can show the visitor the deep appreciation and respect that Taiwanese people have for family identity and roots. If you know a foreign visitor in Taiwan, inviting them to join your Mid-Autumn Festival celebration can give them a deeper understanding of Taiwanese family life.

基本實用會話

Taiwanese (A)　　Westerner (B)

Moon cakes
月餅

B : Thank you. What is this for?
謝謝你，這是做什麼的？

A : This weekend is the Mid-Autumn Festival. Moon cakes are given to all of the teachers.
這個週末是中秋節，月餅是送給所有老師的。

B：It tastes pretty good, and it's not too sweet. But I think I will gain weight if I eat too many.
嚐起來味道很好，而且不會太甜。但我覺得吃太多會變重。

A：Yes. It is a traditional gift given to family members as a gesture of family unity.
對，它是送給家庭成員的傳統禮物，象徵家人團圓。

B：I see. I don't really have family here in Taiwan, so I appreciate the gesture.
我懂了，我其實沒有家人在台灣，所以很感謝你送我月餅。

A：You're welcome. I consider all of our teachers here like a family. Would you like to join our barbecue tonight?
不客氣，我把這裡所有老師都當成家人，你想加入我們今晚的烤肉嗎？

Barbecue
烤肉

B：Wow! I have never seen anyone light charcoal with a blow torch before.
哇！我以前沒看過任何人用焊槍點燃木炭。

A：We don't like to wait too long for the charcoal to be hot. We want to start cooking right away.
我們不想等長時間讓木炭變熱，我們想馬上就開始烤。

B：That's smart. You don't like to waste time. What can I do to help?
真聰明，你們不喜歡浪費時間，我能幫上什麼忙？

A：You can wash these bamboo stalks. And you can bring the meat outside from the kitchen.
你可以洗洗這些竹筍，也可以把肉拿出廚房。

B：No problem. You can barbecue bamboo stalks? And mushrooms, too? I have never seen that.
沒問題，竹筍可以烤？香菇也可以？我從來沒見過。

A：They are just appetizers. We have plenty of meat. Just take your time, and try everything.
這只是開胃菜，我們有很多肉，慢慢來，什麼都試試看。

B：I will. Happy Moon Festival! Thank you for treating me like part of your family.
我會的，中秋節快樂。謝謝你把我當成家人。

NOTES

The Mid-Autumn Festival has its roots almost a thousand years ago in ancient Chinese culture, and it is also know as the "Moon Festival," because of its traditional association with the full moon and moon worship. It is celebrated by ethnic Chinese in China, Taiwan and around the world. The festival celebrates the autumn harvest, and brings families together. Around the world, there are similar festivals during this time related to the autumn harvest, including the Tet Festival or Children's Festival in Vietnam, Chuseok in Korea, Tsukimi in Japan, Lantern Festival in Singapore and Malaysia, and Thanksgiving in the USA.

Sentences a Westerner might say
老外可能會說的句子

Please tell me more about your Mid-Autumn Festival.
請多說說和中秋節有關的事。

That sounds like the American Thanksgiving holiday. That has been around for about 400 years.
聽來很像美國的感恩節，感恩節大約四百年了。

Yes. We have the biggest feast of the year, with many dishes surrounding a large roasted turkey. But there is no barbecue.
是的，我們會舉辦整年最盛大的宴會，有烤火雞，火雞旁還有很多道菜，不過沒有烤肉。

I love barbecue, too. Especially barbecued hamburgers and steak!
我也喜歡烤肉，特別是烤漢堡和牛排！

That's no problem. I am happy to see what your traditions are. What's this?
沒關係，我很高興能看看你們的傳統。這是什麼？

OK. That's not bad. What else is a tradition of the Moon Festival?
好，還不錯。中秋節還有什麼傳統？

Oh, finding a spouse? Have you prayed for that before?
喔，找伴侶？你以前有為此祈禱過嗎？

I don't mind if I do. Can I help with the cooking?
可以啊，我可以幫忙烤嗎？

I have never grilled seafood on a barbecue grill before. That sounds excellent.
我以前沒在烤肉網上烤過海鮮，聽起來好極了。

Now that is definitely something I've never tried before.
這真的是我從來沒試過的東西了。

Sentences a Taiwanese person might say.
台灣人可能會說的句子

It has been around for almost a thousand years. It is a special time for families to gather and give thanks for the harvest.
它已經持續一千年了，它是家人團聚的特殊日子，也是為了感謝豐收。

And what do you do during Thanksgiving? Do you have a feast?
你們感恩節的時候做什麼？會舉辦宴會嗎？

We used to have a big feast at my grandmother's house, but now we have a barbecue.

我們以前會在祖母家吃大餐，可是現在我們會烤肉。

Oh. We won't have hamburgers and steak tonight. I'm sorry.
喔，我們今晚沒有漢堡和牛排，真抱歉。

We're starting with a type of bamboo and mushrooms.
我們一開始先烤竹筍和香菇。

People used to pray for the next season's crops to be successful. Now people pray for finding a spouse, or having good fortune.
人們會祈禱來年豐收，現在人們則會祈禱找到伴侶，或是有好運氣。

I'm not ready for that. Would you like some pork sandwiches with barbecue sauce?
我還沒準備好。你想來點烤豬肉三明治嗎？

Sure. We're going to grill some fish, clams and oysters next.
當然，接下來我們還要烤魚、蛤蜊和牡蠣。

We also have some fish eggs, or maybe you call it roe. We'll barbecue that with some onions.
我們還有魚蛋，或說是魚卵。我們會搭配洋蔥一起烤。

We're honored to share our holiday with our new American friend. Thank you for coming.
我們很榮幸能和新的美國朋友分享我們的節日，謝謝你的光臨。

Featured Vocabulary

harvest (v., n.) 收獲

The Mid-Autumn Festival also has another English name, "The Harvest Moon Festival." This means the festival that occurs during the full moon during the time of harvest. To "harvest" means to gather the food crops when they are ready. In most parts of the Northern Hemisphere, food crops grow during the Summer and are ready to be collected around mid- or late-September. There are many traditional festivals that occur during harvest time, which give people the opportunity to gather to take part in harvesting and activities that give thanks for the life-giving bounty of the earth.

moon cake (n.) 月餅

The making and sharing of moon cakes is an integral tradition of the Mid-Autumn Festival. In Chinese culture, the round shape of the mooncake symbolizes completeness and family unity. That is why the moon cakes are shared with the family during the holiday. Moon cakes have been given during the holiday for hundreds of years, but there are different stories about the origins. Moon cakes are made with flour, oil and egg yolk, and has with different types of filling in the center. One popular filling that is used is lotus seed paste. I believe eating moon cake is even better when accompanied by hot green tea.

barbecue (n.) 燒烤

Barbecue, or BBQ, is a method of cooking over hot coals or flames. It is also referred to as "barby" in Australia. Barbecuing food is very similar to "grilling," but the widely-accepted difference being that grilling is very hot and fast with low-smoke fuel, while barbecuing is low heat and slow, with a fuel that has more smoke. In Taiwan, a family barbecue has become a mainstay in Mid-Autumn Festival celebrations.

UNIT 56

Ghost Festival 中元節

One time, I visited my mother-in-law, and she had a table on the driveway in front of her house. She was preparing for "bai-bai," or the practice of leaving food out for the spirits. This time, she told me it was for wandering ghosts, not her ancestors. That's why the food was placed out near the street, instead of upstairs in the altar room. She asked for my help, and I put my mail down on the table, to help with the food. My mother-in-law screamed, "Take the mail off the table!" I was puzzled, and she explained that it was bad luck for me to reveal my address to the ghosts that may visit. Later, while I was burning joss paper in the garden next to the house, my wife explained the story and superstitions behind the festival known as Ghost Day, and Ghost Month, which is the seventh month of the lunar calendar. I got a list of the many things that I should not do to attract unwanted attention from unfriendly ghosts. I found it a bit funny, but out of respect for their customs and traditions, I promised to do my best not to offend any spirits. After making sure the ghosts had plenty to eat, our family was invited to eat the feast.

Foreigners visiting Taiwan during Ghost Month may be surprised to see tables in front of almost every home and business piled with incense and food. It may be a curiosity to them, because there is nothing like it in their country. Also, many people burn "ghost money" on the side of the street in front of their home or business. This is also another curious custom for Westerners, but it can also be a dangerous one. Many times, while driving on a scooter, I have been burnt by hot flying ashes. One piece of ash in someone's eye can spell disaster.

基本實用會話

Taiwanese (A)　Westerner (B)

Feeding ghosts
祭祀好兄弟

B: Thank you for taking me to the temple to study the details of religious culture.
謝謝你帶我來寺廟，研究宗教文化的細節。

A: This is a special time to bring you here. Do you see all of the food on the tables?
這個時間點很特別。你看到桌上的食物嗎？

B: I do. Why is there so much food? Are they preparing for a feast?
有，為什麼那麼多食物？他們要準備開宴會嗎？

A: These are offerings by the townfolk to the ghosts that may be wandering nearby.
這些是民眾祭祀給附近遊盪的好兄弟的食物。

B : People really believe in ghosts? And, why would they want to feed them?
人們真的相信有鬼？他們為什麼要給他們東西吃？

A : This is one of the traditions of ghost month. I personally believe people just don't want to deal with any hungry, angry ghosts.
這是鬼月的傳統之一。我個人相信人們只是不想面對任何又餓又生氣的鬼。

Burning joss paper
燒紙錢

B : Why are we burning stacks of paper? This looks similar to money.
我們為什麼要燒這堆紙？這和錢好像。

A : This is called "ghost money," or "joss paper." It is for the ghosts of our ancestors.
這稱為「冥紙」，或是「紙錢」。這是獻給祖先的。

B : I see. This is ghost month. I have seen people throw ghost money into incinerators at temples.
我懂了，現在是鬼月，我看到人們把紙錢丟進寺廟的焚化爐。

A : It is a way Taoists and Buddhists show respect for the deceased.
這是道教和佛教對亡者致敬的方式。

B : Interesting. Can you write a message on paper and send it to your deceased relatives?
真有趣。你能在紙上寫下訊息，然後送給亡者嗎？

A : I am not sure. I haven't heard of that custom before. Is that something from your culture?
我不確定。我以前沒聽過這樣的習俗，你的文化裡有嗎？

B : No. You offer food and money, so I just wondered if you also tried to communicate.
不，只有祭祀食物和紙錢，所以我不知道你們會不會試著溝通。

NOTES

The Ghost Festival, or Hungry Ghost Festival, is observed by Chinese people in China and Taiwan. There is really nothing like it in Western culture. Halloween celebrates the deceased, but does not require people to make offerings to the dead. The fifteenth day of the seventh month is called Ghost Day, and the seventh month is referred to as the Ghost Month. According to folklore, on the fifteenth day, the gates of Heaven and Hell and the gates of the living world are open, and the spirits are free to wander. Buddhists and Taoists make offerings to reduce the suffering of the deceased. Rituals include burning incense, joss paper, and other objects made of paper. Of course, a lot of food is offered to feed the great hunger of these wandering ghosts. During Ghost Month, many Chinese people are very superstitious.

Sentences a Westerner might say
老外可能會說的句子

You didn't tell me that there would be a show with this dinner. I didn't know that temples held concerts.
你沒告訴我晚餐還有節目表演。我不知道廟裡會舉辦音樂會。

Are you serious? That bag of groceries we bought are for ghosts? What's going on?
真的嗎？那袋雜貨店裡買的東西是給鬼的？怎麼回事？

OK. I thought we came here to enjoy a relaxing dinner at a temple.
好，我以為我們是來寺廟享受一頓輕鬆的晚餐。

What about our food? Will everyone share their food?
那我們的食物呢？大家都會分享他們的食物嗎？

That looks like Chinese opera. That's interesting. Should we get a front row seat?
看來像國劇，真有趣，我們可以坐前排嗎？

Wow! I see. That is quite respectful. I didn't know that temples provide live shows.
哇！我懂了。真恭敬。我不知道寺廟會有現場表演。

I can't believe my eyes! Do you see what I see? That woman is taking her clothes off.
我不敢相信我的眼睛！你看到我看到的東西嗎？那女人正在脫衣服。

This is not bad. I think this show pleases the living as well.
還不錯，我想這些節目也能取悅活人。

But, this is not something people can see every day. My friends won't believe it.
可是這不是一般人天天會看到的東西，我的朋友不會相信的。

Relax. I didn't know you were so superstitious.
放輕鬆，我不知道你這麼迷信。

Sentences a Taiwanese person might say.
台灣人可能會說的句子

Yes, there will be singing and performances on stage. Did you bring the food to offer to the ghosts?
是的，會有歌唱和舞台表演，你有帶祭祀好兄弟的食物嗎？

This temple celebration is for Ghost Day. The locals bring a lot of food to please the wandering ghosts.
這項寺廟慶典是為鬼月而辦。當地人會帶很多食物來取悅遊蕩的鬼魂。

I'm sure you won't see any ghosts. This is just a show of respect. It is our ancient tradition.
我確定你不會看到鬼，只是為了表現尊重的節目，是我們古老的傳統。

No. That is for us to take home later. But, it's for us to offer to the ghosts. The temple will provide a meal for everyone.
不會，我們的食物晚點可以帶回家，不過這是為了祭祀鬼魂的，廟裡會為每個人準備餐點。

No! Stay out of those seats. The best seats are provided to any ghosts that may come.
不！那些位置不能坐。最好的任置是留給可能來參加的鬼魂。

Only on special occasions. This show is to provide entertainment for the ghosts. They wander during Ghost Month searching for food and entertainment.
只有在特殊情況才有。這節目是為了提供鬼魂娛樂，他們在鬼月時四處遊蕩，尋找食物和娛樂。

It's OK. Some places offer burlesque shows to please the ghosts.
沒問題的，有些地方提供脫衣舞，取悅那些鬼魂。

Hey! Put that camera away. I don't think the performers, or ghosts, would be comfortable.
嘿！把相機收起來，我想表演者和鬼魂都會不高興的。

Just be discreet. You don't want to anger any ghosts. You may have bad luck this year.
小心點，你不會想惹怒鬼魂的，否則今年會運氣不好。

I think most religious people in Taiwan are. Let's go. It's time to eat.
我想台灣大部分有信仰的人都這樣，我們走吧，該去吃東西了。

Featured Vocabulary

haunt (v., n.) 出沒

In English, the word, "haunt" can refer to a place that is frequently visited by a person. Someone might say, "During my college years, that bar was my old haunt." The word, "haunt," is more frequently used as a verb that means the actions of a ghost in a place. A ghost can haunt a house, or a church or a graveyard. If people believe that a ghost frequently haunts a house, they can say the house is "haunted." In Western culture, many people believe in ghosts and tell "horror" stories about haunted places to scare people. Creating sensationalized fear is a form of entertainment in the West.

curse (v., n.) 詛咒

Chinese people may worry about running into a ghost and getting bad luck. In English, Westerners would describe obtaining bad luck as being cursed. Being cursed is a supernatural phenomenon, whereas a ghost or spirit may cast a spell to punish a living person. It is the curse, or spell, which attracts bad luck for the person. Some famous documented cases reveal curses received by people who discovered the tombs of ancient Egyptian pharoahs. Many of them died of mysterious causes soon afterwards.

57

Dragon Boat 端午節

I had my first taste of the Dragon Boat Festival living in Orlando, Florida. Like Chinese New Year and the Moon Festival, the Dragon Boat Festival is widely celebrated in the USA by the Asian-American community. These three Chinese holidays have been opportunities for non-Asians to experience Chinese culture. From my experience, more Americans came out to enjoy the Dragon Boat Festival activities than any other Chinese holiday. I believe the main reason was the spirit of athletic competition. Many companies throughout Florida trained their own teams to compete in the Dragon Boat races in Orlando, Tampa and Miami, Florida. Most competitors were not even Asian. But they enjoyed the competitive spirit, and the experience of ethnic and cultural diversity. I even enjoyed paddling in the long decorative canoes with my friends and family, even though we were nowhere close to being champions.

Foreigners visiting Taiwan during the Dragon Boat Festival may be prone to staying indoors to avoid the severe heat of the summer sun, but the festival activities are worth coming out for. First, there are usually cultural parades in the streets, where you can see many colorful costumes, and dragon symbolism, including the well-known dragon dance. The parades usually lead to the center of activity, which is near a body of water. That is where the excitement of dragon boat races occur. Athletes train year-round to try to win the honor of being champions. It is also the best opportunity to try "zhongshi" sticky rice dumplings, which aren't really available at any other time.

基本實用會話

Taiwanese (A)  Westerner (B)

Eating sticky rice dumplings
吃粽子

B: So, I unwrap the bamboo leaves like this?
我要像這樣解開竹葉？

A: Yes. The bamboo leaves hold the sticky rice, so your fingers won't get sticky.
對，竹葉包住糯米，你的手指才不會黏。

B: Mmmm. Not bad. What's inside the glutinous rice? That's how we say sticky rice in English.
嗯，不錯，糯米裡面是什麼？英文的糯米叫glutinous rice。

A：A bit of everything, perhaps. Pork belly, mushrooms, peanuts, egg, mung beans, or taro.
或許什麼都包一點。五花肉，香菇，花生，蛋，毛豆或芋頭。

B：Interesting combinations. Perhaps what makes it fun to eat is not knowing what you'll get.
有趣的組合。或許不知道會吃到什麼，才是它有趣的地方。

A：I agree. It's fun to be surprised.
我同意，驚喜都很有趣。

Dragon boat racing
划龍舟

B：This is much harder than it looks.
這比看起來難多。

A：It's not only the strength of your paddling that matters. It also takes teamwork.
重要的不只是你自己划槳的力量，也需要團隊合作。

B：I know what you mean now. We can only travel straight to our goal by paddling in unison.
我知道你的意思了，我們只有齊心划槳，才能向前到達目標。

A：Right. Just follow the beat of the drum and synchronize with the people around you.
對，只要跟著鼓的節奏，和身邊的人同步。

B：OK. I think we can win the next race. We were so close last time.
好，我想我們下場比賽就能贏，上場比賽很接近了。

A：You have a good competitive spirit. If we win, the sticky rice dumplings will be on me.
你的競賽精神很好。如果我們贏了，我請大家吃粽子。

B：And I'll buy the bubble milk tea for our team.
我請大家喝珍珠奶茶。

NOTES

The Dragon Boat Festival (端午節), or Duanwu Festival, is one of the four major holidays observed by ethnic Chinese people. Duanwu means "double five," becaue the holiday occurs on the 5th day of the 5th month of the lunar calendar. This festival corresponds with the summer solstice, the longest day of the year in the Northern Hemisphere. In Chinese culture, the dragon represents, like the sun, represents male energy, whereas the phoenix and the moon represent feminine energy. The Summer Solstice is a time represented as the peak of the dragon's strength. The celebrations that occur during the Dragon Boat Festival include eating sticky rice dumplings (粽子), drinking realgear wine, and racing dragon boats. There are several folk tales describing the origins of the Dragon Boat celebrations. However, the origins may have just begun in ancient times as a celebration of the annual harvest of winter wheat.

Sentences a Westerner might say
老外可能會說的句子

I don't know if I want to go outdoors to attend any festivals. Do you know how hot it is today?
我不知道我今天想不想出門參加任何節慶。你知道今天有多熱嗎？

Are you serious? I have a day off from work. I can sleep longer and rest in air-conditioned comfort.
你是認真的嗎？我今天放假，我可以在舒適的冷氣房裡睡久一點。

Yes. But I can experience Chinese culture any time in Taiwan.
對，但我在台灣任何時候都能體驗中華文化。

No. What's so special about it?
沒有，它有什麼特別的？

I've always liked dragons. But it will take something exciting to get me out of bed today.
我一直很喜歡龍，但今天得有更刺激的東西才能讓我離開床。

It's going to be 32 degrees Celsius today. Cultural dances are not enough.
今天的溫度是攝氏32度，文化舞蹈的理由還不夠充足。

Athletic competition is something I really enjoy.
我真的很喜歡運動競賽。

That is something I would be interested in. Count me in.
那是我會有興趣的事，算我一份。

I'd appreciate having that new experience. Thank you.
能有這份新體驗，我會很感激的，謝謝你。

Celebrating with your friends also sounds like a worthwhile reason to go.
和你朋友一起慶祝，聽來也是值得出門的理由。

Sentences a Taiwanese person might say.
台灣人可能會說的句子

It might be hot, but I don't think you'll want to miss out on the activities of this important holiday.
或許是很熱，但我覺得你不想錯過這個重要節日的活動。

Aren't you always interested in experiencing Chinese culture?
你不是一直想體驗中華文化嗎？

That's true, but have you ever experienced this festival?
這是真的，但你體驗過這個節慶嗎？

It is a celebration of the Summer Solstice and the sun's energy, symbolized by the dragon.
這是慶祝夏至和太陽能量的節慶，它的象徵是龍。

If it's excitement you want, you'll see lion dances and dragon dances.
如果你想要刺激，應該看看舞龍舞獅。

There will be some exciting dragon boat racing on the river.
河上還有刺激的龍舟競賽。

There are athletes from all over Taiwan in the competition. I think you may even have a chance to show your skills, too.
會有來自台灣各地的運動員參加競賽。我想你或許也有機會大展身手。

All right. I will see if I can give you a chance to paddle on my company's dragon boat team.
好，看看我能不能安排你加入我公司的龍舟隊。

After the races, we will celebrate with a dinner of sticky rice dumplings and a special type of wine.
在比賽後，我們會吃粽子、喝特殊的酒慶祝。

OK. We'll need to bring plenty of water, comfortable clothes and sunblock.
好，我們得帶大量的水、穿上舒服的衣服和防晒油。

Featured Vocabulary

dragon boat race (n.) 龍舟賽

A dragon boat race is a competition between canoe-like boats powered by teams of people using paddles. This had long been a popular sport in Chinese-speaking countries. Surprisingly, this sport has become very popular in Western countries, with many people participating who are not of Chinese ethnicity. Dragon boat racing has its roots in ancient times with the Dragon Boat Festival. According to one folk story, this custom of paddling canoes come from the story of Qu Yuan (屈原). When this beloved hero took his own life in the Miluo River, his countrymen searched for his body in the river paddling in boats. This act of racing around the river, evolved into today's Dragon Boat Race.

summer solstice (n.) 夏至

The Dragon Boat Festival takes place annually during or near the summer solstice, which is the day in which the sun is considered the strongest in the Northern Hemisphere. Likewise, the winter solstice is the day that there is the least amount of sunlight in the Northern Hemisphere. This is caused by the annual tilting of the axis of the rotation of the Earth. This tilting is so predictable, that scientists can predict the exact date and time of the solstices every year for many years to come. One of the customs of the Summer Solstice Day in Taiwan is balancing raw eggs to stand upright. It is said that raw eggs cannot stand upright like boiled eggs can. This is true, except for around noon on the Summer Solstice, when the sun is at its strongest. Apparently, the effect of the Sun's gravity is at its strongest during this time. I personally agree with this theory, as I won an egg-standing contest at a grocery store during the Summer Solstice of 2014, standing 12 eggs within 2 minutes.

UNIT 58

New Year 新年

My first Lunar New Year experience in Taiwan surpassed all of my expectations. The household was very active leading up to the first day of the new year. There was a lot of cleaning and shopping done before the first day. Then, on the first day, the feasting and celebrations began. My children received red envelopes for the first time, and they were so happy, they forgave us for not having a Christmas holiday. We ate and ate and ate, and stayed up late to light fireworks. We didn't see my wife's sisters until the second day. When they arrived with their children, there was more feasting and more red envelopes for the children. The two-week holiday was the first time we spent considerable time with my wife's family. We ate, visited temples, ate and traveled. By the 15th day, we had many cherished memories together and I had to buy a new belt for my pants.

Foreigners visiting Taiwan during the Lunar New Year can see many interesting traditions. However, since this is a time of family reunions, visitors may not have the opportunity to experience these traditions, unless they are invited by a host family. It can be a very uneventful and lonely time for foreigners, since many people have returned to their families and many businesses are closed. So, if you know any visitors, you have the opportunity to give them the most special cultural experience possible by inviting them to celebrate the holiday with your family.

基本實用會話

Taiwanese (A)　Westerner (B)

Cleaning the house
打掃房子

B：Why do we have to set aside the entire weekend to clean our apartment?
我們為什麼要把整個週末拿來打掃公寓？

A：Lunar New Year is almost here. It is tradition to clean your entire home before the new year.
農曆新年快到的。傳統上要在新年前大掃除。

B：I appreciate having a clean house, but why must we be so thorough?
我很重視家裡要乾淨，但為什麼要打掃這麼徹底？

A：According to custom, we need to clean to clear out all of the bad luck from the previous year to attract more good luck for the new year.
根據習俗，我們要把前一年的壞運氣徹底掃出門，才能吸引新年的好運氣。

B: OK. I will call my friends to cancel my weekend plans.
好，我打電話給朋友取消週末計畫。

A: I promise that it will be worth it. Lunar New Year will hold many surprises for you.
我保證一切會值得的。農曆新年將會給你帶來許多驚喜。

Wearing red clothes
穿紅衣

B: Do I really have to wear this? I feel silly wearing these red Chinese-style clothes.
我一定要穿這件嗎？穿這種紅色中國服，覺得自己好蠢。

A: Come on! It's your first Lunar New Year celebration with my family. I want you to surprise them.
拜託！這是你第一次和我家人過農曆新年，我希望你讓他們驚訝一下。

B: I will surprise them all right. They'll be surprised by the crazy foreigner in red clothes.
我會整晚都讓他們很驚訝，他們會被一個紅衣外國人驚嚇。

A: It's not that bad. Your outfit will match mine. Everyone will wear red clothes tonight.
沒那麼糟，你的衣服和我的很搭，大家今晚都穿紅衣。

B: You did tell me that I would be surprised by the Lunar New Year customs, so you are right.
你說我會對農曆新年的習俗感到驚訝，你說得對。

A: Wearing red clothes is our custom. The red color is supposed to scare away evil spirits.
穿紅衣是我們的習俗，紅色可以嚇跑邪惡的鬼魂。

B: OK. But, I am not going to wear this little Chinese hat. That is where I draw the line.
好，但我不會戴這頂小中國帽，這是我的界線。

 NOTES

The Lunar New Year is also referred to as the Chinese New Year or also Spring Festival. It is the most revered and widely celebrated of the Chinese holidays. People travel near and far to reunite with their families for the two-week holiday. In China, the largest annual migration of human beings takes place every year during this time, as hundreds of millions of people travel back home. For over two weeks, families take part in many activities and traditions to clear away the previous year's bad luck and attract good fortune for the new year. It is a happy time of feasting, celebration, and the sharing of kinship. On the first day of the new year, families share feasts to welcome the deities, and light firecrackers to scare away the evil spirits. On the second day, married daughters have the opportunity to visit their parents. Each day afterwards has significant meanings and traditions. The holiday concludes on the fifteenth day, which is a holiday known as the Lantern Festival. By that time, every has usually gained a few kilograms and vows to go on a diet.

Sentences a Westerner might say
老外可能會說的句子

Oh my gracious! I can't eat another bite. Please thank your mother for the feast.
我的天啊！我一口都吃不下了，謝謝你母親準備這頓餐點。

Your mother and brother have given our children red envelopes. That is so nice of them. They shouldn't have given them so much.
你母親和哥哥給我們小孩紅包，他們人真好，他們不該給小孩那麼多錢。

I guess it should be OK to let our children spend some of it during their vacation. Do we need to give them red envelopes, too?
我想讓我們的孩子在假期時使用這些錢也沒關係。我們也要給他們紅包嗎？

I didn't realize this holiday would be so expensive. It's a good thing I received a bonus at work.
我不知道這個假期會這麼昂貴。還好我的工作有獎金。

Does that mean your sisters will be here tomorrow with their families?
這表示你的姐妹們明天會和家人回來這裡？

Are you serious? Do we have enough? I guess our kids will have a lot of money. Maybe I can borrow some from them.
真的嗎？我們的錢夠嗎？我猜我的孩子也會很有錢。或許我能跟他們借？

Thank goodness. I will be better prepared next year.
謝天謝地。我最好為明年做準備了。

I told you. I am stuffed. What is "niangao?"
我說過了，我好撐，什麼是「年糕」？

No, thank you. What will we be doing after dinner?
不，謝謝你。我們晚餐後要做什麼？

OK, I could use more good fortune, so next year I can be ready to give red envelopes.
好，我需要更多好運，明年我才能準備紅包。

Sentences a Taiwanese person might say.
台灣人可能會說的句子

She is happy you can join the family celebration for the first time.
你是第一次加入我們的家庭聚餐，她很高興。

That's our custom. We should put most of it away for their future needs.
那是我們的習俗，我們應該為他們的未來存起來。

Of course. We didn't give them any presents for Christmas. And, we should also give a red envelope to my mother, because she does not work.
當然，我們聖誕節沒給他們禮物，我們也給母親紅包，因為她沒有工作。

On the second day of the new year, married daughters are supposed to return home.
在新年第二天，出嫁的女兒會回家。

Exactly. So we will need to prepare red envelopes for all of their kids, too.
沒錯。我們也會為所有的孩子準備紅包。

Don't worry, I have been saving all year for this holiday. I have enough for everyone.
別擔心，我為了這個假日存了一整年。我的錢夠包給大家。

Are you sure you don't have room for dessert? My mom makes really good "niangao."
你確定你沒有肚子吃甜點，我媽做的年糕非常好吃。

It is a type of pudding made from rice flour and sugar.
那是一種用米粉和糖做的布丁。

All of us will walk to the local temple and pray to have good fortune this year.
我們大家都要走到當地的廟宇去，祈禱今年好運。

You're funny. After that, you and our kids can light the fireworks.
你真有趣。在晚餐後，你可以和我們的孩子去放煙火。

Featured Vocabulary

red envelope (n.) 紅包

The most anticipated custom of the Lunar New Year festivities, especially with children, is the receiving of the "red envelope." It is also described as "lucky money," and is offered by the working adults of the family to children and elders who no longer can work. In Taiwan, the amount varies, but I have seen many parents put all or most of the money aside for the students' education. This may take the excitement out of the custom, but an important philosophy of Taiwanese people is "saving for a rainy day." The red envelope is also used to give money for weddings or other special occasions. Giving money to children for a holiday or special occasion seems strange to Americans, because gifts for children are almost always toys and consumer goods. There is no American tradition that I know of involving giving money to children as gifts.

resolution (n.) 決議

Westerners do not typically celebrate Lunar New Year. Instead, they celebrate "ringing in the new year" on New Year's Eve and on New Year's Day. "Ringing in" means "to welcome." Their traditions include, attending a party and staying up until midnight on New Year's Eve (December 31). They will watch the clock count down, and then cheer while fireworks go off. Many adults will use this opportunity kiss someone standing next to them at exactly midnight. One of the customs for New Year's Day is making a "New Year's resolution" and starting on it. A resolution is a firm decision to do something. A person usually chooses a resolution that is that is beneficial, but difficult for the person to do. For example, a common New Year's resolution could be declaring to lose weight or giving up on sweets.

UNIT 59

Yuenshui 鹽水蜂炮

I first visited the Yuenshui Beehive Fireworks Festival wearing protective gear and armed with my camera, ready to document the experience for CNN iReport. I did not know what to expect. Before dark, my family and I toured the quaint Old Street, touring shops that seemed unchanged after 100 years. After dark, my family retreated to safety at the edge of town, while I walked towards the center of activity. There were hundreds of vendors lining the streets, selling local specialties and drinks. After enjoying the opening ceremonies at a large temple, people wandered the streets looking for the beehives, which are carts with thousands of bottle rockets inside. I followed the crowd and stood about 20 feet away from a beehive on the street. All of a sudden, the fuse was lit, and thousands of bottle rockets were flying right at us. People started dancing and jumping, while the firworks exploded all around them. I tried to take photos, but the explosions kept hitting my helmet and my camera, so I decided to run back to find my family. As I ran, I realized that my heart raced with excitement and I never felt more exhilerated. I finally knew what thrillseekers felt like.

The Yuenshui Beehive Fireworks Festival is famous worldwide, and attracts many foreign visitors every year, because there is nothing like it anywhere else in the world. Whether you are a thrillseeker or a casual observer, the fireworks and cultural activities make this festival a must-see event in Taiwan. There will be thousands of people wandering the streets sampling delicious snacks and treats, drinking beverages, and avoiding flying fireworks. There is much to see in this city, and a beautiful old section of town greets visitors with its rustic charm. After dark, the energy starts to sizzle. Fireworks light up the sky, and around the corner may be a "beehive" ready to shoot thousands of bottle rockets AT YOU.

基本實用會話

Taiwanese (A)  Westerner (B)

Yuenshui Old Street
鹽水老街

B : Where are we? These building looks so architecturally different that those in our city.
這裡是哪裡？這些建築看來和我們城市很不一樣。

A : This is Yuenshui Old District. These buildings are the traditional style from 100 years ago.
這裡是鹽水老街。這些大樓是一百年前的傳統建築。

B : I can't believe how well-preserved they are. Some of the buildings are shops.
我不敢相信他們保存得這麼好。有些建築是商店。

A : Check out this shop. This family makes hand-made knives just like they did a long time ago.
你看這家商店，這家人製作手工刀，就跟他們以前一樣。

B : That's cool. But I'm hungry. There are just hundreds of food stalls outside.
酷。但我餓了，外面有上百個食物攤。

A : OK. Let me show you some local specialties. Let's grab dinner before the fireworks start.
好，我帶你去看看地方特產，在煙火開始前先吃點晚餐吧。

Wearing proper clothing
穿著適當的服裝

B : I really want to stand close to the beehives tonight. Am I wearing enough clothing?
我今晚真的想靠蜂炮近一點。這樣穿夠嗎？

A : Well, your helmet doesn't provide full facial protection, so you'll have to buy a new one.
你的安全帽不是全罩的，所以你得買頂新的。

B : OK. They're pretty cheap. Is there anything else I should wear?
好，這些很便宜，我還要穿戴什麼嗎？

A : You should have a heavy coat over your clothes, but it can't be rubber or plastic. That may catch fire.
你的衣服外要再加件厚外套，但不能是塑膠或橡膠，否則可能會起火。

B : Got it. I have long pants and boots, too. I hope I can still see where I'm going.
知道了，我也穿了長褲和靴子，希望我還能看得到路。

A : You're not quite finished. You should wear a towel under your helmet to protect your neck.
這樣還不夠，你的安全帽下要圍一條圍巾保護脖子。

B : All right. I'm getting hot already. I think I am wearing enough gear. Let's go!
好，我準備好了，我想我的設備齊全了，走吧！

NOTES

According to folk stories, the Yuenshui Beehive Fireworks Festival began over 100 years ago when there was an outbreak of the deadly disease, cholera, in Yuenshui. The residents called on the deity, Guān Dì (關帝), the God of War, to help give them strength against the disease. They used fireworks to attract the attention of the deity, and have done so ever since. This event takes place on the 14th and 15th day of the new lunar year, and it concludes with the Lantern Festival. What makes this festival unique is that there are "beehives" containing thousands of bottle rockets that are shot into the crowd. Because of the danger levels of this activity, the festival has been voted worldwide as the 3rd Most Dangerous Folk Festival in the World. The city also does a beautiful job during the Lantern Festival, and its decorative lanterns, alone, are worth visiting.

Sentences a Westerner might say
老外可能會說的句子

That was a beautiful opening ceremony. The fireworks were amazing! Where are we going now?
這個開幕儀式很美，煙火也很棒！我們現在要去哪裡？

What are beehives? Do they have bees?
什麼是蜂炮？有蜜蜂嗎？

OK. But, what's so special about bottle rockets? They just make a loud noise.
好，可是沖天炮有什麼特別的？他們只會發出噪音。

Are the bottle rockets really going to fly towards us? I hope I'm wearing enough.
沖天炮真的會朝我們飛過來嗎？希望我穿得夠多。

Wow! Oh my! This is crazy!
哇，我的天啊！太瘋狂了！

What? I can't hear you! It is so loud! This is lasting a long time.
什麼？我聽不到！好大聲！這維持好久。

I'm good. No damage here. But my coat has a lot of burn marks on it. And I felt a lot of the explosions. That was... invigorating!
我很好，沒受傷。但我的外套上有好多燒焦的痕跡，我也感覺到爆炸的威力，太刺激了。

Are you serious? I'm ready to do it again. But, I'll probably have enough energy only until midnight.
你是認真的嗎？我準備好了。可是我的體力可能只夠維持到午夜。

That's fine. But I think we should hit the food stalls to try more delicious food.
好，但我想我們該去食物攤，嘗試更多美食。

You were right about coming here. It is nothing like anything I have experienced before. Thank you.
來這裡是正確的選擇。這和我以前的體驗都不一樣，謝謝你。

Sentences a Taiwanese person might say.
台灣人可能會說的句子

You haven't seen anything yet. We're following the crowds looking for beehives.
你還沒看到重點呢，我們要跟著人群去看蜂炮。

No. But maybe they look something like beehives, because they hold thousands of bottle rockets that will fly like angry bees.
沒有，不過是像蜂巢般的東西，因為裡面會飛出上千隻沖天炮，跟憤怒的蜜蜂一樣亂竄。

You will see what's so special. Look! They're rolling a beehive out to the middle of the street. Let's get closer.
你會看到它的特別之處。你看！他們把蜂炮車推到街道中央了，我們靠近一點。

Yes, you're well-prepared. Get ready to enjoy the experience.
會，你準備得很好。準備好好體驗吧。

Do what everyone else is doing. Jump! It might prevent a firecracker from sticking onto you.
跟其他人一起做，跳！這樣能預防炮火黏在你身上。

Are you OK? How do you feel? Did any fireworks get under your clothes?
你還好嗎？感覺怎麼樣？有炮火鑽到你的衣服底下嗎？

Are you ready for more? It's only 10:30 pm. This will go on all night until morning.
準備好繼續了嗎？現在才十點半，這活動會維持一整晚，直到天亮。

That's fine. You'll see an incredible fireworks show in a park in the middle of town.
沒關係，在城市中央，你可以看到驚人的煙火。

Eat up. Maybe you'll have more energy to stay out later.
吃吧，或許這樣你才有體力可以熬夜。

You're welcome. It's my pleasure to show people why I love Taiwan.
不客氣，這是我的榮幸，讓朋友了解我對台灣的愛。

Featured Vocabulary

fireworks (n.) 煙火

Fireworks is a general terms to describe the explosive devices that are used for celebration. Fireworks give off a loud sound when they explode, but can also provide colorful illumination as well. Firecrackers (鞭炮) are a type of fireworks, which are small and only make noise when they explode. In Chinese culture, they are typically placed together in a string, and are exploded consecutively to scare away "evil spirits." There are many festivals in Taiwan that show fireworks, but during the Yuenshui Beehive Fireworks Festival, millions of fireworks light up the sky, and a million more are shot at the visitors.

protective gear (n.) 保護的服裝

Another word for "clothing" is "gear," especially when referring to clothing meant to perform a specific function. For example, during a thunderstorm, a person should wear rain gear, and a person going fishing should wear fishing gear. Fishing gear may include waterproof boots, heavy pants, jacket and hat. One a person goes to participate in the Yuenshui Beehive Fireworks Festival, it is recommended that he or she wear protective gear, or clothing that will protect the person from the firecrackers. A person will need a heavy non-flammable coat, long pants, gloves socks, and motorcycle helmet. One should cover every inch of skin, because I have seen bottle rockets fly into a helmet and blow up in someone's ear. Every year, people need to be hospitalized, so the danger is real.

thrillseekers (n.) 追求冒險的人

Why do so many foreigners enjoy going to the Yuenshui Beehive Fireworks Festival? Because many foreigners enjoy facing dangerous situation to be entertained. You can say that they are seeking thrills. In English, people who seek dangerous situations for fun are thrillseeking, and you can call them thrillseekers.

Politics 政治

60

As a democratic state that is evolving and exploring its democratic nature, politics seem to be pervasive throughout society. The Taiwanese people I have met were very passionate about their political affiliation, and seemed to take on the ideologies of their political parties as part of the own personal identities. When I met people for the first time, many proudly told me that they were Pan-Blue, supporting the Kuomingtang Party (中國國民黨), or Pan-Green, supporting the Democratic Progressive Party (民主進步黨). I have met more Pan-Green supporters in Southern Taiwan, who referred to themselves as "Taiwanese" and more Pan-Blue supporters in the Taipei area, who referred to themselves as "Chinese." There are also other established political parties in Taiwan, such as the Taiwan Solidarity Union (台灣團結聯盟), People's First Party (親民黨), and the Non-Partisan Solidarity Union (無黨團結聯盟). As an outsider, I have tried to stay non-affiliated or unbiased. But being raised USA, I personally like any representative who can support democratic principals for the benefit of the majority of the people, and who can show a track record of honesty and integrity.

The way foreigners percieve the political environment in Taiwan will vary, depending on the country they come from. A person from Canada or the USA will view things differently than someone from Russia or Iran. But, they all may agree that the Taiwanese people are very passionate about their views, and thanks to democracy, they can share their views freely. Political passions in Taiwan can spin out of control, as many people have witnessed internationally the fist fights that have occurred in Taiwan's legislature.

基本實用會話

Taiwanese (A) : Westerner (B) :

News Reporting
新聞報導

B : I would like to read more about presidential candidates. Where can I find a newspaper?
我想更了解總統選舉的事，哪裡可以找到報紙？

A : Well, the perspective of the news you read depends on the newspaper. Some newspapers are Pan Green, while most are Pan Blue.
各個報紙會有不同的觀點。有些報紙是泛綠的，大部分是泛藍的。

B : What does that mean, Pan Green and Pan Blue?
泛綠和泛藍是什麼意思？

A : Pan Green means they lean towards the views of the Democratic Progressive Party and Pan Blue leans towards the views of the Kuomingtang Party. They are the two main parties here.

泛綠表示他們偏向民進黨的觀點，而泛藍則偏向國民黨的觀點。他們是這裡的兩大政黨。

B : But, I thought newspapers should be unbiased, and not favor any party.

但我以為報紙應該中立，沒有偏好任何政黨。

A : Hey! Let's face it. The media everywhere have always been political tools for people in power.

面對現實吧，每個地方的媒體都是掌權者的政治工具。

Elections
選舉

B : Are you going to vote today? Can I join you? I am very curious.

你今天要去投票嗎？我能和你一起去嗎？我非常好奇。

A : Sure, but there won't be much to see. I need to stand in that line and vote in that building.

當然，不過沒什麼好看的。我得在那棟大樓排隊投票。

B : That man says I can't go in. I'll just wait outside.

那個人說我不能進去，我只能在外面等。

A : (Later) I just voted on a card in a voting booth for different candidates for different positions.

（稍後）我剛在投票亭，為不同職位投票給不同的候選人。

B : That sounds similar to the American way. While you were inside, a man yelled at me to put my camera away.

聽起來和美國的方式很像。你在裡面的時候，有個男人對我大吼，叫我收起相機。

A : You're not allowed to take photos anywhere near a voting area. That's just the way it is.

在投票區附近不能照相，規定就是這樣。

NOTES

The people of Taiwan are truly a multicultural melting pot, with different backgrounds and opinions. Historically, Taiwan has been ruled by outside powers, that have dominated the majority of the population to protect the interests of the few. Throughout its history, Taiwanese people have fought for their self-determination, in order to have the right to live free from corruption and abuse. In the past, the fight for democracy and self-rule has been met with severe repression and tragedy. From an American's point of view, I believe that people should not forget these tragedies, and there should always be public awareness of these historic lessons, so people can appreciate the democracy Taiwan currently enjoys, and to avoid repeating past mistakes. Americans have been taught about their government's historical wrongdoings, and have seen the public apologies as a big step towards healing and reconciliation of the nation. I hope to see Taiwan follow in these footsteps to have a stronger, more self-determined future.

Sentences a Westerner might say
老外可能會說的句子

The coffee is delicious here. What did you do yesterday?
這裡的咖啡很好喝。你昨天做了什麼事？

Oh! Well, let's talk about something else. I try to stay out of politics.
喔！我們聊點別的事，我盡量不碰政治。

In my country, most people avoid political discussion, because it can lead to arguments and fights. People can lose their friends over their political views.
在我的國家，大部分的人都避免談論政治，因為它會導致爭吵，人們因為政治觀點不同而失去朋友。

OK. I don't know much about Taiwanese politics, but I have seen the Taiwanese legislators fight each other on TV.
好，我不太了解台灣的政治，但我在電視上看過台灣的立法委員吵架。

I don't really know enough about Taiwanese politics to have a serious discussion.
我其實不太了解台灣政治，無法做什麼嚴肅的討論。

OK. I come from a democratic country, so I believe that every citizen should have a voice in the decisions and laws of their country.
好，我來自一個民主的國家，所以我相信每個市民對國家的決策和法律，都有發言權。

What is your view about the democratic process?
你對民主過程的觀點是什麼？

Well that view will challenge the principles of democracy.
這觀點將會挑戰民主的原則。

Please give me an example.
請舉例說明。

I also agree that greater trade with China is important to Taiwan's economy, but, I also believe that relying so much on one trading partner is very risky. Taiwan should expand its international relations.
我也同意和中國有更多貿易，對台灣的經濟很重要，但我也相信過度依賴單一貿易對象非常危險。台灣應該擴展它的國際關係。

Sentences a Taiwanese person might say.
台灣人可能會說的句子

I just voted for the local legislature candidates. The elections are very important.
我去投地方議會候選人了，這選舉非常重要。

I love to talk about politics. It is so important to our future here in Taiwan.
我喜歡談政治，這對台灣的未來很重要。

Learning about Taiwan — History, Culture, Scenery...

You won't have to worry about losing me as a friend because of your political views.
你不用擔心因為你的政治觀點，失去我這個朋友。

True. That is extreme, and most people in Taiwan are passionate about their views.
真的，那是極端的情況，台灣大部分的人對自己的觀點都抱持熱情。

Well, we can learn from what you know, and I can teach you about what I know.
我們可能聊聊你知道的，我也可以告訴你我知道的。

I agree with you. And Taiwan struggles with their different voices.
我同意，而台灣不同的聲音之間常有爭斗。

It's a relatively new form of government here. I am not always sure that the people know what's best for them.
這裡的政府算是相對較新的形式，我不太相信人們總是知道什麼才是最好的。

People sometimes base their decisions on their emotions, instead of the bigger picture. They may not make choices that are in the best interest of the whole island.
人們有時候會以情緒做選擇，而非大局。他們或許不是基於對台灣的最佳利益做出選擇。

Freedom doesn't put food on the table. Without a strong economy, there won't be enough jobs. So, we should pursue a strong economic relationship with China.
自由不是桌上的食物，沒有強大的經濟，就沒有足夠的工作。所以我們要追求與中國建立強大的經濟關係。

I can see your point. That's why I am learning English.
我明白你的觀點，所以我才要學習英文。

Featured Vocabulary

politics (n.) 政治

The word "politics" comes from the Greek word "politikos," which means relating to citizens. There are two definitions of this word. First, politics means the activities associated with the governance of a country or area, especially the debate when there are multiple parties having power. An example of this is a discussion of "Taiwan's party politics." Second, politics can mean the activities that are associated with improving someone's status or increasing power within an organization. An example of this is an examination of "office politics" within a company. Any discussion or evaluation of politics reveals people trying to influence others to get what they want. When decisions are made politically, there are usually winners and losers. Only through democratic debate, negotiation and compromise can the political process create a win-win situation. I believe that in today's society, there are fewer people with the patience and sense of responsibility needed to democratize this process.

democracy (n.) 民主

The word "democracy" also comes from a Greek word, "demokratia," which means the rule of the people. Ancient Greece was the birthplace of modern democracy. Democracy is a form of government where all eligible citizens are able to participate equally in the decision-making, by electing representatives. According to the "Economist Intelligence Unit," there are only 25 fully democratic nations in the world. The same organization lists 53 countries with flawed democracies, with Taiwan being in this category. The fact that Taiwan has been able to institute democratic reform through the will of its people has been a major achievment, but the Taiwanese people should not forget that there is still room to improve, and the achievement are fragile. This means they can be lost more quickly that they were achieved. It hs been my observation that insecurity, fear, and lack of responsibility are the biggest factors in the loss of any democracy.

國家圖書館出版品預行編目資料

遇到老外英語這樣說／Tony Coolidge 陳華友著；－
－初版 . － －臺中市：晨星，2015.09
面； 公分 . － －（Guide book；353）

ISBN 978-986-443-012-3（平裝）

1. 英語 2. 會話

805.188   104008676

Guide Book 353
遇到老外英語這樣說

作者	Tony Coolidge 陳華友
編輯	林千裕
封面設計	許芷婷
內頁繪圖	腐貓君
美術編輯	曾麗香
錄音老師	Tony Coolidge 陳華友、徐淑敏
創辦人	陳銘民
發行所	晨星出版有限公司
	台中市 407 工業區 30 路 1 號
	TEL：(04)23595820　FAX：(04)23550581
	E-mail：service@morningstar.com.tw
	http：//www.morningstar.com.tw
	行政院新聞局局版台業字第 2500 號
法律顧問	陳思成律師
初版	西元 2015 年 9 月 15 日
郵政劃撥	22326758（晨星出版有限公司）
讀者服務專線	(04)23595819＃230
印刷	上好印刷股份有限公司

定價 290 元
（如書籍有缺頁或破損，請寄回更換）
ISBN：978-986-443-012-3

Published by Morning Star Publishing Inc.
Printed in Taiwan
All rights reserved.

以下資料或許太過繁瑣，但卻是我們了解您的唯一途徑

誠摯期待能與您在下一本書中相逢，讓我們一起從閱讀中尋找樂趣吧！

姓名：＿＿＿＿＿＿　　性別：□ 男 □ 女　　生日： ／ ／

教育程度：＿＿＿＿＿＿＿＿＿＿＿＿＿＿＿＿

職業：□ 學生　□ 教師　　□ 內勤職員　□ 家庭主婦　□ SOHO 族　□ 企業主管
　　　□ 服務業　　□ 製造業 □ 醫藥護理　□ 軍警　　　□ 資訊業　　□ 銷售業務
　　　□ 其他＿＿＿＿＿＿＿＿＿＿＿＿＿＿＿＿＿＿
E-mail：＿＿＿＿＿＿＿＿＿＿＿＿＿＿＿＿＿
聯絡電話：＿＿＿＿＿＿＿＿＿＿＿＿＿＿＿＿
聯絡地址：□□□ ＿＿＿＿＿＿＿＿＿＿＿＿＿

購買書名：遇到老外英語這樣說＿＿＿＿＿＿＿＿＿＿＿＿＿

· 本書中最吸引您的是哪一篇文章或哪一段話呢？ ＿＿＿＿＿＿＿＿＿＿＿

· 誘使您購買此書的原因？
□ 於 ＿＿＿＿＿ 書店尋找新知時□ 看 ＿＿＿＿＿ 報時瞄到□ 受海報或文案吸引
□ 翻閱 ＿＿＿＿＿ 雜誌時□ 親朋好友拍胸脯保證□ ＿＿＿＿＿電台 DJ 熱情推薦
□ 其他編輯萬萬想不到的過程：＿＿＿＿＿＿＿＿＿＿＿＿＿

· 對於本書的評分？（請填代號：1. 很滿意 2. OK 啦！ 3. 尚可 4.需改進）
　　封面設計 ＿＿＿＿版面編排 ＿＿＿＿　內容 ＿＿＿＿文／譯筆 ＿＿＿

· 美好的事物、聲音或影像都很吸引人，但究竟是怎樣的書最能吸引您呢？
□ 自然科學 □ 生命科學 □ 動物 □ 植物 □ 物理 □ 化學 □ 天文／宇宙
□ 數學 □ 地球科學 □ 醫學 □電子／科技 □ 機械 □ 建築 □ 心理學
□ 食品科學 □ 其他 ＿＿＿＿＿＿＿＿＿＿＿＿＿＿

· 您是在哪裡購買本書？（單選）
□ 博客來 □ 金石堂 □ 誠品書店 □ 晨星網路書店 □ 其他

· 您與眾不同的閱讀品味，也請務必與我們分享：
□ 哲學　　　□ 心理學　　□ 宗教　　　□ 自然生態 □ 流行趨勢 □ 醫療保健
□ 財經企管 □ 史地　　　□ 傳記　　　□ 文學　　　□ 散文　　　□ 原住民
□ 小說　　　□ 親子叢書 □ 休閒旅遊 □ 其他＿＿＿＿＿＿＿＿＿

以上問題想必耗去您不少心力，為免這份心血白費

請務必將此回函郵寄回本社，或傳真至（04）2359-7123，感謝！

若行有餘力，也請不吝賜教，好讓我們可以出版更多更好的書！

· 其他意見：

晨星出版有限公司 編輯群，感謝您！

廣告回函
台灣中區郵政管理局
登記證第 267 號
免貼郵票

407
台中市工業區 30 路 1 號

晨星出版有限公司

更方便的購書方式：

(1) 網站：http://www.morningstar.com.tw
(2) 郵政劃撥　帳號：22326758
　　　　　　戶名：晨星出版有限公司
　　請於通信欄中註明欲購買之書名及數量
(3) 電話訂購：如為大量團購可直接撥客服專線洽詢

◎ 如需詳細書目可上網查詢或來電索取。
◎ 客服專線：04-23595819#230　傳真：04-23597123
◎ 客戶信箱：service@morningstar.com.tw